my brain hurts

BY LIZ BAILLIE VOLUME TWO

First Edition, December 1, 2009

This is Microcosm #76094

ISBN 978-1-934620-44-1

Microcosm Publishing

222 S Rogers St.

Bloomington, IN 47404

www.microcosmpublishing.com

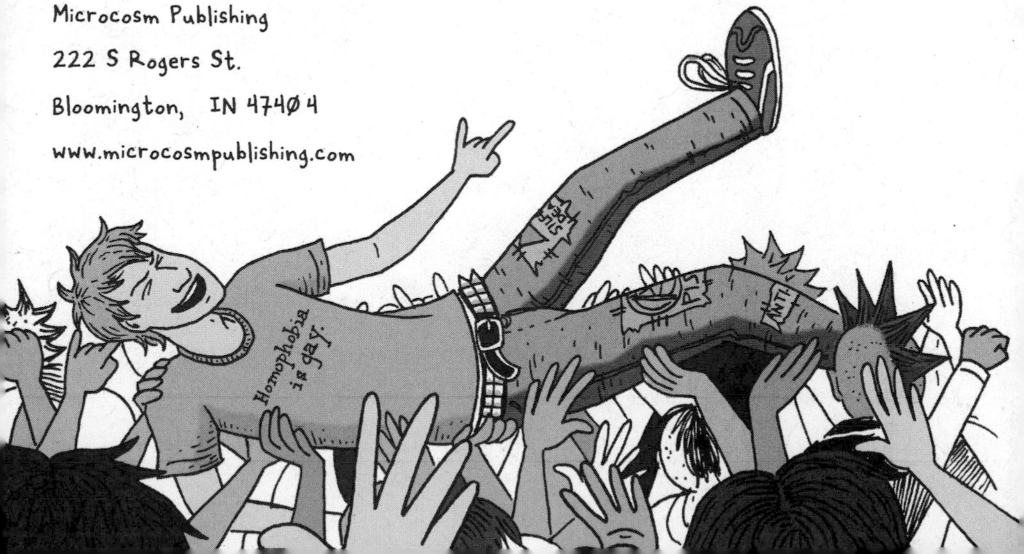
Homophobia is gay.
ANTI

DEDICATED TO THE ST. MARK'S PLACE CLASS OF 1994 - 2001
(especially the ones who didn't make it)

AND WITH LOVE TO ZANE
(without you, nothing is possible)

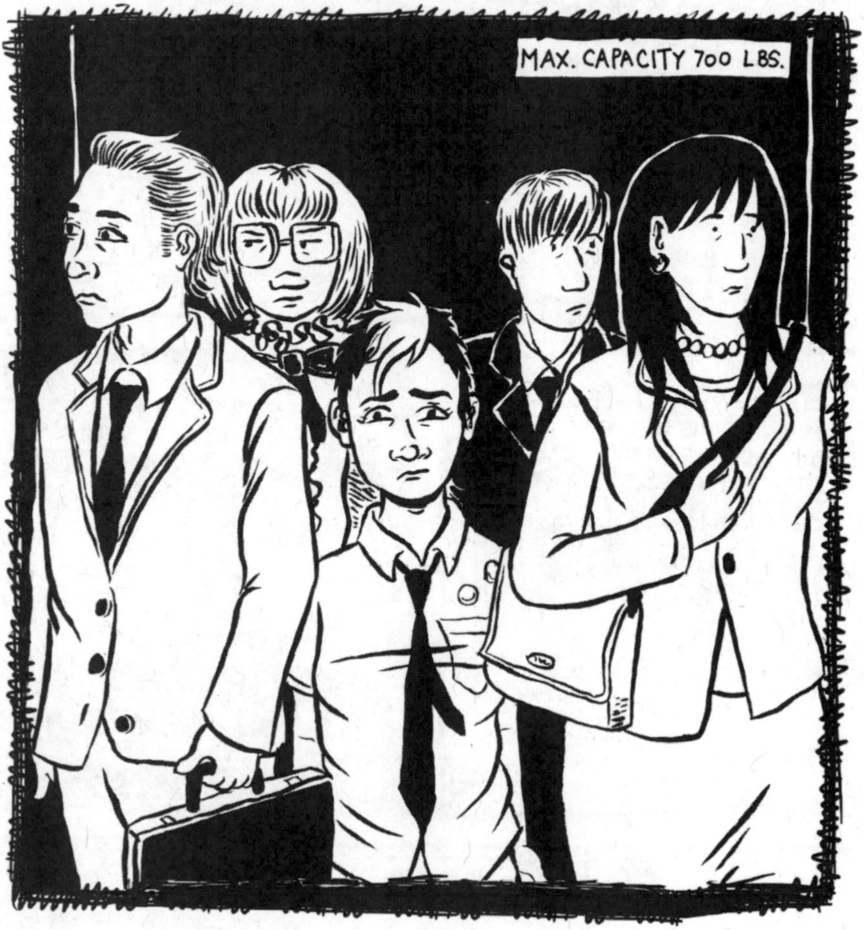
MAX. CAPACITY 700 LBS.

CHAPTER ONE

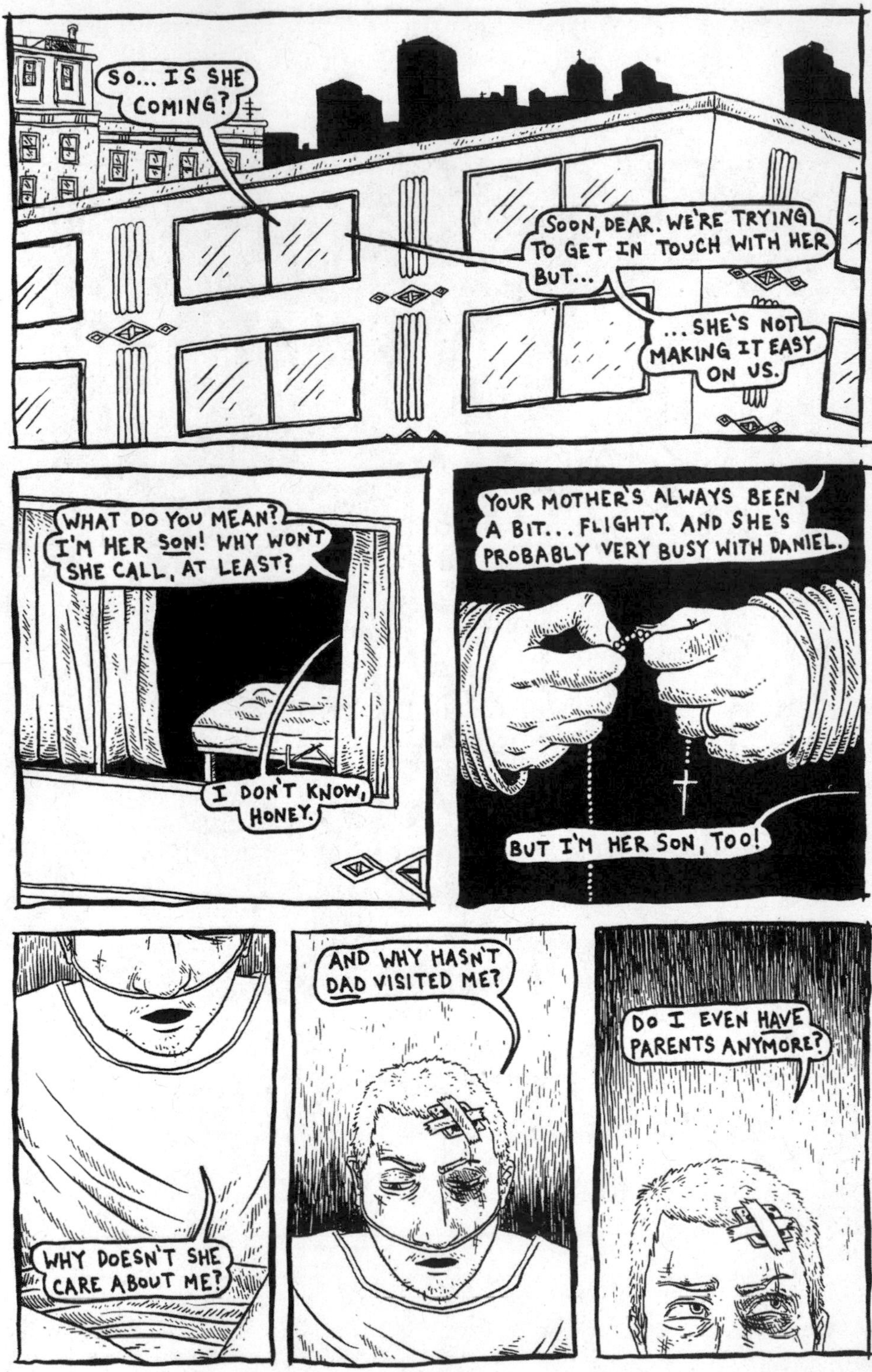
SO... IS SHE COMING?
SOON, DEAR. WE'RE TRYING TO GET IN TOUCH WITH HER BUT...
...SHE'S NOT MAKING IT EASY ON US.
WHAT DO YOU MEAN? I'M HER SON! WHY WON'T SHE CALL, AT LEAST?
I DON'T KNOW, HONEY.
YOUR MOTHER'S ALWAYS BEEN A BIT... FLIGHTY. AND SHE'S PROBABLY VERY BUSY WITH DANIEL.
BUT I'M HER SON, TOO!
WHY DOESN'T SHE CARE ABOUT ME?
AND WHY HASN'T DAD VISITED ME?
DO I EVEN HAVE PARENTS ANYMORE?

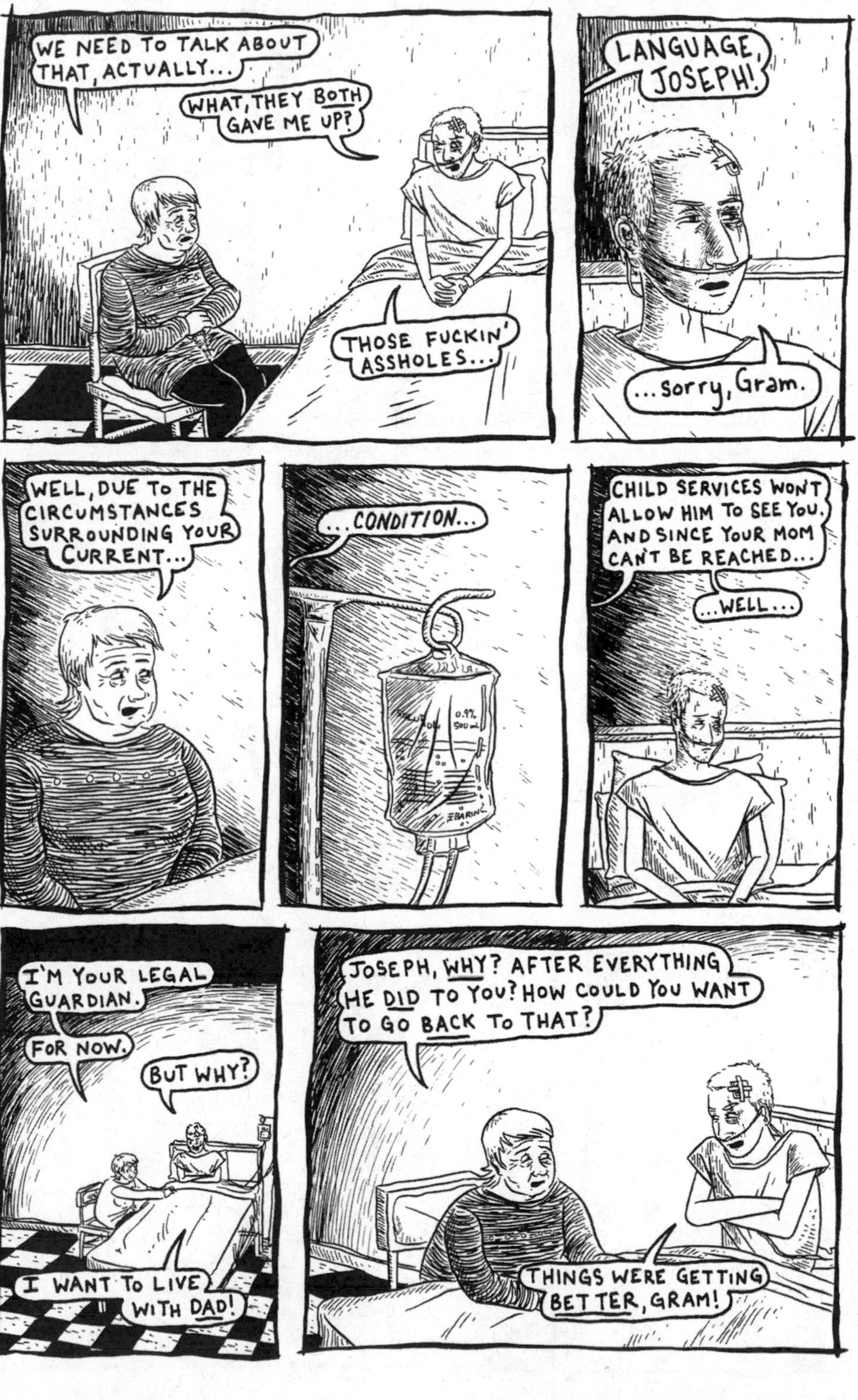
WE NEED TO TALK ABOUT THAT, ACTUALLY...
WHAT, THEY BOTH GAVE ME UP?
THOSE FUCKIN' ASSHOLES...
LANGUAGE, JOSEPH!
...Sorry, Gram.
WELL, DUE TO THE CIRCUMSTANCES SURROUNDING YOUR CURRENT...
...CONDITION...
0.9%
500 ml
CHILD SERVICES WON'T ALLOW HIM TO SEE YOU. AND SINCE YOUR MOM CAN'T BE REACHED...
...WELL...
I'M YOUR LEGAL GUARDIAN.
FOR NOW.
BUT WHY?
I WANT TO LIVE WITH DAD!
JOSEPH, WHY? AFTER EVERYTHING HE DID TO YOU? HOW COULD YOU WANT TO GO BACK TO THAT?
THINGS WERE GETTING BETTER, GRAM!

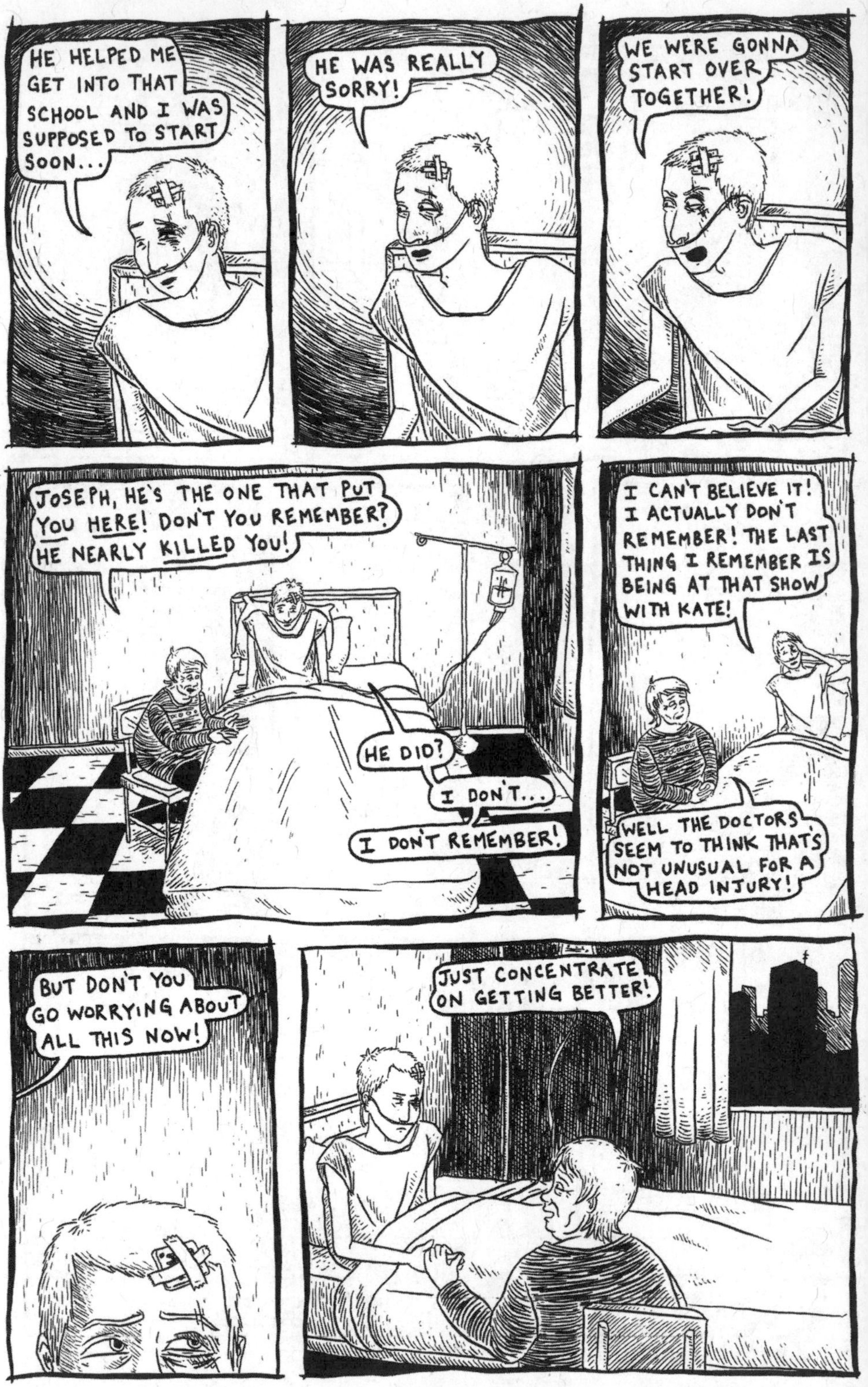
HE HELPED ME GET INTO THAT SCHOOL AND I WAS SUPPOSED TO START SOON...
HE WAS REALLY SORRY!
WE WERE GONNA START OVER TOGETHER!
JOSEPH, HE'S THE ONE THAT PUT YOU HERE! DON'T YOU REMEMBER? HE NEARLY KILLED YOU!
HE DID?
I DON'T...
I DON'T REMEMBER!
I CAN'T BELIEVE IT! I ACTUALLY DON'T REMEMBER! THE LAST THING I REMEMBER IS BEING AT THAT SHOW WITH KATE!
WELL THE DOCTORS SEEM TO THINK THAT'S NOT UNUSUAL FOR A HEAD INJURY!
BUT DON'T YOU GO WORRYING ABOUT ALL THIS NOW!
JUST CONCENTRATE ON GETTING BETTER!

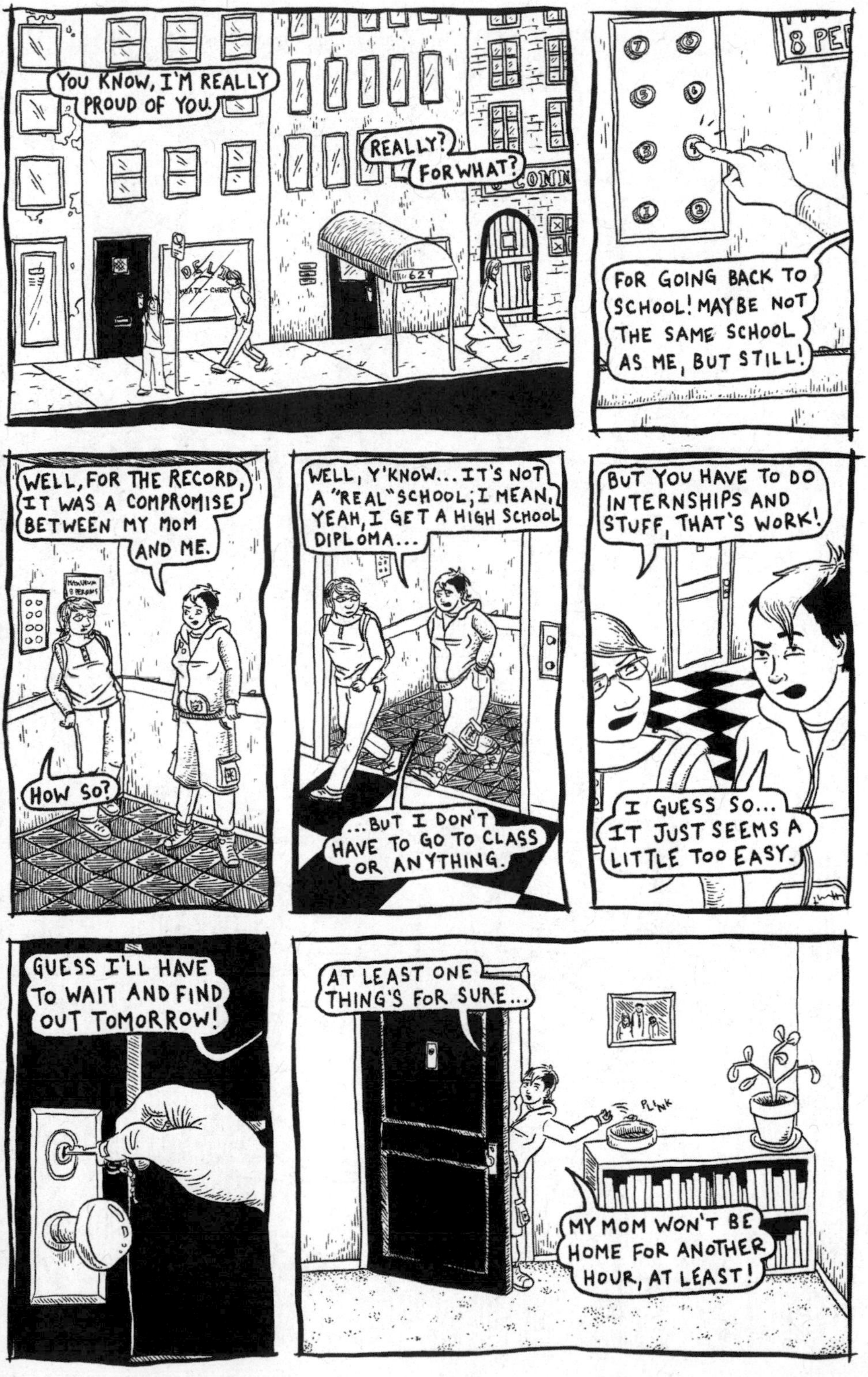
YOU KNOW, I'M REALLY PROUD OF YOU.
REALLY? FOR WHAT?
DELI
629
FOR GOING BACK TO SCHOOL! MAYBE NOT THE SAME SCHOOL AS ME, BUT STILL!
WELL, FOR THE RECORD, IT WAS A COMPROMISE BETWEEN MY MOM AND ME.
HOW SO?
WELL, Y'KNOW... IT'S NOT A "REAL" SCHOOL; I MEAN, YEAH, I GET A HIGH SCHOOL DIPLOMA...
...BUT I DON'T HAVE TO GO TO CLASS OR ANYTHING.
BUT YOU HAVE TO DO INTERNSHIPS AND STUFF, THAT'S WORK!
I GUESS SO... IT JUST SEEMS A LITTLE TOO EASY.
GUESS I'LL HAVE TO WAIT AND FIND OUT TOMORROW!
AT LEAST ONE THING'S FOR SURE...
PLINK
MY MOM WON'T BE HOME FOR ANOTHER HOUR, AT LEAST!

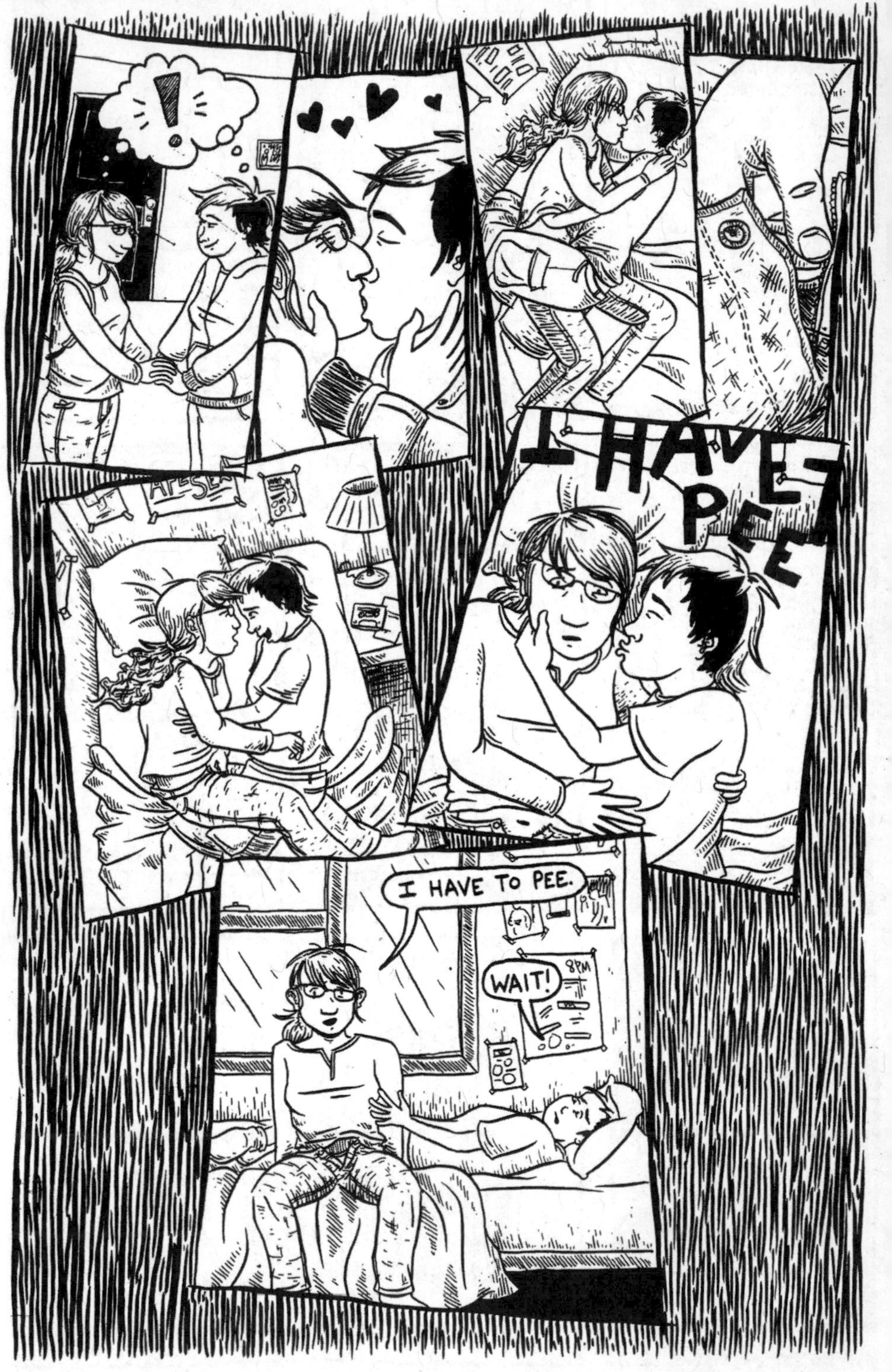
!
I HAVE
PEE
I HAVE TO PEE.
WAIT!
8PM

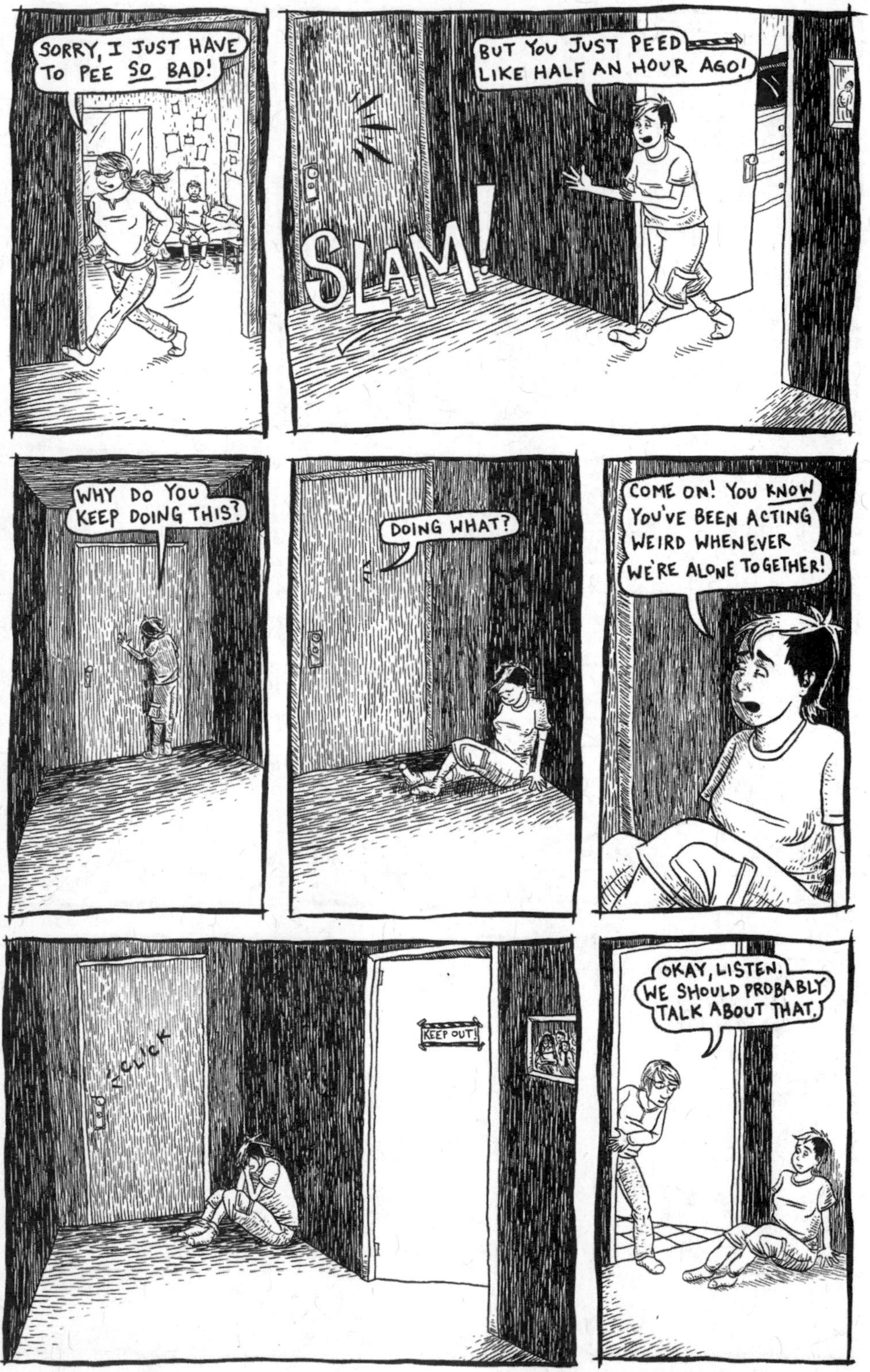
SORRY, I JUST HAVE TO PEE SO BAD!
BUT YOU JUST PEED LIKE HALF AN HOUR AGO!
SLAM!
WHY DO YOU KEEP DOING THIS?
DOING WHAT?
COME ON! YOU KNOW YOU'VE BEEN ACTING WEIRD WHENEVER WE'RE ALONE TOGETHER!
CLICK
KEEP OUT!
OKAY, LISTEN. WE SHOULD PROBABLY TALK ABOUT THAT.

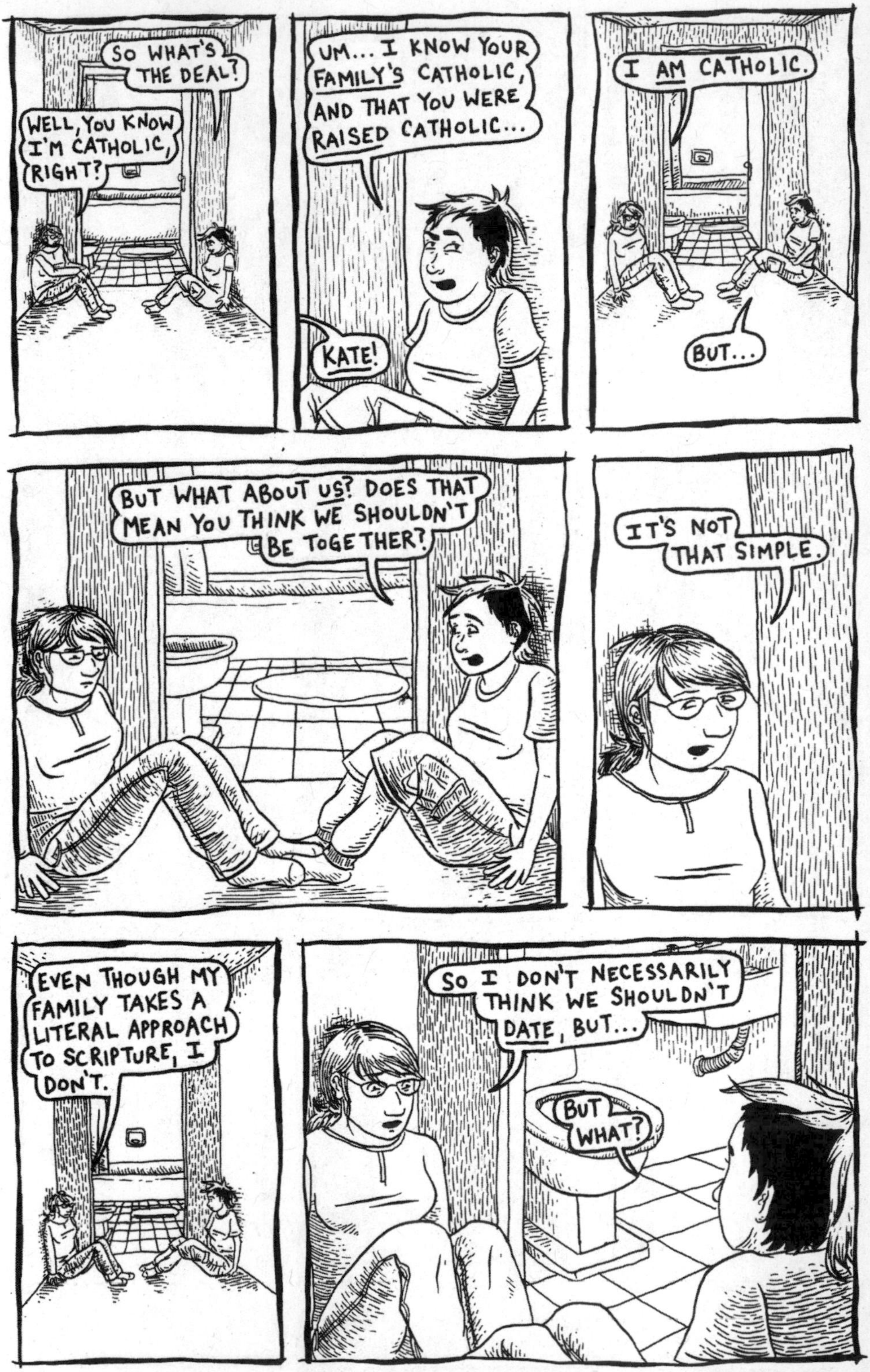
SO WHAT'S THE DEAL?
WELL, YOU KNOW I'M CATHOLIC, RIGHT?
UM... I KNOW YOUR FAMILY'S CATHOLIC, AND THAT YOU WERE RAISED CATHOLIC...
KATE!
I AM CATHOLIC.
BUT...
BUT WHAT ABOUT US? DOES THAT MEAN YOU THINK WE SHOULDN'T BE TOGETHER?
IT'S NOT THAT SIMPLE.
EVEN THOUGH MY FAMILY TAKES A LITERAL APPROACH TO SCRIPTURE, I DON'T.
SO I DON'T NECESSARILY THINK WE SHOULDN'T DATE, BUT...
BUT WHAT?

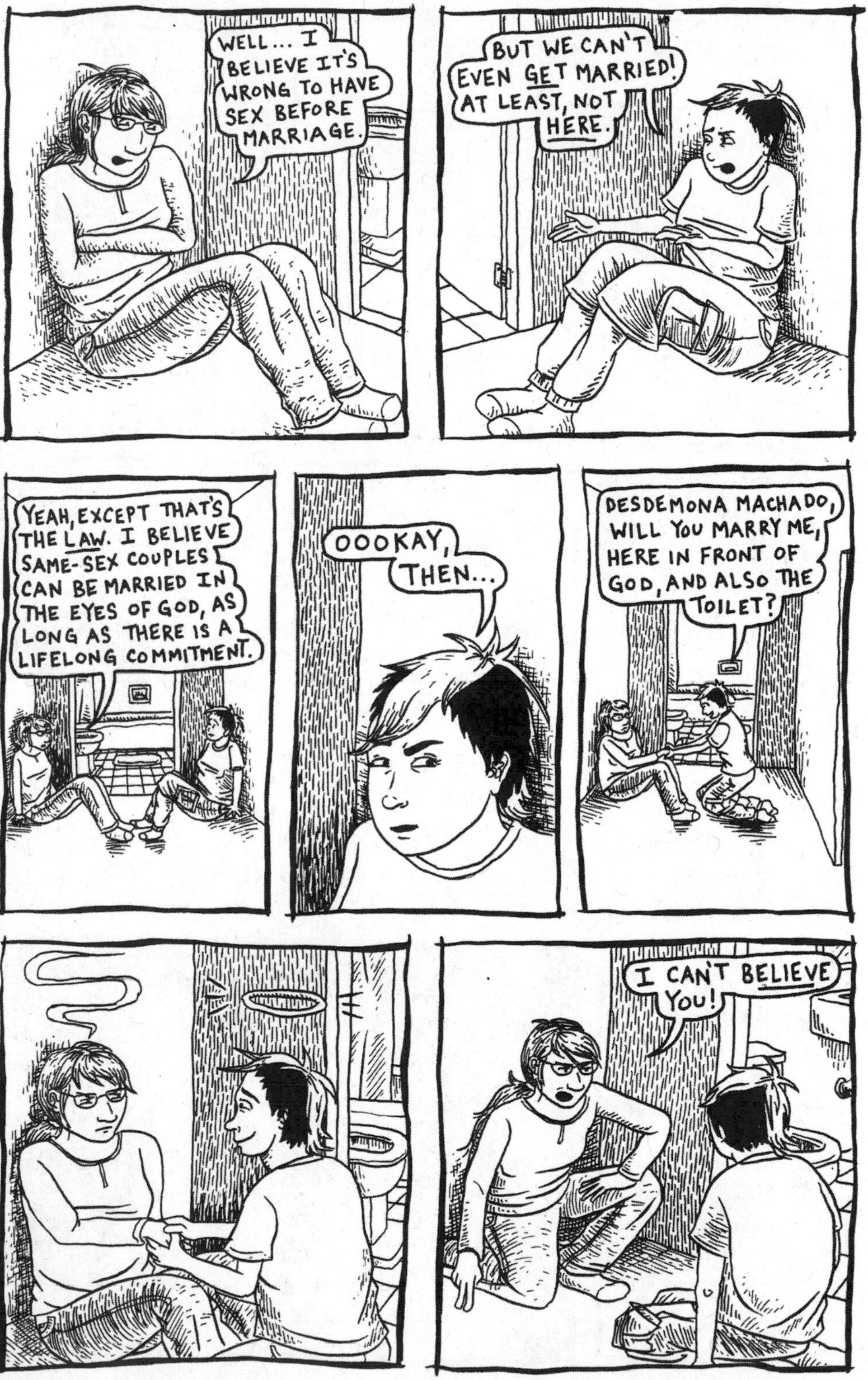
WELL... I BELIEVE IT'S WRONG TO HAVE SEX BEFORE MARRIAGE.
BUT WE CAN'T EVEN GET MARRIED! AT LEAST, NOT HERE.
YEAH, EXCEPT THAT'S THE LAW. I BELIEVE SAME-SEX COUPLES CAN BE MARRIED IN THE EYES OF GOD, AS LONG AS THERE IS A LIFELONG COMMITMENT.
OOOKAY, THEN...
DESDEMONA MACHADO, WILL YOU MARRY ME, HERE IN FRONT OF GOD, AND ALSO THE TOILET?
I CAN'T BELIEVE YOU!

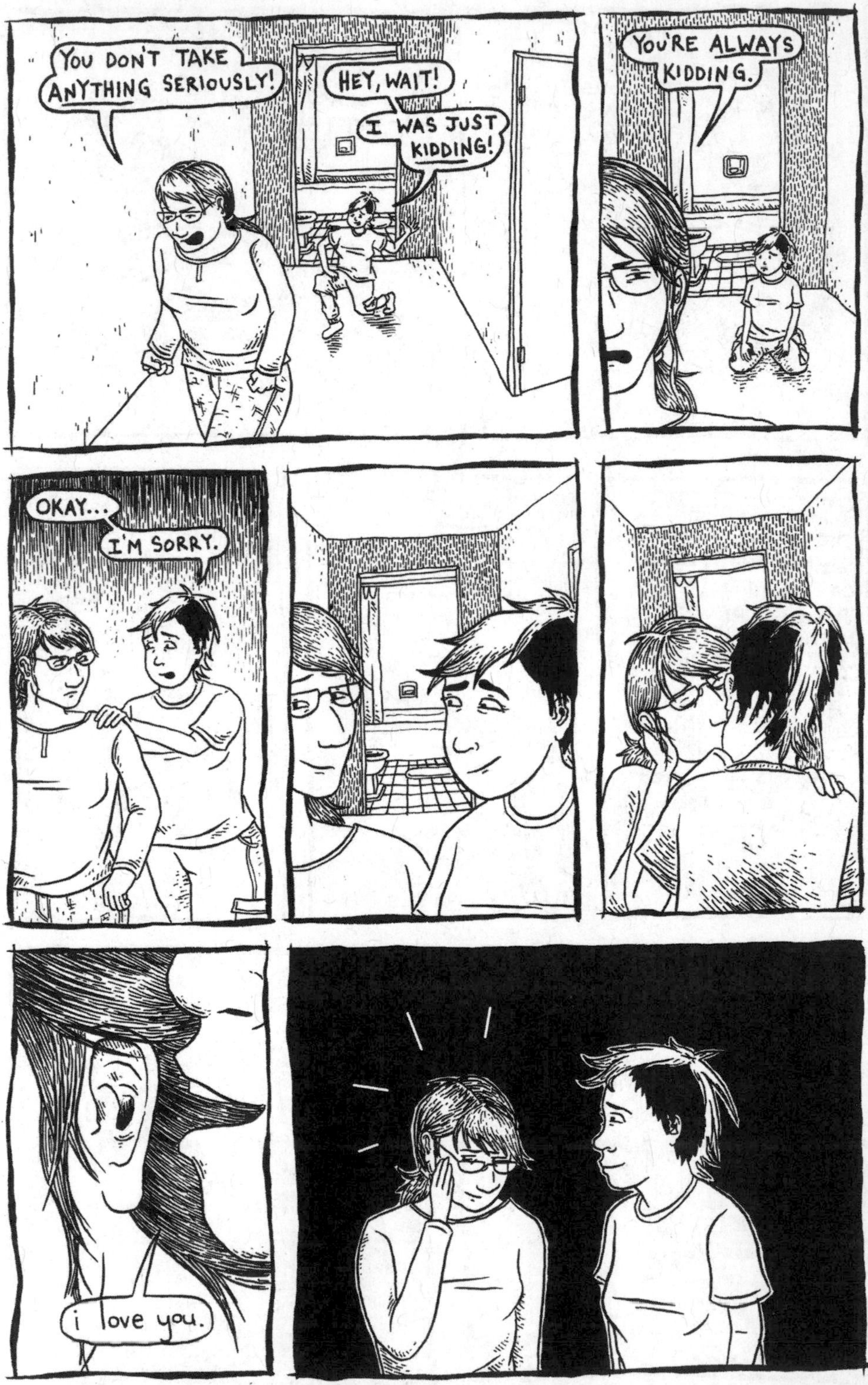
YOU DON'T TAKE ANYTHING SERIOUSLY!
HEY, WAIT!
I WAS JUST KIDDING!
YOU'RE ALWAYS KIDDING.
OKAY...
I'M SORRY.
i love you.

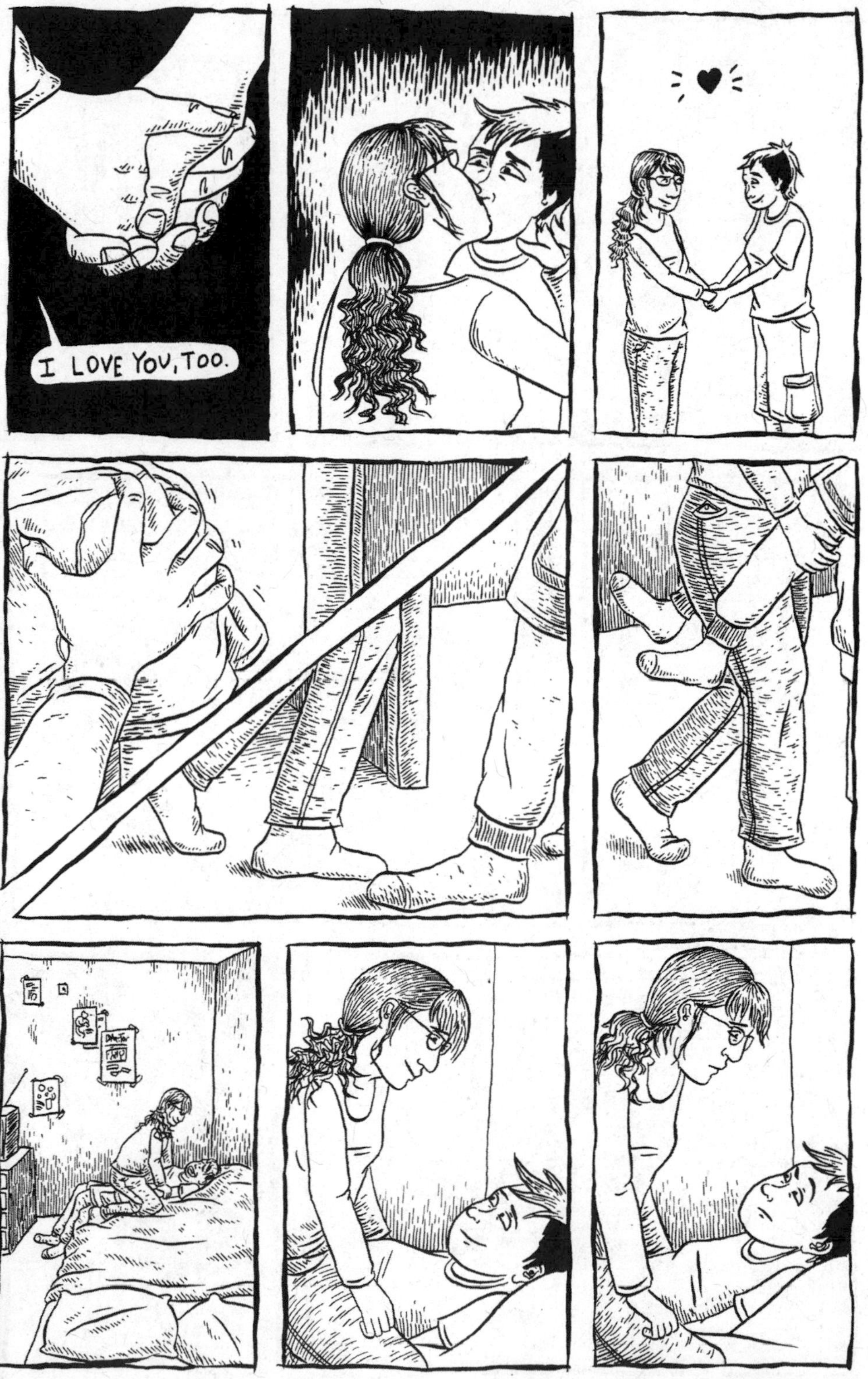
I LOVE YOU, TOO.

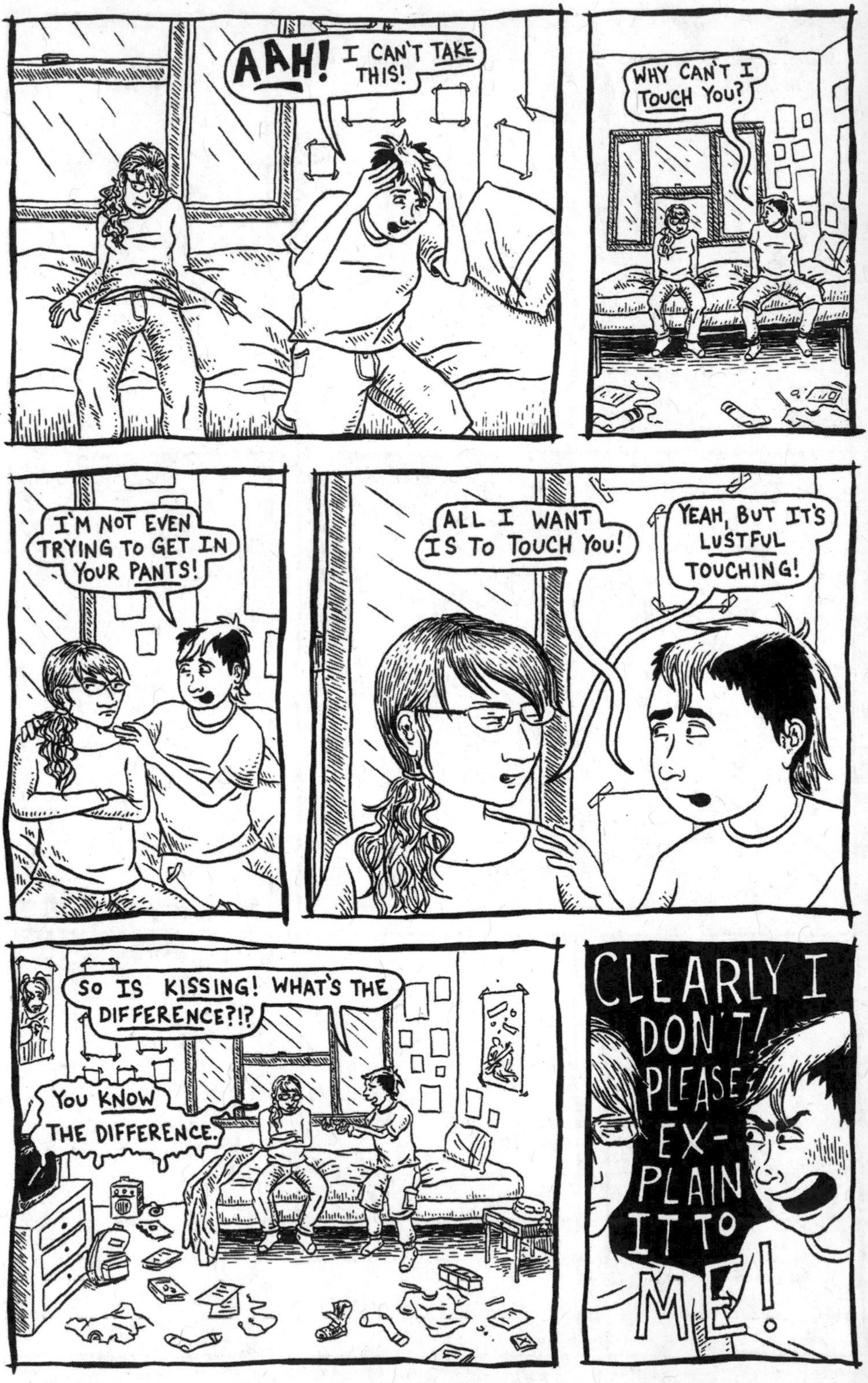
AAH! I CAN'T TAKE THIS!
WHY CAN'T I TOUCH YOU?
I'M NOT EVEN TRYING TO GET IN YOUR PANTS!
ALL I WANT IS TO TOUCH YOU!
YEAH, BUT IT'S LUSTFUL TOUCHING!
SO IS KISSING! WHAT'S THE DIFFERENCE?!?
YOU KNOW THE DIFFERENCE.
CLEARLY I DON'T! PLEASE EX-PLAIN IT TO ME!

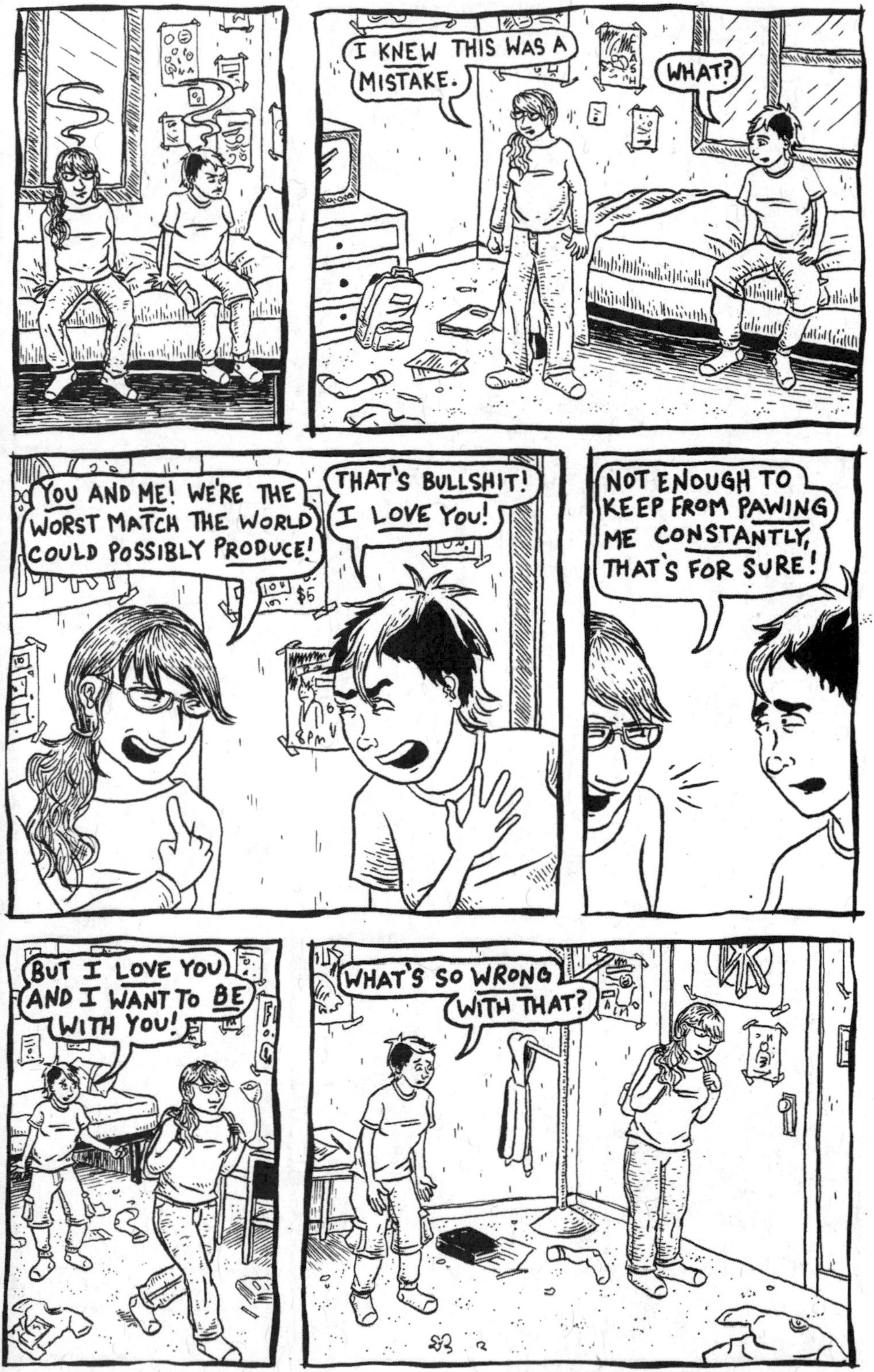
I KNEW THIS WAS A MISTAKE.
WHAT?
YOU AND ME! WE'RE THE WORST MATCH THE WORLD COULD POSSIBLY PRODUCE!
THAT'S BULLSHIT! I LOVE YOU!
NOT ENOUGH TO KEEP FROM PAWING ME CONSTANTLY, THAT'S FOR SURE!
BUT I LOVE YOU AND I WANT TO BE WITH YOU!
WHAT'S SO WRONG WITH THAT?

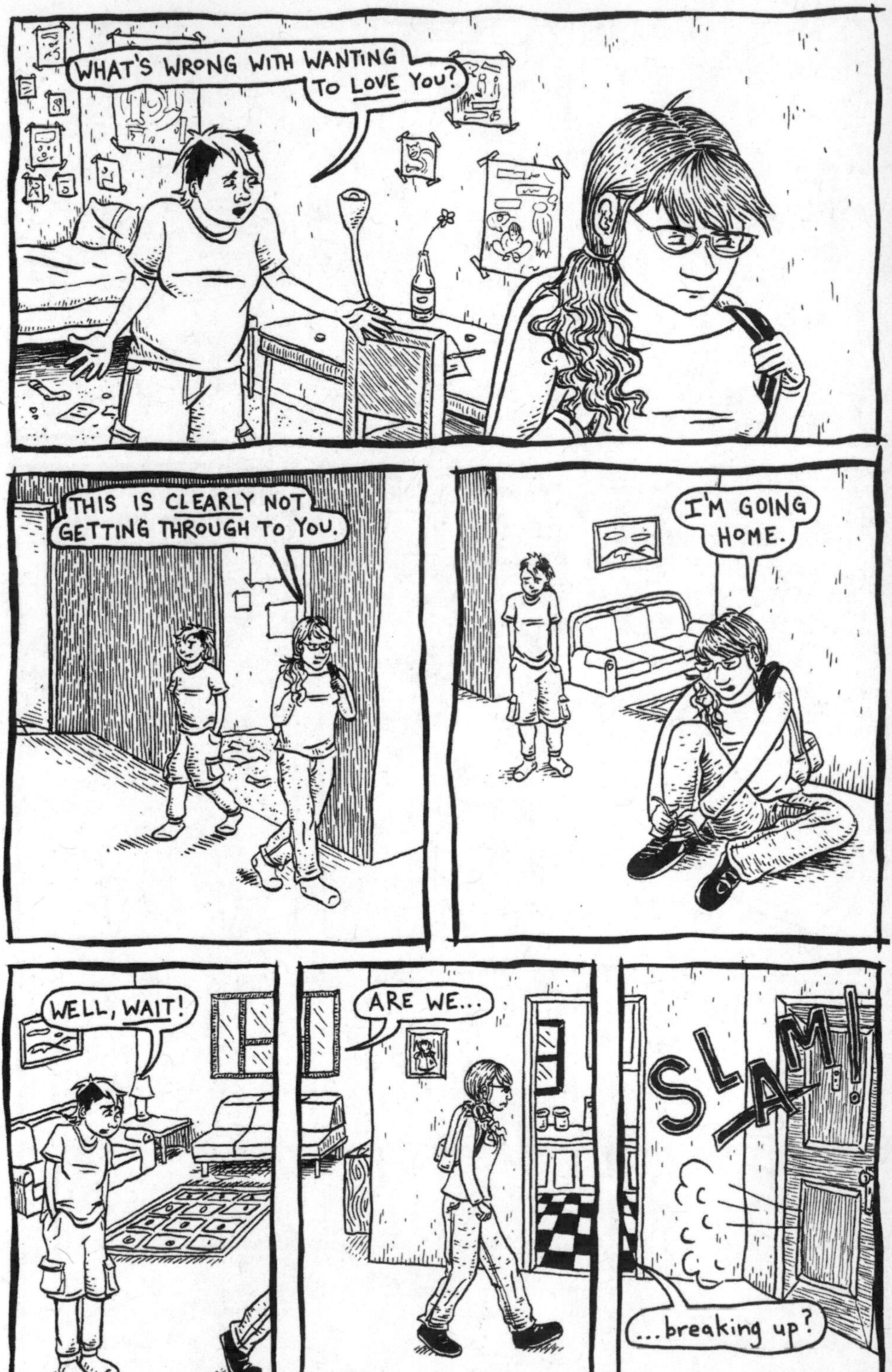
WHAT'S WRONG WITH WANTING TO LOVE YOU?
THIS IS CLEARLY NOT GETTING THROUGH TO YOU.
I'M GOING HOME.
WELL, WAIT!
ARE WE...
SLAM!
...breaking up?

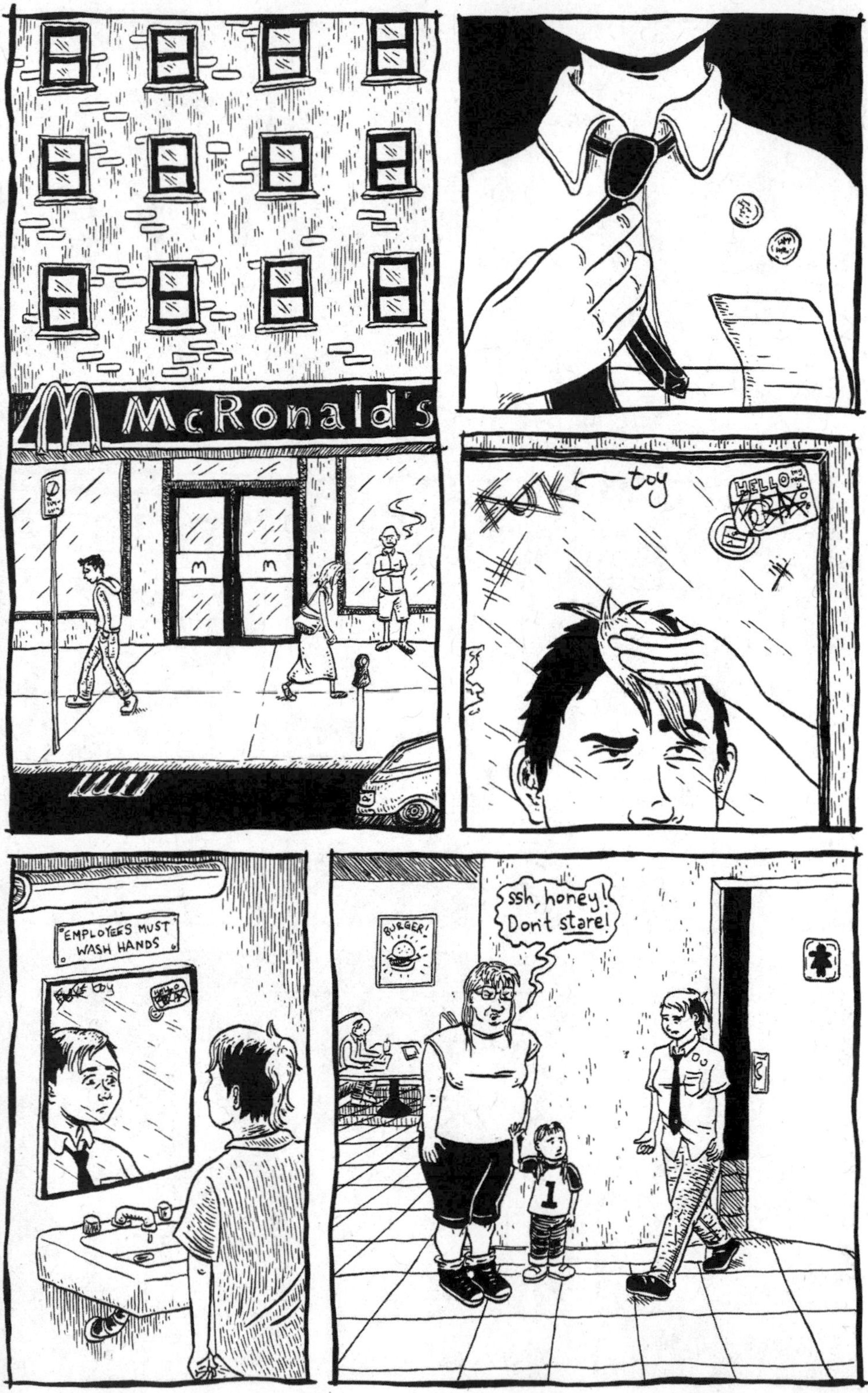
McRonald's
toy
HELLO my name is
EMPLOYEES MUST WASH HANDS
BURGER!
ssh, honey! Don't stare!
1

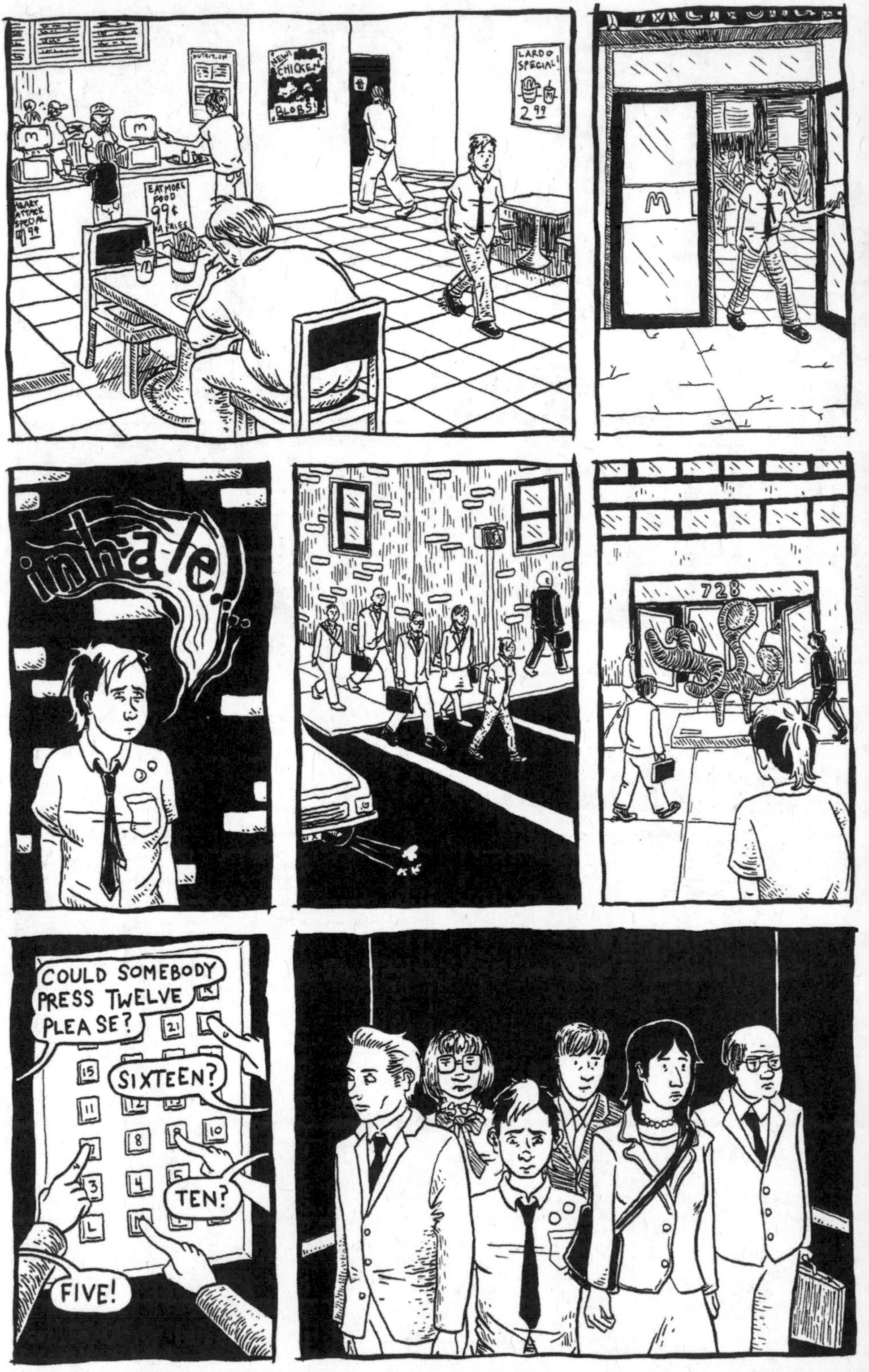

NUTRITION
NEW! CHICKEN BLOBS!
LARDO SPECIAL 2.99
HEART ATTACK SPECIAL 4.99
EAT MORE FOOD 99¢
inhale.
728
COULD SOMEBODY PRESS TWELVE PLEASE?
SIXTEEN?
TEN?
FIVE!

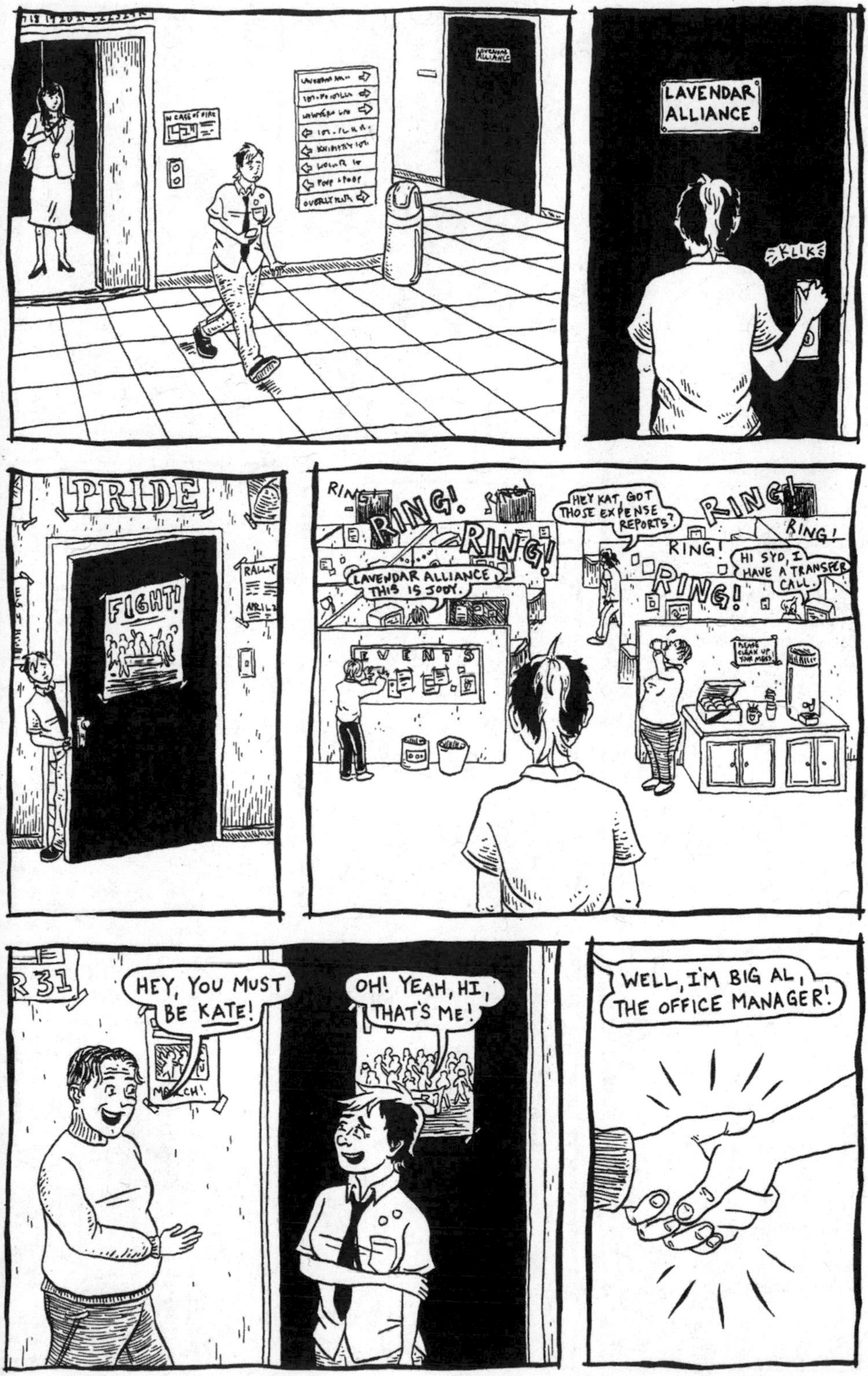
LAVENDAR ALLIANCE
KLIK
PRIDE
FIGHT!
RING!
RING!
RING!
HEY KAT, GOT THOSE EXPENSE REPORTS?
RING!
RING!
RING!
LAVENDAR ALLIANCE, THIS IS JODY.
HI SYD, I HAVE A TRANSFER CALL.
RING!
EVENTS
HEY, YOU MUST BE KATE!
OH! YEAH, HI, THAT'S ME!
WELL, I'M BIG AL, THE OFFICE MANAGER!

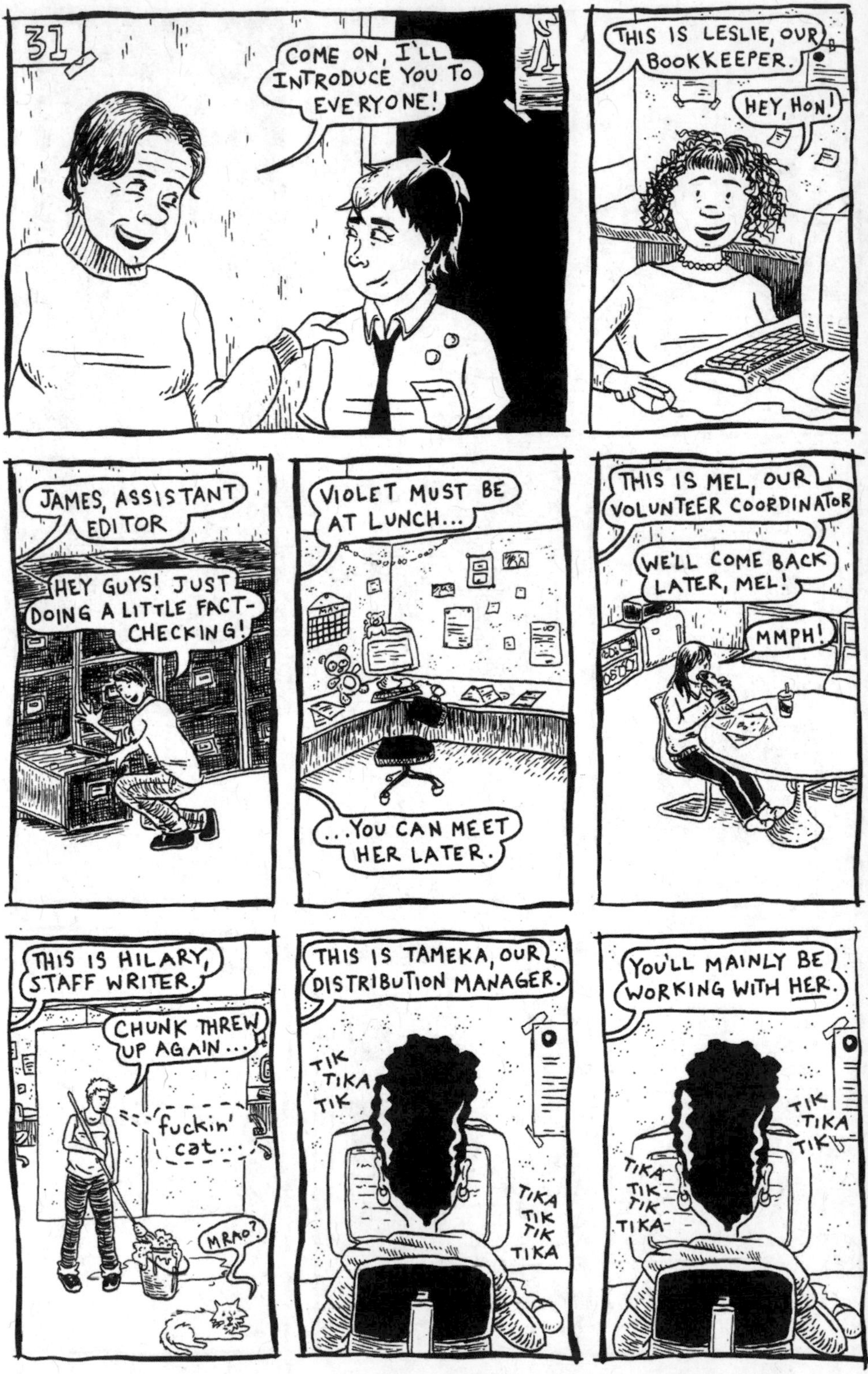
31
COME ON, I'LL INTRODUCE YOU TO EVERYONE!
THIS IS LESLIE, OUR BOOKKEEPER.
HEY, HON!
JAMES, ASSISTANT EDITOR
HEY GUYS! JUST DOING A LITTLE FACT-CHECKING!
VIOLET MUST BE AT LUNCH...
...YOU CAN MEET HER LATER.
THIS IS MEL, OUR VOLUNTEER COORDINATOR
WE'LL COME BACK LATER, MEL!
MMPH!
THIS IS HILARY, STAFF WRITER.
CHUNK THREW UP AGAIN...
fuckin' cat...
MRAO?
THIS IS TAMEKA, OUR DISTRIBUTION MANAGER.
TIK TIKA TIK
TIKA TIK TIK TIKA
YOU'LL MAINLY BE WORKING WITH HER.
TIK TIKA TIK
TIKA TIK TIK TIKA

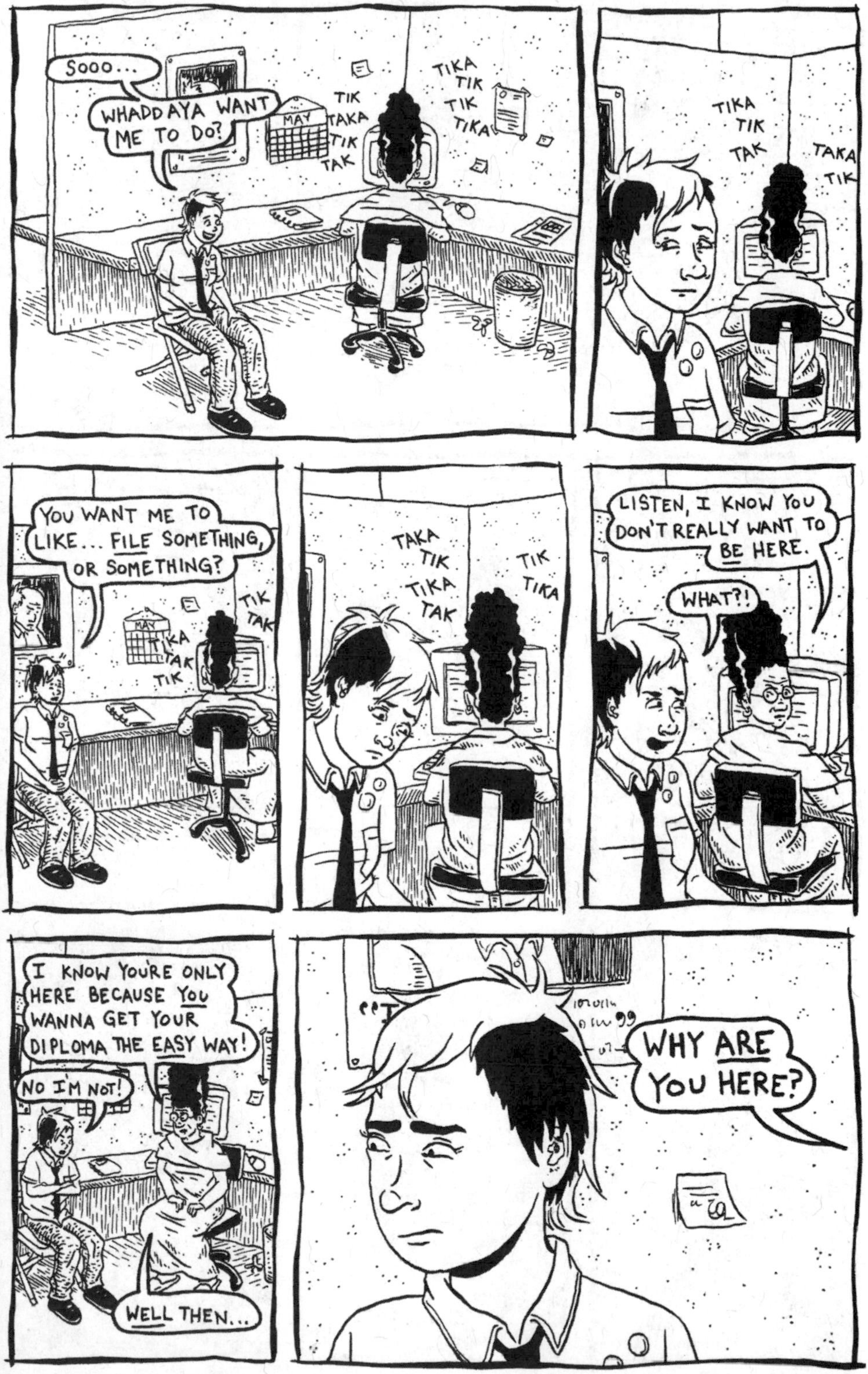
SOOO...
WHADDAYA WANT ME TO DO?
MAY
TIK TAKA TIK TAK
TIKA TIK TIK TIKA
TIKA TIK TAK
TAKA TIK
YOU WANT ME TO LIKE... FILE SOMETHING, OR SOMETHING?
MAY
TIK TAK
TIKA TAK TIK
TAKA TIK TIKA TAK
TIK TIKA
LISTEN, I KNOW YOU DON'T REALLY WANT TO BE HERE.
WHAT?!
I KNOW YOU'RE ONLY HERE BECAUSE YOU WANNA GET YOUR DIPLOMA THE EASY WAY!
NO I'M NOT!
WELL THEN...
WHY ARE YOU HERE?

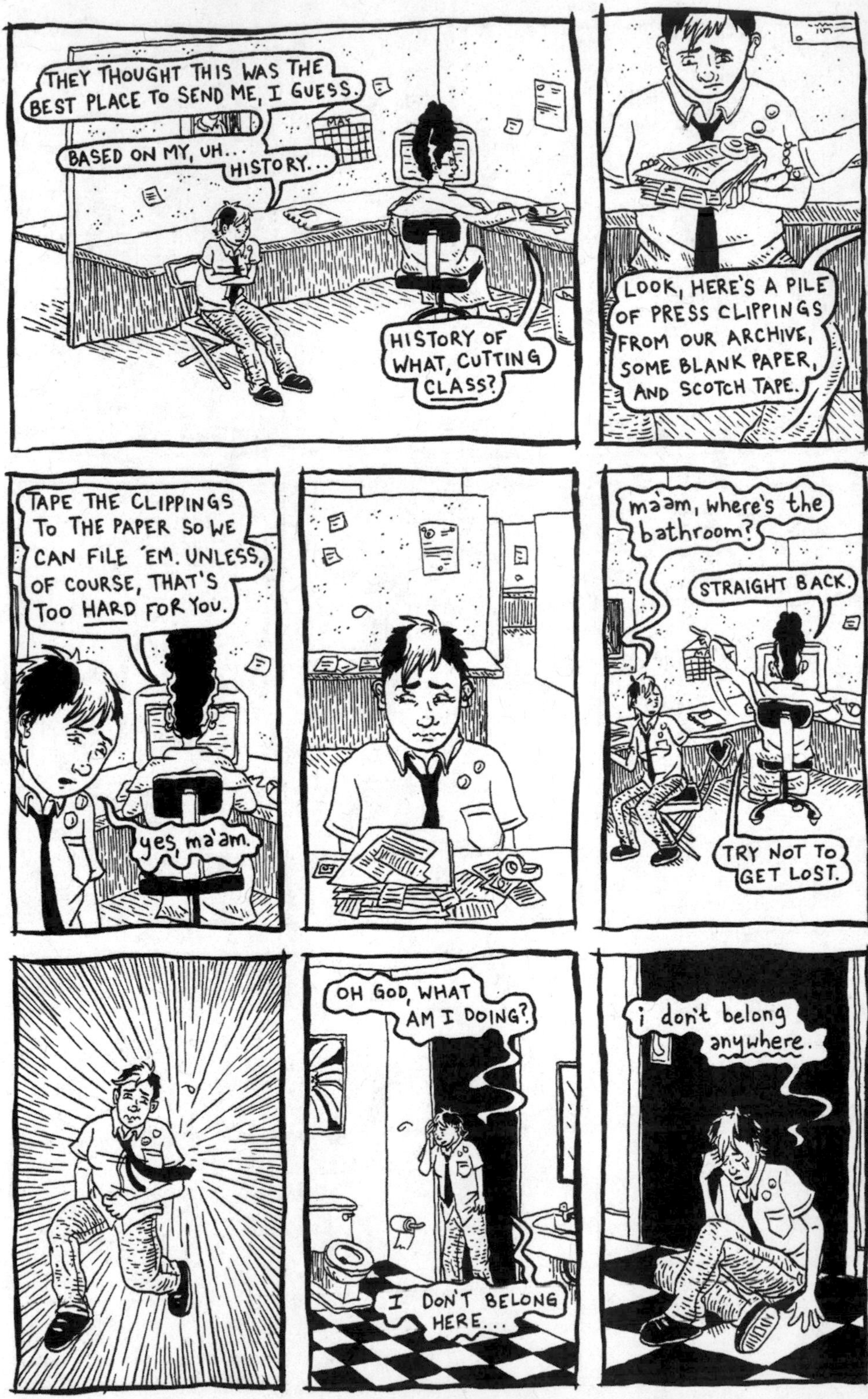
THEY THOUGHT THIS WAS THE BEST PLACE TO SEND ME, I GUESS.
BASED ON MY, UH... HISTORY...
HISTORY OF WHAT, CUTTING CLASS?
LOOK, HERE'S A PILE OF PRESS CLIPPINGS FROM OUR ARCHIVE, SOME BLANK PAPER, AND SCOTCH TAPE.
TAPE THE CLIPPINGS TO THE PAPER SO WE CAN FILE 'EM. UNLESS, OF COURSE, THAT'S TOO HARD FOR YOU.
yes, ma'am.
ma'am, where's the bathroom?
STRAIGHT BACK.
TRY NOT TO GET LOST.
OH GOD, WHAT AM I DOING?
I DON'T BELONG HERE...
i don't belong anywhere.

CHAPTER TWO

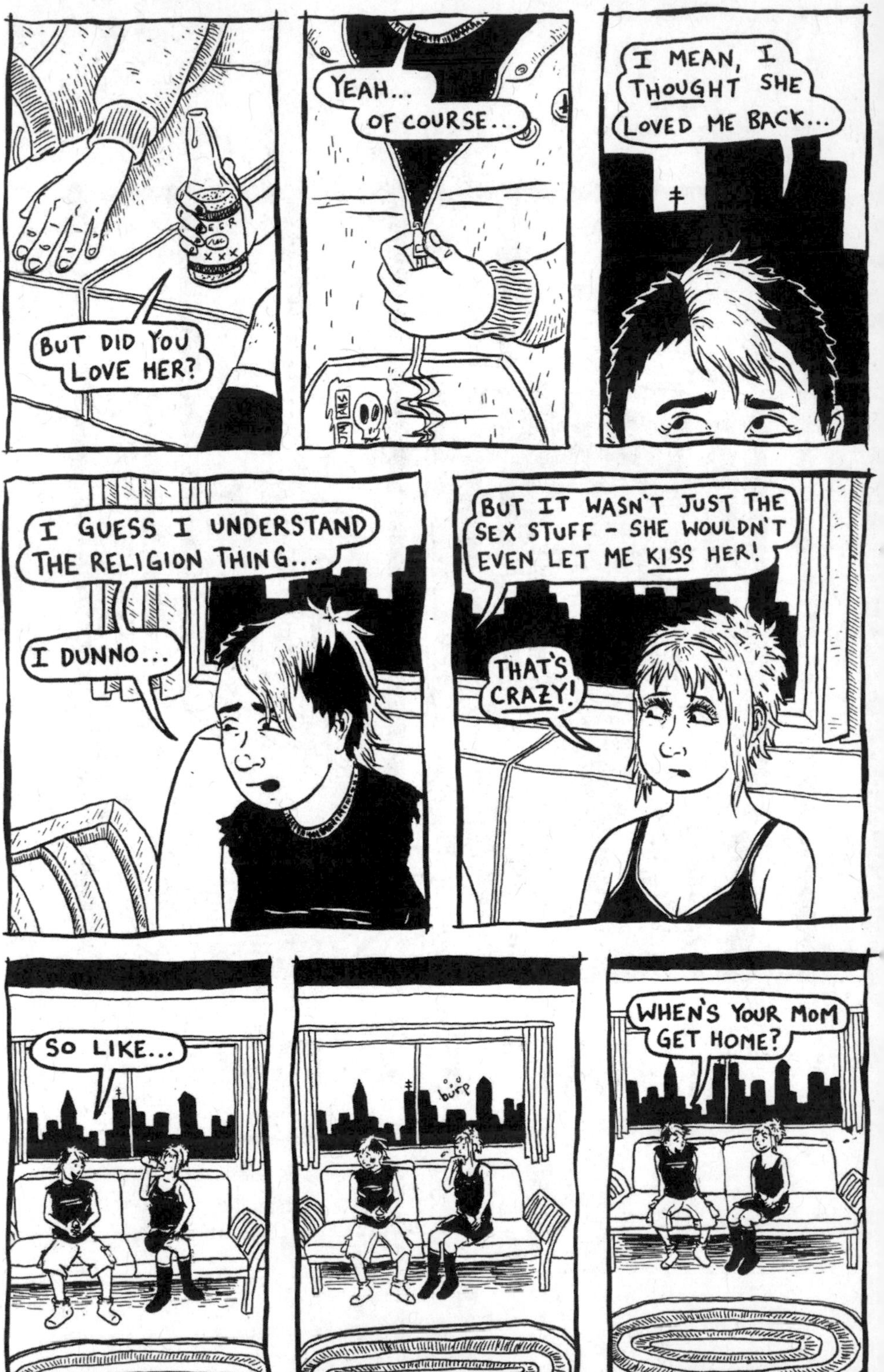
BUT DID YOU LOVE HER?
YEAH... OF COURSE...
I MEAN, I THOUGHT SHE LOVED ME BACK...
I GUESS I UNDERSTAND THE RELIGION THING...
I DUNNO...
BUT IT WASN'T JUST THE SEX STUFF - SHE WOULDN'T EVEN LET ME KISS HER!
THAT'S CRAZY!
SO LIKE...
BURP
WHEN'S YOUR MOM GET HOME?

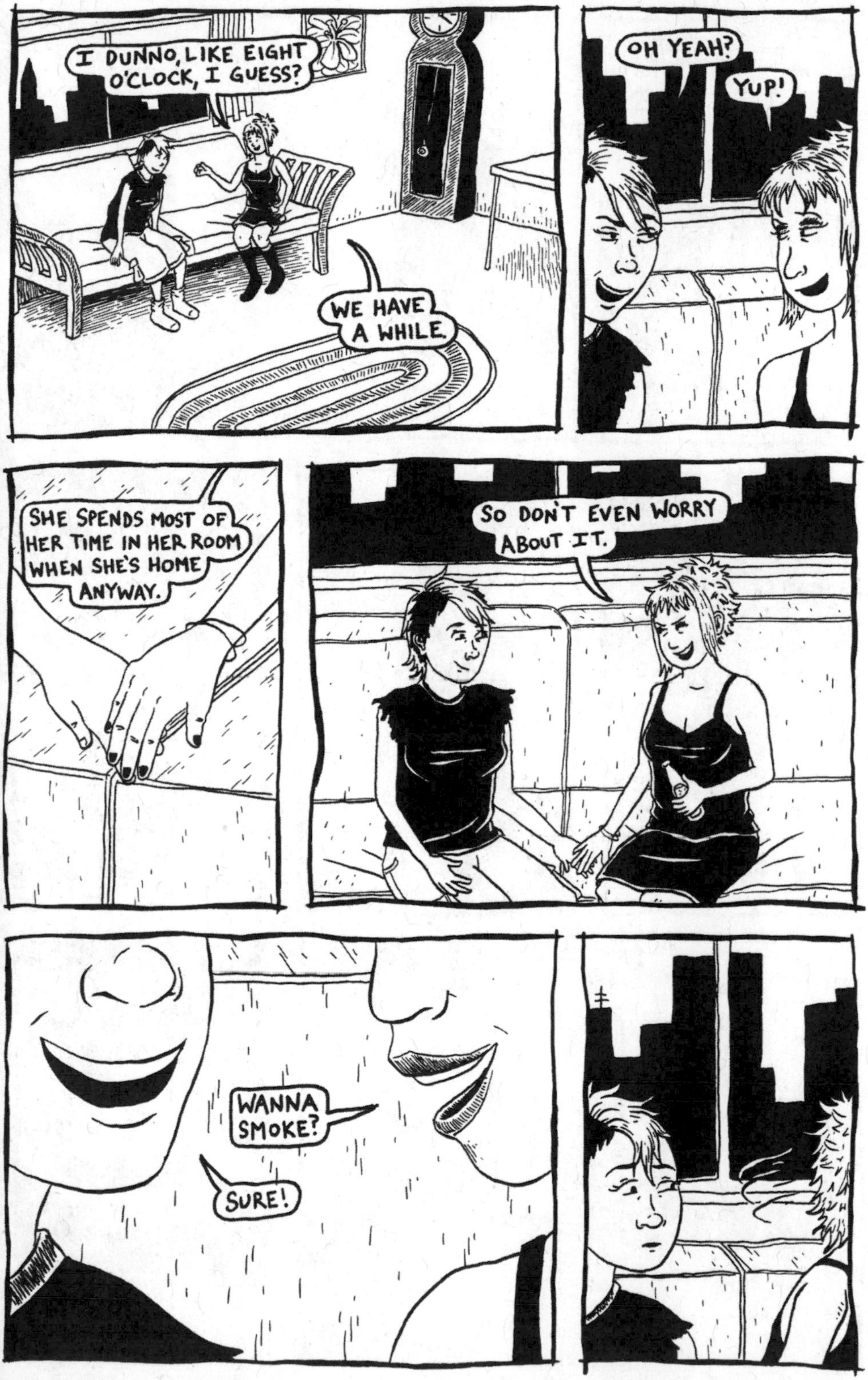
I DUNNO, LIKE EIGHT O'CLOCK, I GUESS?
WE HAVE A WHILE.
OH YEAH?
YUP!
SHE SPENDS MOST OF HER TIME IN HER ROOM WHEN SHE'S HOME ANYWAY.
SO DON'T EVEN WORRY ABOUT IT.
WANNA SMOKE?
SURE!

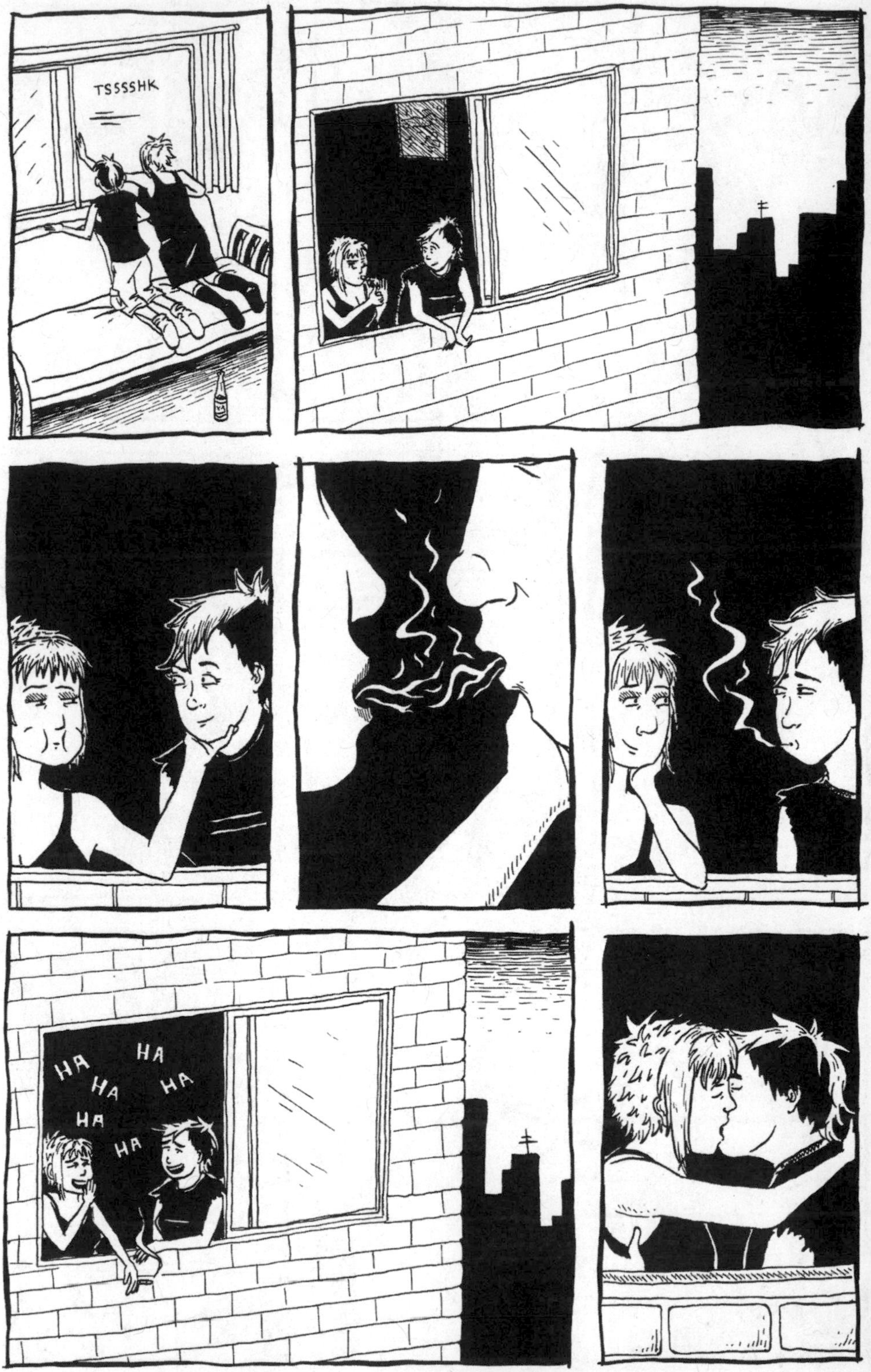
TSSSSHK
HA
HA
HA
HA
HA
HA

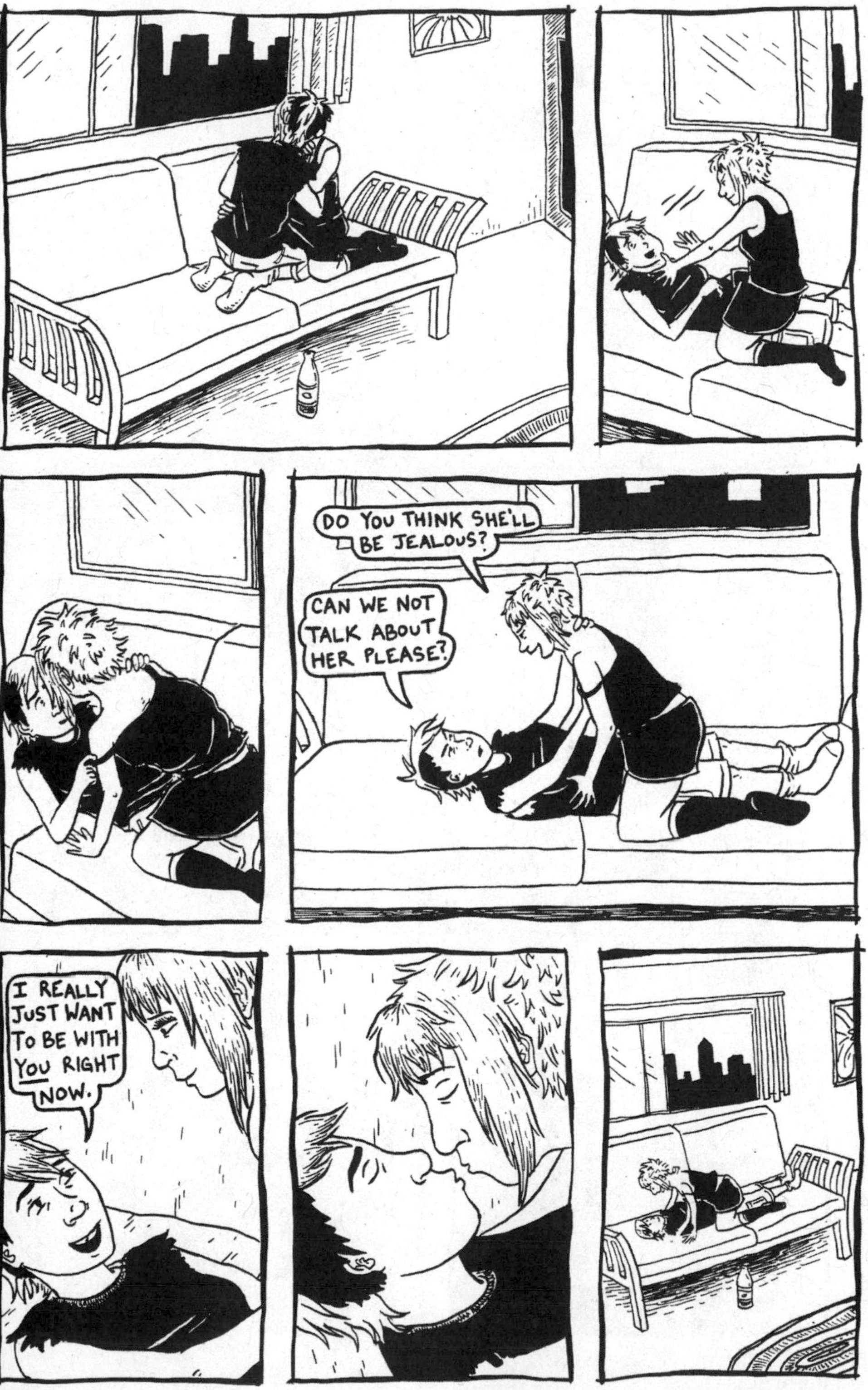
DO YOU THINK SHE'LL BE JEALOUS?
CAN WE NOT TALK ABOUT HER PLEASE?
I REALLY JUST WANT TO BE WITH YOU RIGHT NOW.

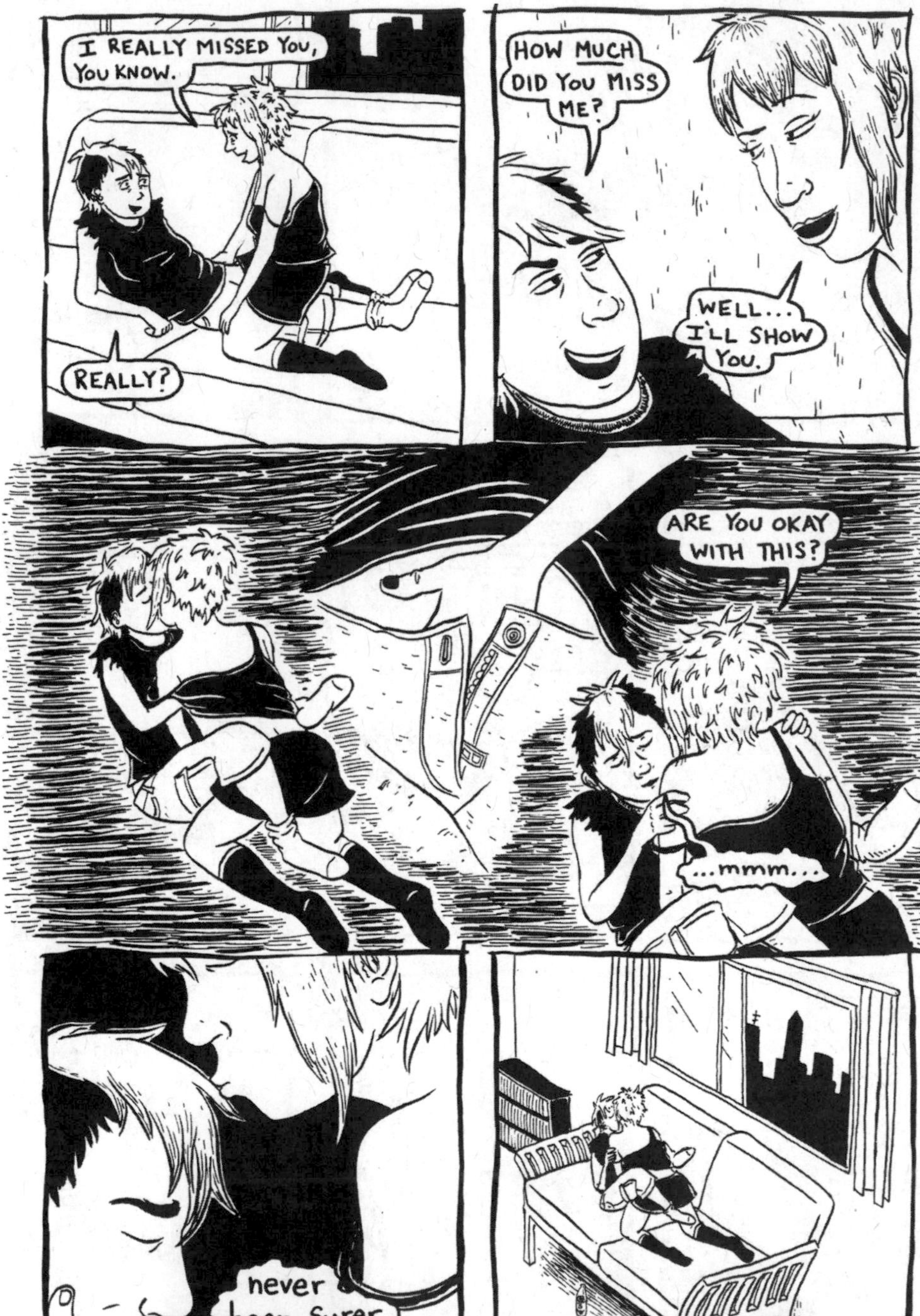
I REALLY MISSED YOU, YOU KNOW.
REALLY?
HOW MUCH DID YOU MISS ME?
WELL... I'LL SHOW YOU.
ARE YOU OKAY WITH THIS?
...mmm...
never been Surer.

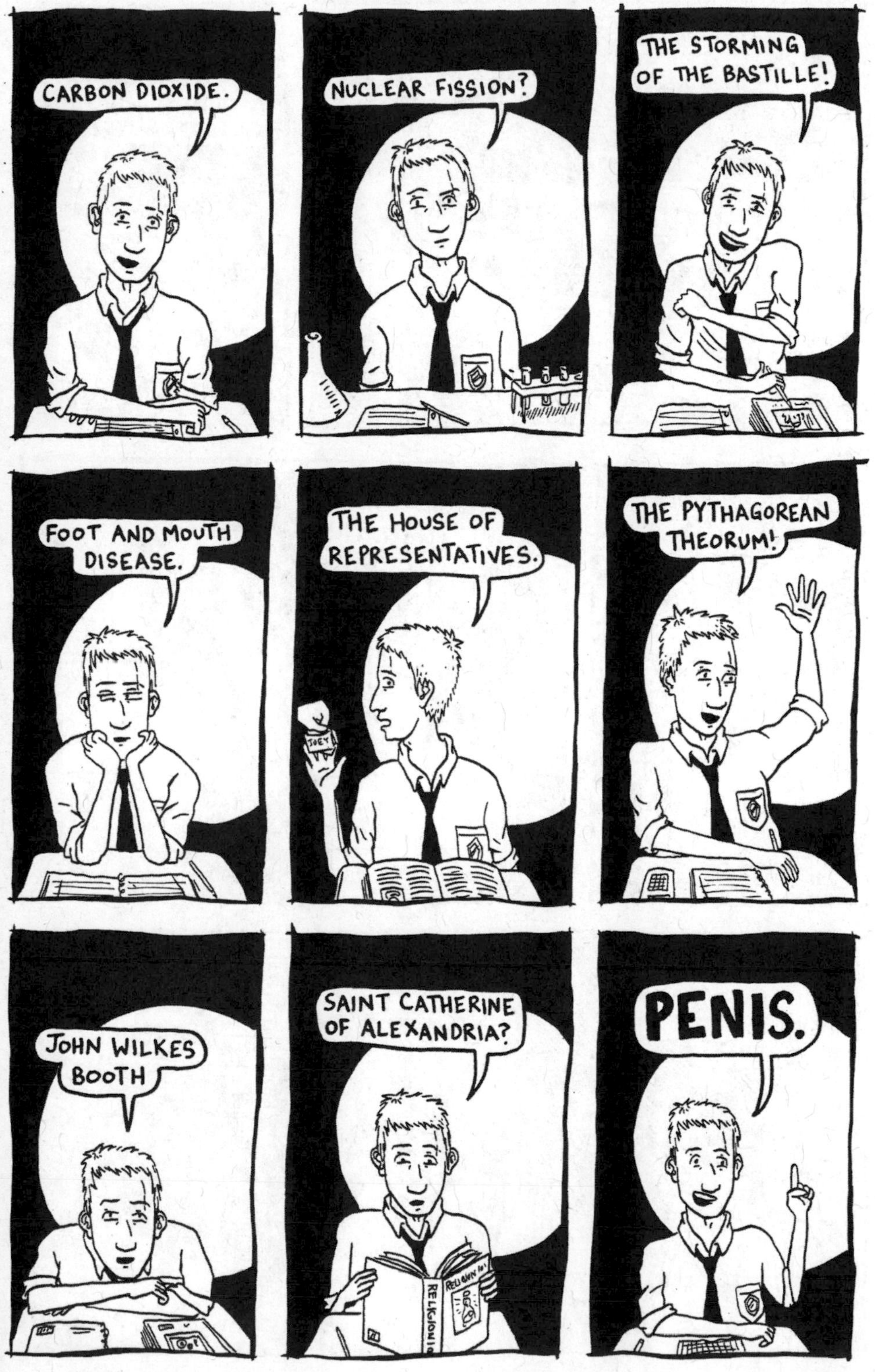
CARBON DIOXIDE.
NUCLEAR FISSION?
THE STORMING OF THE BASTILLE!
FOOT AND MOUTH DISEASE.
THE HOUSE OF REPRESENTATIVES.
THE PYTHAGOREAN THEORUM!
JOHN WILKES BOOTH
SAINT CATHERINE OF ALEXANDRIA?
PENIS.

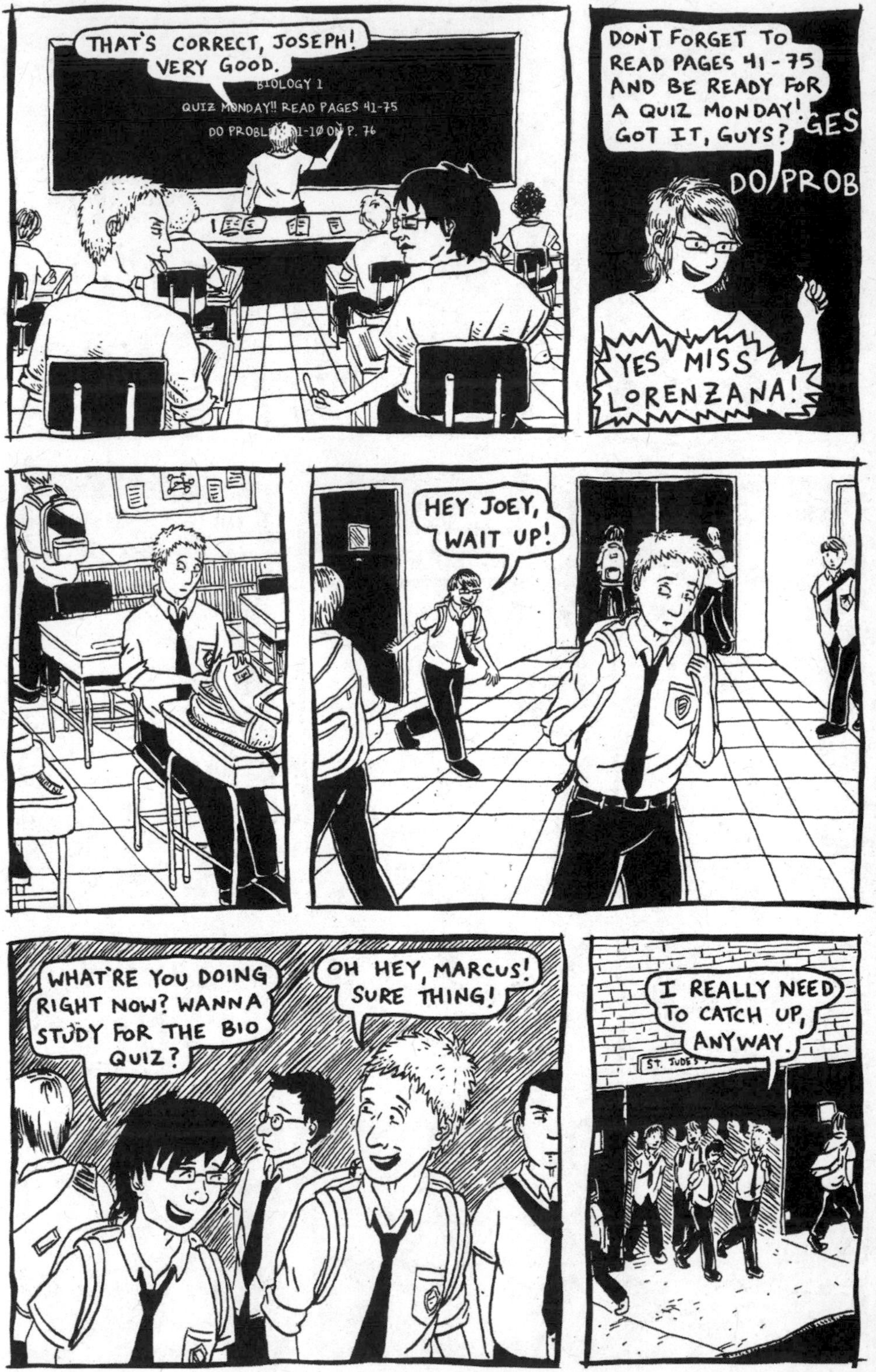
THAT'S CORRECT, JOSEPH! VERY GOOD.
BIOLOGY 1
QUIZ MONDAY!! READ PAGES 41-75
DON'T FORGET TO READ PAGES 41 - 75 AND BE READY FOR A QUIZ MONDAY! GOT IT, GUYS?
GES
DO PROB
YES MISS LORENZANA!
HEY JOEY, WAIT UP!
WHAT'RE YOU DOING RIGHT NOW? WANNA STUDY FOR THE BIO QUIZ?
OH HEY, MARCUS! SURE THING!
I REALLY NEED TO CATCH UP, ANYWAY.
ST. JUDE'S

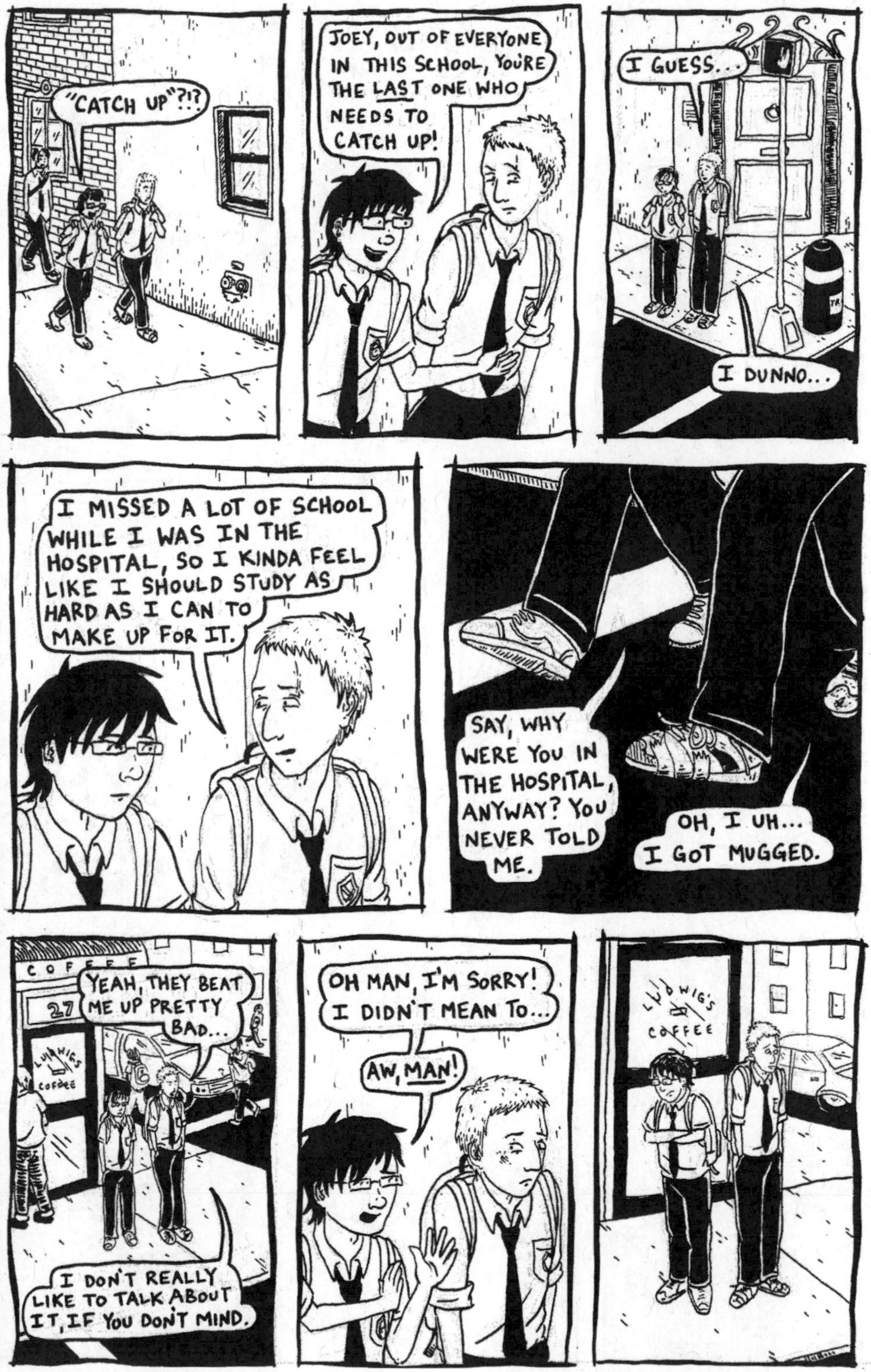
"CATCH UP"?!?
JOEY, OUT OF EVERYONE IN THIS SCHOOL, YOU'RE THE LAST ONE WHO NEEDS TO CATCH UP!
I GUESS...
I DUNNO...
I MISSED A LOT OF SCHOOL WHILE I WAS IN THE HOSPITAL, SO I KINDA FEEL LIKE I SHOULD STUDY AS HARD AS I CAN TO MAKE UP FOR IT.
SAY, WHY WERE YOU IN THE HOSPITAL, ANYWAY? YOU NEVER TOLD ME.
OH, I UH... I GOT MUGGED.
27
YEAH, THEY BEAT ME UP PRETTY BAD...
I DON'T REALLY LIKE TO TALK ABOUT IT, IF YOU DON'T MIND.
OH MAN, I'M SORRY! I DIDN'T MEAN TO...
AW, MAN!
LUDWIG'S COFFEE

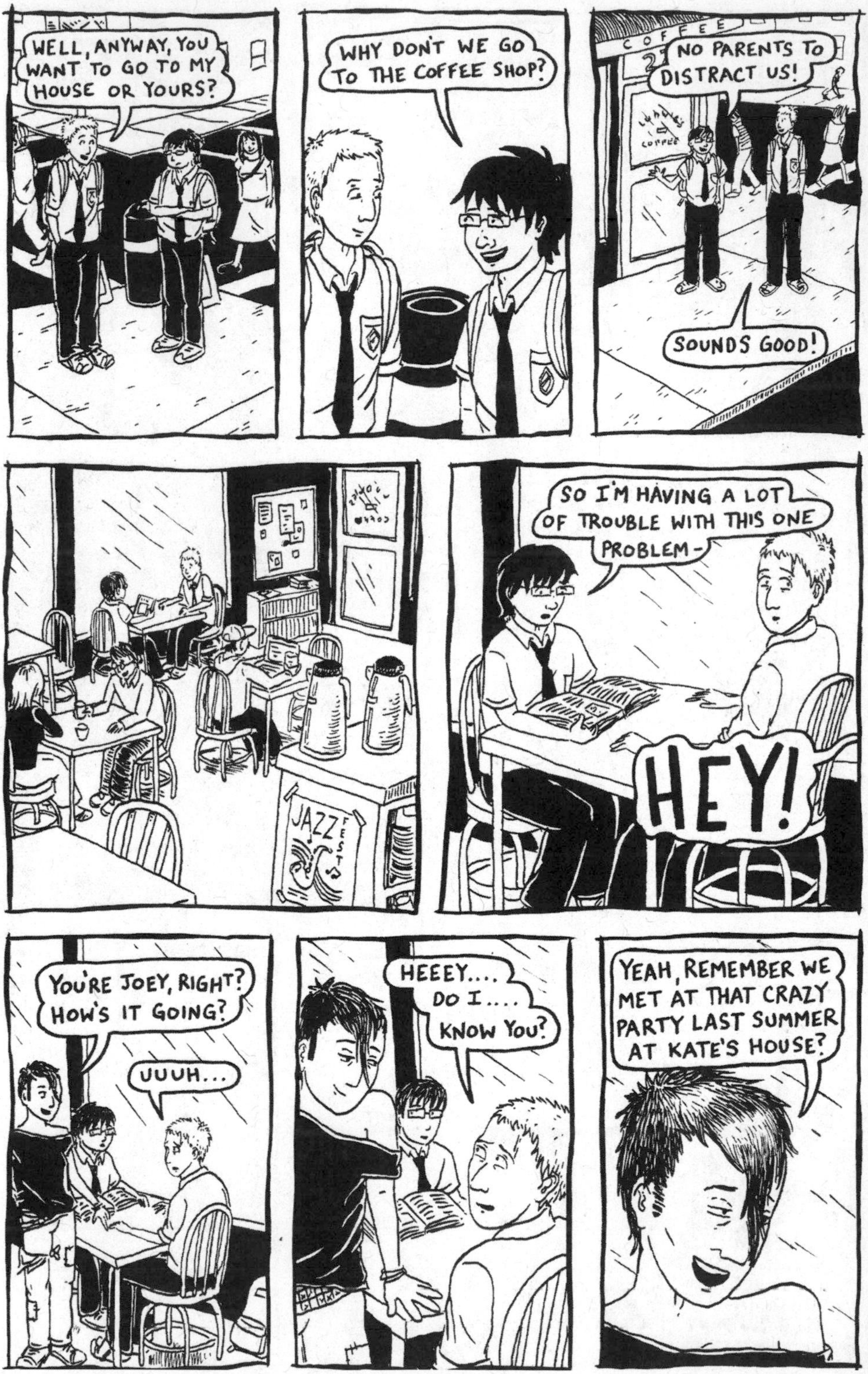
WELL, ANYWAY, YOU WANT TO GO TO MY HOUSE OR YOURS?
WHY DON'T WE GO TO THE COFFEE SHOP?
COFFEE
NO PARENTS TO DISTRACT US!
SOUNDS GOOD!
JAZZ FEST
SO I'M HAVING A LOT OF TROUBLE WITH THIS ONE PROBLEM-
HEY!
YOU'RE JOEY, RIGHT? HOW'S IT GOING?
UUUH...
HEEEY.... DO I.... KNOW YOU?
YEAH, REMEMBER WE MET AT THAT CRAZY PARTY LAST SUMMER AT KATE'S HOUSE?

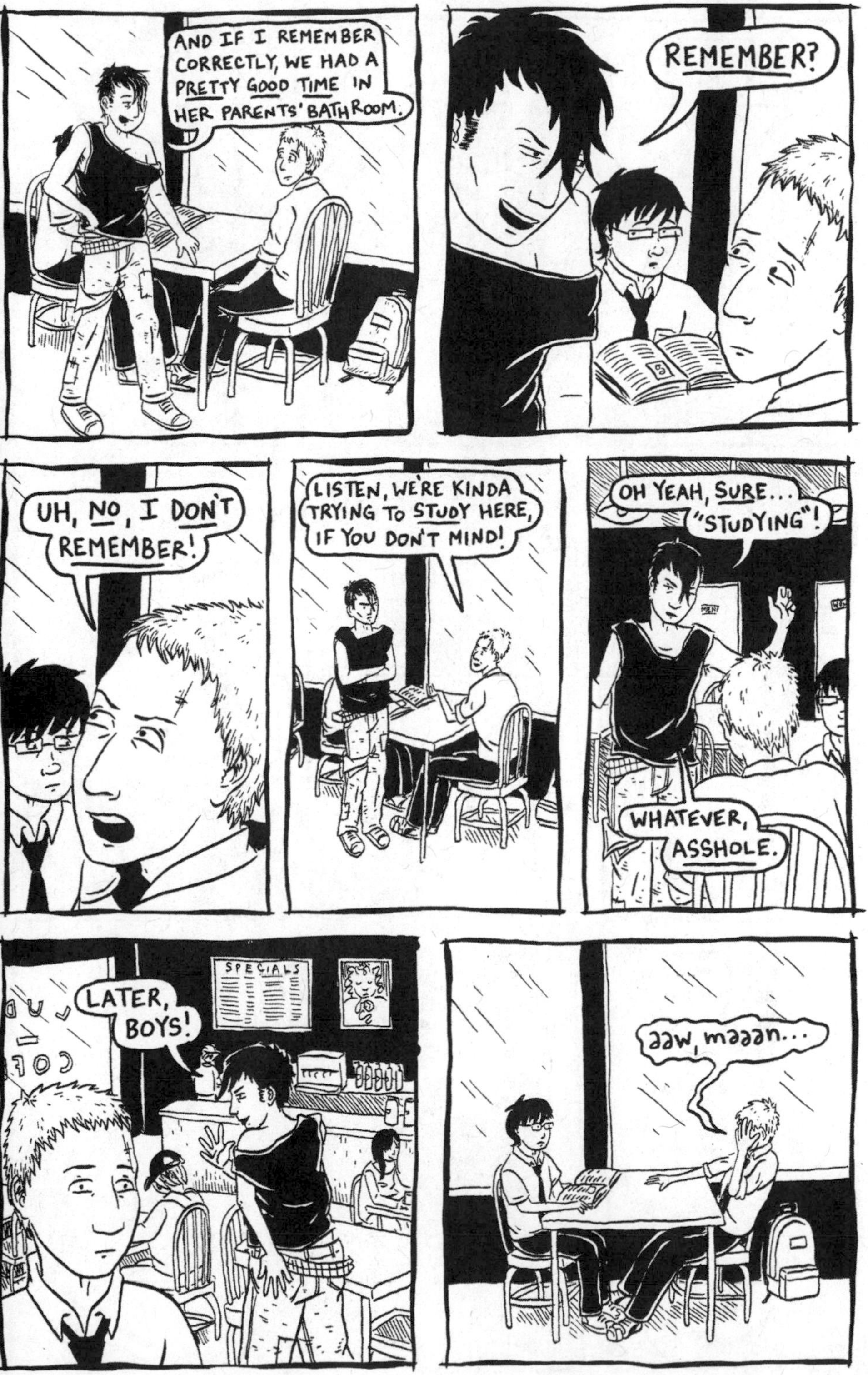
AND IF I REMEMBER CORRECTLY, WE HAD A PRETTY GOOD TIME IN HER PARENTS' BATHROOM.
REMEMBER?
UH, NO, I DON'T REMEMBER!
LISTEN, WE'RE KINDA TRYING TO STUDY HERE, IF YOU DON'T MIND!
OH YEAH, SURE... "STUDYING"!
WHATEVER, ASSHOLE.
SPECIALS
LATER, BOYS!
aaw, maaan...

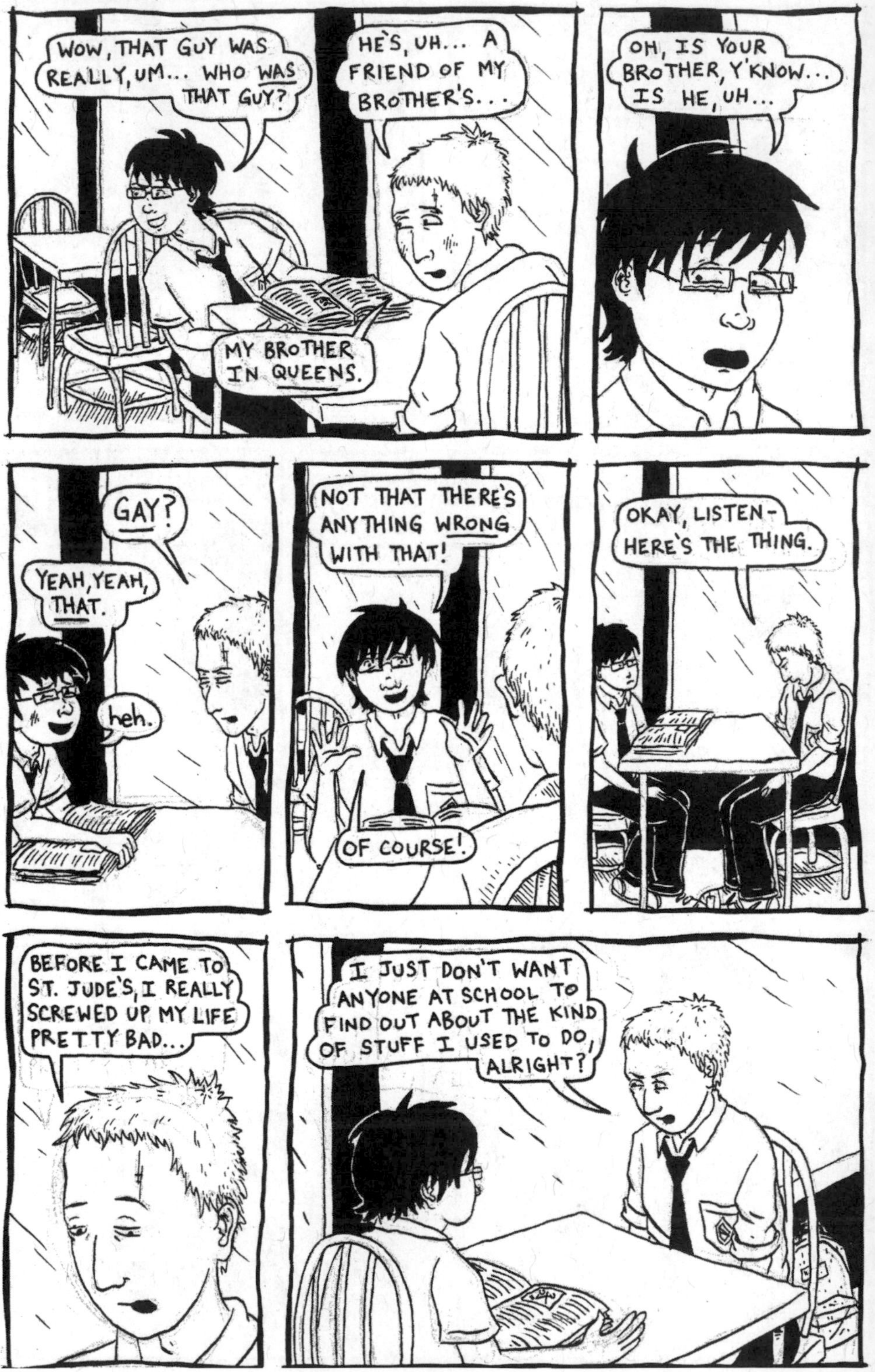
WOW, THAT GUY WAS REALLY, UM... WHO WAS THAT GUY?
HE'S, UH... A FRIEND OF MY BROTHER'S...
MY BROTHER IN QUEENS.
OH, IS YOUR BROTHER, Y'KNOW... IS HE, UH...
GAY?
YEAH, YEAH, THAT.
heh.
NOT THAT THERE'S ANYTHING WRONG WITH THAT!
OF COURSE!
OKAY, LISTEN- HERE'S THE THING.
BEFORE I CAME TO ST. JUDE'S, I REALLY SCREWED UP MY LIFE PRETTY BAD...
I JUST DON'T WANT ANYONE AT SCHOOL TO FIND OUT ABOUT THE KIND OF STUFF I USED TO DO, ALRIGHT?

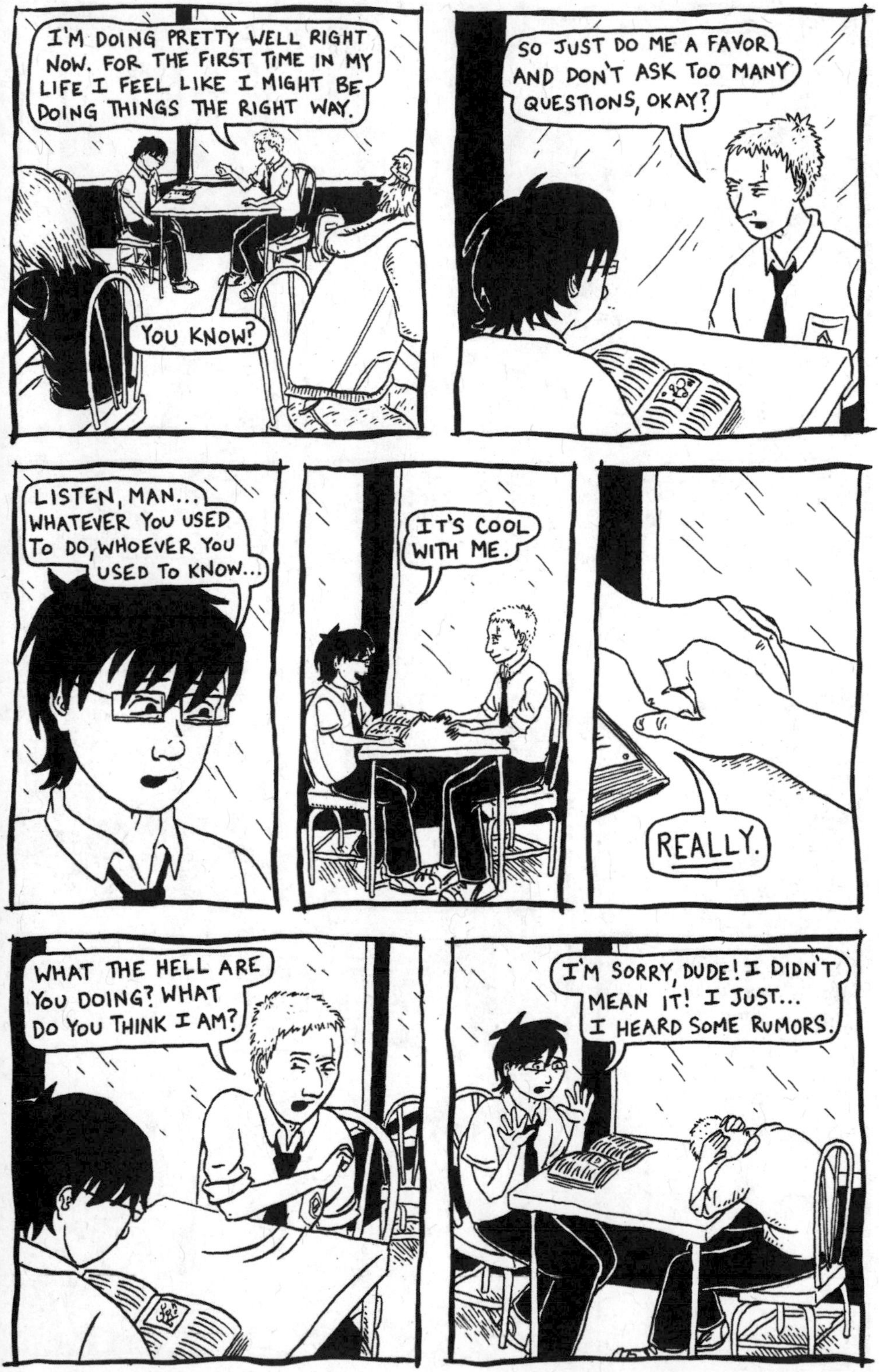
I'M DOING PRETTY WELL RIGHT NOW. FOR THE FIRST TIME IN MY LIFE I FEEL LIKE I MIGHT BE DOING THINGS THE RIGHT WAY.
YOU KNOW?
SO JUST DO ME A FAVOR AND DON'T ASK TOO MANY QUESTIONS, OKAY?
LISTEN, MAN... WHATEVER YOU USED TO DO, WHOEVER YOU USED TO KNOW...
IT'S COOL WITH ME.
REALLY.
WHAT THE HELL ARE YOU DOING? WHAT DO YOU THINK I AM?
I'M SORRY, DUDE! I DIDN'T MEAN IT! I JUST... I HEARD SOME RUMORS.

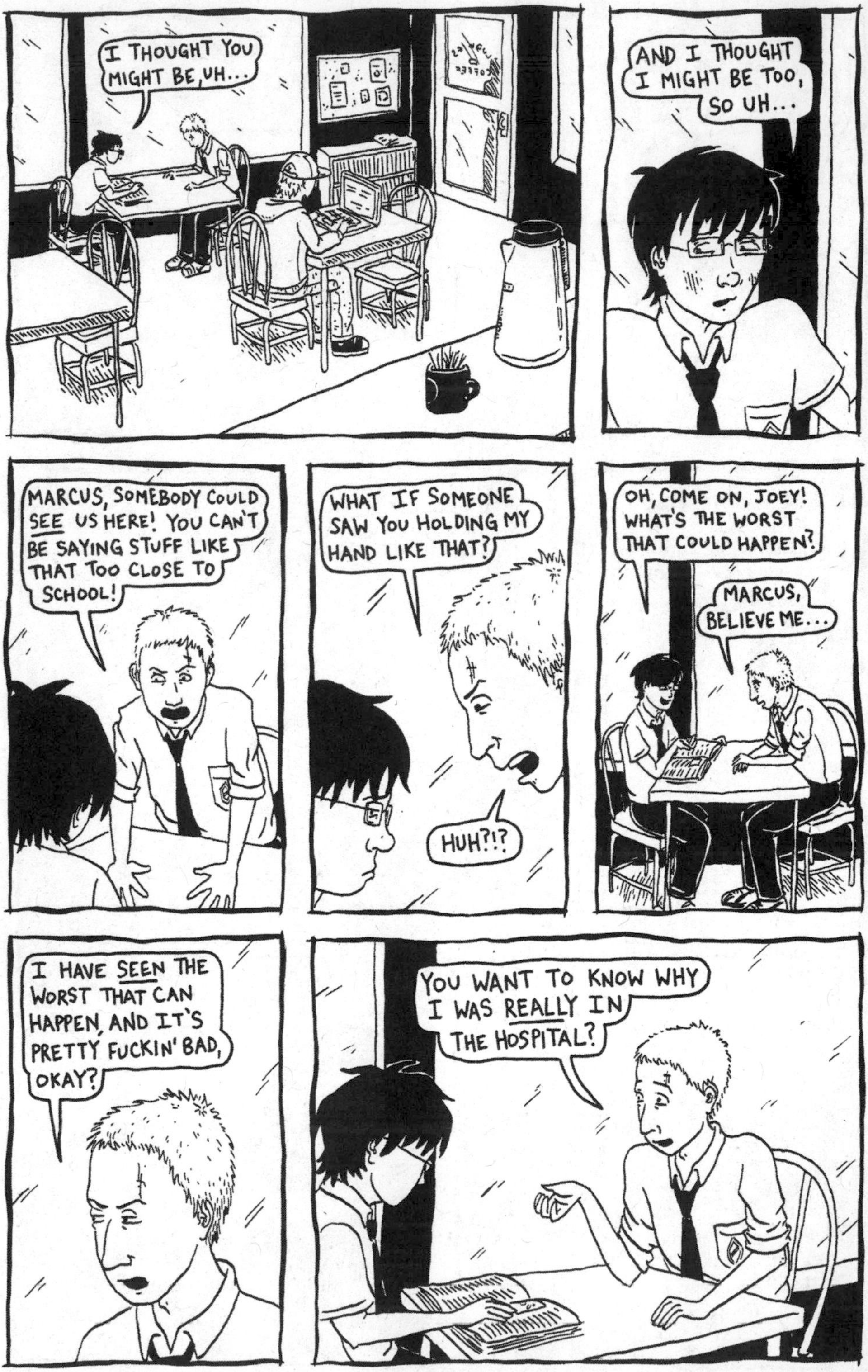
I THOUGHT YOU MIGHT BE, UH...
COFFEE
AND I THOUGHT I MIGHT BE TOO, SO UH...
MARCUS, SOMEBODY COULD SEE US HERE! YOU CAN'T BE SAYING STUFF LIKE THAT TOO CLOSE TO SCHOOL!
WHAT IF SOMEONE SAW YOU HOLDING MY HAND LIKE THAT?
HUH?!?
OH, COME ON, JOEY! WHAT'S THE WORST THAT COULD HAPPEN?
MARCUS, BELIEVE ME...
I HAVE SEEN THE WORST THAT CAN HAPPEN, AND IT'S PRETTY FUCKIN' BAD, OKAY?
YOU WANT TO KNOW WHY I WAS REALLY IN THE HOSPITAL?

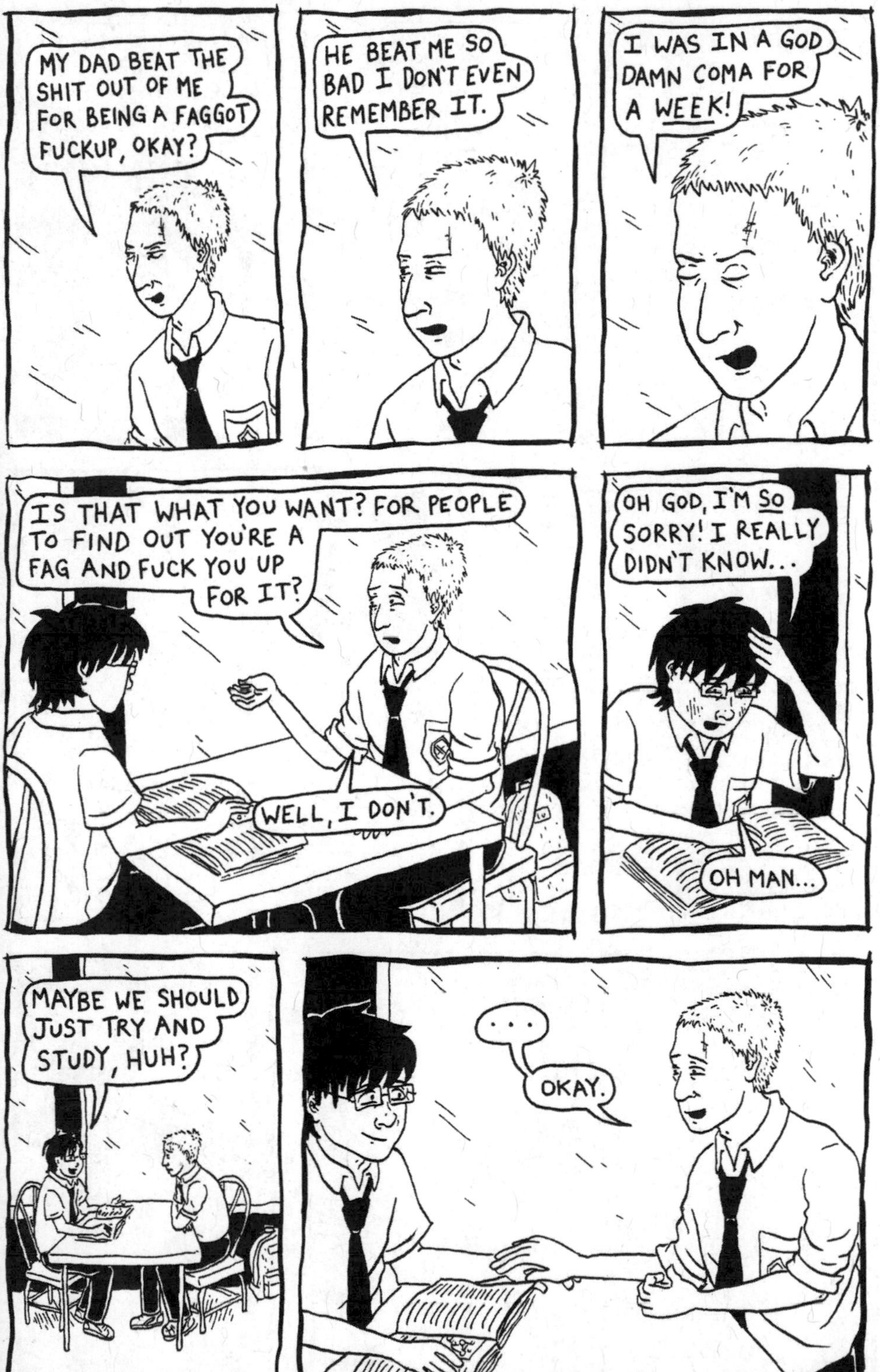
MY DAD BEAT THE SHIT OUT OF ME FOR BEING A FAGGOT FUCKUP, OKAY?
HE BEAT ME SO BAD I DON'T EVEN REMEMBER IT.
I WAS IN A GOD DAMN COMA FOR A WEEK!
IS THAT WHAT YOU WANT? FOR PEOPLE TO FIND OUT YOU'RE A FAG AND FUCK YOU UP FOR IT?
WELL, I DON'T.
OH GOD, I'M SO SORRY! I REALLY DIDN'T KNOW...
OH MAN...
MAYBE WE SHOULD JUST TRY AND STUDY, HUH?
...
OKAY.

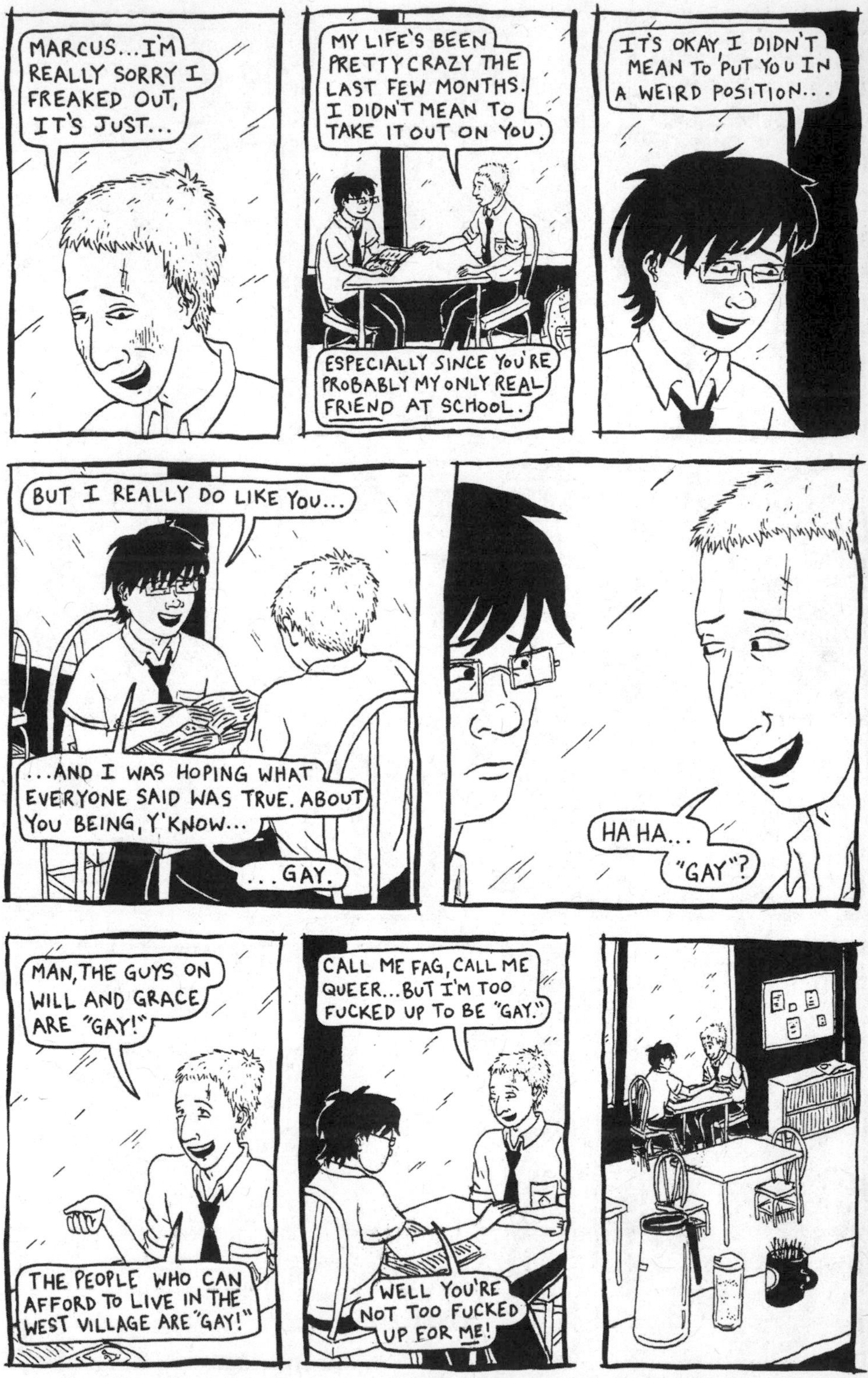
MARCUS...I'M REALLY SORRY I FREAKED OUT, IT'S JUST...
MY LIFE'S BEEN PRETTY CRAZY THE LAST FEW MONTHS. I DIDN'T MEAN TO TAKE IT OUT ON YOU.
ESPECIALLY SINCE YOU'RE PROBABLY MY ONLY REAL FRIEND AT SCHOOL.
IT'S OKAY, I DIDN'T MEAN TO PUT YOU IN A WEIRD POSITION...
BUT I REALLY DO LIKE YOU...
...AND I WAS HOPING WHAT EVERYONE SAID WAS TRUE. ABOUT YOU BEING, Y'KNOW...
...GAY.
HA HA...
"GAY"?
MAN, THE GUYS ON WILL AND GRACE ARE "GAY!"
THE PEOPLE WHO CAN AFFORD TO LIVE IN THE WEST VILLAGE ARE "GAY!"
CALL ME FAG, CALL ME QUEER...BUT I'M TOO FUCKED UP TO BE "GAY."
WELL YOU'RE NOT TOO FUCKED UP FOR ME!

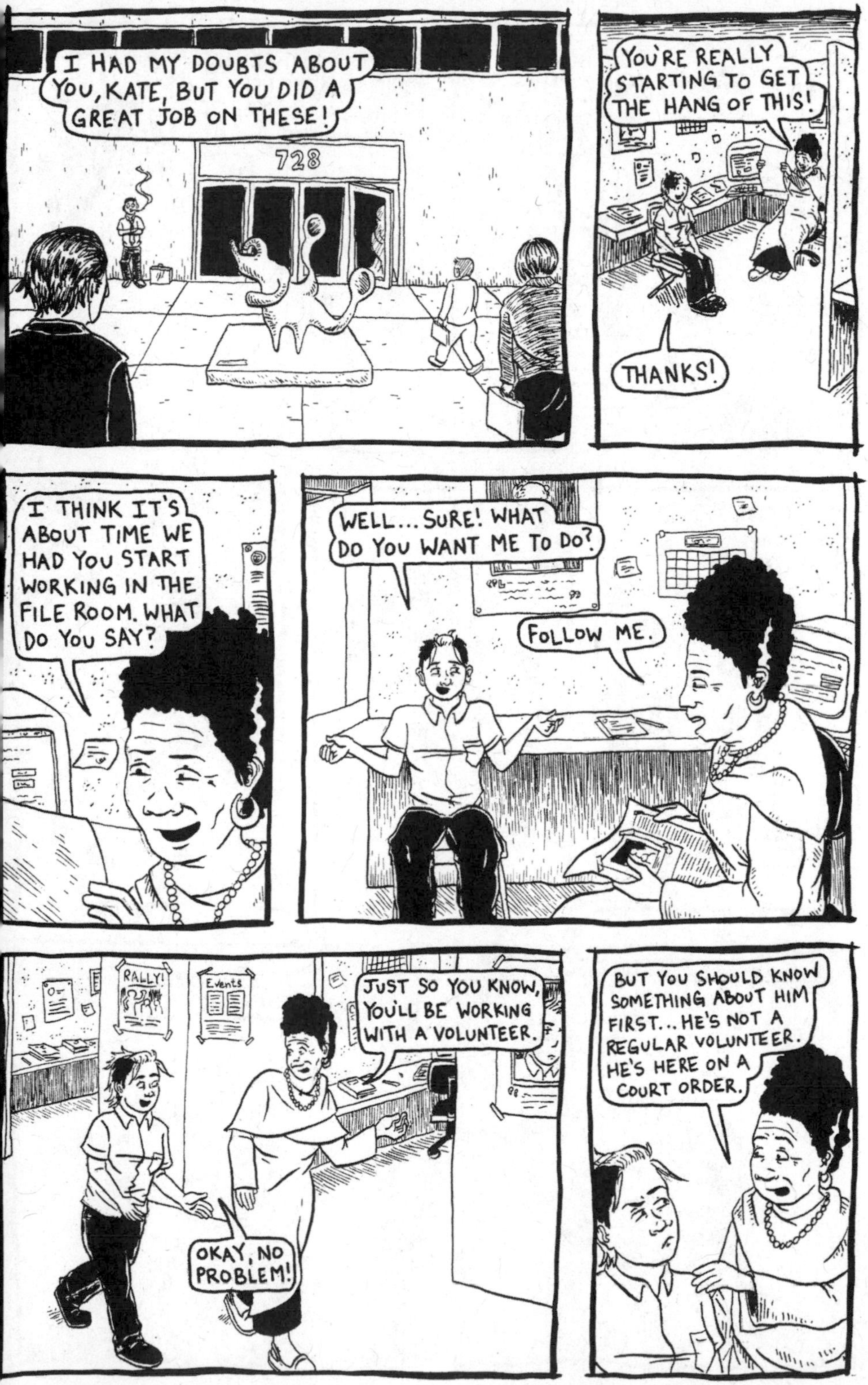
I HAD MY DOUBTS ABOUT YOU, KATE, BUT YOU DID A GREAT JOB ON THESE!
728
YOU'RE REALLY STARTING TO GET THE HANG OF THIS!
THANKS!
I THINK IT'S ABOUT TIME WE HAD YOU START WORKING IN THE FILE ROOM. WHAT DO YOU SAY?
WELL... SURE! WHAT DO YOU WANT ME TO DO?
FOLLOW ME.
RALLY!
Events
JUST SO YOU KNOW, YOU'LL BE WORKING WITH A VOLUNTEER.
OKAY, NO PROBLEM!
BUT YOU SHOULD KNOW SOMETHING ABOUT HIM FIRST... HE'S NOT A REGULAR VOLUNTEER. HE'S HERE ON A COURT ORDER.

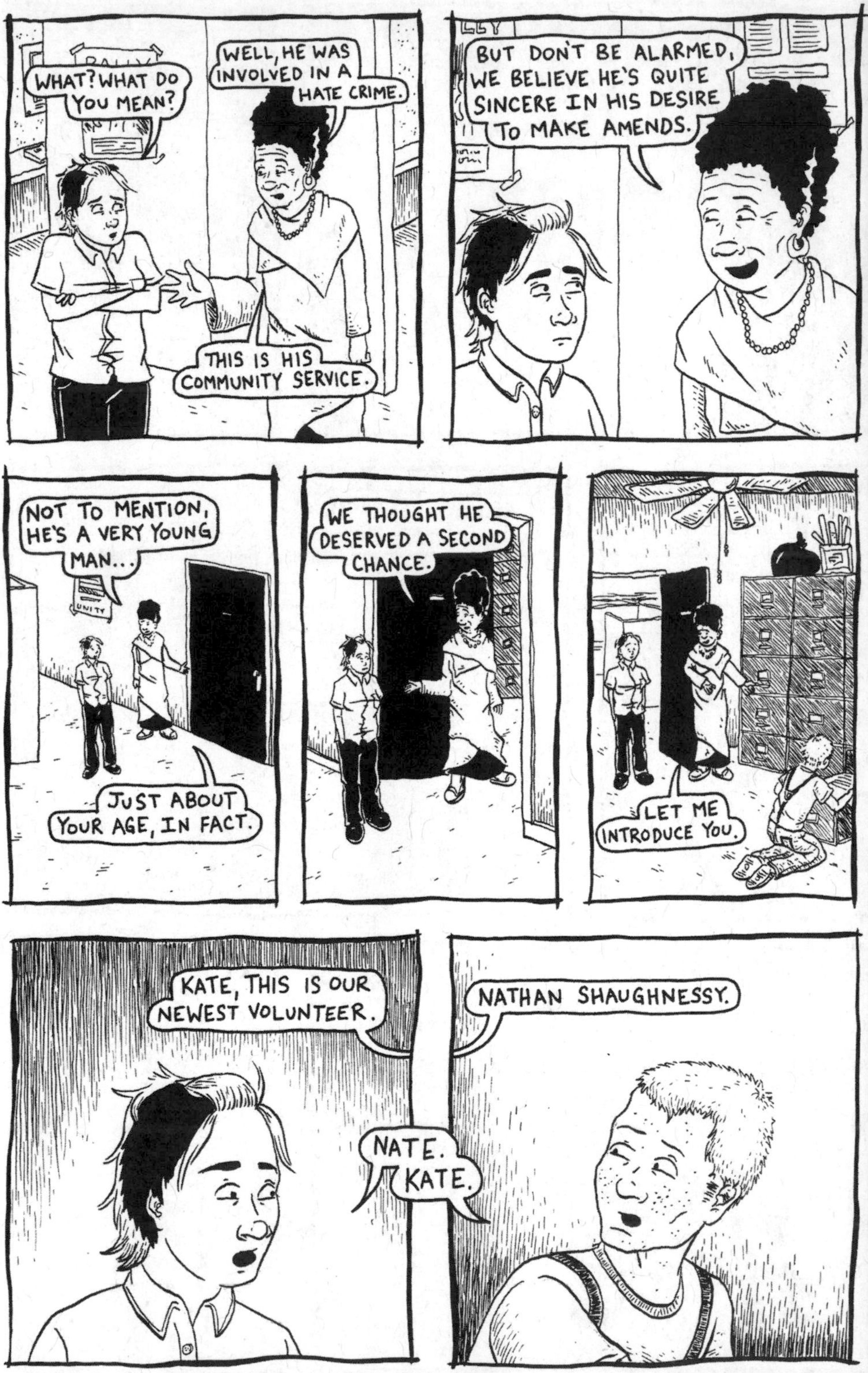
WHAT? WHAT DO YOU MEAN?
WELL, HE WAS INVOLVED IN A HATE CRIME.
THIS IS HIS COMMUNITY SERVICE.
BUT DON'T BE ALARMED, WE BELIEVE HE'S QUITE SINCERE IN HIS DESIRE TO MAKE AMENDS.
NOT TO MENTION, HE'S A VERY YOUNG MAN...
UNITY
JUST ABOUT YOUR AGE, IN FACT.
WE THOUGHT HE DESERVED A SECOND CHANCE.
LET ME INTRODUCE YOU.
KATE, THIS IS OUR NEWEST VOLUNTEER.
NATHAN SHAUGHNESSY.
NATE.
KATE.

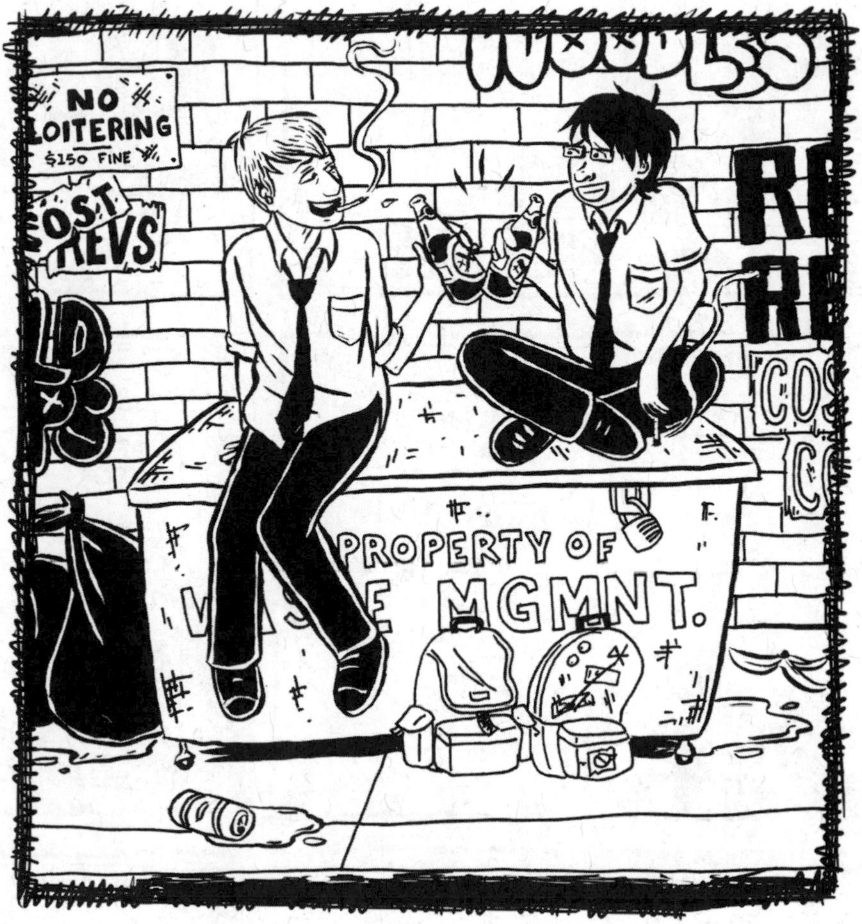
NO
LOITERING
$150 FINE
PROPERTY OF
MGMNT.

CHAPTER THREE

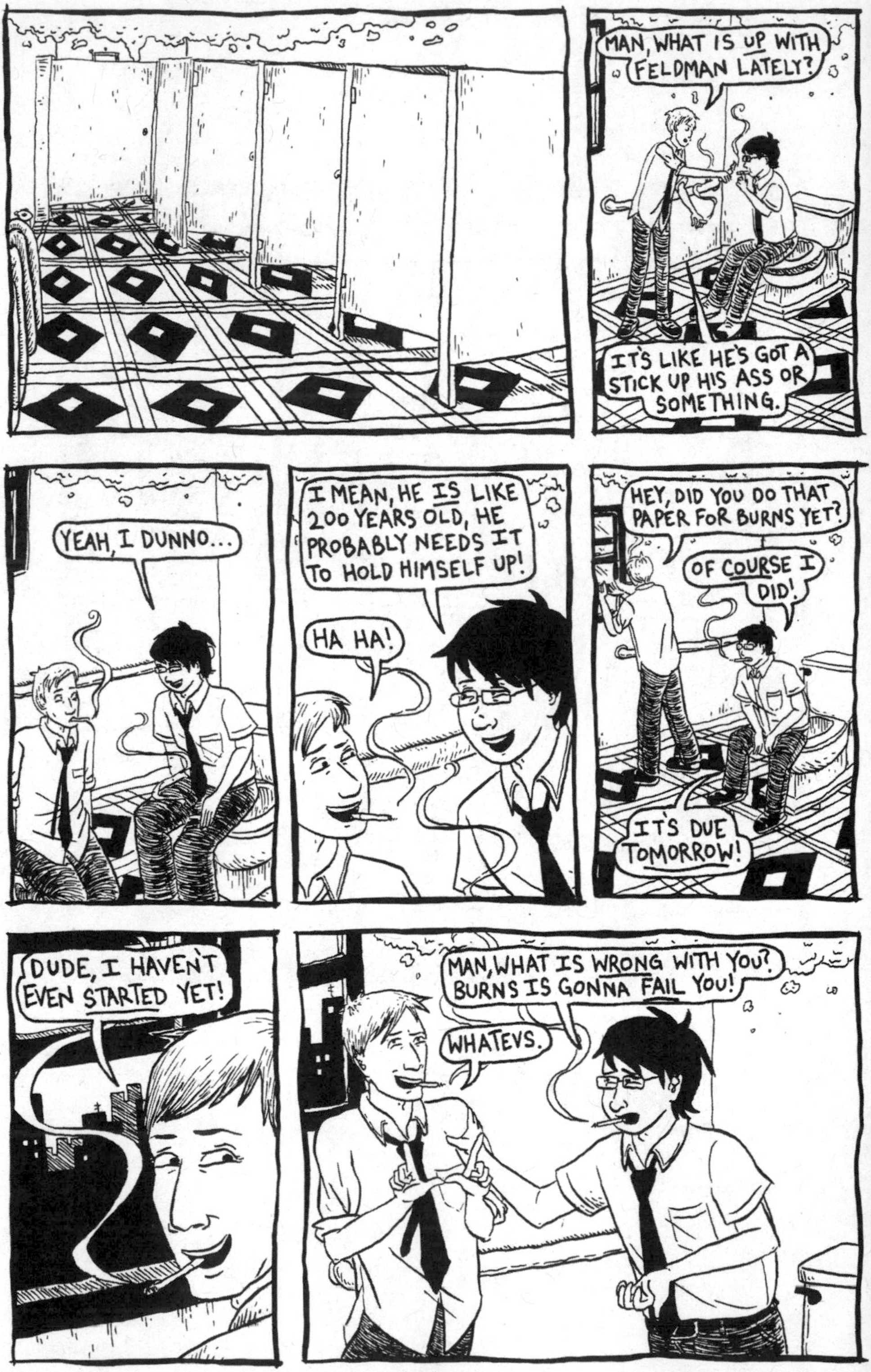
MAN, WHAT IS UP WITH FELDMAN LATELY?
IT'S LIKE HE'S GOT A STICK UP HIS ASS OR SOMETHING.
YEAH, I DUNNO...
I MEAN, HE IS LIKE 200 YEARS OLD, HE PROBABLY NEEDS IT TO HOLD HIMSELF UP!
HA HA!
HEY, DID YOU DO THAT PAPER FOR BURNS YET?
OF COURSE I DID!
IT'S DUE TOMORROW!
DUDE, I HAVEN'T EVEN STARTED YET!
MAN, WHAT IS WRONG WITH YOU? BURNS IS GONNA FAIL YOU!
WHATEVS.

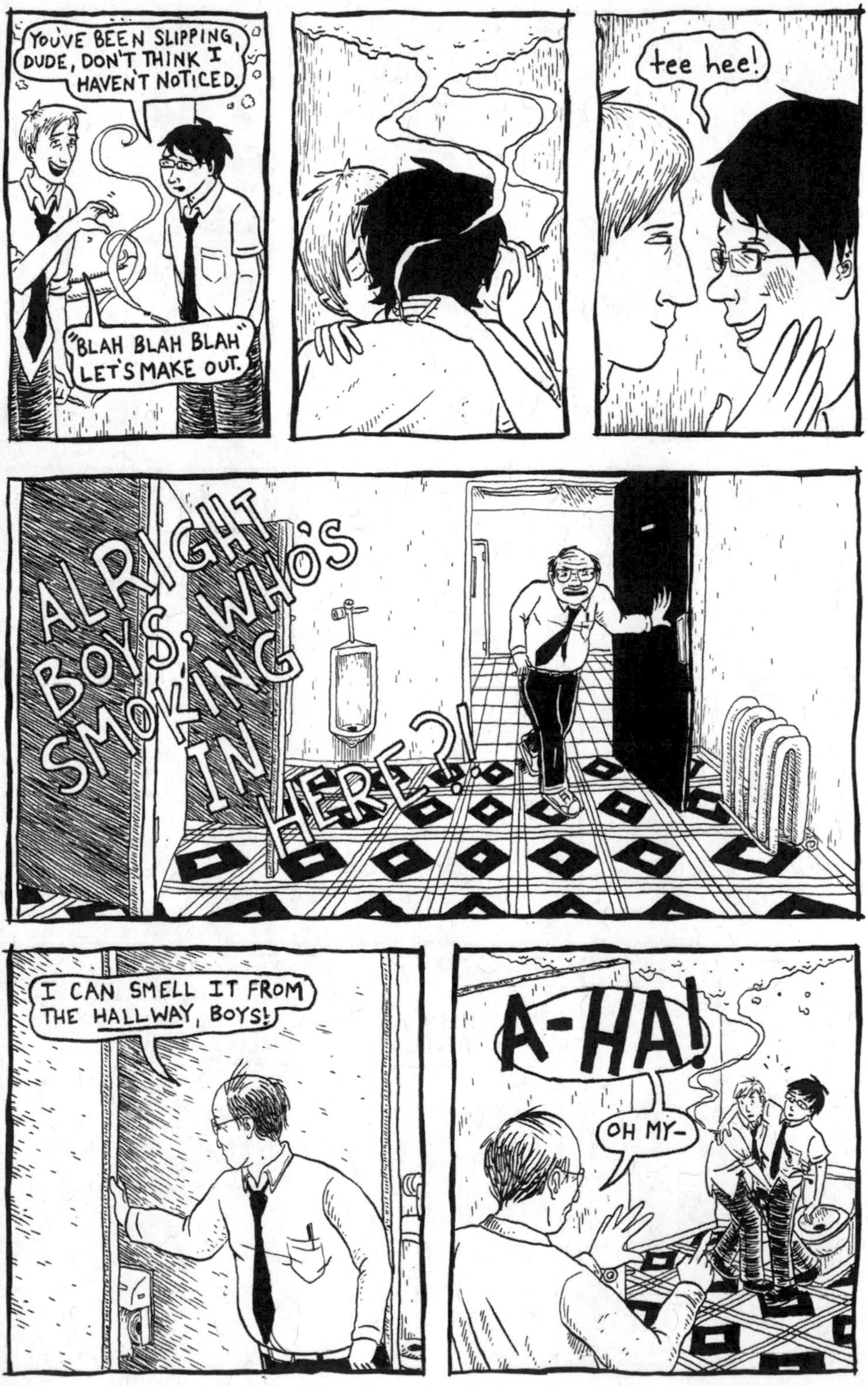
YOU'VE BEEN SLIPPING, DUDE, DON'T THINK I HAVEN'T NOTICED.
"BLAH BLAH BLAH" LET'S MAKE OUT.
tee hee!
ALRIGHT BOYS, WHO'S SMOKING IN HERE?!
I CAN SMELL IT FROM THE HALLWAY, BOYS!
A-HA!
OH MY-

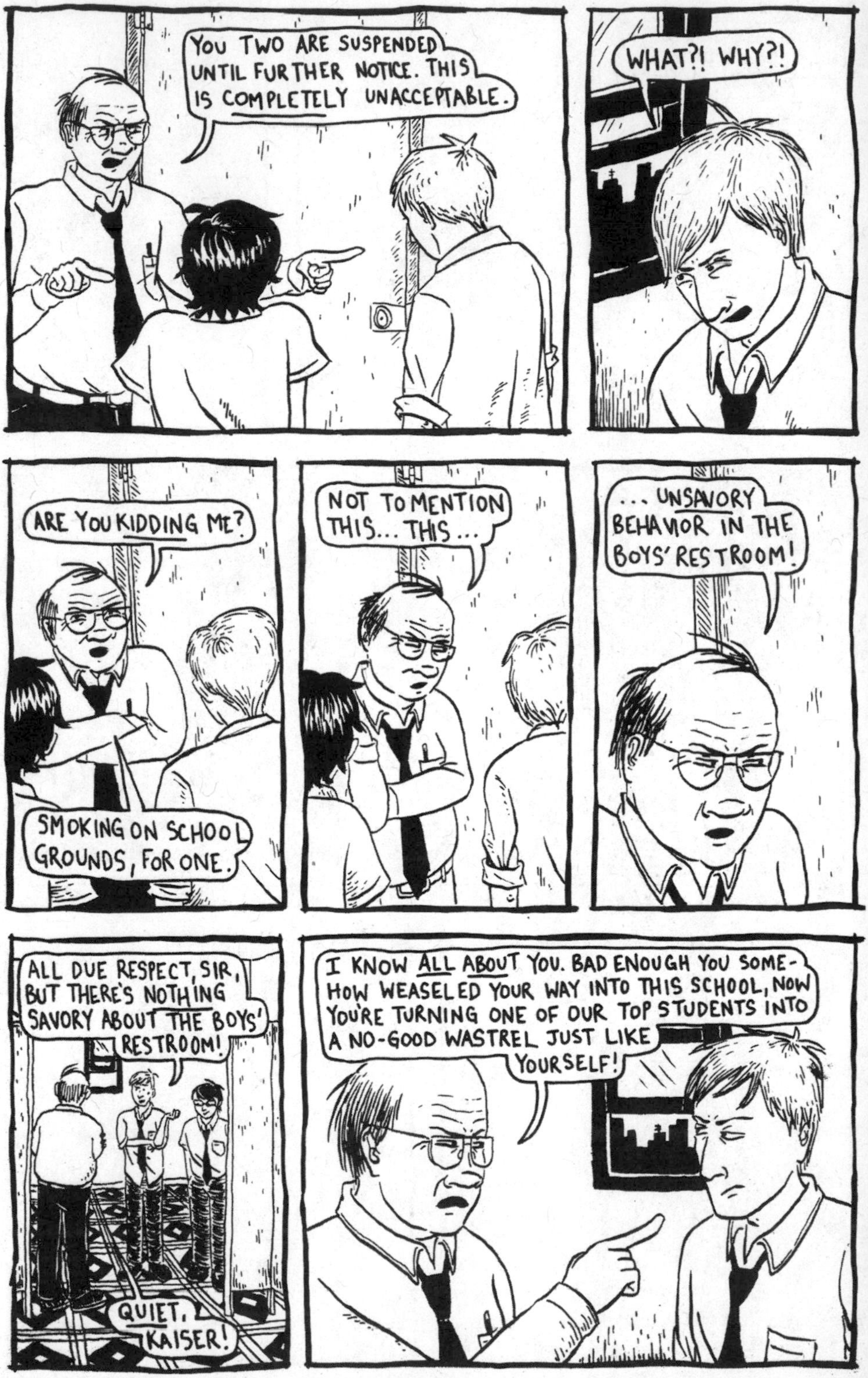
YOU TWO ARE SUSPENDED UNTIL FURTHER NOTICE. THIS IS COMPLETELY UNACCEPTABLE.
WHAT?! WHY?!
ARE YOU KIDDING ME?
SMOKING ON SCHOOL GROUNDS, FOR ONE.
NOT TO MENTION THIS... THIS...
... UNSAVORY BEHAVIOR IN THE BOYS' RESTROOM!
ALL DUE RESPECT, SIR, BUT THERE'S NOTHING SAVORY ABOUT THE BOYS' RESTROOM!
QUIET, KAISER!
I KNOW ALL ABOUT YOU. BAD ENOUGH YOU SOMEHOW WEASELED YOUR WAY INTO THIS SCHOOL, NOW YOU'RE TURNING ONE OF OUR TOP STUDENTS INTO A NO-GOOD WASTREL JUST LIKE YOURSELF!

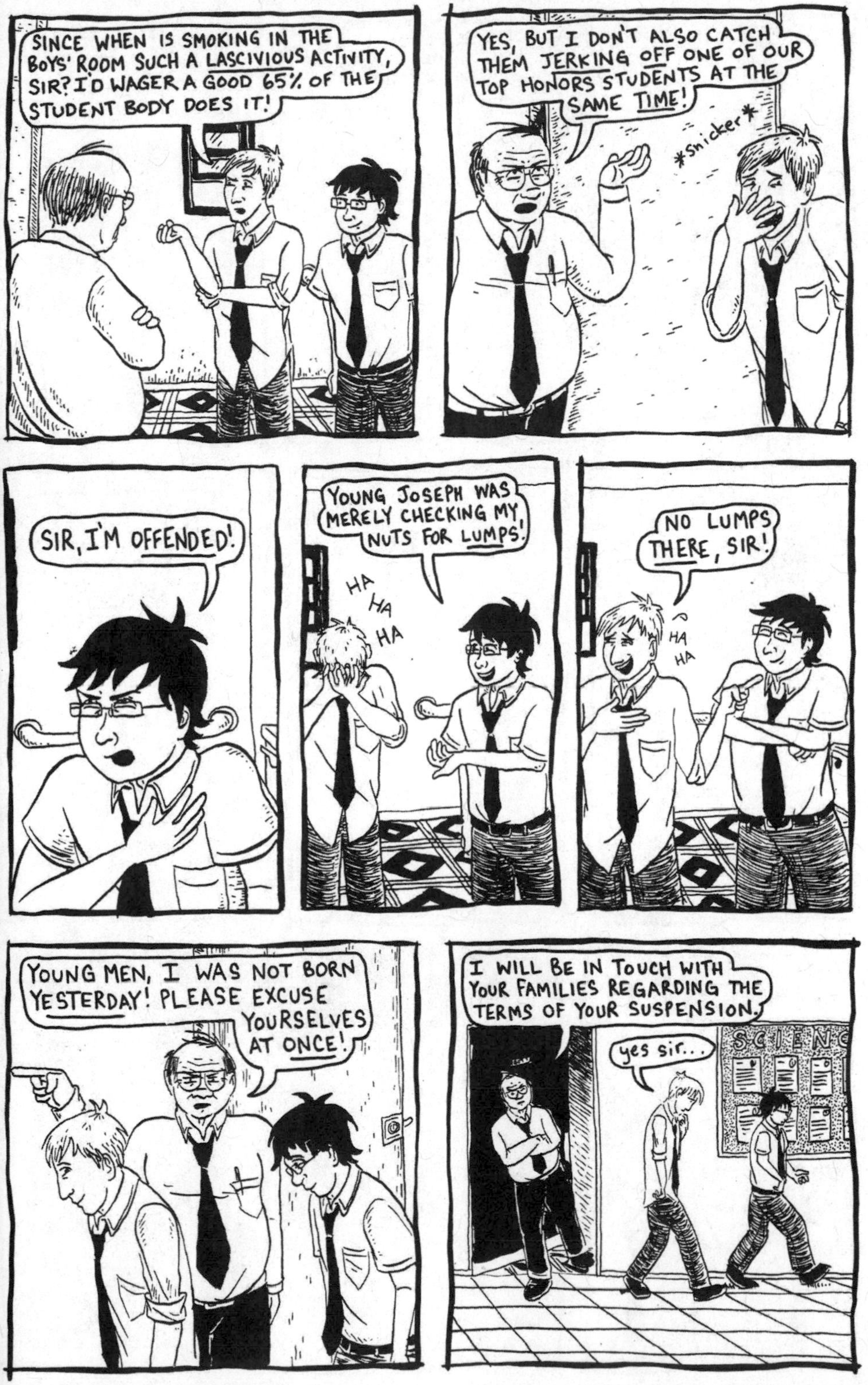
SINCE WHEN IS SMOKING IN THE BOYS' ROOM SUCH A LASCIVIOUS ACTIVITY, SIR? I'D WAGER A GOOD 65% OF THE STUDENT BODY DOES IT!
YES, BUT I DON'T ALSO CATCH THEM JERKING OFF ONE OF OUR TOP HONORS STUDENTS AT THE SAME TIME!
snicker
SIR, I'M OFFENDED!
YOUNG JOSEPH WAS MERELY CHECKING MY NUTS FOR LUMPS!
HA HA HA
NO LUMPS THERE, SIR!
HA HA
YOUNG MEN, I WAS NOT BORN YESTERDAY! PLEASE EXCUSE YOURSELVES AT ONCE!
I WILL BE IN TOUCH WITH YOUR FAMILIES REGARDING THE TERMS OF YOUR SUSPENSION.
yes sir...

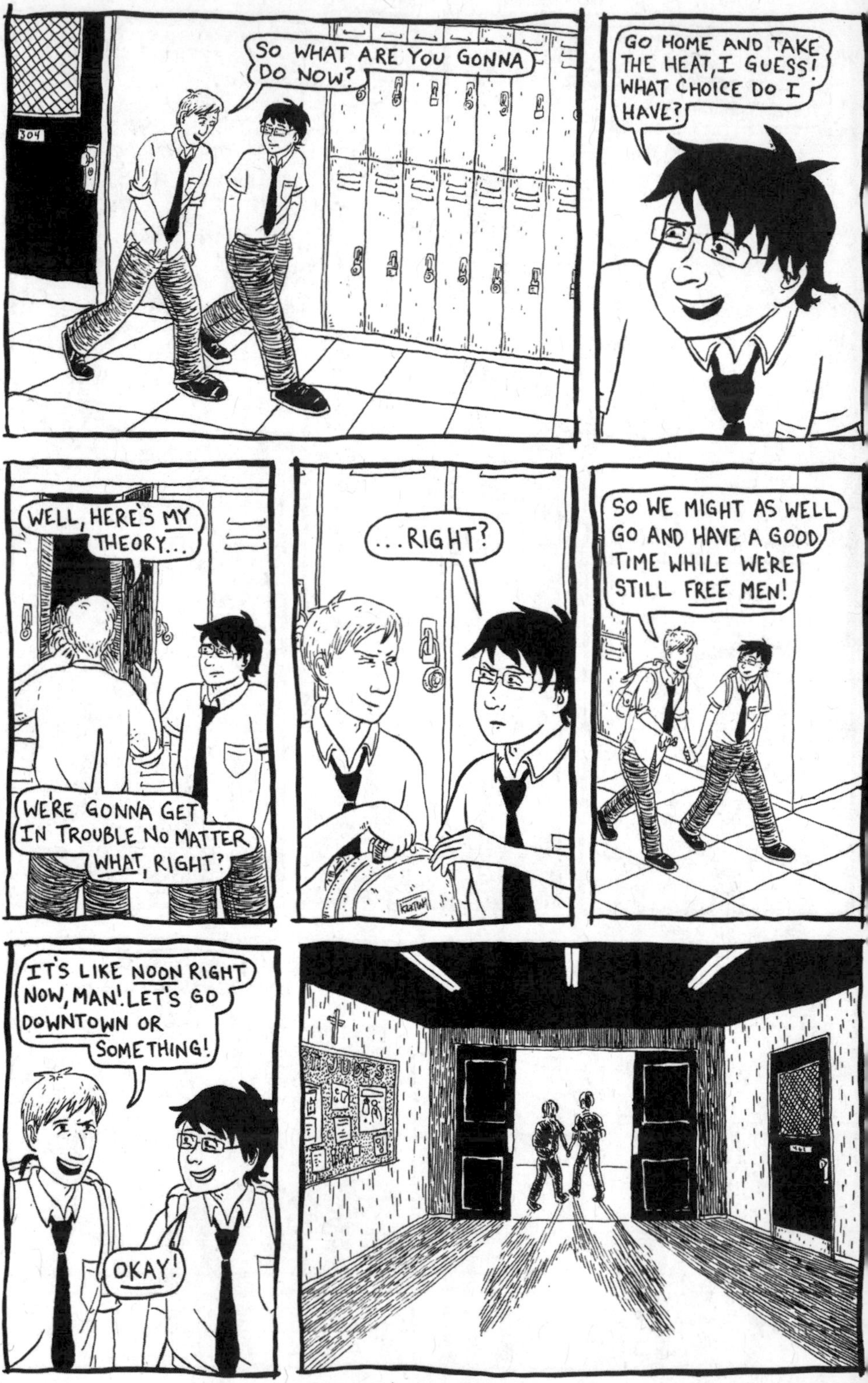

304
SO WHAT ARE YOU GONNA DO NOW?
GO HOME AND TAKE THE HEAT, I GUESS! WHAT CHOICE DO I HAVE?
WELL, HERE'S MY THEORY...
WE'RE GONNA GET IN TROUBLE NO MATTER WHAT, RIGHT?
...RIGHT?
SO WE MIGHT AS WELL GO AND HAVE A GOOD TIME WHILE WE'RE STILL FREE MEN!
IT'S LIKE NOON RIGHT NOW, MAN! LET'S GO DOWNTOWN OR SOMETHING!
OKAY!
ST. JUDE'S

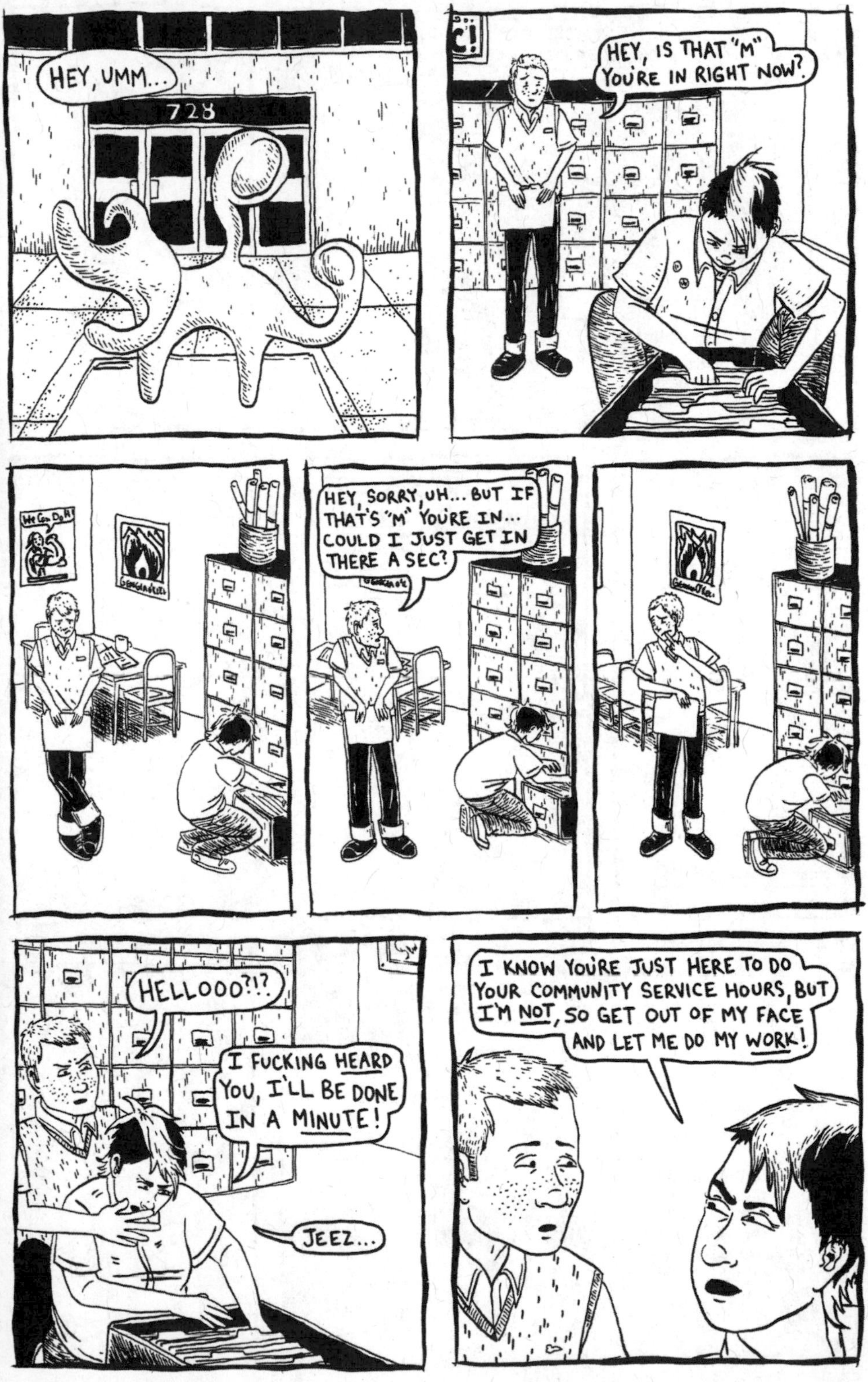
HEY, UMM...
728
HEY, IS THAT "M" YOU'RE IN RIGHT NOW?
HEY, SORRY, UH... BUT IF THAT'S "M" YOU'RE IN... COULD I JUST GET IN THERE A SEC?
HELLOOO?!?
I FUCKING HEARD YOU, I'LL BE DONE IN A MINUTE!
JEEZ...
I KNOW YOU'RE JUST HERE TO DO YOUR COMMUNITY SERVICE HOURS, BUT I'M NOT, SO GET OUT OF MY FACE AND LET ME DO MY WORK!

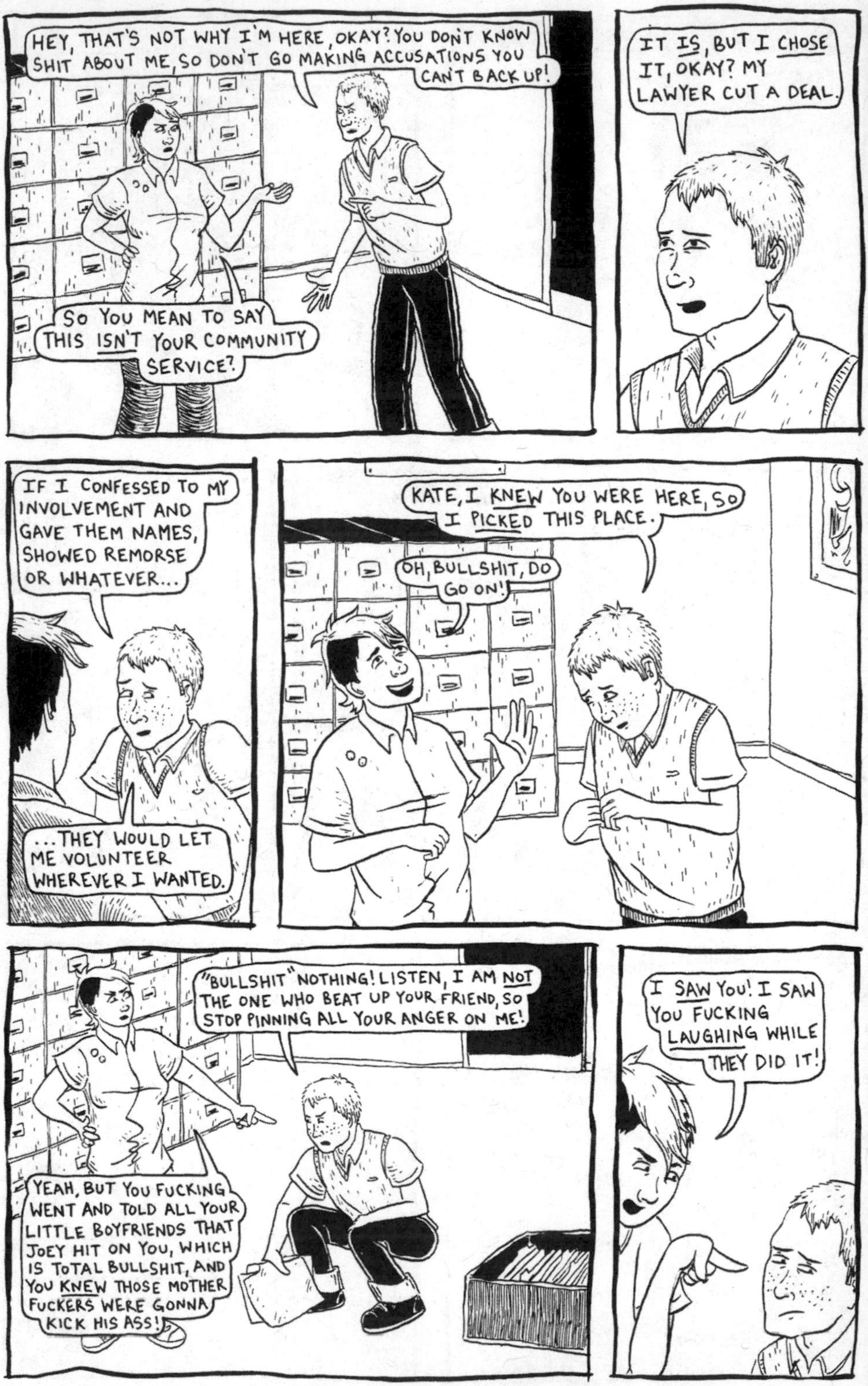
HEY, THAT'S NOT WHY I'M HERE, OKAY? YOU DON'T KNOW SHIT ABOUT ME, SO DON'T GO MAKING ACCUSATIONS YOU CAN'T BACK UP!
SO YOU MEAN TO SAY THIS ISN'T YOUR COMMUNITY SERVICE?
IT IS, BUT I CHOSE IT, OKAY? MY LAWYER CUT A DEAL.
IF I CONFESSED TO MY INVOLVEMENT AND GAVE THEM NAMES, SHOWED REMORSE OR WHATEVER...
...THEY WOULD LET ME VOLUNTEER WHEREVER I WANTED.
KATE, I KNEW YOU WERE HERE, SO I PICKED THIS PLACE.
OH, BULLSHIT, DO GO ON!
"BULLSHIT" NOTHING! LISTEN, I AM NOT THE ONE WHO BEAT UP YOUR FRIEND, SO STOP PINNING ALL YOUR ANGER ON ME!
YEAH, BUT YOU FUCKING WENT AND TOLD ALL YOUR LITTLE BOYFRIENDS THAT JOEY HIT ON YOU, WHICH IS TOTAL BULLSHIT, AND YOU KNEW THOSE MOTHER FUCKERS WERE GONNA KICK HIS ASS!
I SAW YOU! I SAW YOU FUCKING LAUGHING WHILE THEY DID IT!

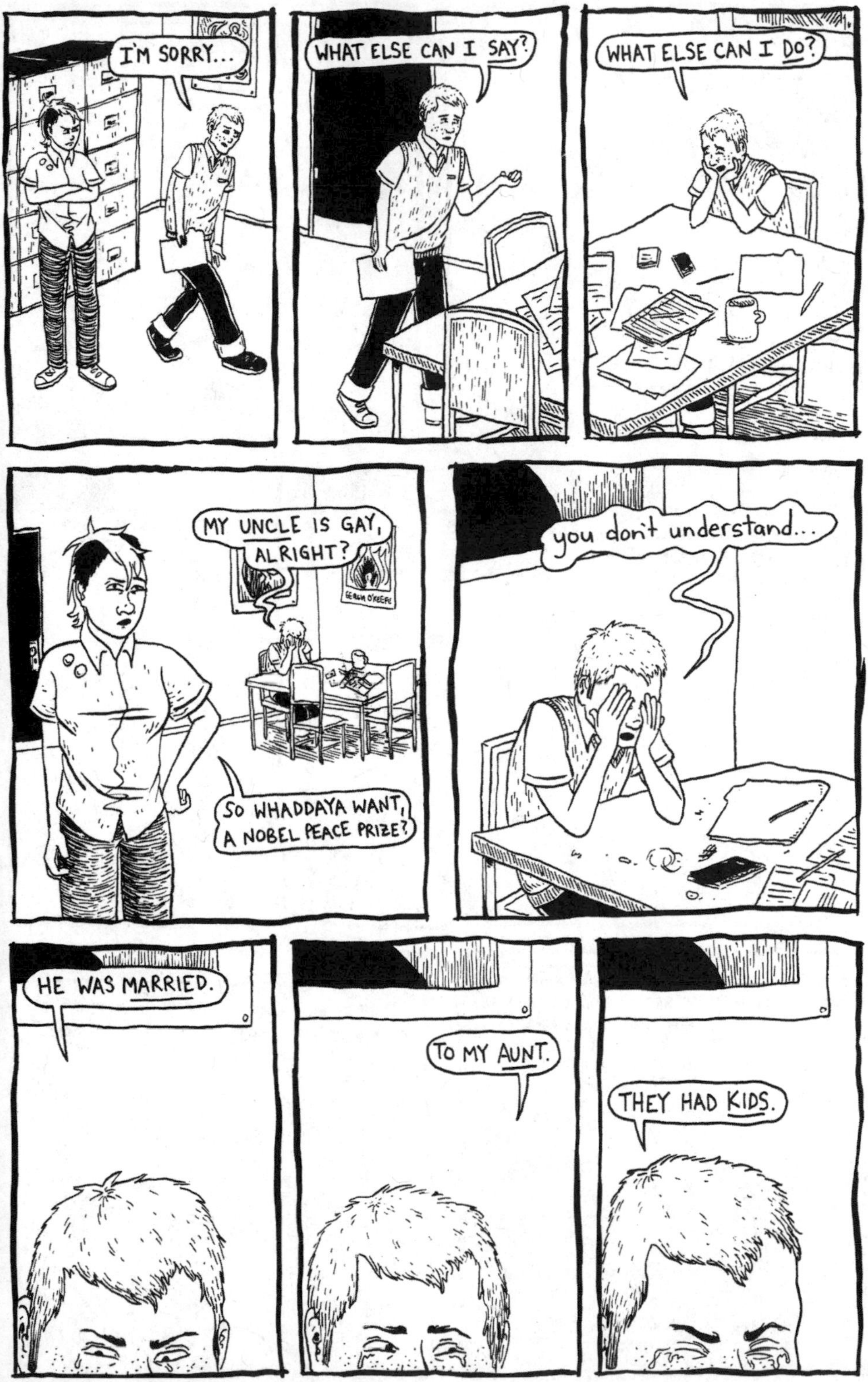
I'M SORRY...
WHAT ELSE CAN I SAY?
WHAT ELSE CAN I DO?
MY UNCLE IS GAY, ALRIGHT?
GEORGIA O'KEEFE
SO WHADDAYA WANT, A NOBEL PEACE PRIZE?
you don't understand...
HE WAS MARRIED.
TO MY AUNT.
THEY HAD KIDS.

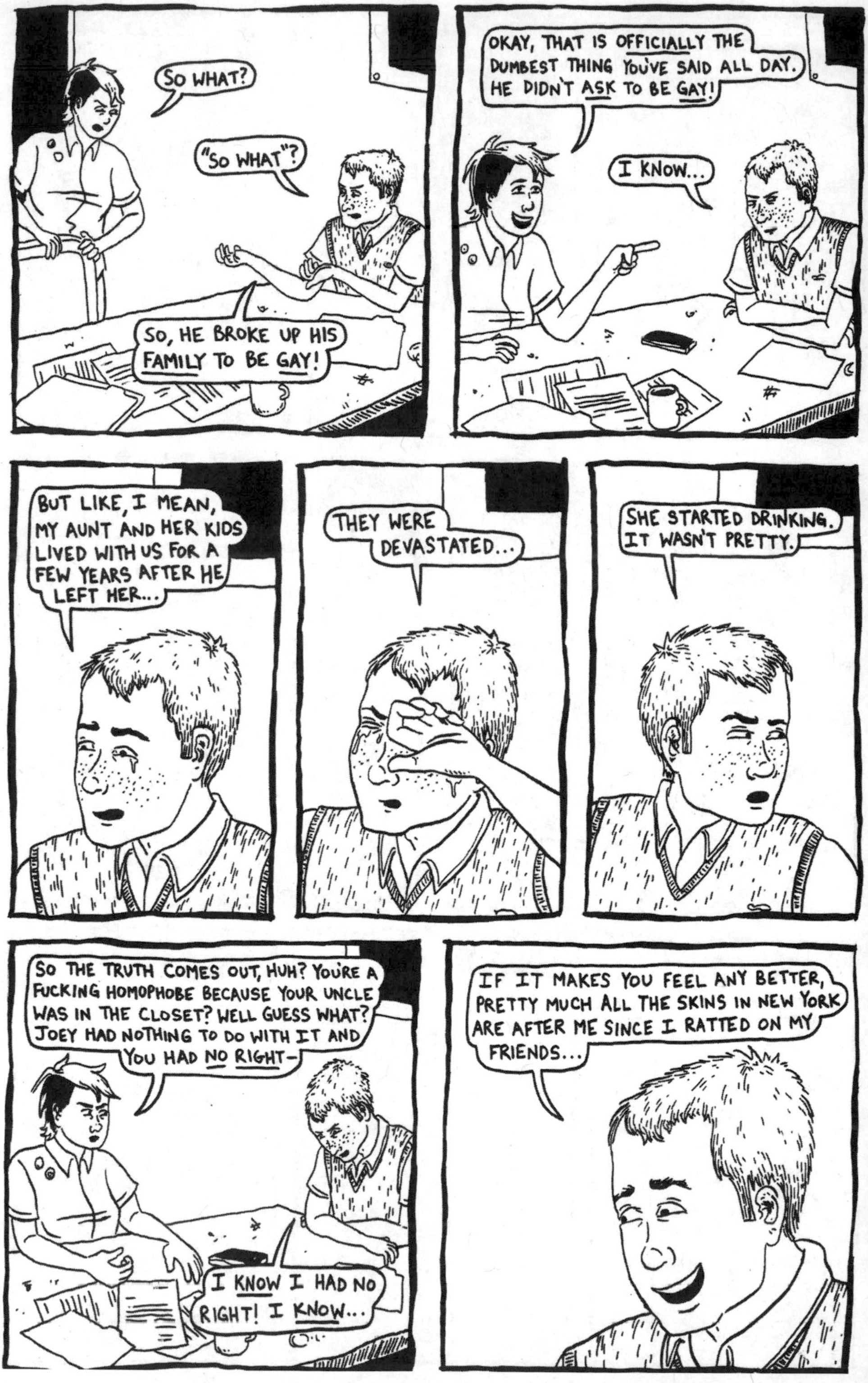
SO WHAT?
"SO WHAT"?
SO, HE BROKE UP HIS FAMILY TO BE GAY!
OKAY, THAT IS OFFICIALLY THE DUMBEST THING YOU'VE SAID ALL DAY. HE DIDN'T ASK TO BE GAY!
I KNOW...
BUT LIKE, I MEAN, MY AUNT AND HER KIDS LIVED WITH US FOR A FEW YEARS AFTER HE LEFT HER...
THEY WERE DEVASTATED...
SHE STARTED DRINKING. IT WASN'T PRETTY.
SO THE TRUTH COMES OUT, HUH? YOU'RE A FUCKING HOMOPHOBE BECAUSE YOUR UNCLE WAS IN THE CLOSET? WELL GUESS WHAT? JOEY HAD NOTHING TO DO WITH IT AND YOU HAD NO RIGHT-
I KNOW I HAD NO RIGHT! I KNOW...
IF IT MAKES YOU FEEL ANY BETTER, PRETTY MUCH ALL THE SKINS IN NEW YORK ARE AFTER ME SINCE I RATTED ON MY FRIENDS...

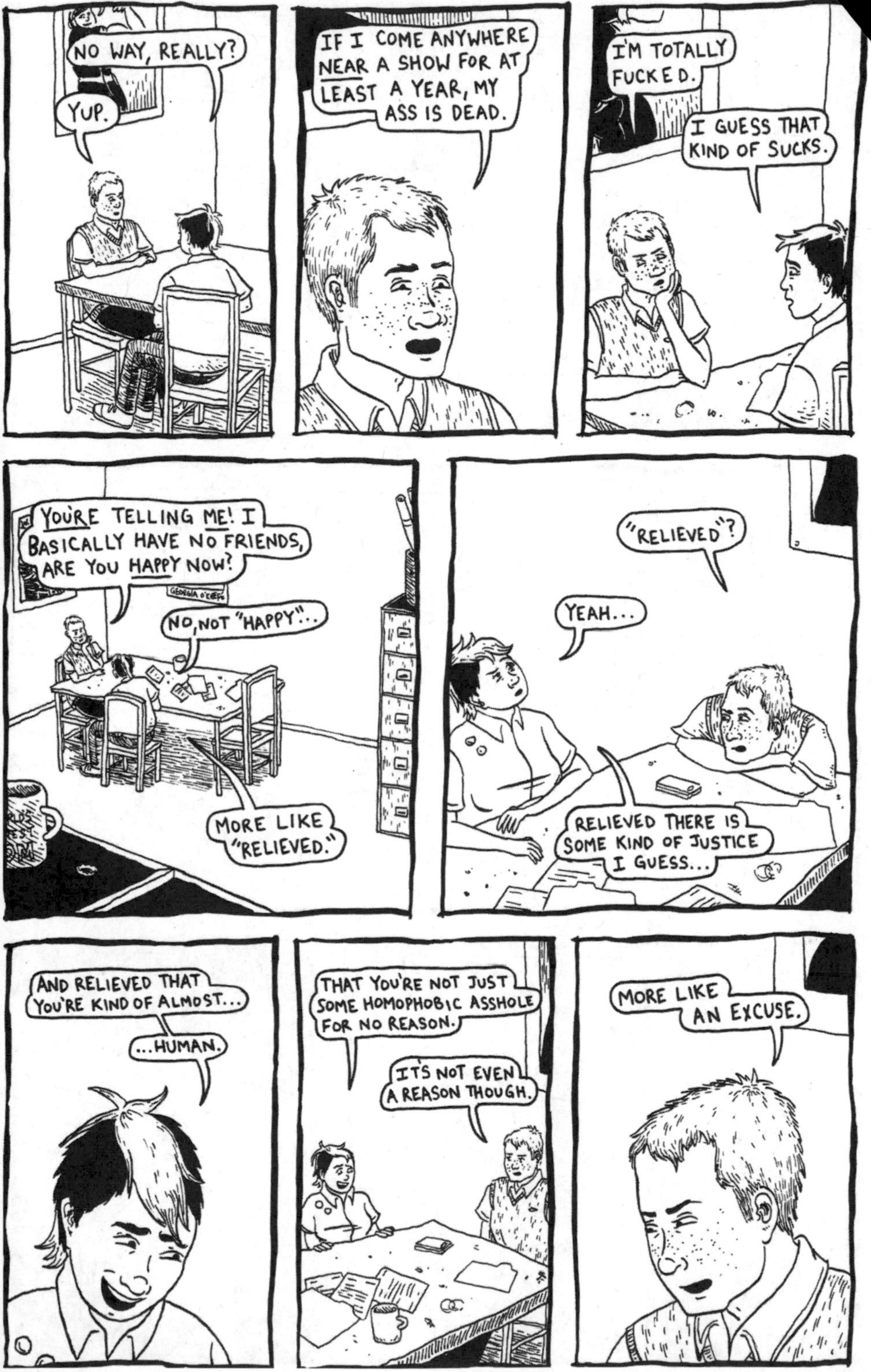
NO WAY, REALLY?
YUP.
IF I COME ANYWHERE NEAR A SHOW FOR AT LEAST A YEAR, MY ASS IS DEAD.
I'M TOTALLY FUCKED.
I GUESS THAT KIND OF SUCKS.
YOU'RE TELLING ME! I BASICALLY HAVE NO FRIENDS, ARE YOU HAPPY NOW?
NO, NOT "HAPPY"...
MORE LIKE "RELIEVED."
"RELIEVED"?
YEAH...
RELIEVED THERE IS SOME KIND OF JUSTICE I GUESS...
AND RELIEVED THAT YOU'RE KIND OF ALMOST...
...HUMAN.
THAT YOU'RE NOT JUST SOME HOMOPHOBIC ASSHOLE FOR NO REASON.
IT'S NOT EVEN A REASON THOUGH.
MORE LIKE AN EXCUSE.

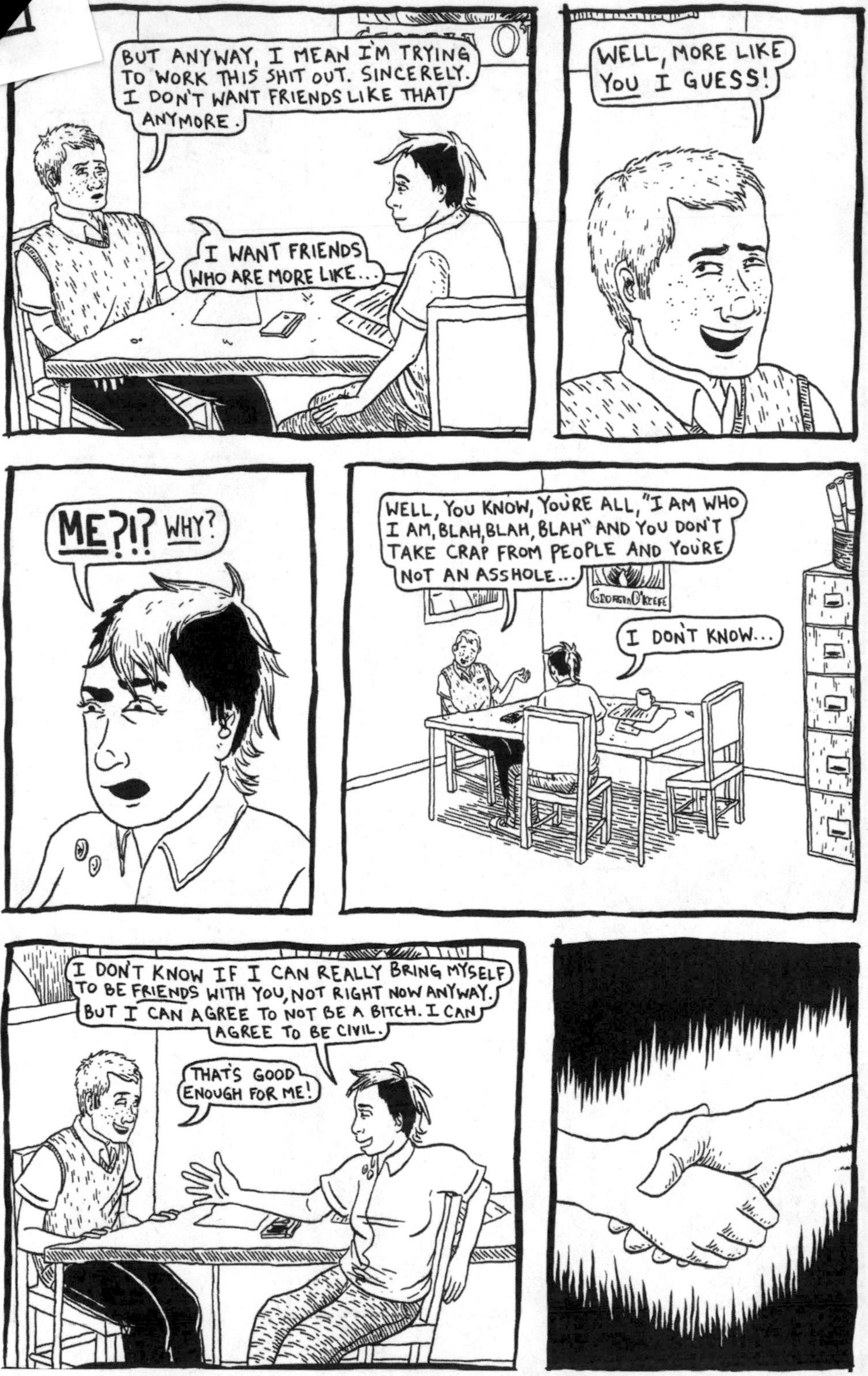
BUT ANYWAY, I MEAN I'M TRYING TO WORK THIS SHIT OUT. SINCERELY. I DON'T WANT FRIENDS LIKE THAT ANYMORE.
I WANT FRIENDS WHO ARE MORE LIKE...
WELL, MORE LIKE YOU I GUESS!
ME?!? WHY?
WELL, YOU KNOW, YOU'RE ALL, "I AM WHO I AM, BLAH, BLAH, BLAH" AND YOU DON'T TAKE CRAP FROM PEOPLE AND YOU'RE NOT AN ASSHOLE...
GEORGIA O'KEEFE
I DON'T KNOW...
I DON'T KNOW IF I CAN REALLY BRING MYSELF TO BE FRIENDS WITH YOU, NOT RIGHT NOW ANYWAY. BUT I CAN AGREE TO NOT BE A BITCH. I CAN AGREE TO BE CIVIL.
THAT'S GOOD ENOUGH FOR ME!

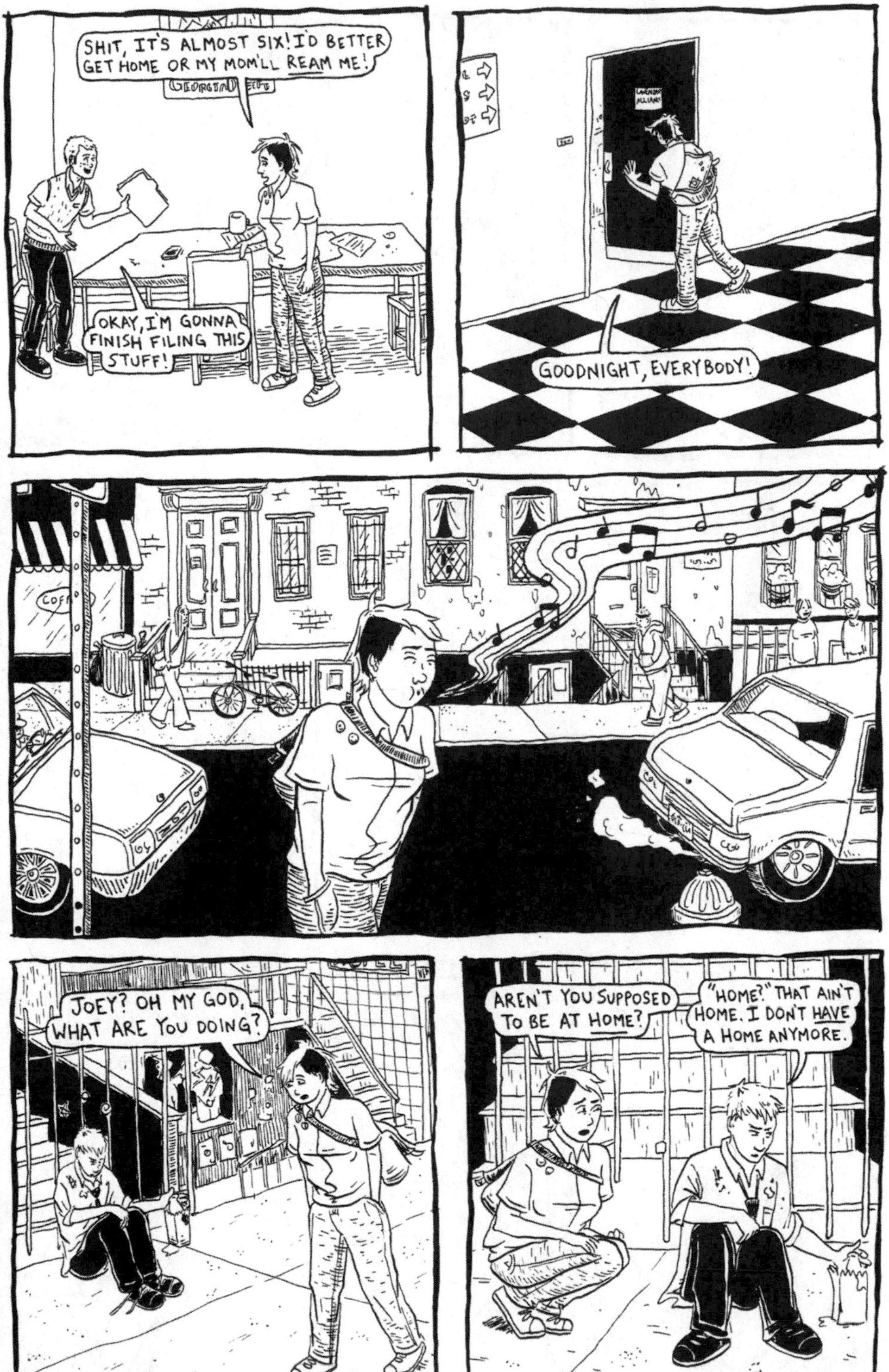
SHIT, IT'S ALMOST SIX! I'D BETTER GET HOME OR MY MOM'LL REAM ME!
OKAY, I'M GONNA FINISH FILING THIS STUFF!
GOODNIGHT, EVERYBODY!
JOEY? OH MY GOD, WHAT ARE YOU DOING?
AREN'T YOU SUPPOSED TO BE AT HOME?
"HOME?" THAT AIN'T HOME. I DON'T HAVE A HOME ANYMORE.

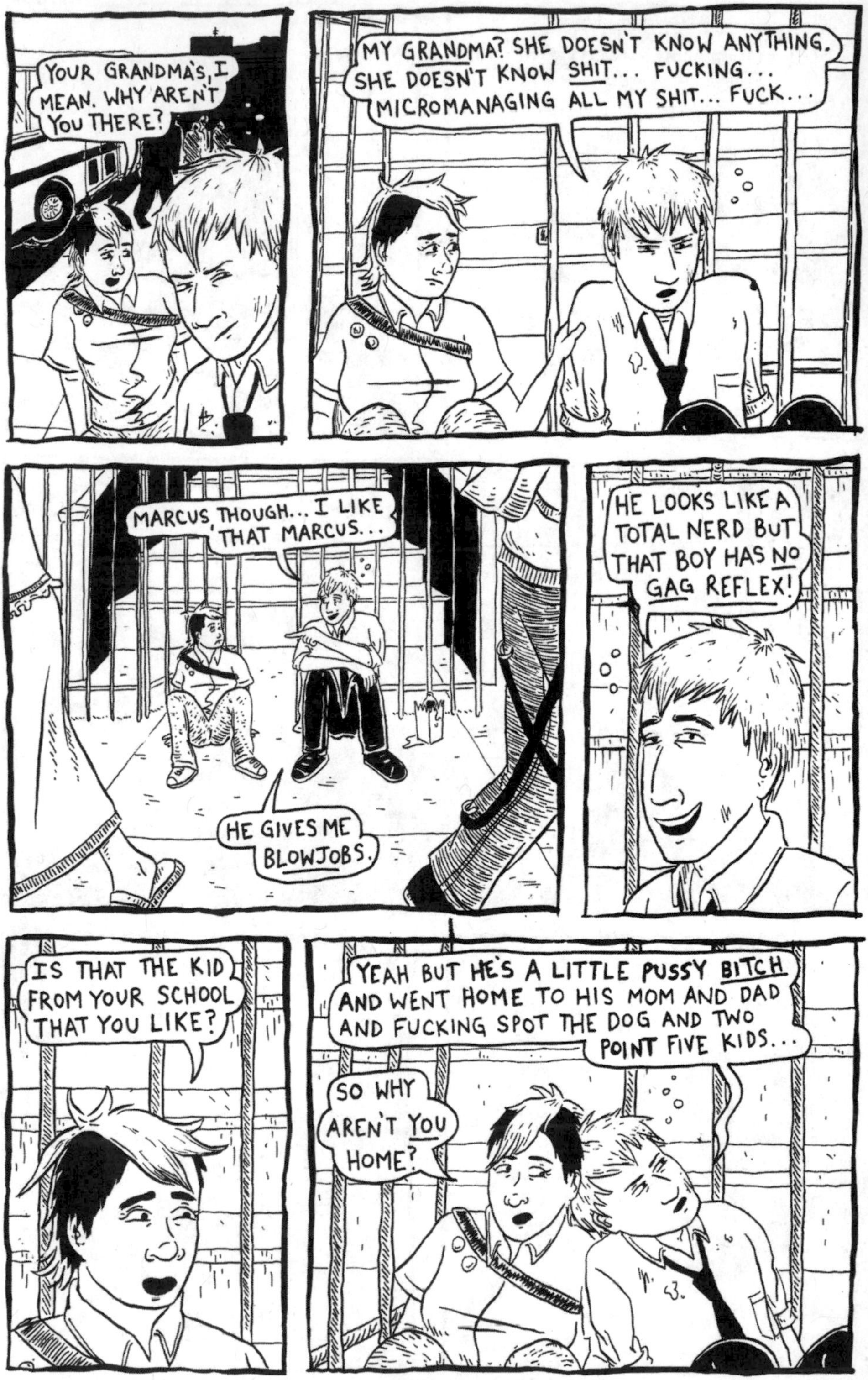
YOUR GRANDMA'S, I MEAN. WHY AREN'T YOU THERE?
MY GRANDMA? SHE DOESN'T KNOW ANYTHING. SHE DOESN'T KNOW SHIT... FUCKING... MICROMANAGING ALL MY SHIT... FUCK...
MARCUS, THOUGH... I LIKE THAT MARCUS...
HE GIVES ME BLOWJOBS.
HE LOOKS LIKE A TOTAL NERD BUT THAT BOY HAS NO GAG REFLEX!
IS THAT THE KID FROM YOUR SCHOOL THAT YOU LIKE?
YEAH BUT HE'S A LITTLE PUSSY BITCH AND WENT HOME TO HIS MOM AND DAD AND FUCKING SPOT THE DOG AND TWO POINT FIVE KIDS...
SO WHY AREN'T YOU HOME?

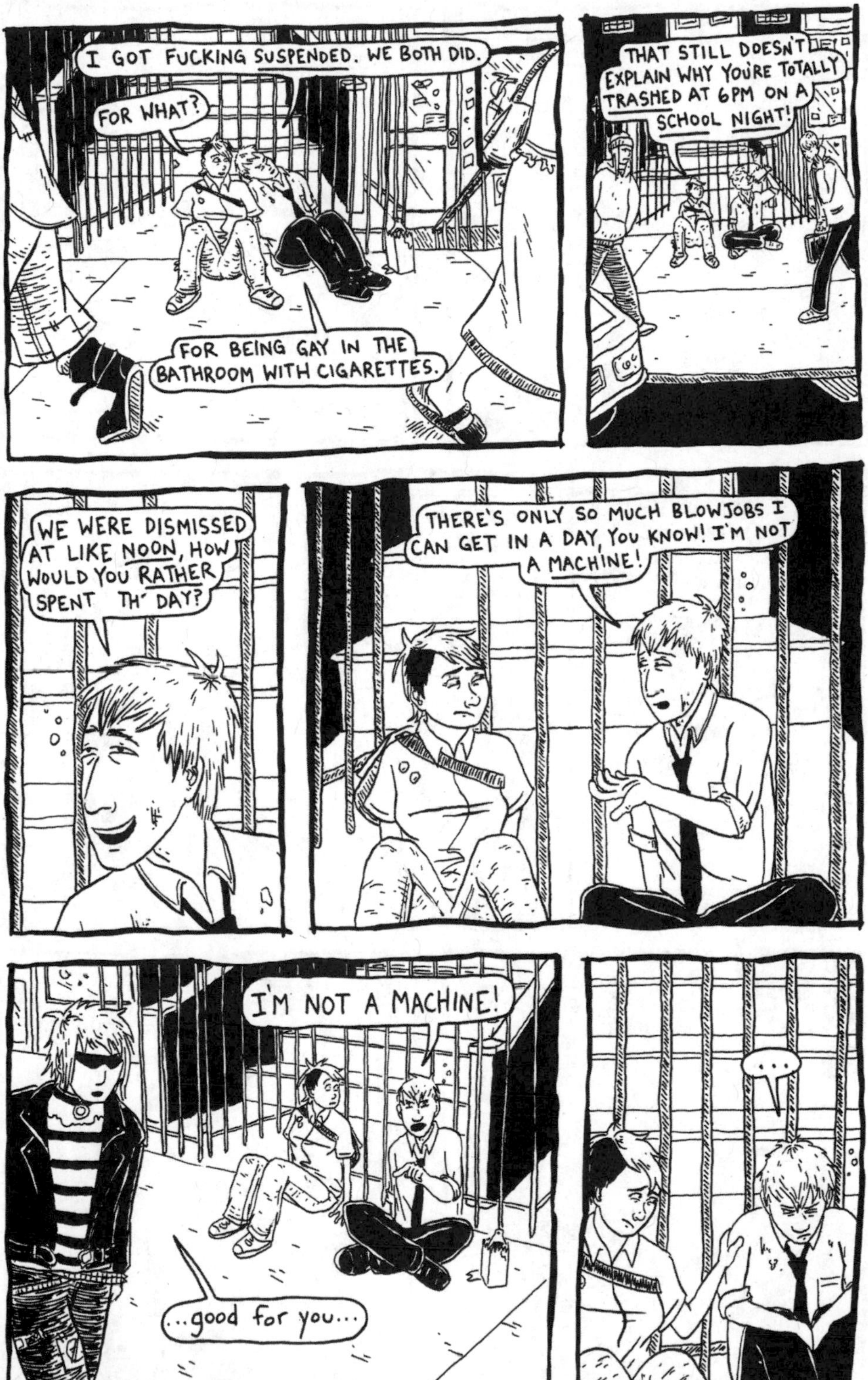
I GOT FUCKING SUSPENDED. WE BOTH DID.
FOR WHAT?
FOR BEING GAY IN THE BATHROOM WITH CIGARETTES.
THAT STILL DOESN'T EXPLAIN WHY YOU'RE TOTALLY TRASHED AT 6PM ON A SCHOOL NIGHT!
WE WERE DISMISSED AT LIKE NOON, HOW WOULD YOU RATHER SPENT TH' DAY?
THERE'S ONLY SO MUCH BLOWJOBS I CAN GET IN A DAY, YOU KNOW! I'M NOT A MACHINE!
I'M NOT A MACHINE!
...good for you...
...

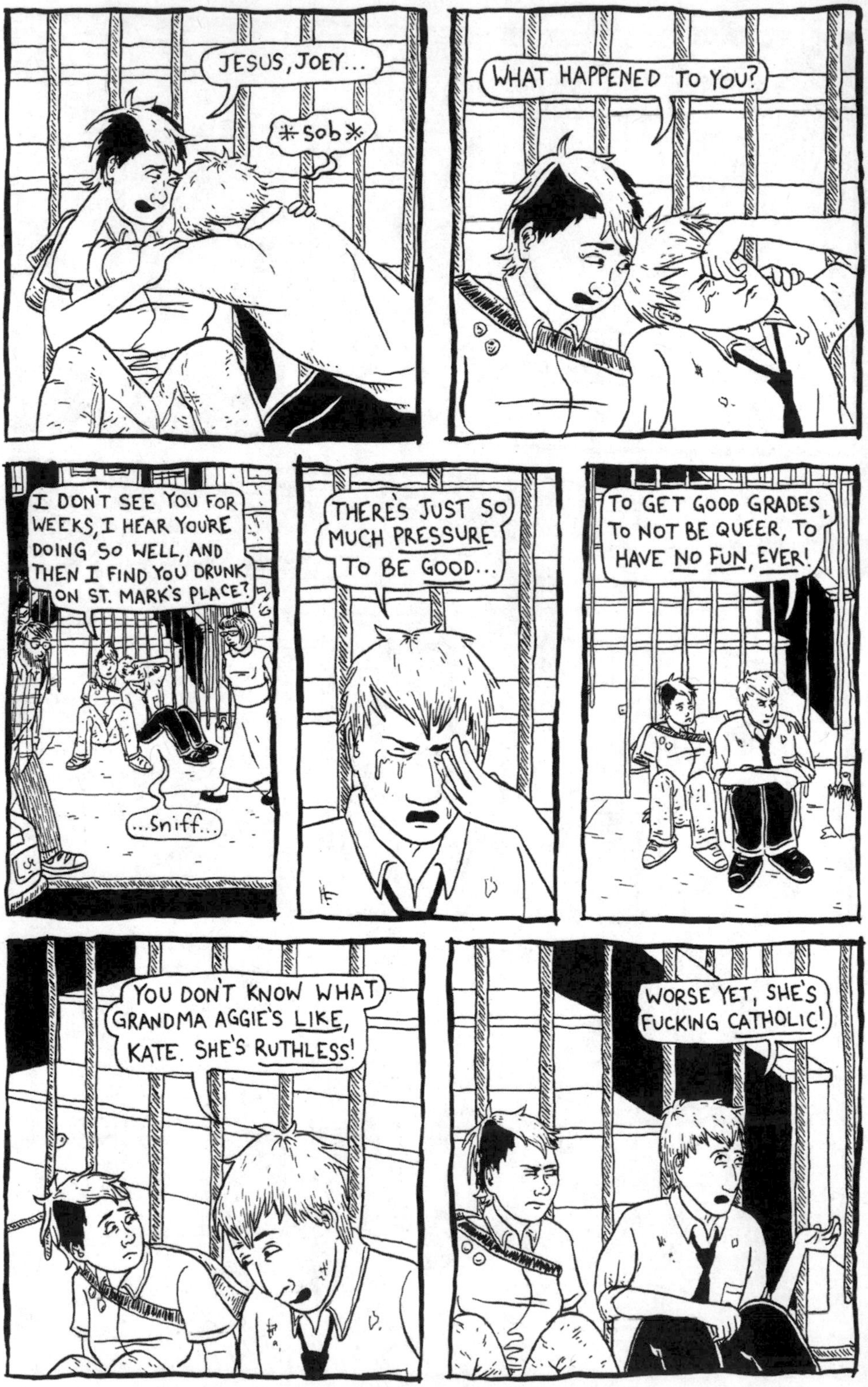
JESUS, JOEY...
sob
WHAT HAPPENED TO YOU?
I DON'T SEE YOU FOR WEEKS, I HEAR YOU'RE DOING SO WELL, AND THEN I FIND YOU DRUNK ON ST. MARK'S PLACE?
...Sniff...
THERE'S JUST SO MUCH PRESSURE TO BE GOOD...
TO GET GOOD GRADES, TO NOT BE QUEER, TO HAVE NO FUN, EVER!
YOU DON'T KNOW WHAT GRANDMA AGGIE'S LIKE, KATE. SHE'S RUTHLESS!
WORSE YET, SHE'S FUCKING CATHOLIC!

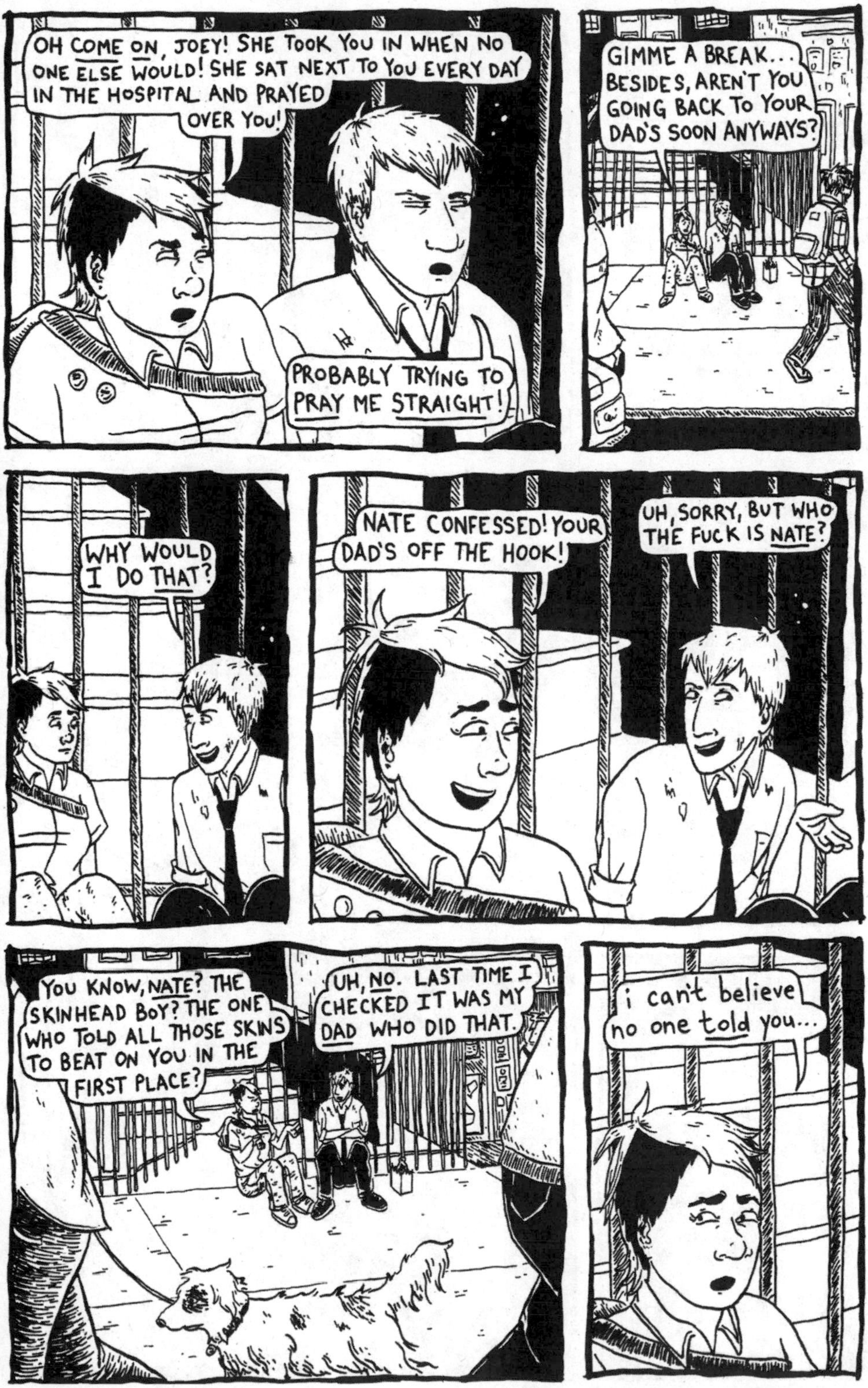
OH COME ON, JOEY! SHE TOOK YOU IN WHEN NO ONE ELSE WOULD! SHE SAT NEXT TO YOU EVERY DAY IN THE HOSPITAL AND PRAYED OVER YOU!
PROBABLY TRYING TO PRAY ME STRAIGHT!
GIMME A BREAK... BESIDES, AREN'T YOU GOING BACK TO YOUR DAD'S SOON ANYWAYS?
WHY WOULD I DO THAT?
NATE CONFESSED! YOUR DAD'S OFF THE HOOK!
UH, SORRY, BUT WHO THE FUCK IS NATE?
YOU KNOW, NATE? THE SKINHEAD BOY? THE ONE WHO TOLD ALL THOSE SKINS TO BEAT ON YOU IN THE FIRST PLACE?
UH, NO. LAST TIME I CHECKED IT WAS MY DAD WHO DID THAT.
i can't believe no one told you...

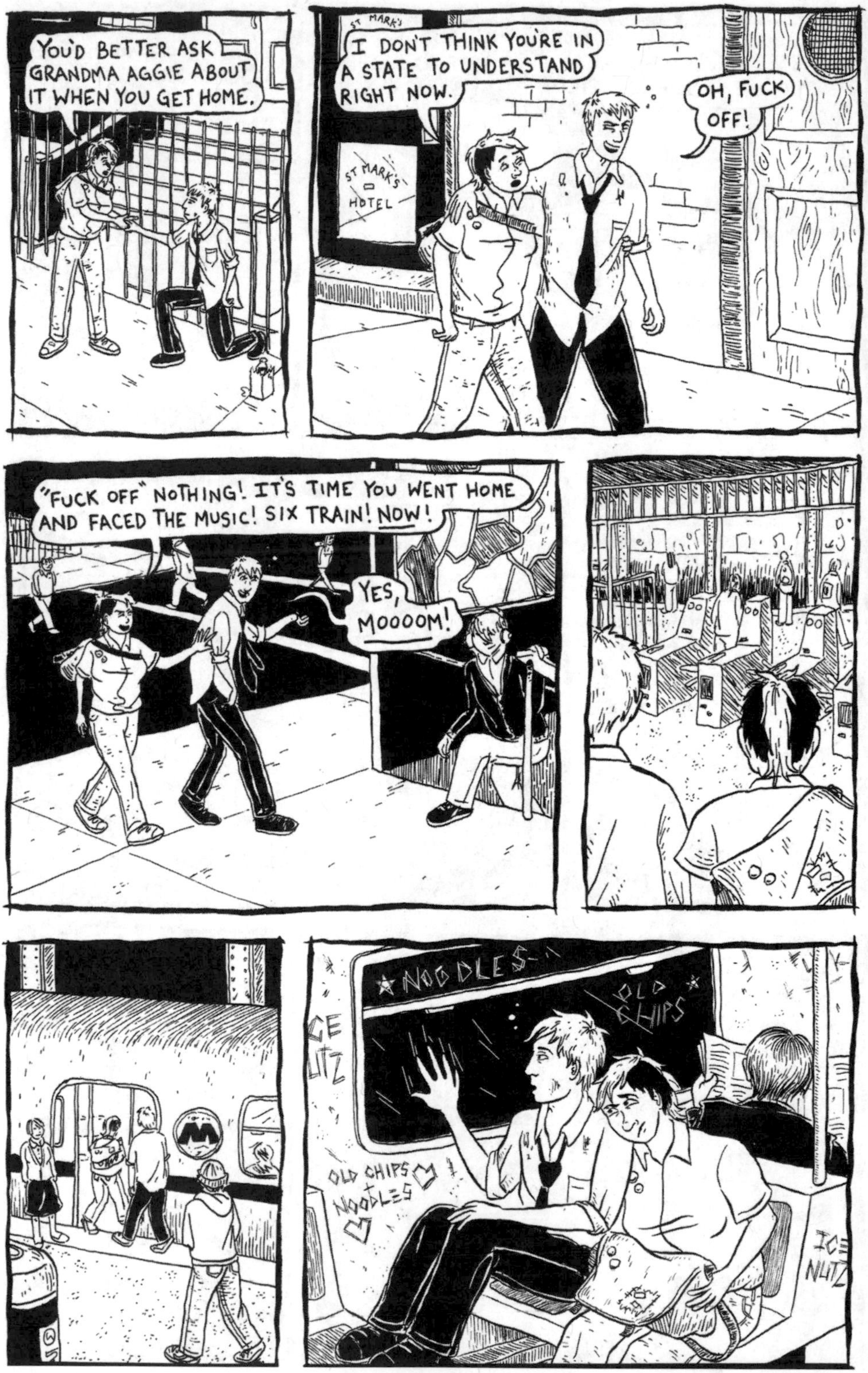
YOU'D BETTER ASK GRANDMA AGGIE ABOUT IT WHEN YOU GET HOME.
ST MARK'S
I DON'T THINK YOU'RE IN A STATE TO UNDERSTAND RIGHT NOW.
OH, FUCK OFF!
ST MARK'S HOTEL
"FUCK OFF" NOTHING! IT'S TIME YOU WENT HOME AND FACED THE MUSIC! SIX TRAIN! NOW!
YES, MOOOOM!
NOODLES
OLD CHIPS
ICE NUTZ
OLD CHIPS + NOODLES

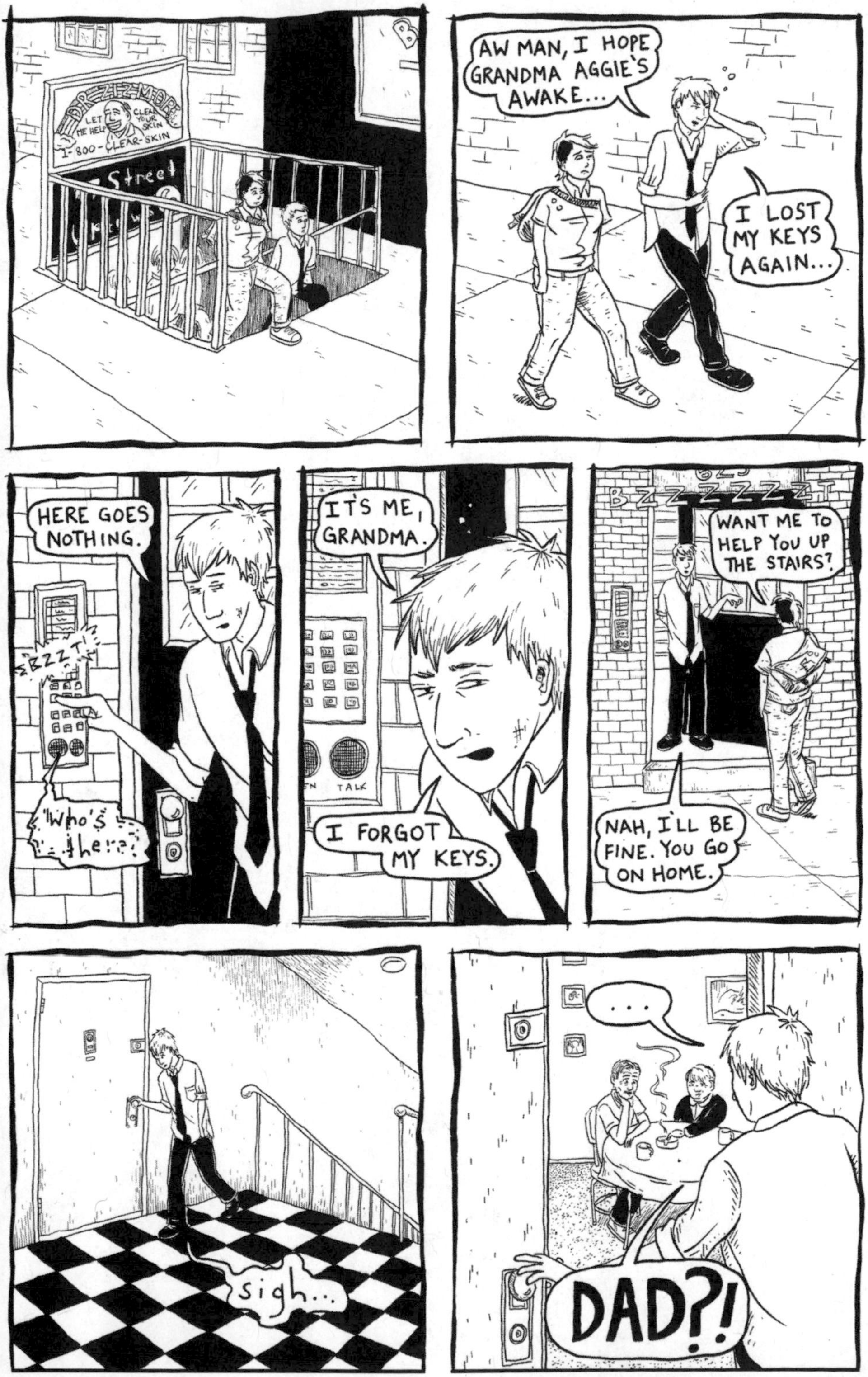
DR. ZITZ-MORE
LET ME HELP CLEAR YOUR SKIN
1-800-CLEAR-SKIN
Street
AW MAN, I HOPE GRANDMA AGGIE'S AWAKE...
I LOST MY KEYS AGAIN...
HERE GOES NOTHING.
BZZZT!
"Who's there?"
IT'S ME, GRANDMA.
TALK
I FORGOT MY KEYS.
BZZZZZZZZT
WANT ME TO HELP YOU UP THE STAIRS?
NAH, I'LL BE FINE. YOU GO ON HOME.
sigh...
...
DAD?!

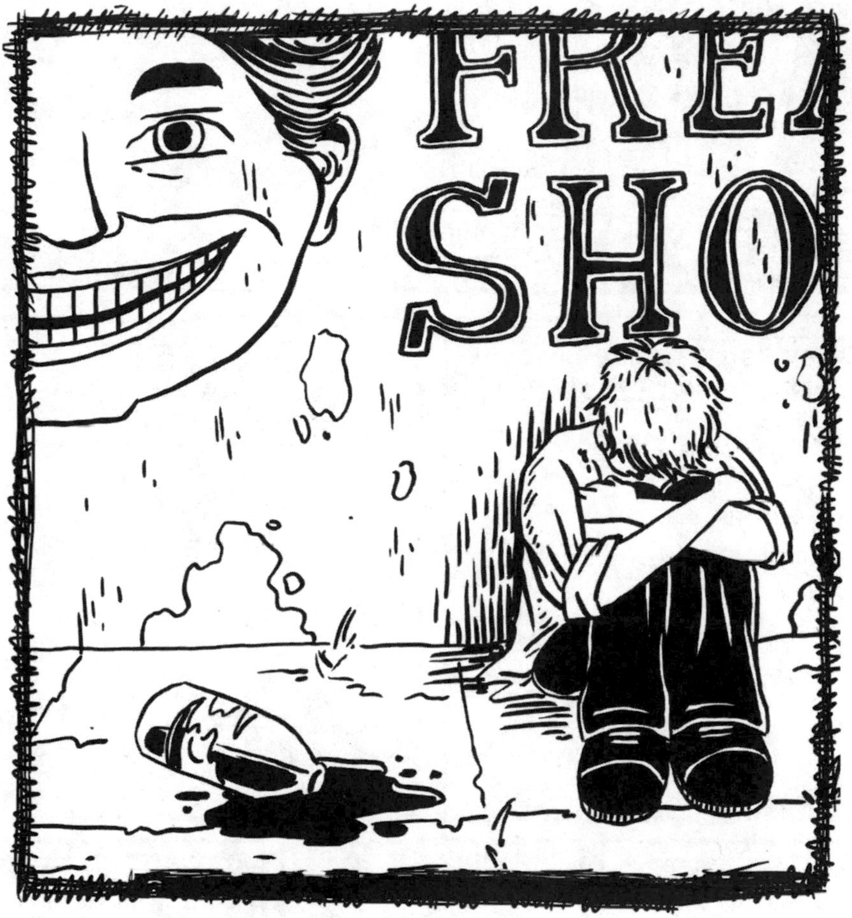
FREA
SHO

CHAPTER FOUR

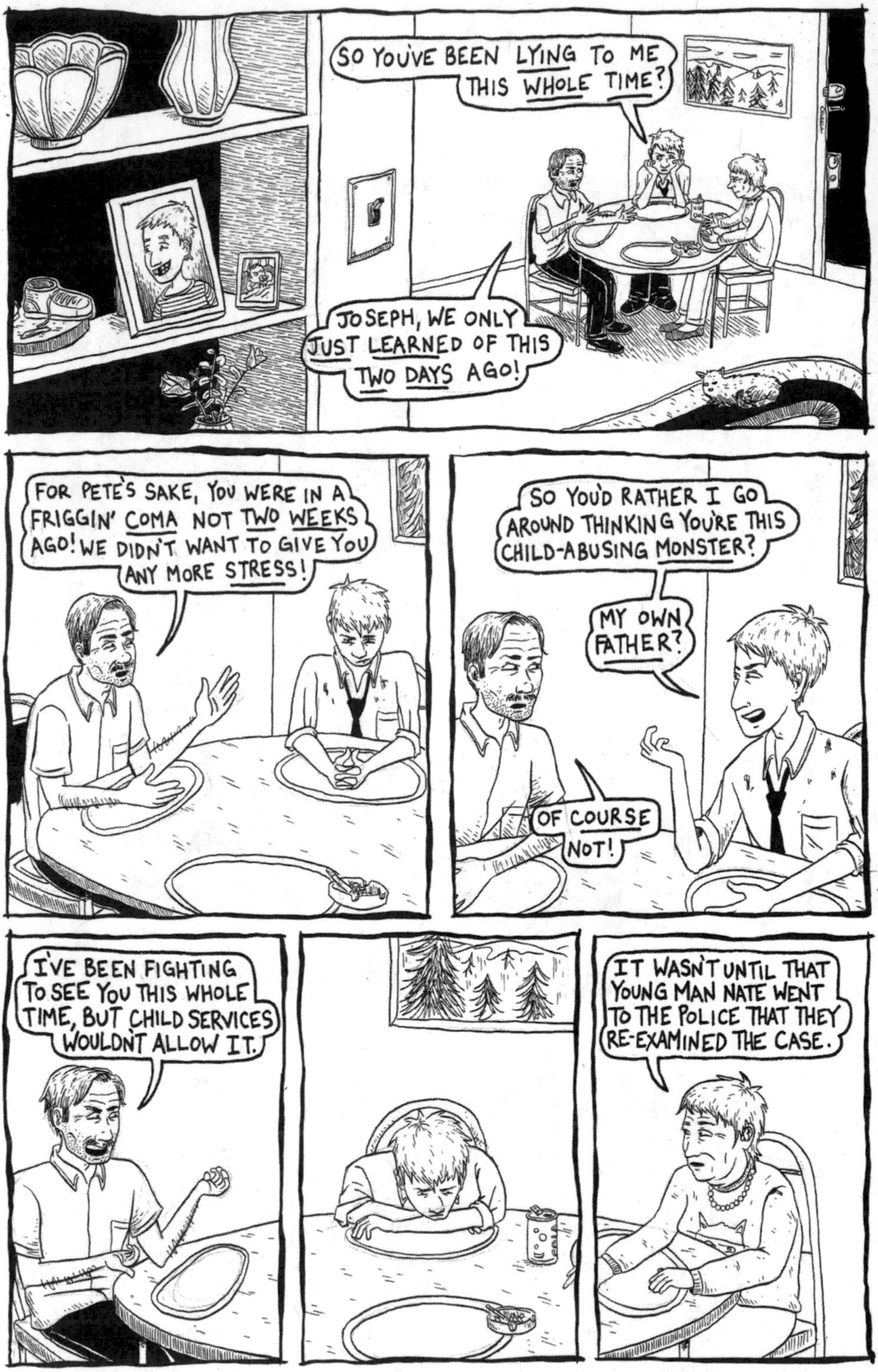
SO YOU'VE BEEN LYING TO ME THIS WHOLE TIME?
JOSEPH, WE ONLY JUST LEARNED OF THIS TWO DAYS AGO!
FOR PETE'S SAKE, YOU WERE IN A FRIGGIN' COMA NOT TWO WEEKS AGO! WE DIDN'T WANT TO GIVE YOU ANY MORE STRESS!
SO YOU'D RATHER I GO AROUND THINKING YOU'RE THIS CHILD-ABUSING MONSTER?
MY OWN FATHER?
OF COURSE NOT!
I'VE BEEN FIGHTING TO SEE YOU THIS WHOLE TIME, BUT CHILD SERVICES WOULDN'T ALLOW IT.
IT WASN'T UNTIL THAT YOUNG MAN NATE WENT TO THE POLICE THAT THEY RE-EXAMINED THE CASE.

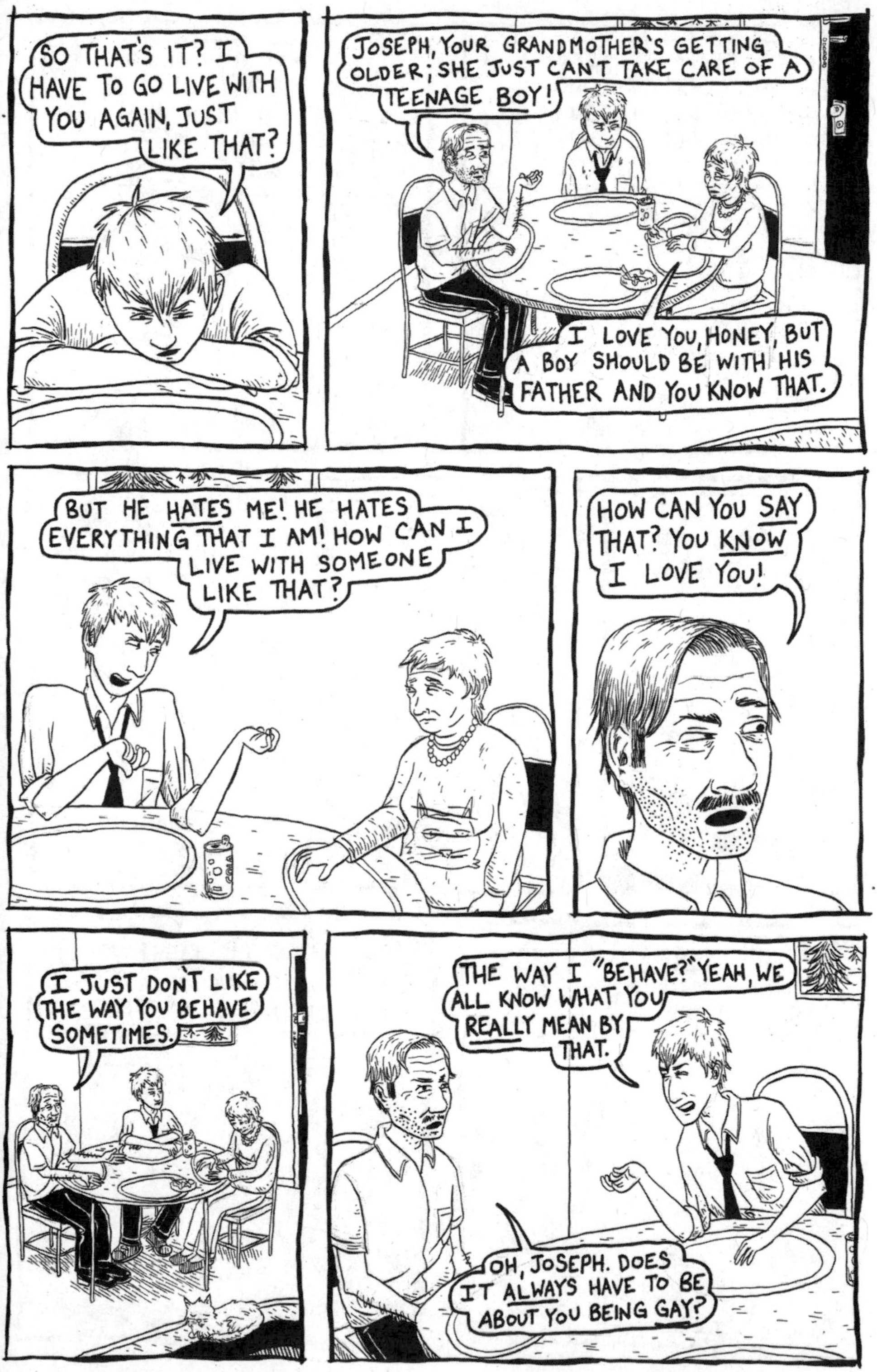
SO THAT'S IT? I HAVE TO GO LIVE WITH YOU AGAIN, JUST LIKE THAT?
JOSEPH, YOUR GRANDMOTHER'S GETTING OLDER; SHE JUST CAN'T TAKE CARE OF A TEENAGE BOY!
I LOVE YOU, HONEY, BUT A BOY SHOULD BE WITH HIS FATHER AND YOU KNOW THAT.
BUT HE HATES ME! HE HATES EVERYTHING THAT I AM! HOW CAN I LIVE WITH SOMEONE LIKE THAT?
HOW CAN YOU SAY THAT? YOU KNOW I LOVE YOU!
I JUST DON'T LIKE THE WAY YOU BEHAVE SOMETIMES.
THE WAY I "BEHAVE?" YEAH, WE ALL KNOW WHAT YOU REALLY MEAN BY THAT.
OH, JOSEPH. DOES IT ALWAYS HAVE TO BE ABOUT YOU BEING GAY?

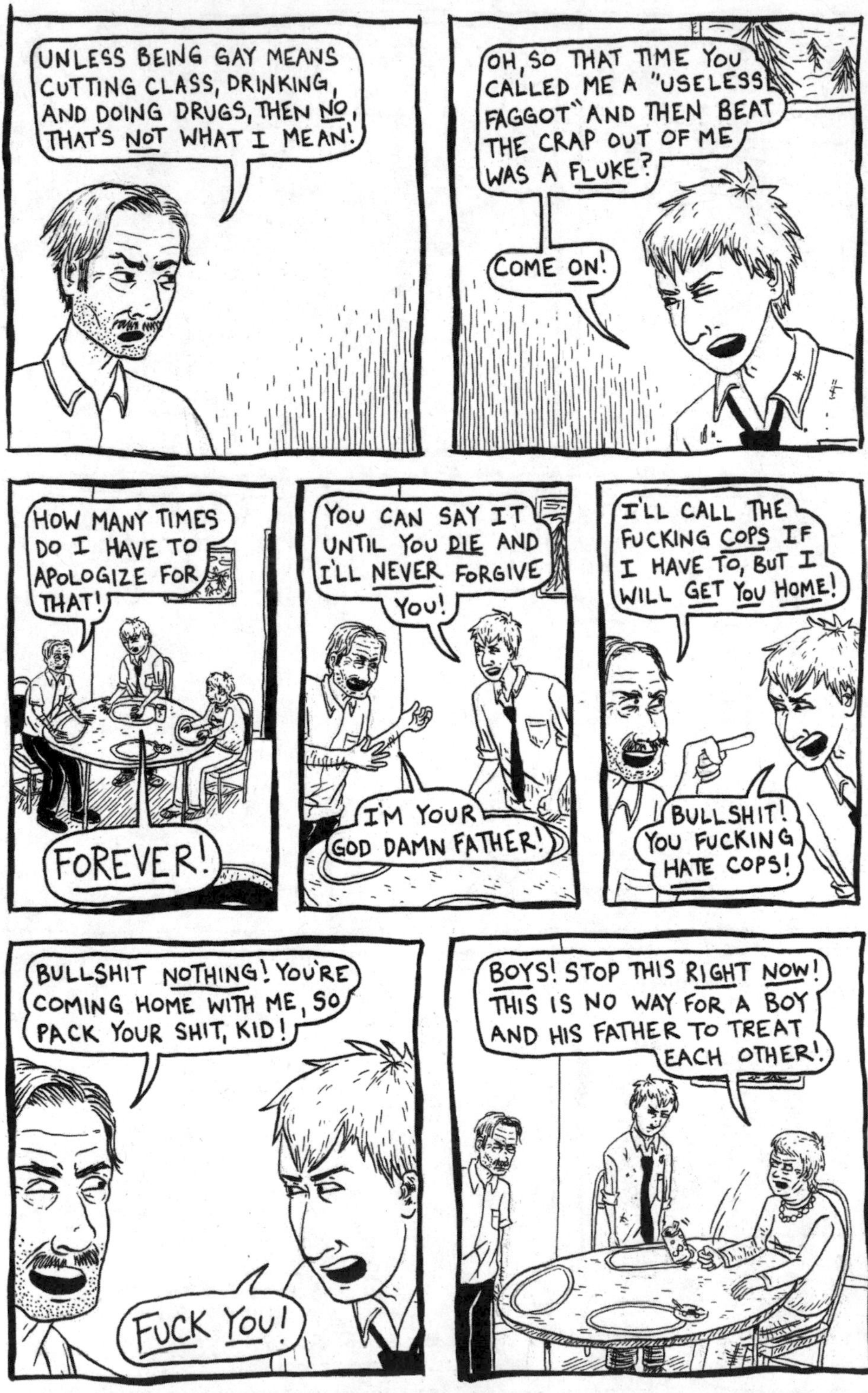
UNLESS BEING GAY MEANS CUTTING CLASS, DRINKING, AND DOING DRUGS, THEN NO, THAT'S NOT WHAT I MEAN!
OH, SO THAT TIME YOU CALLED ME A "USELESS FAGGOT" AND THEN BEAT THE CRAP OUT OF ME WAS A FLUKE?
COME ON!
HOW MANY TIMES DO I HAVE TO APOLOGIZE FOR THAT!
FOREVER!
YOU CAN SAY IT UNTIL YOU DIE AND I'LL NEVER FORGIVE YOU!
I'M YOUR GOD DAMN FATHER!
I'LL CALL THE FUCKING COPS IF I HAVE TO, BUT I WILL GET YOU HOME!
BULLSHIT! YOU FUCKING HATE COPS!
BULLSHIT NOTHING! YOU'RE COMING HOME WITH ME, SO PACK YOUR SHIT, KID!
FUCK YOU!
BOYS! STOP THIS RIGHT NOW! THIS IS NO WAY FOR A BOY AND HIS FATHER TO TREAT EACH OTHER!

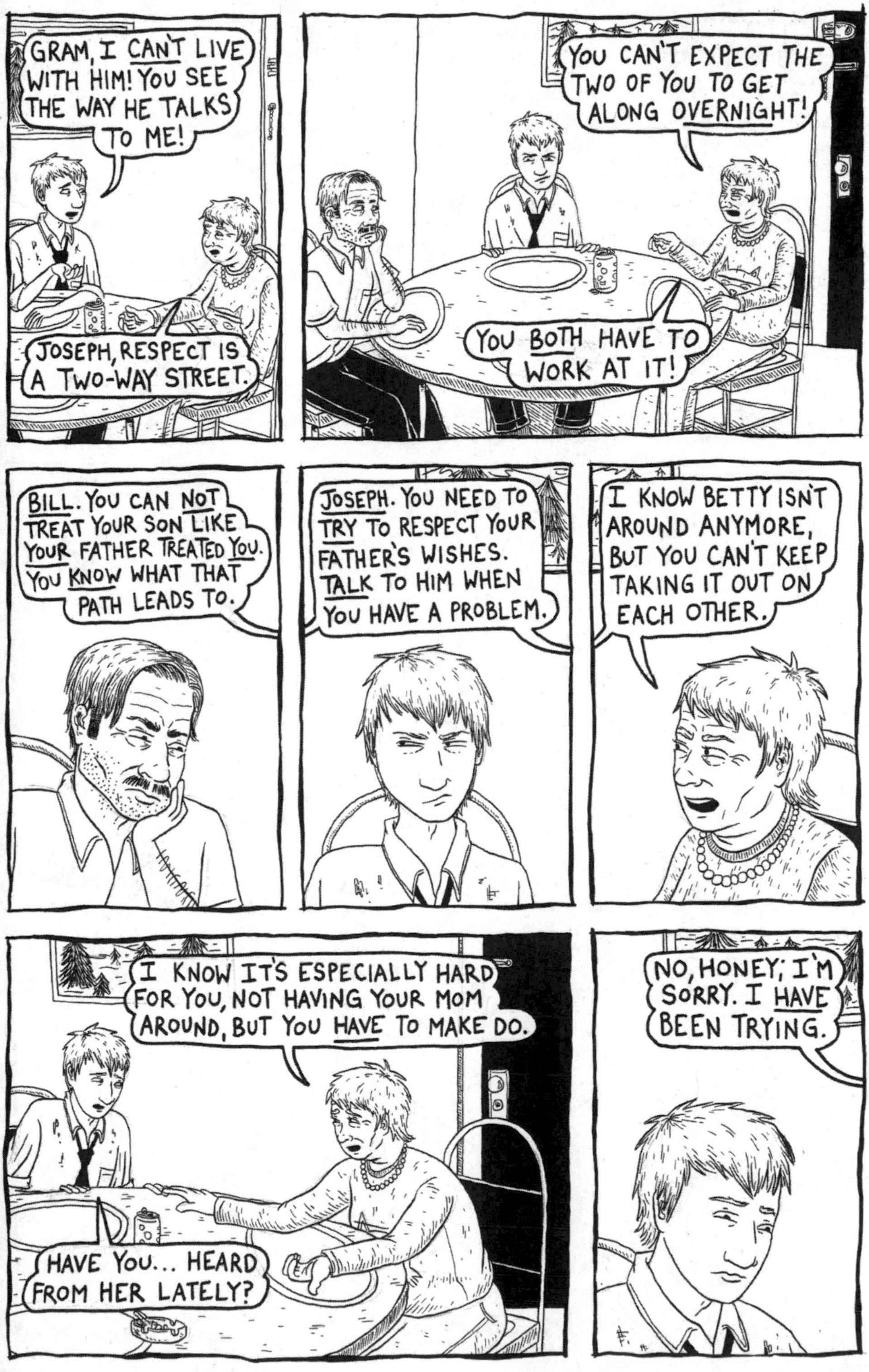
GRAM, I CAN'T LIVE WITH HIM! YOU SEE THE WAY HE TALKS TO ME!
JOSEPH, RESPECT IS A TWO-WAY STREET.
YOU CAN'T EXPECT THE TWO OF YOU TO GET ALONG OVERNIGHT!
YOU BOTH HAVE TO WORK AT IT!
BILL. YOU CAN NOT TREAT YOUR SON LIKE YOUR FATHER TREATED YOU. YOU KNOW WHAT THAT PATH LEADS TO.
JOSEPH. YOU NEED TO TRY TO RESPECT YOUR FATHER'S WISHES. TALK TO HIM WHEN YOU HAVE A PROBLEM.
I KNOW BETTY ISN'T AROUND ANYMORE, BUT YOU CAN'T KEEP TAKING IT OUT ON EACH OTHER.
I KNOW IT'S ESPECIALLY HARD FOR YOU, NOT HAVING YOUR MOM AROUND, BUT YOU HAVE TO MAKE DO.
HAVE YOU... HEARD FROM HER LATELY?
NO, HONEY; I'M SORRY. I HAVE BEEN TRYING.

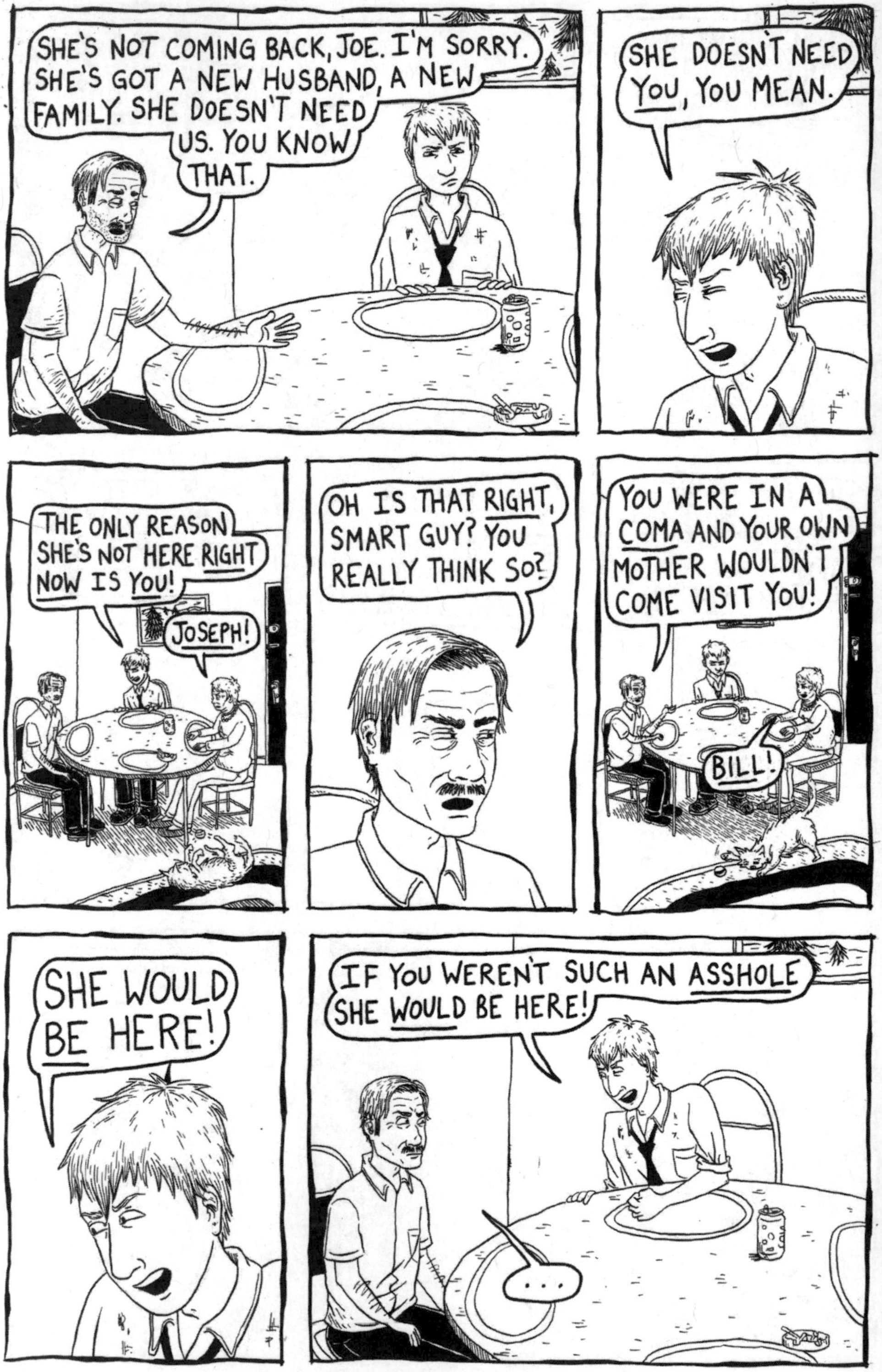

SHE'S NOT COMING BACK, JOE. I'M SORRY. SHE'S GOT A NEW HUSBAND, A NEW FAMILY. SHE DOESN'T NEED US. YOU KNOW THAT.
SHE DOESN'T NEED YOU, YOU MEAN.
THE ONLY REASON SHE'S NOT HERE RIGHT NOW IS YOU!
JOSEPH!
OH IS THAT RIGHT, SMART GUY? YOU REALLY THINK SO?
YOU WERE IN A COMA AND YOUR OWN MOTHER WOULDN'T COME VISIT YOU!
BILL!
SHE WOULD BE HERE!
IF YOU WEREN'T SUCH AN ASSHOLE SHE WOULD BE HERE!
...

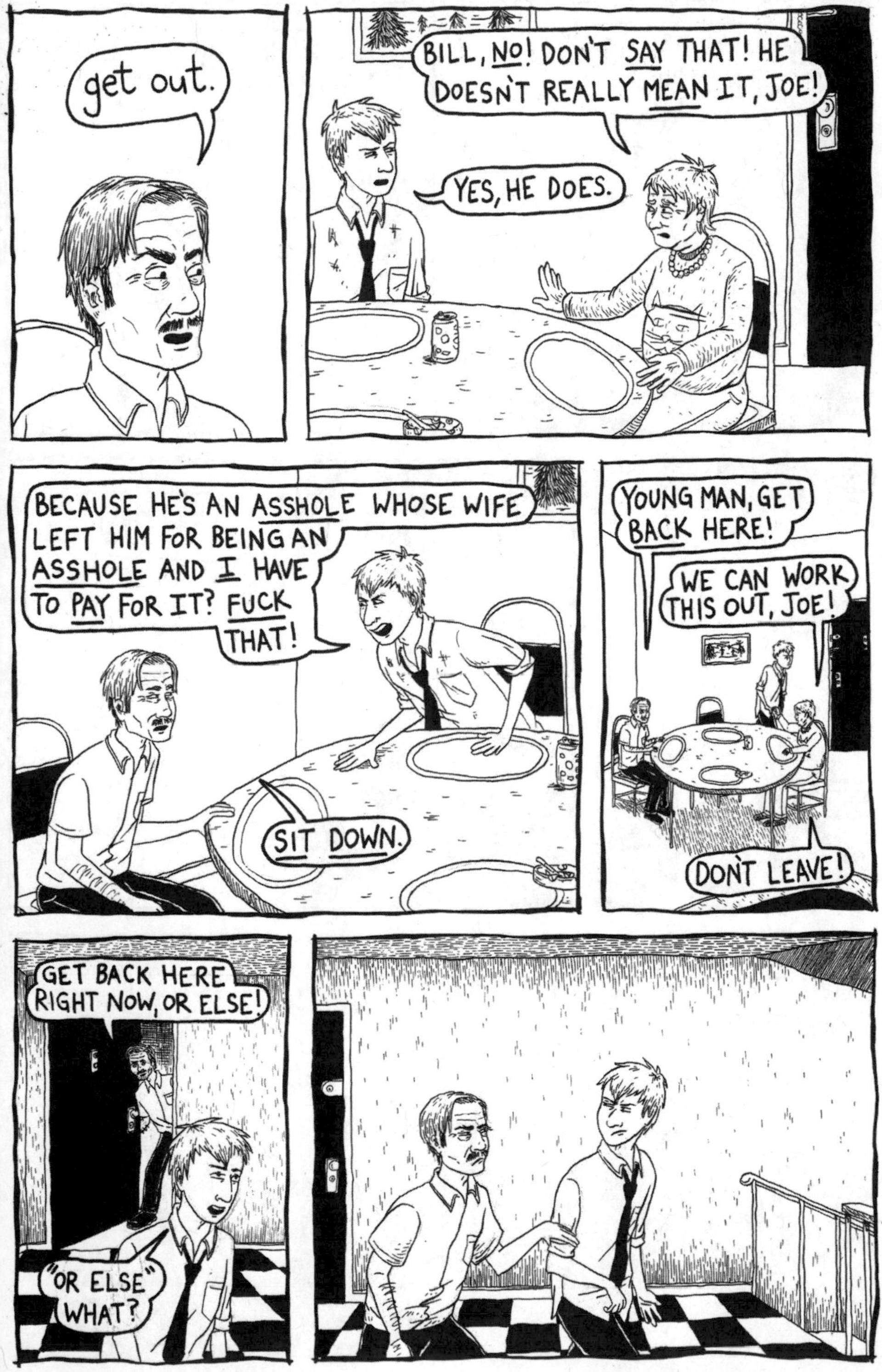
get out.
BILL, NO! DON'T SAY THAT! HE DOESN'T REALLY MEAN IT, JOE!
YES, HE DOES.
BECAUSE HE'S AN ASSHOLE WHOSE WIFE LEFT HIM FOR BEING AN ASSHOLE AND I HAVE TO PAY FOR IT? FUCK THAT!
SIT DOWN.
YOUNG MAN, GET BACK HERE!
WE CAN WORK THIS OUT, JOE!
DON'T LEAVE!
GET BACK HERE RIGHT NOW, OR ELSE!
"OR ELSE" WHAT?

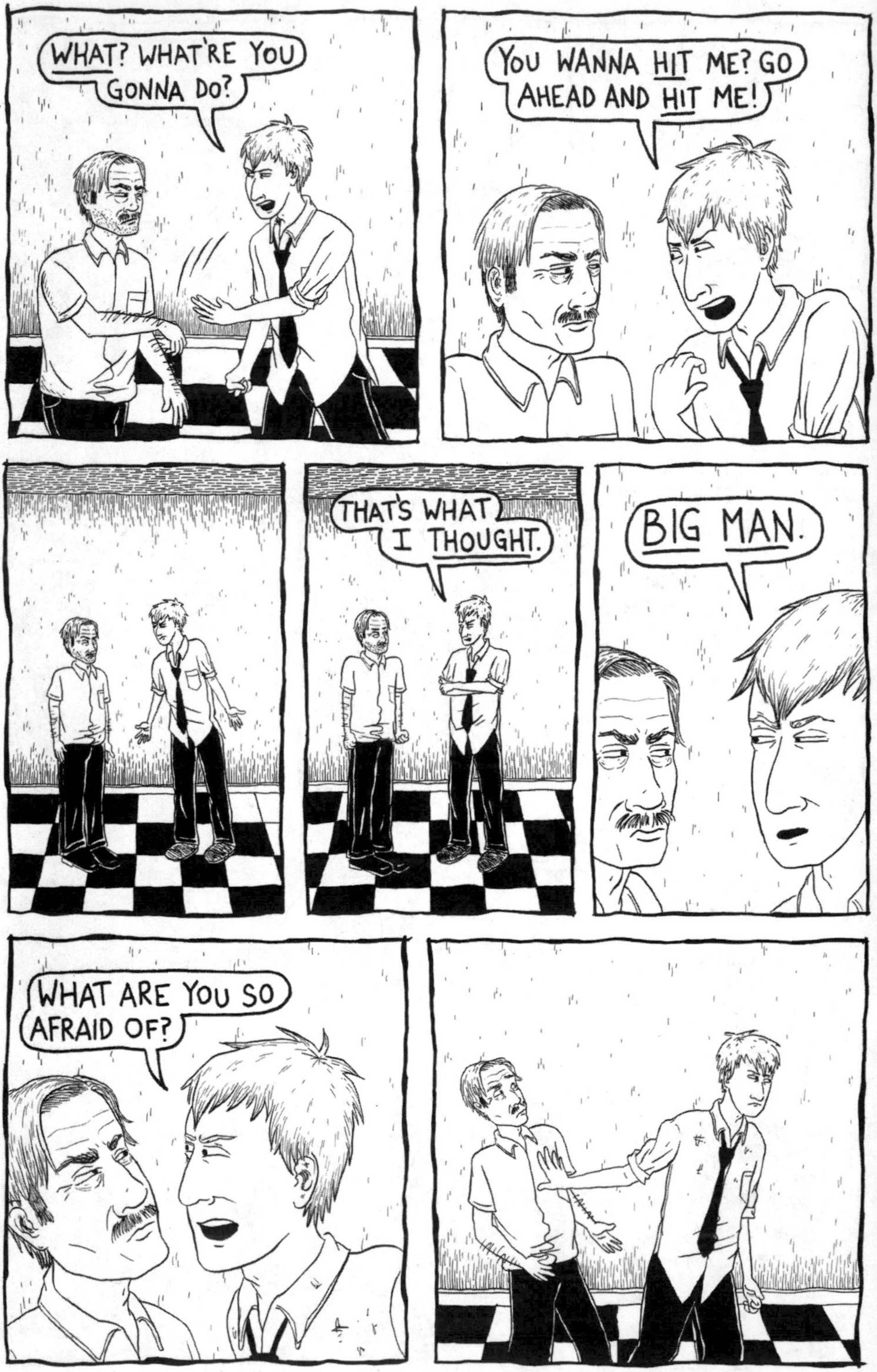
WHAT? WHAT'RE YOU GONNA DO?
YOU WANNA HIT ME? GO AHEAD AND HIT ME!
THAT'S WHAT I THOUGHT.
BIG MAN.
WHAT ARE YOU SO AFRAID OF?

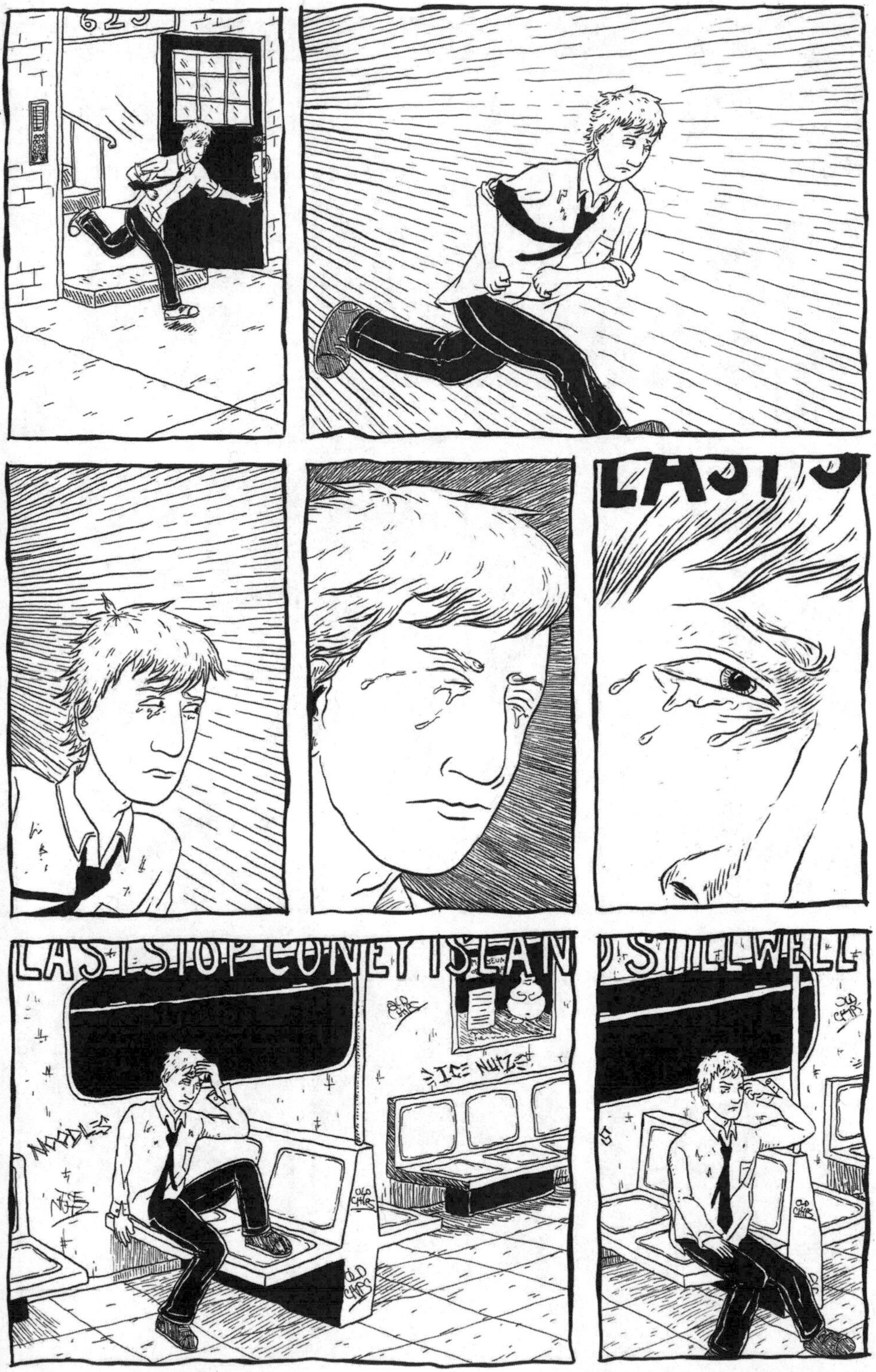
625
LAST STOP CONEY ISLAND STILLWELL
ICE NUTZ
NOODLES

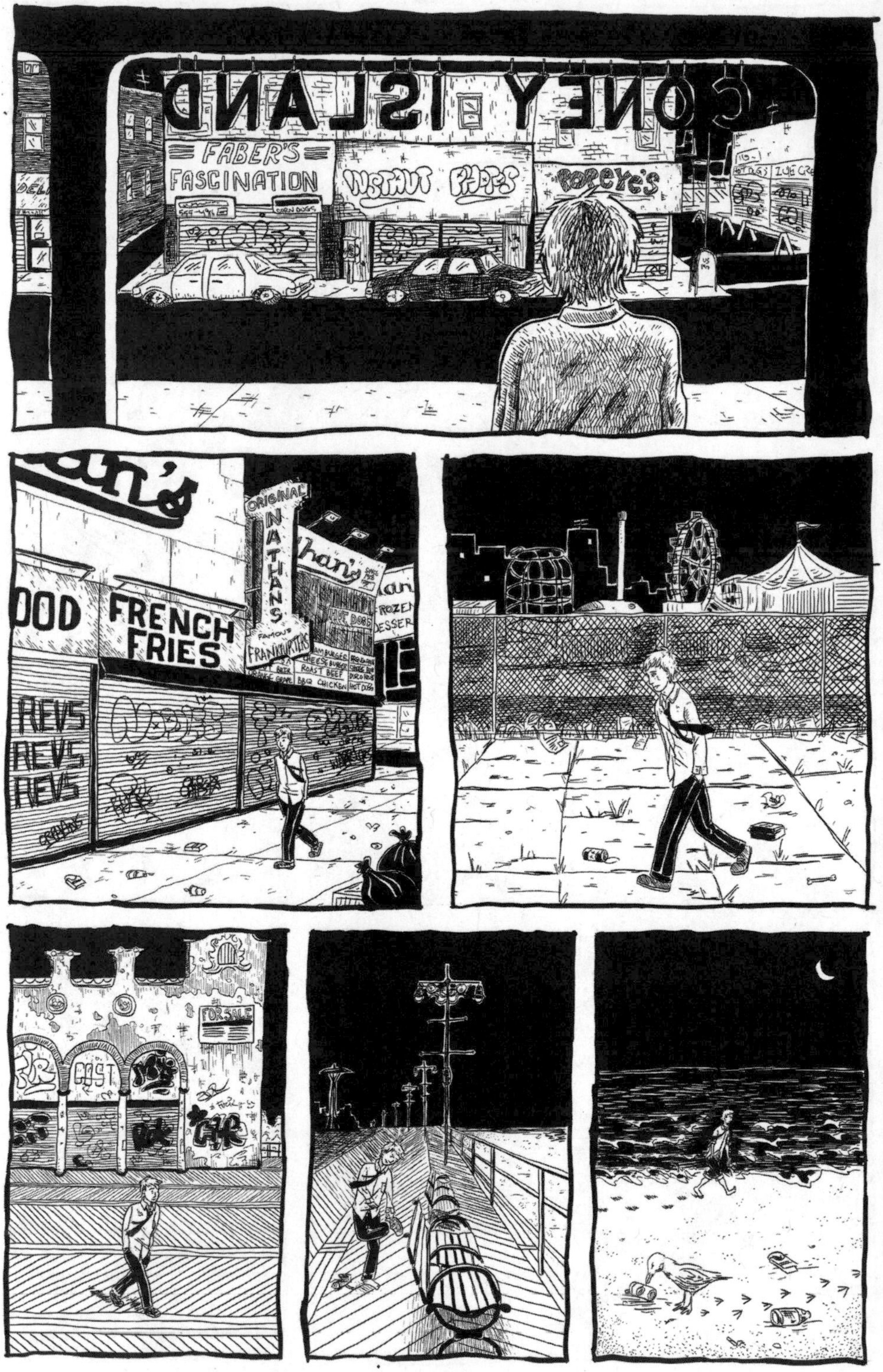
CONEY ISLAND
FABER'S
FASCINATION
CORN DOGS
INSTANT PHOTOS
POPEYE'S
DELI
FRENCH
FRIES
ORIGINAL
NATHAN'S
FAMOUS
FRANKFURTERS
HAMBURGER
CHEESEBURGER
ROAST BEEF
BBQ CHICKEN
HOT DOGS
FROZEN
DESSER
REVS
REVS
REVS
FOR SALE
COST

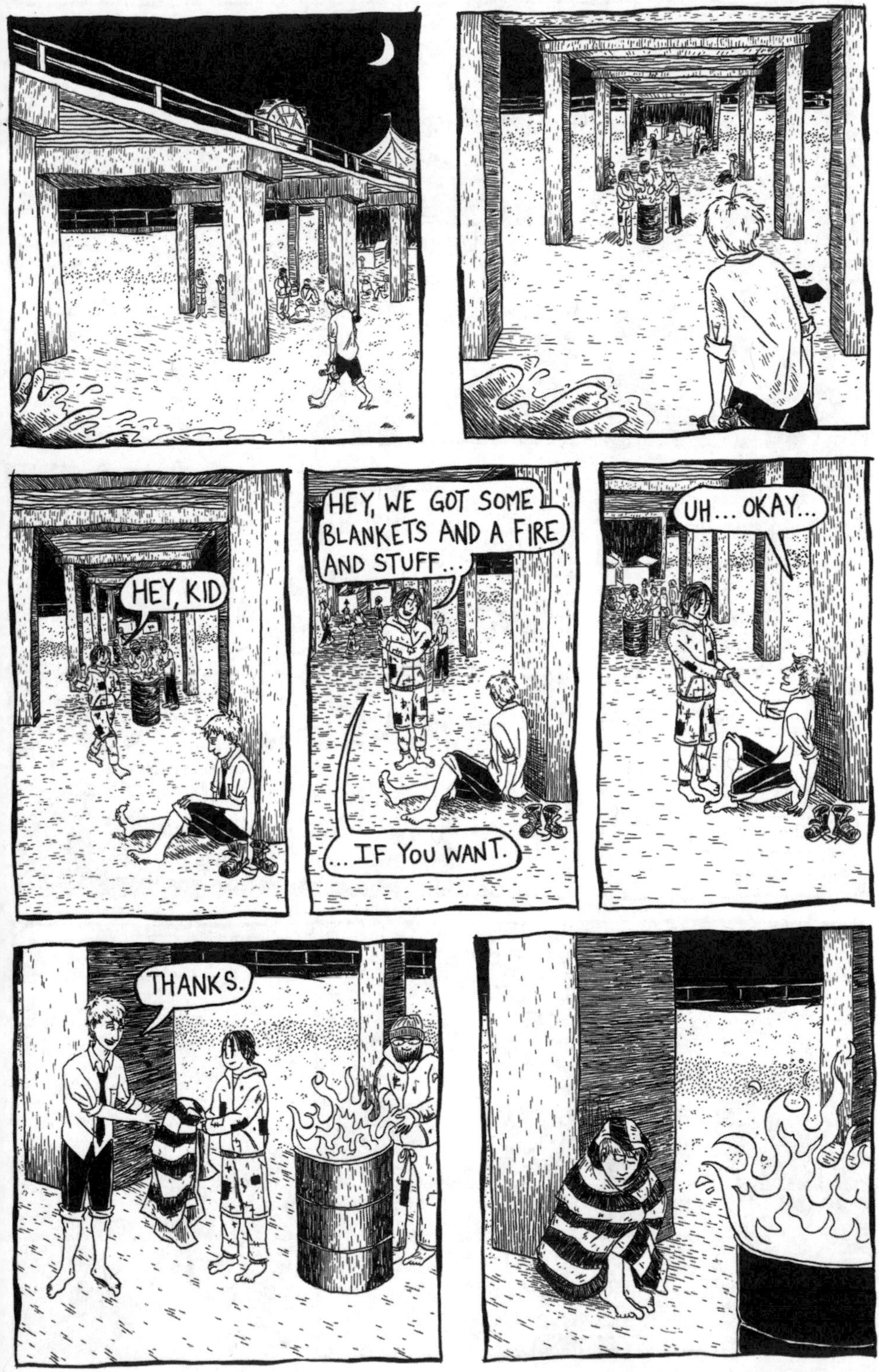
HEY, KID
HEY, WE GOT SOME BLANKETS AND A FIRE AND STUFF...
...IF YOU WANT.
UH... OKAY...
THANKS.

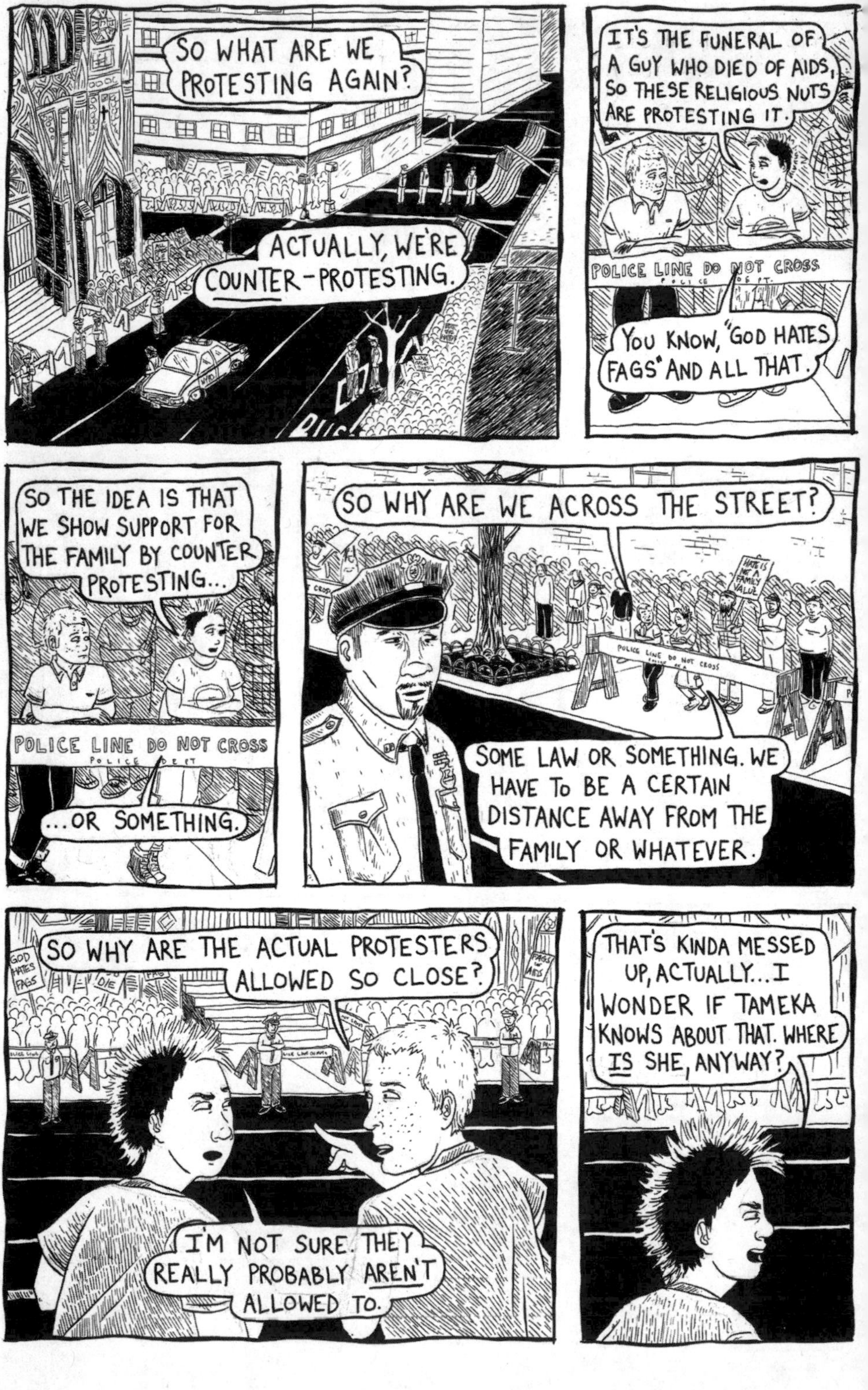
SO WHAT ARE WE PROTESTING AGAIN?
ACTUALLY, WE'RE COUNTER-PROTESTING.
IT'S THE FUNERAL OF A GUY WHO DIED OF AIDS, SO THESE RELIGIOUS NUTS ARE PROTESTING IT.
POLICE LINE DO NOT CROSS
YOU KNOW, "GOD HATES FAGS" AND ALL THAT.
SO THE IDEA IS THAT WE SHOW SUPPORT FOR THE FAMILY BY COUNTER PROTESTING...
POLICE LINE DO NOT CROSS
...OR SOMETHING.
SO WHY ARE WE ACROSS THE STREET?
HATE IS NOT A FAMILY VALUE
POLICE LINE DO NOT CROSS
SOME LAW OR SOMETHING. WE HAVE TO BE A CERTAIN DISTANCE AWAY FROM THE FAMILY OR WHATEVER.
GOD HATES FAGS
DIE
FAGS AIDS
SO WHY ARE THE ACTUAL PROTESTERS ALLOWED SO CLOSE?
I'M NOT SURE. THEY REALLY PROBABLY AREN'T ALLOWED TO.
THAT'S KINDA MESSED UP, ACTUALLY... I WONDER IF TAMEKA KNOWS ABOUT THAT. WHERE IS SHE, ANYWAY?

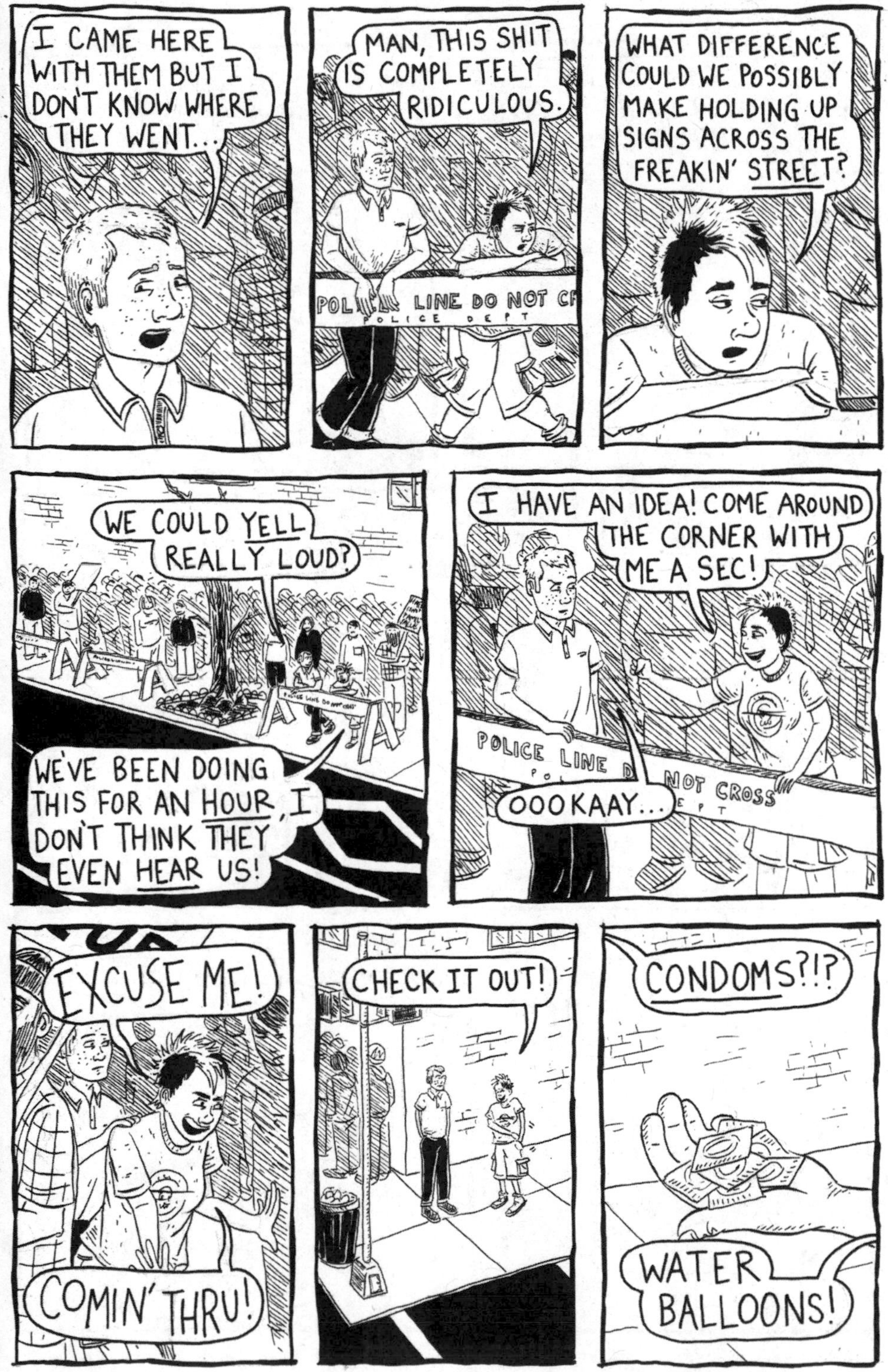
I CAME HERE WITH THEM BUT I DON'T KNOW WHERE THEY WENT...
MAN, THIS SHIT IS COMPLETELY RIDICULOUS.
POLICE LINE DO NOT CR
POLICE DEPT
WHAT DIFFERENCE COULD WE POSSIBLY MAKE HOLDING UP SIGNS ACROSS THE FREAKIN' STREET?
WE COULD YELL REALLY LOUD?
WE'VE BEEN DOING THIS FOR AN HOUR, I DON'T THINK THEY EVEN HEAR US!
I HAVE AN IDEA! COME AROUND THE CORNER WITH ME A SEC!
POLICE LINE DO NOT CROSS
OOOKAAY...
EXCUSE ME!
COMIN' THRU!
CHECK IT OUT!
CONDOMS?!?
WATER BALLOONS!

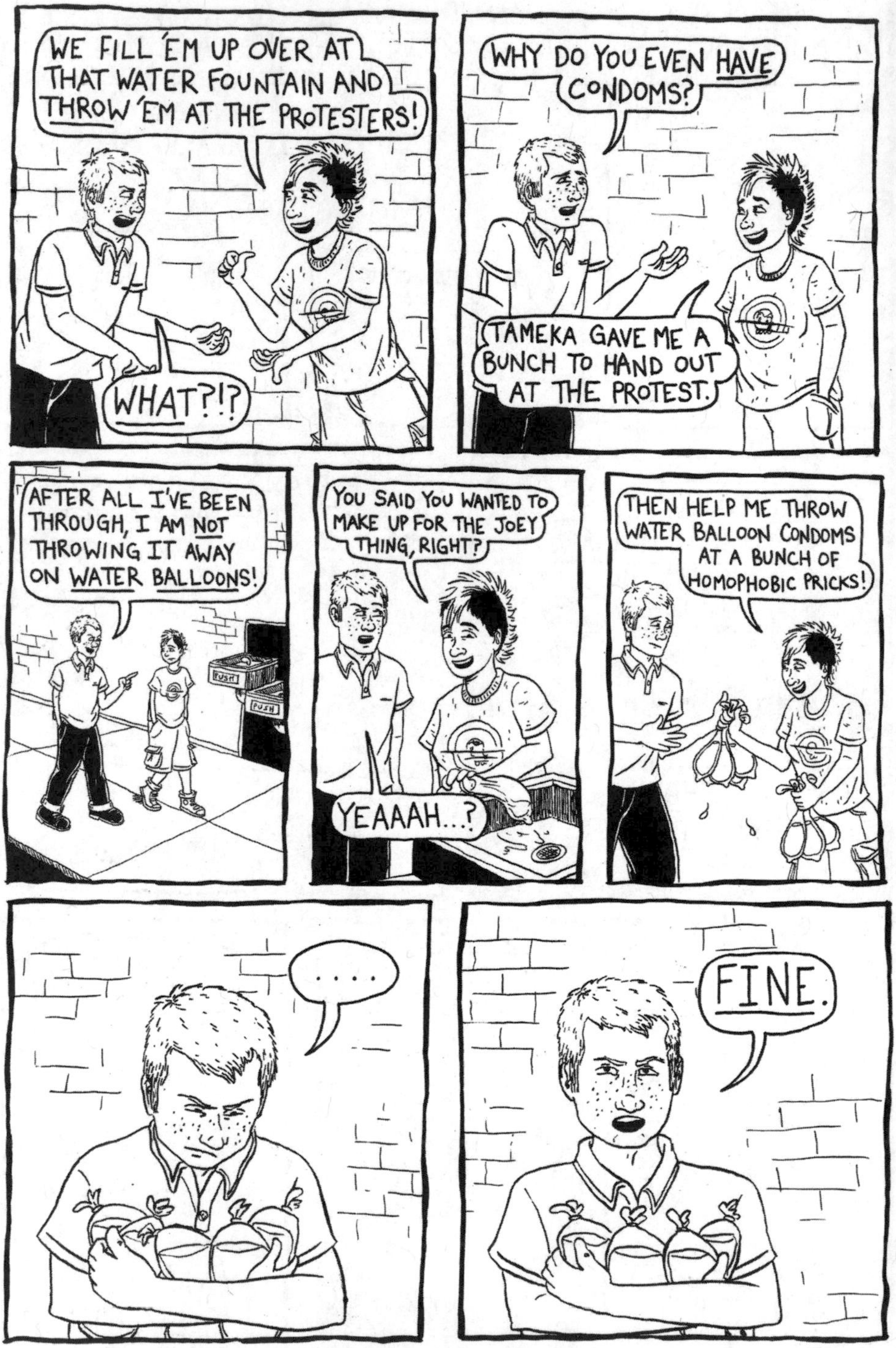
WE FILL 'EM UP OVER AT THAT WATER FOUNTAIN AND THROW 'EM AT THE PROTESTERS!
WHAT?!?
WHY DO YOU EVEN HAVE CONDOMS?
TAMEKA GAVE ME A BUNCH TO HAND OUT AT THE PROTEST.
AFTER ALL I'VE BEEN THROUGH, I AM NOT THROWING IT AWAY ON WATER BALLOONS!
PUSH
PUSH
YOU SAID YOU WANTED TO MAKE UP FOR THE JOEY THING, RIGHT?
YEAAAH...?
THEN HELP ME THROW WATER BALLOON CONDOMS AT A BUNCH OF HOMOPHOBIC PRICKS!
.....
FINE.

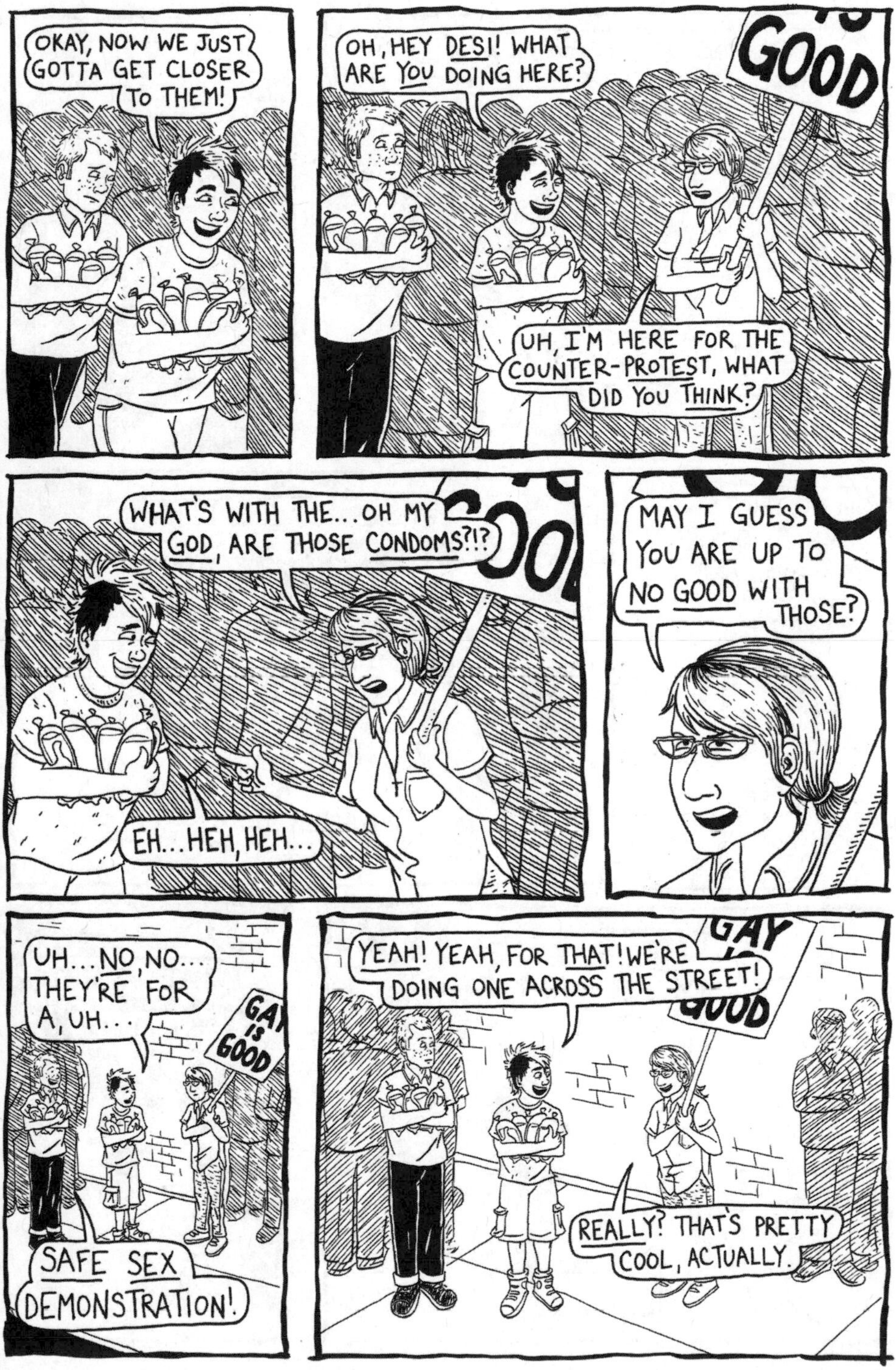
OKAY, NOW WE JUST GOTTA GET CLOSER TO THEM!
OH, HEY DESI! WHAT ARE YOU DOING HERE?
GOOD
UH, I'M HERE FOR THE COUNTER-PROTEST, WHAT DID YOU THINK?
WHAT'S WITH THE... OH MY GOD, ARE THOSE CONDOMS?!?
EH... HEH, HEH...
MAY I GUESS YOU ARE UP TO NO GOOD WITH THOSE?
UH... NO, NO... THEY'RE FOR A, UH...
GAY IS GOOD
SAFE SEX DEMONSTRATION!
YEAH! YEAH, FOR THAT! WE'RE DOING ONE ACROSS THE STREET!
REALLY? THAT'S PRETTY COOL, ACTUALLY.

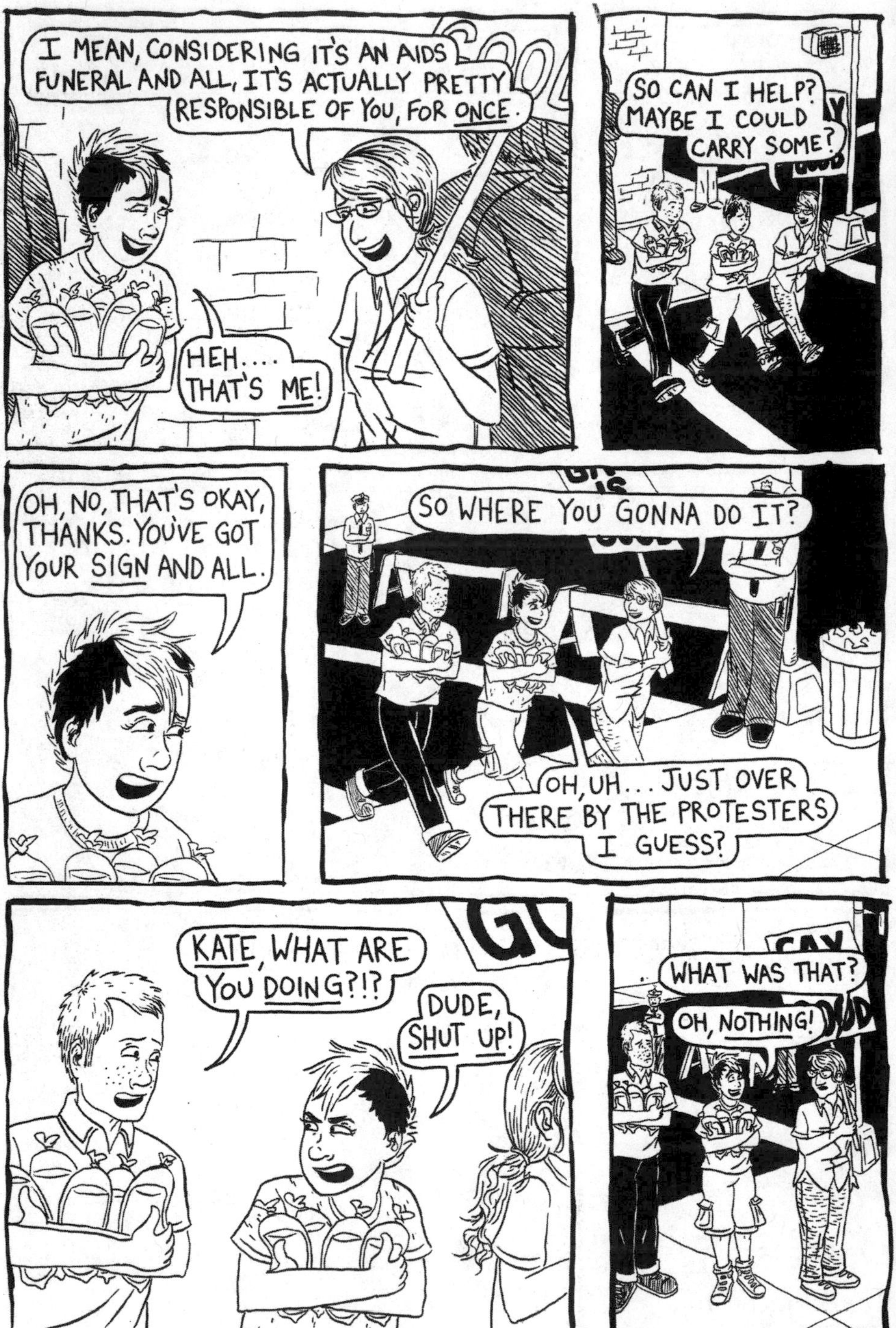
I MEAN, CONSIDERING IT'S AN AIDS FUNERAL AND ALL, IT'S ACTUALLY PRETTY RESPONSIBLE OF YOU, FOR ONCE.
HEH.... THAT'S ME!
SO CAN I HELP? MAYBE I COULD CARRY SOME?
OH, NO, THAT'S OKAY, THANKS. YOU'VE GOT YOUR SIGN AND ALL.
SO WHERE YOU GONNA DO IT?
OH, UH... JUST OVER THERE BY THE PROTESTERS I GUESS?
KATE, WHAT ARE YOU DOING?!?
DUDE, SHUT UP!
WHAT WAS THAT?
OH, NOTHING!

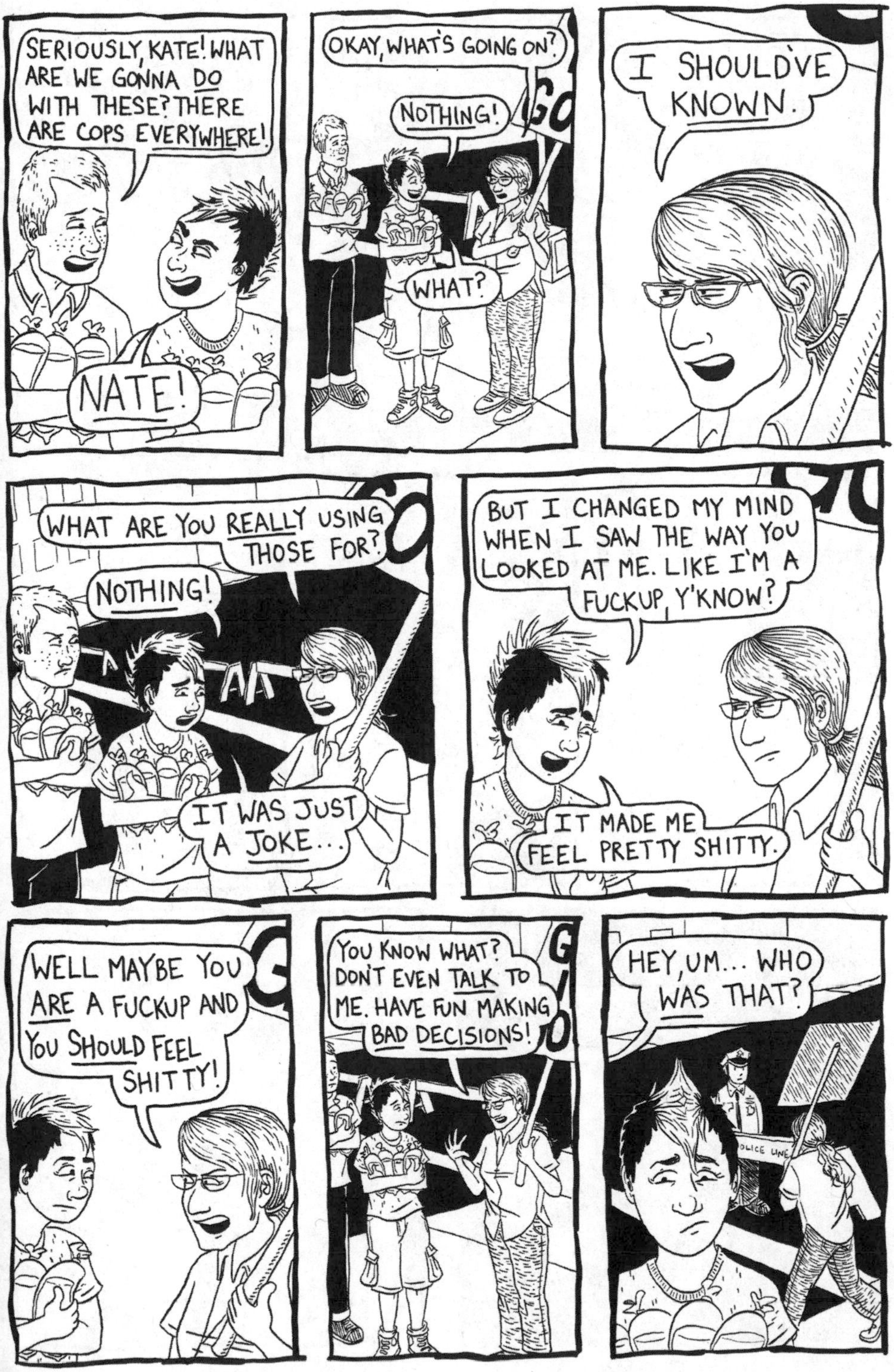
SERIOUSLY, KATE! WHAT ARE WE GONNA DO WITH THESE? THERE ARE COPS EVERYWHERE!
NATE!
OKAY, WHAT'S GOING ON?
NOTHING!
WHAT?
I SHOULD'VE KNOWN.
WHAT ARE YOU REALLY USING THOSE FOR?
NOTHING!
IT WAS JUST A JOKE...
BUT I CHANGED MY MIND WHEN I SAW THE WAY YOU LOOKED AT ME. LIKE I'M A FUCKUP, Y'KNOW?
IT MADE ME FEEL PRETTY SHITTY.
WELL MAYBE YOU ARE A FUCKUP AND YOU SHOULD FEEL SHITTY!
YOU KNOW WHAT? DON'T EVEN TALK TO ME. HAVE FUN MAKING BAD DECISIONS!
HEY, UM... WHO WAS THAT?

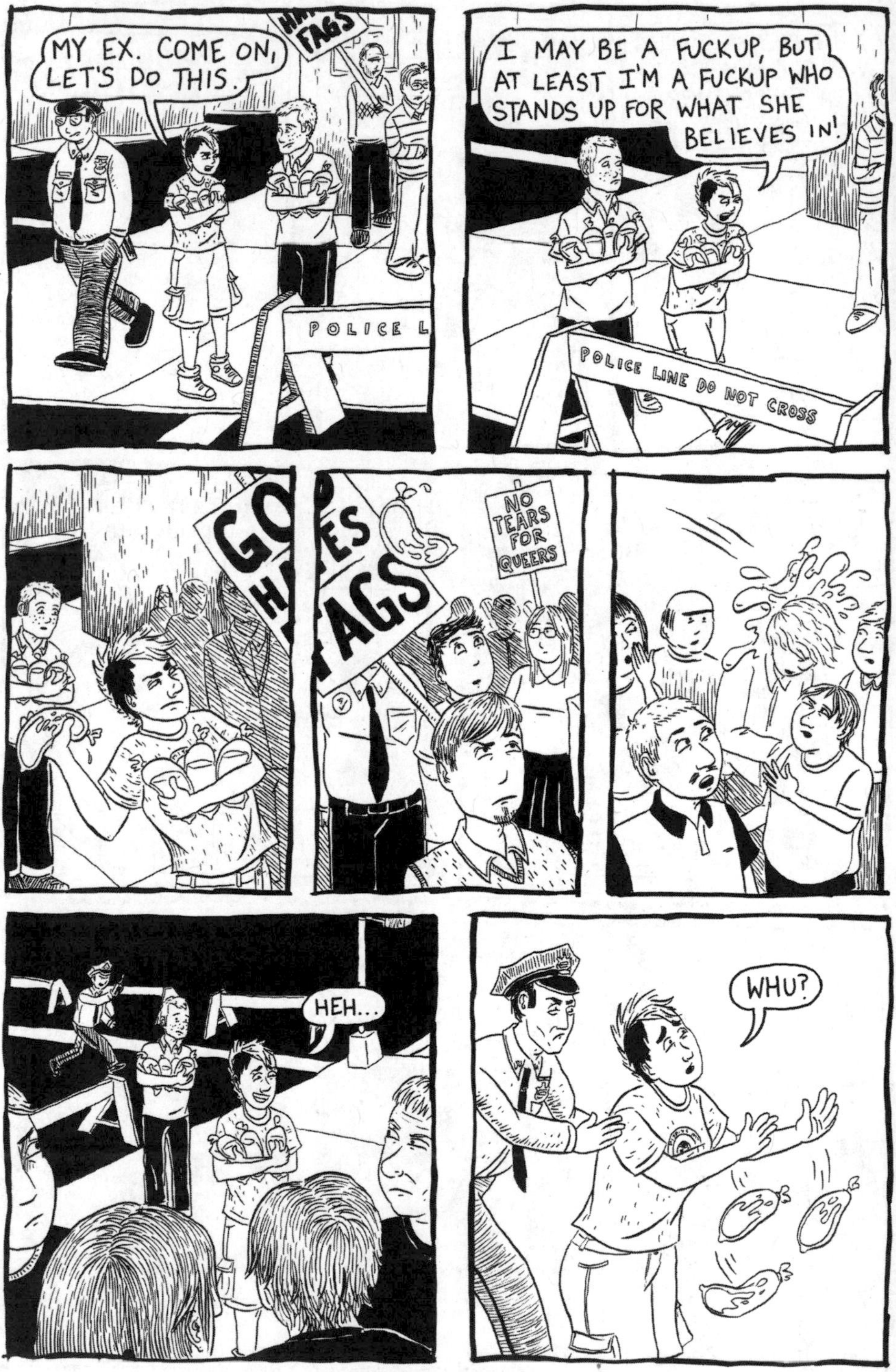
MY EX. COME ON, LET'S DO THIS.
FAGS
POLICE L
I MAY BE A FUCKUP, BUT AT LEAST I'M A FUCKUP WHO STANDS UP FOR WHAT SHE BELIEVES IN!
POLICE LINE DO NOT CROSS
GOD HATES FAGS
NO TEARS FOR QUEERS
HEH...
WHU?

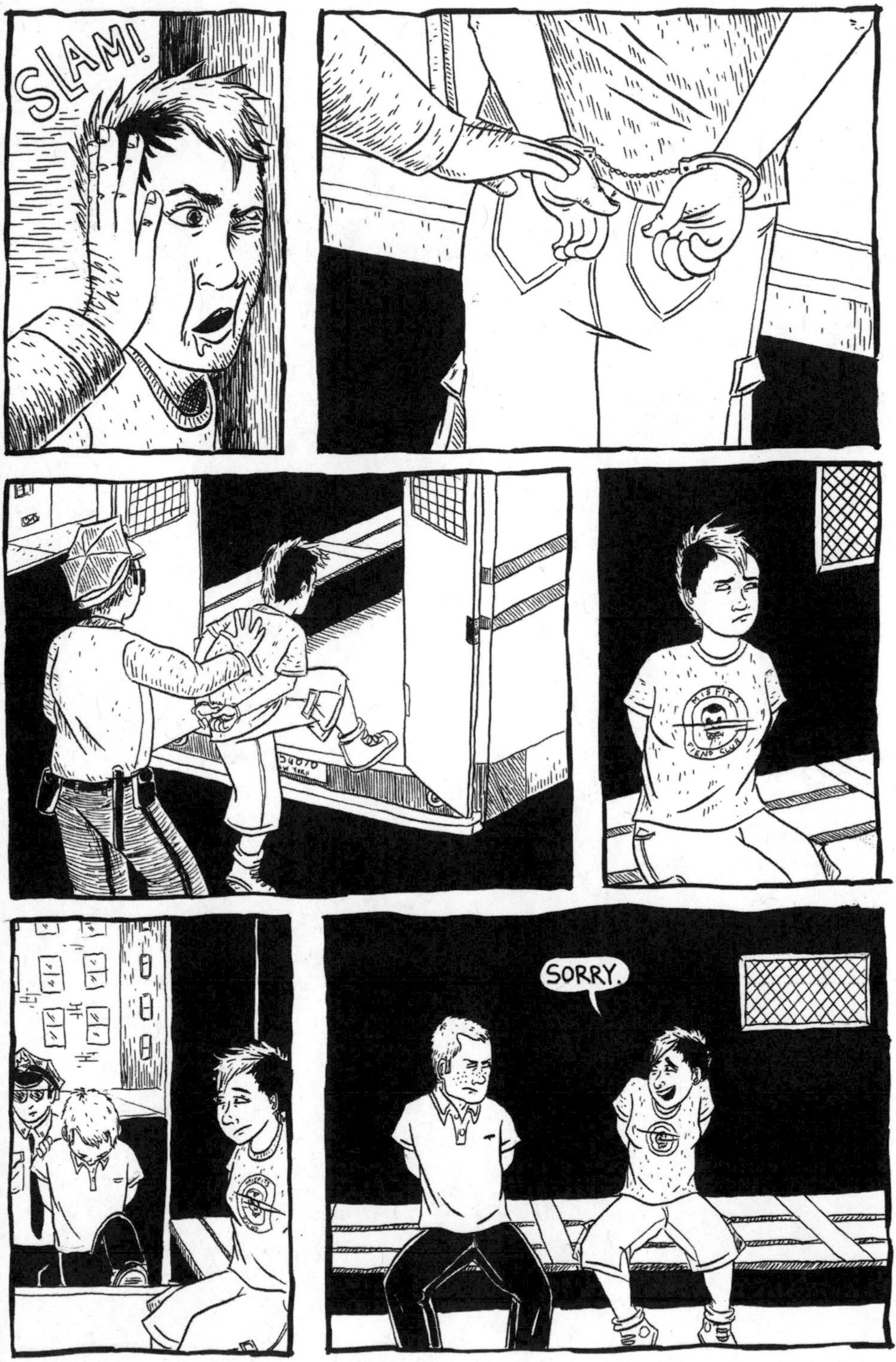
SLAM!
SORRY.

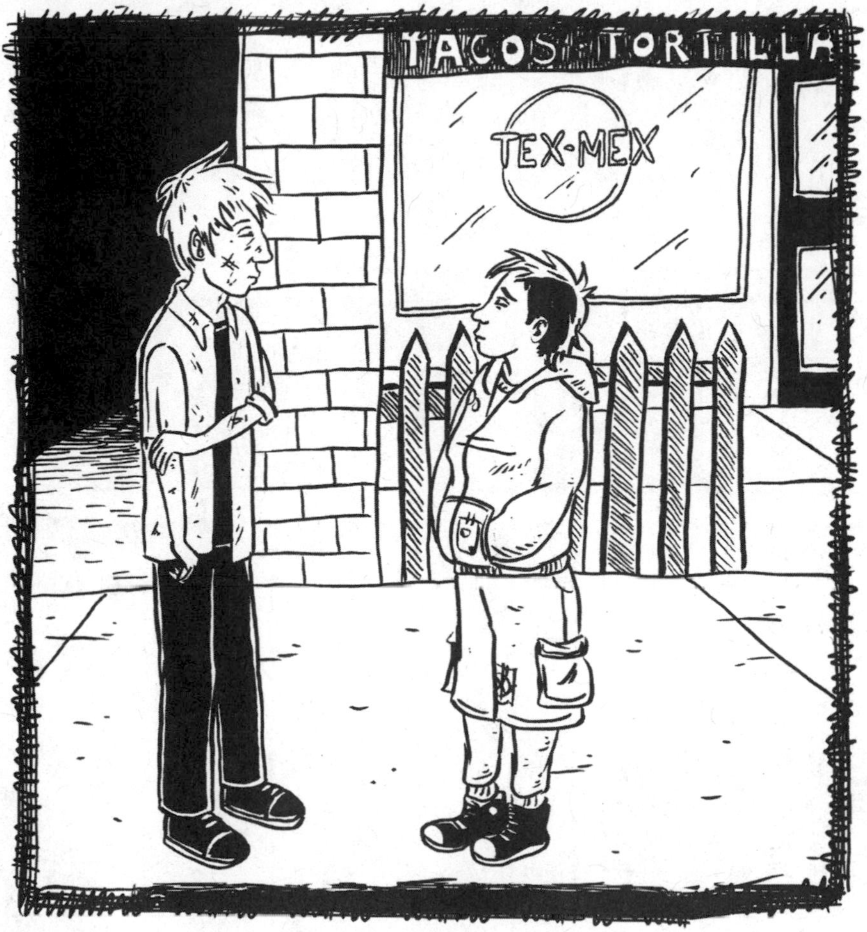
TACOS·TORTILLA
TEX-MEX

CHAPTER FIVE

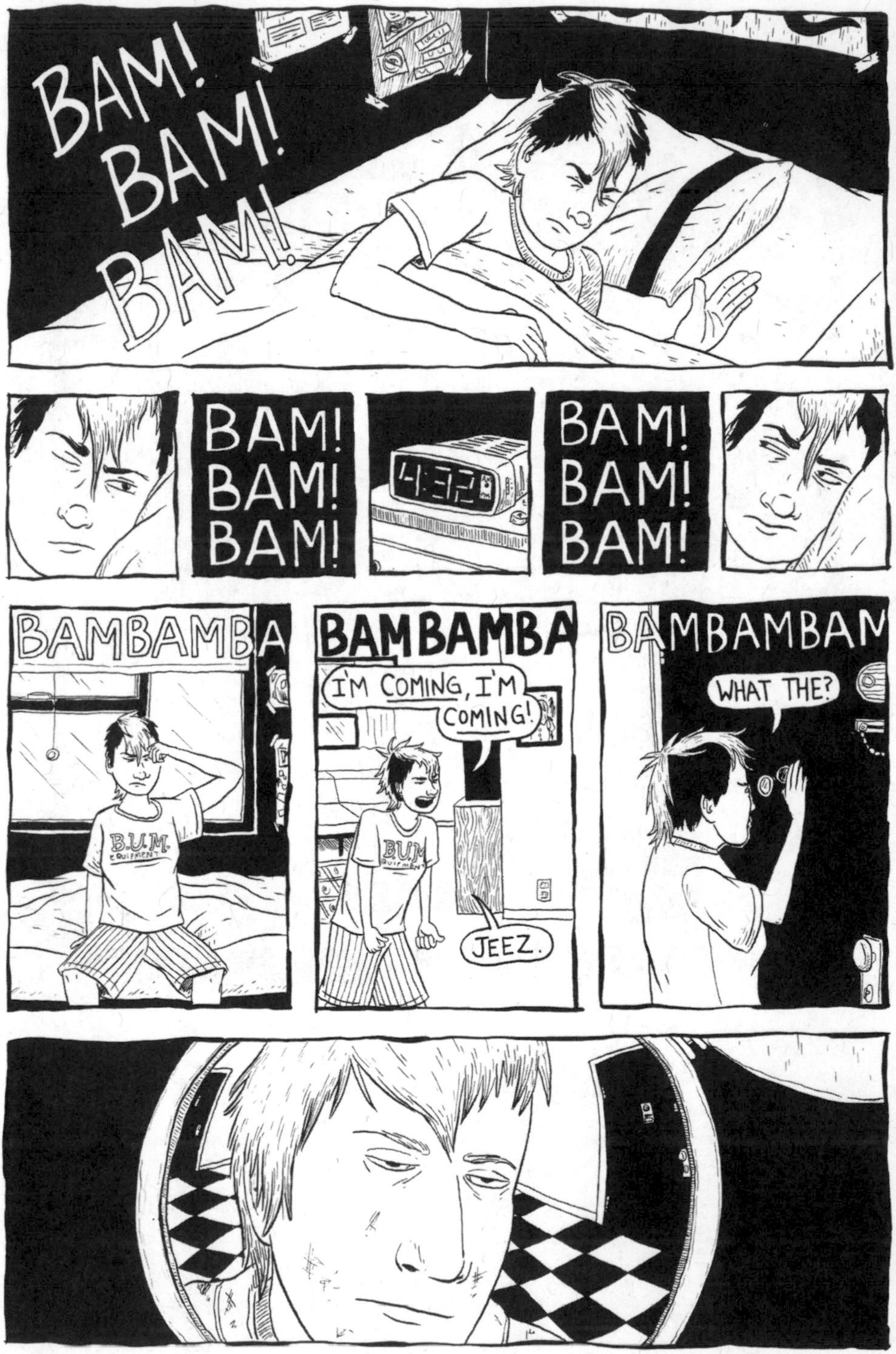
BAM! BAM! BAM!
BAM! BAM! BAM!
4:32
BAM! BAM! BAM!
BAMBAMBA
BAMBAMBA
I'M COMING, I'M COMING!
JEEZ.
BAMBAMBAM
WHAT THE?

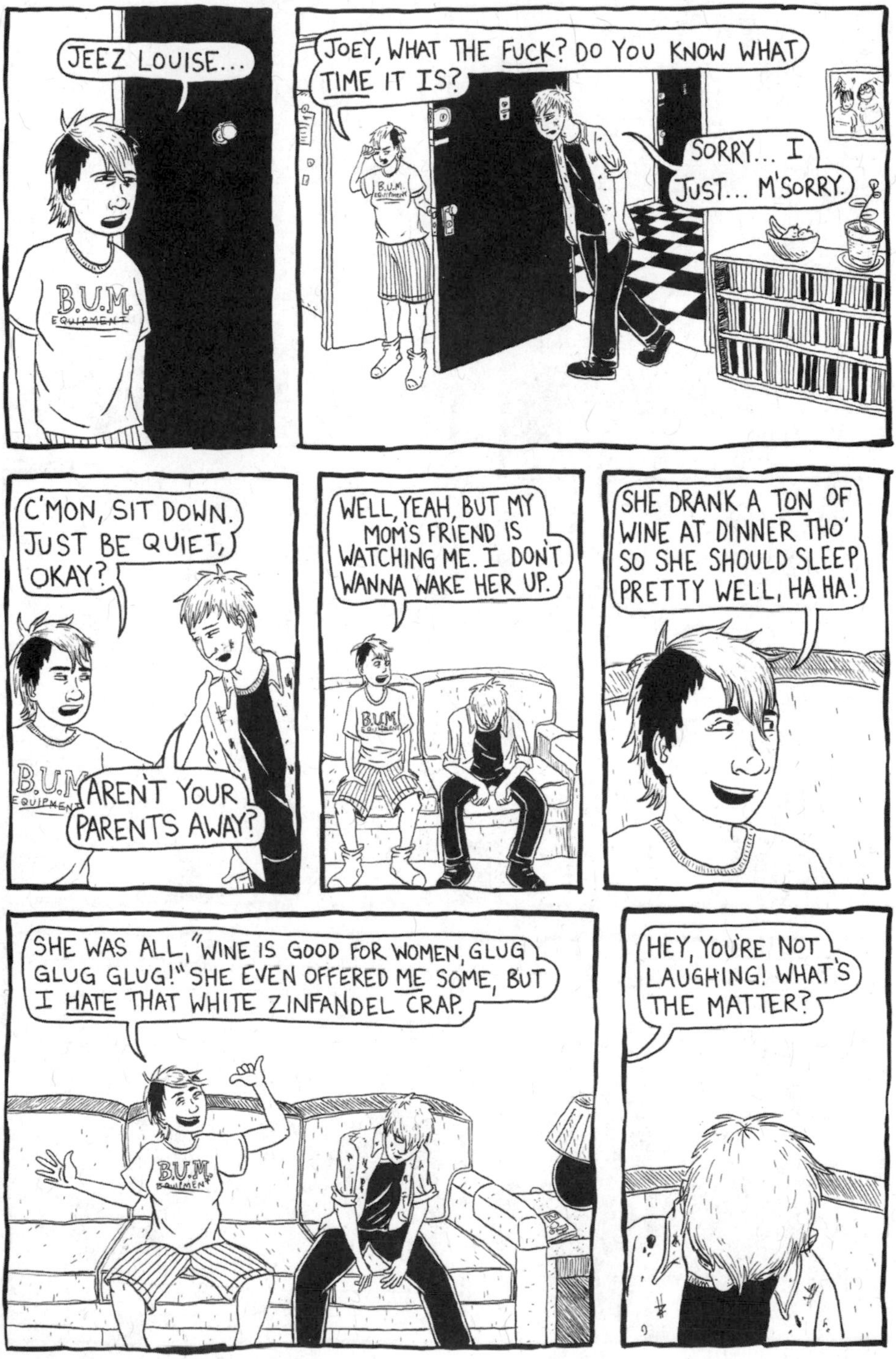
JEEZ LOUISE...
JOEY, WHAT THE FUCK? DO YOU KNOW WHAT TIME IT IS?
SORRY... I JUST... M'SORRY.
C'MON, SIT DOWN. JUST BE QUIET, OKAY?
AREN'T YOUR PARENTS AWAY?
WELL, YEAH, BUT MY MOM'S FRIEND IS WATCHING ME. I DON'T WANNA WAKE HER UP.
SHE DRANK A TON OF WINE AT DINNER THO' SO SHE SHOULD SLEEP PRETTY WELL, HA HA!
SHE WAS ALL, "WINE IS GOOD FOR WOMEN, GLUG GLUG GLUG!" SHE EVEN OFFERED ME SOME, BUT I HATE THAT WHITE ZINFANDEL CRAP.
HEY, YOU'RE NOT LAUGHING! WHAT'S THE MATTER?

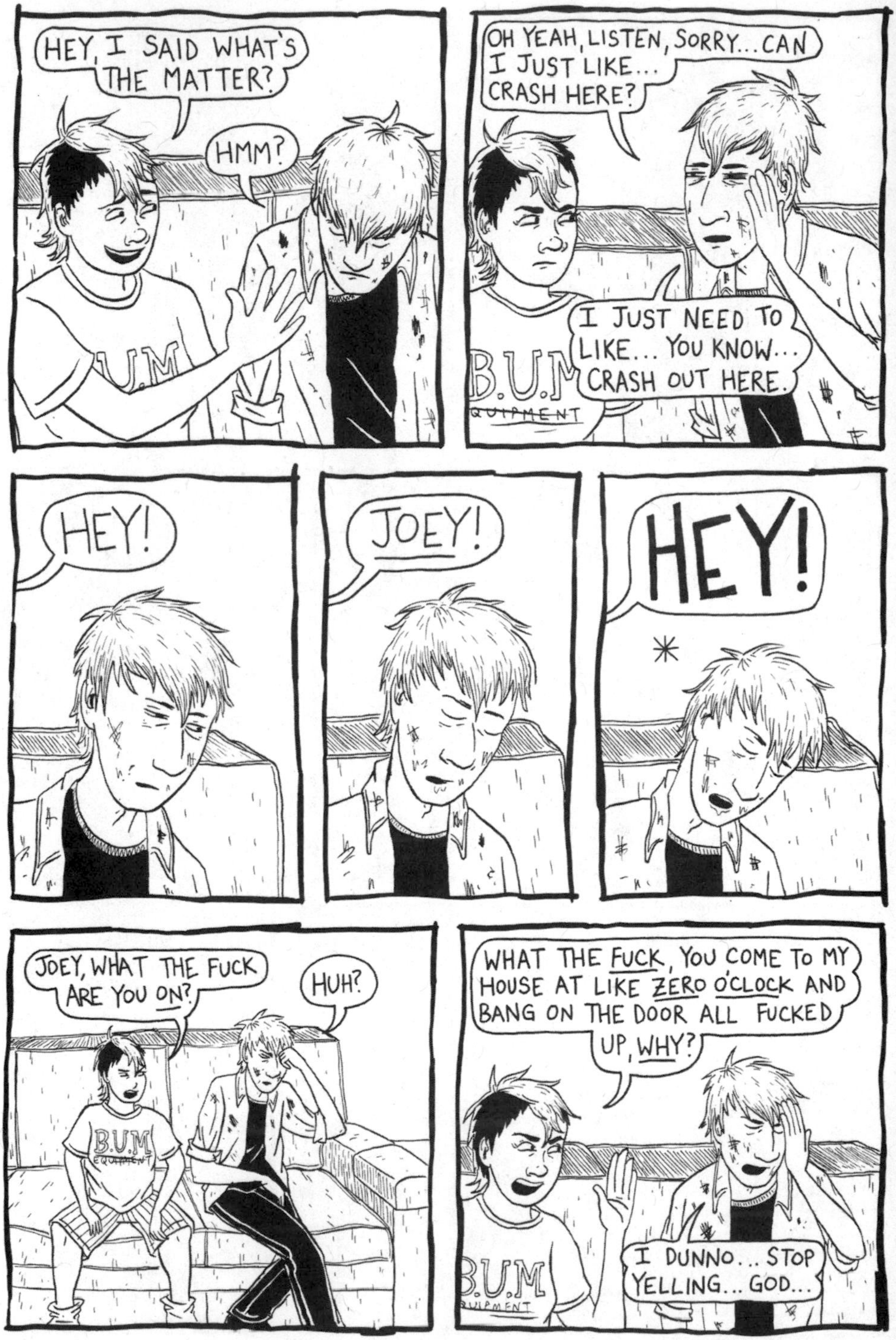
HEY, I SAID WHAT'S THE MATTER?
HMM?
OH YEAH, LISTEN, SORRY... CAN I JUST LIKE... CRASH HERE?
I JUST NEED TO LIKE... YOU KNOW... CRASH OUT HERE.
B.U.M EQUIPMENT
HEY!
JOEY!
HEY!
JOEY, WHAT THE FUCK ARE YOU ON?
HUH?
B.U.M EQUIPMENT
WHAT THE FUCK, YOU COME TO MY HOUSE AT LIKE ZERO O'CLOCK AND BANG ON THE DOOR ALL FUCKED UP, WHY?
I DUNNO... STOP YELLING... GOD...
B.U.M EQUIPMENT

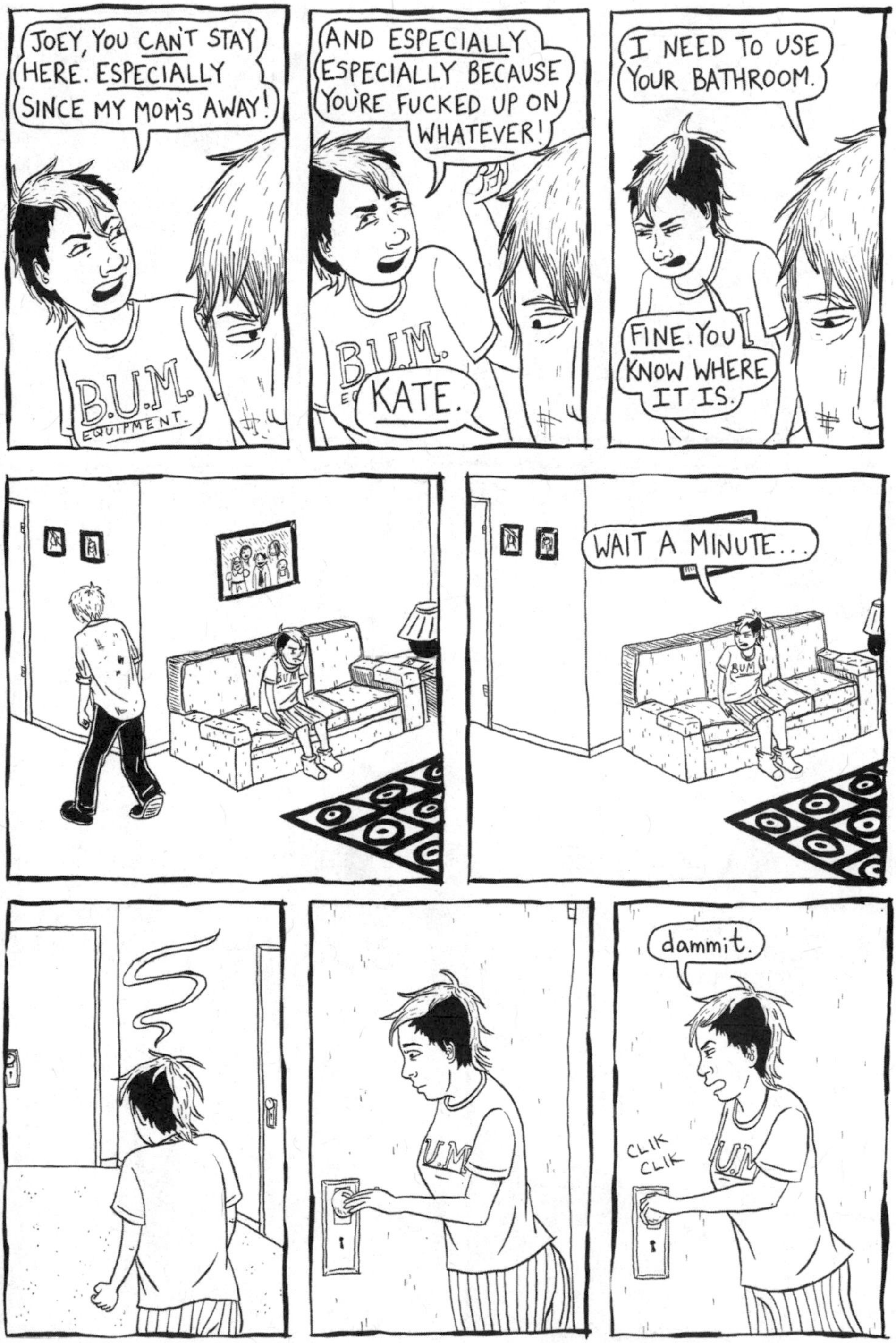
JOEY, YOU CAN'T STAY HERE. ESPECIALLY SINCE MY MOM'S AWAY!
B.U.M. EQUIPMENT
AND ESPECIALLY ESPECIALLY BECAUSE YOU'RE FUCKED UP ON WHATEVER!
KATE.
I NEED TO USE YOUR BATHROOM.
FINE. YOU KNOW WHERE IT IS.
WAIT A MINUTE...
dammit.
CLIK CLIK

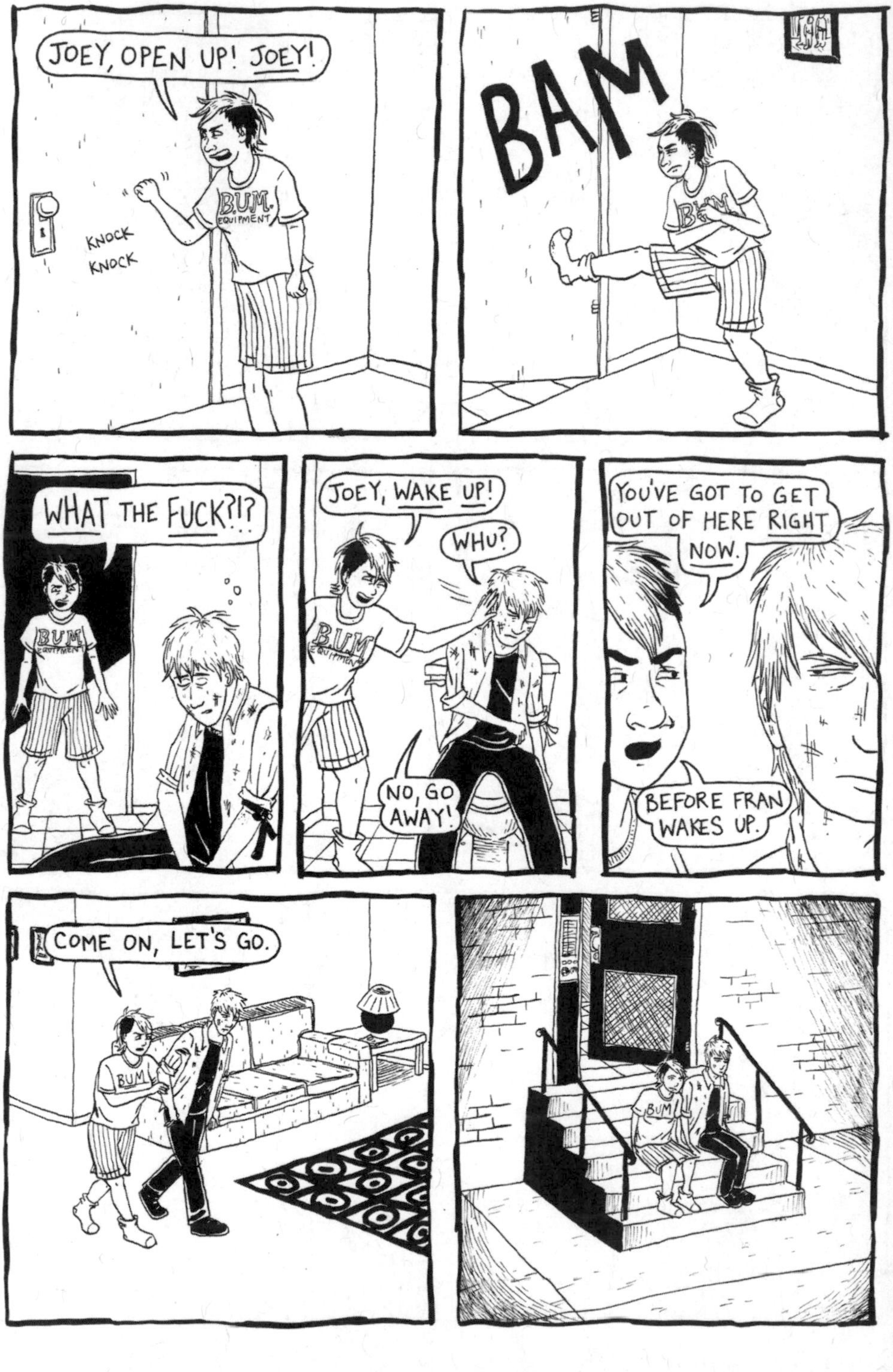
JOEY, OPEN UP! JOEY!
KNOCK KNOCK
B.U.M. EQUIPMENT
BAM
WHAT THE FUCK?!?...
JOEY, WAKE UP!
WHU?
NO, GO AWAY!
YOU'VE GOT TO GET OUT OF HERE RIGHT NOW.
BEFORE FRAN WAKES UP.
COME ON, LET'S GO.
BUM

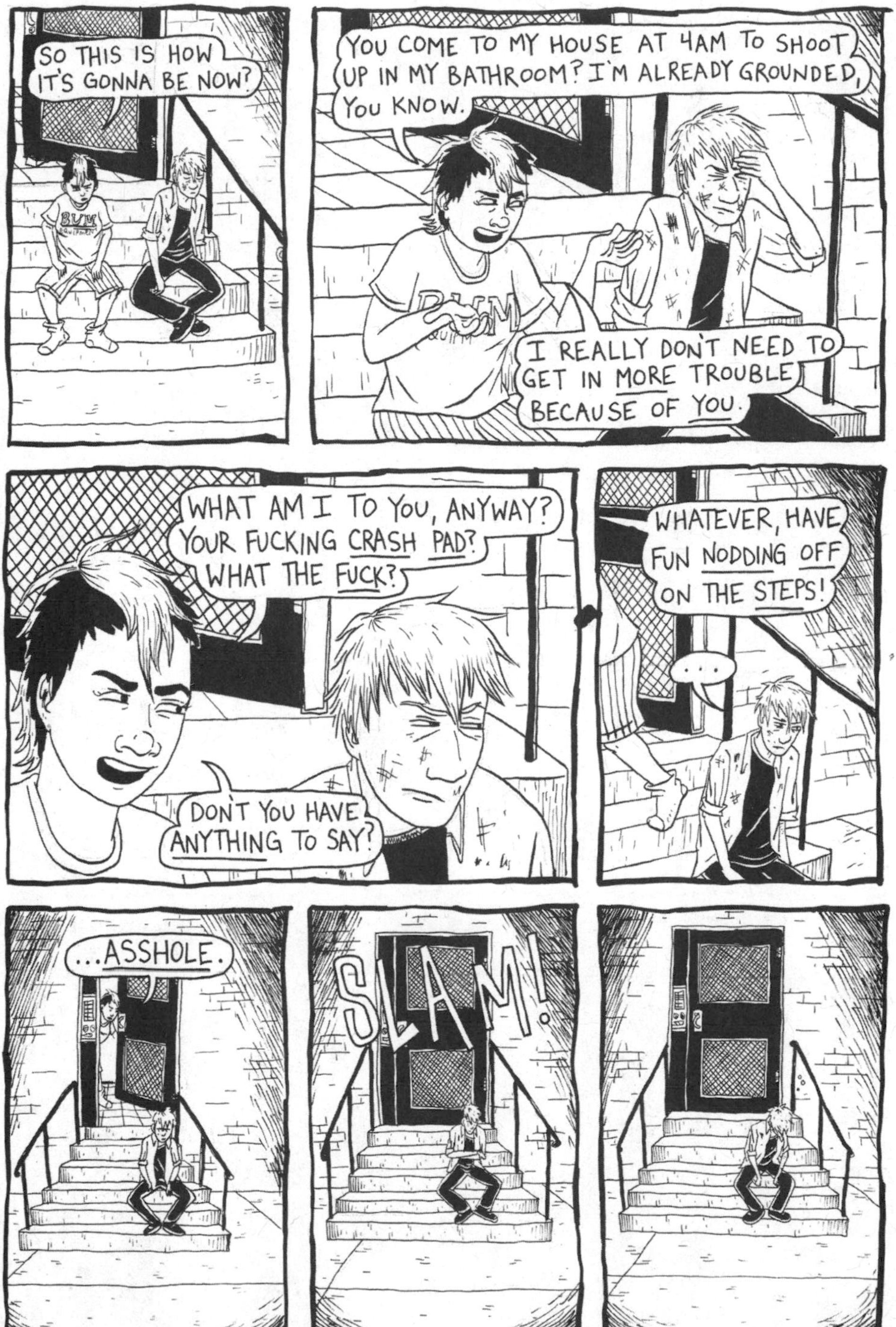
SO THIS IS HOW IT'S GONNA BE NOW?
BUM
YOU COME TO MY HOUSE AT 4AM TO SHOOT UP IN MY BATHROOM? I'M ALREADY GROUNDED, YOU KNOW.
I REALLY DON'T NEED TO GET IN MORE TROUBLE BECAUSE OF YOU.
WHAT AM I TO YOU, ANYWAY? YOUR FUCKING CRASH PAD? WHAT THE FUCK?
DON'T YOU HAVE ANYTHING TO SAY?
WHATEVER, HAVE FUN NODDING OFF ON THE STEPS!
...
...ASSHOLE.
SLAM!

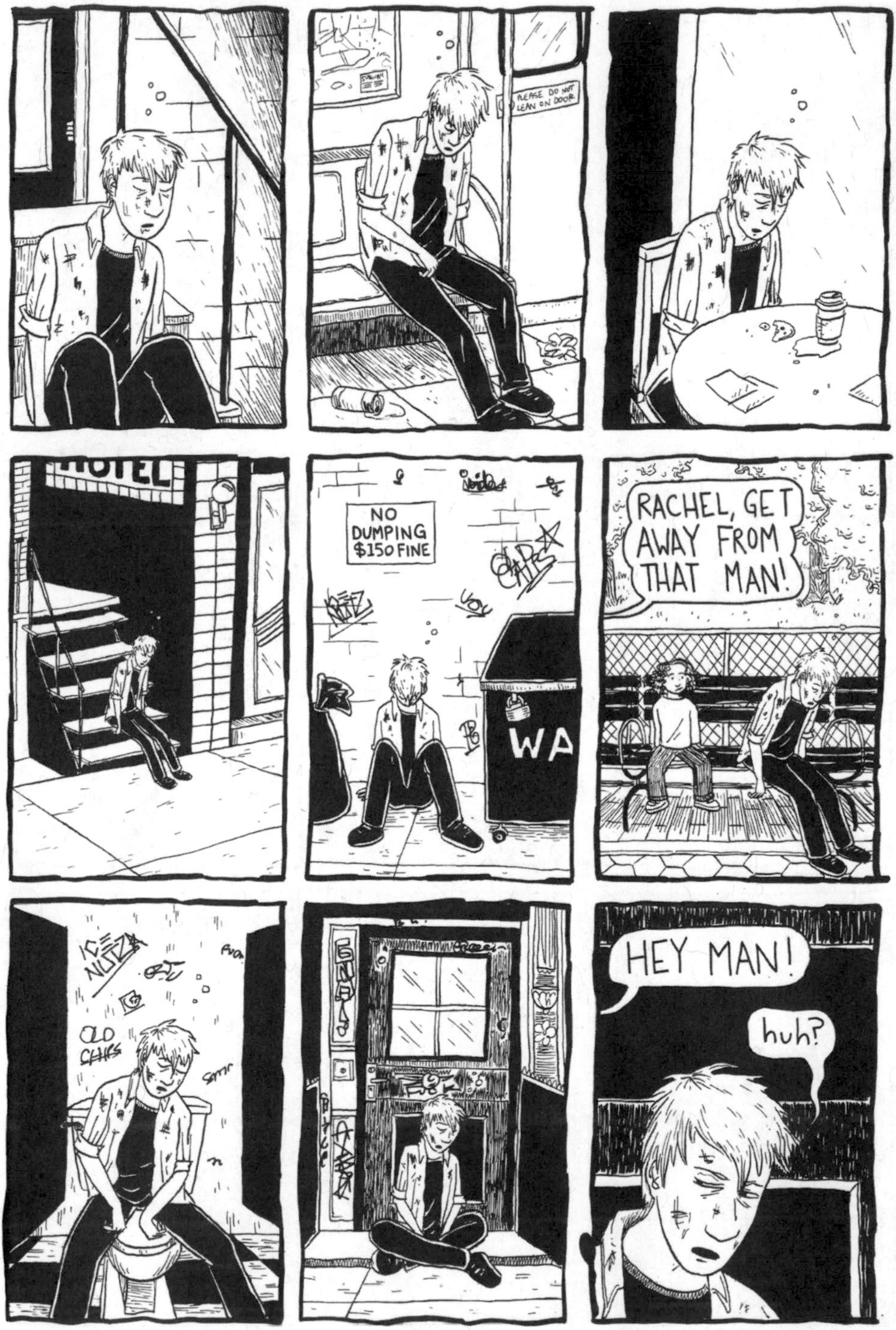
PLEASE DO NOT LEAN ON DOOR
HOTEL
NO DUMPING $150 FINE
WA
RACHEL, GET AWAY FROM THAT MAN!
HEY MAN!
huh?

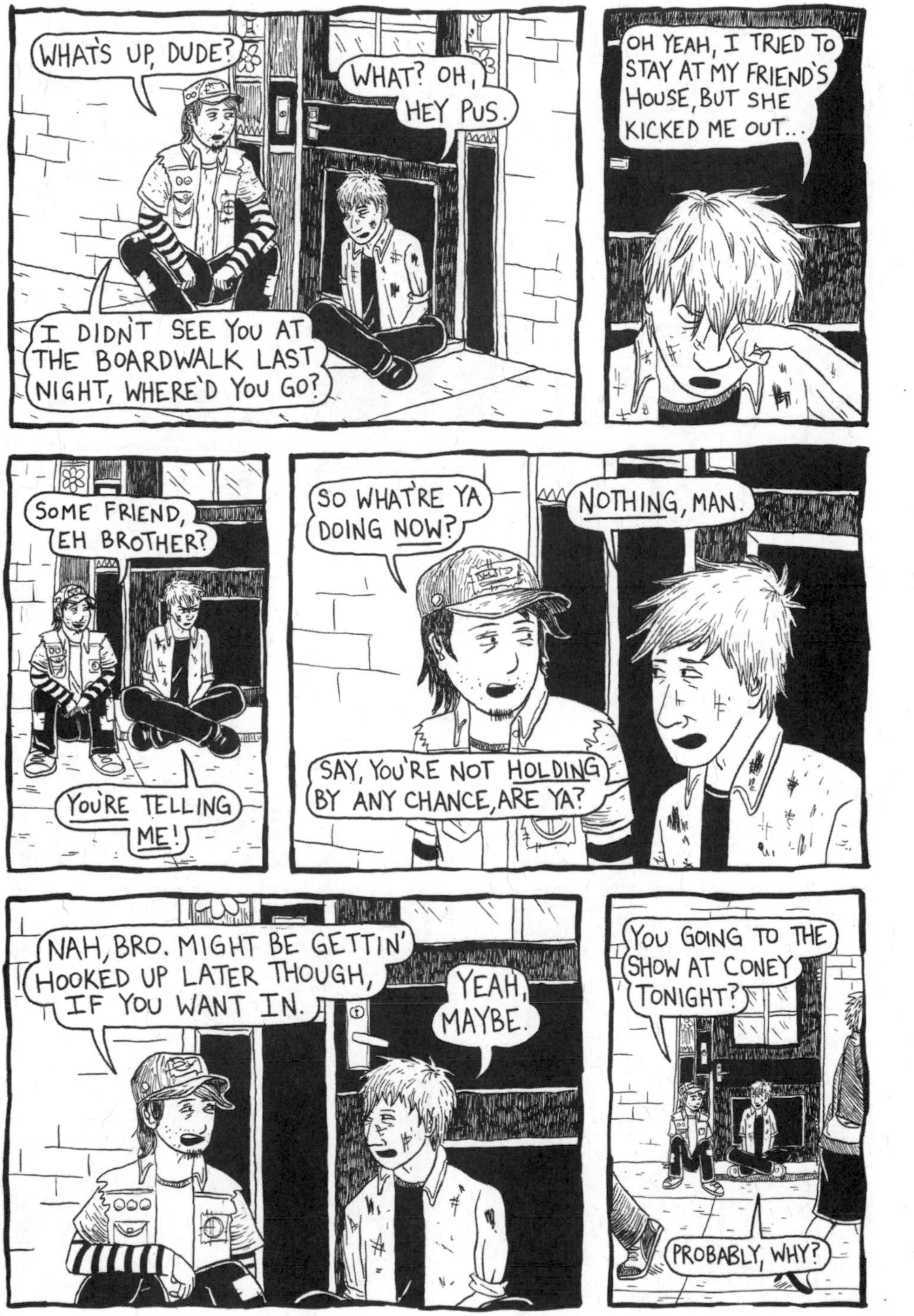
WHAT'S UP, DUDE?
WHAT? OH, HEY PUS.
I DIDN'T SEE YOU AT THE BOARDWALK LAST NIGHT, WHERE'D YOU GO?
OH YEAH, I TRIED TO STAY AT MY FRIEND'S HOUSE, BUT SHE KICKED ME OUT...
SOME FRIEND, EH BROTHER?
YOU'RE TELLING ME!
SO WHAT'RE YA DOING NOW?
NOTHING, MAN.
SAY, YOU'RE NOT HOLDING BY ANY CHANCE, ARE YA?
NAH, BRO. MIGHT BE GETTIN' HOOKED UP LATER THOUGH, IF YOU WANT IN.
YEAH, MAYBE.
YOU GOING TO THE SHOW AT CONEY TONIGHT?
PROBABLY, WHY?

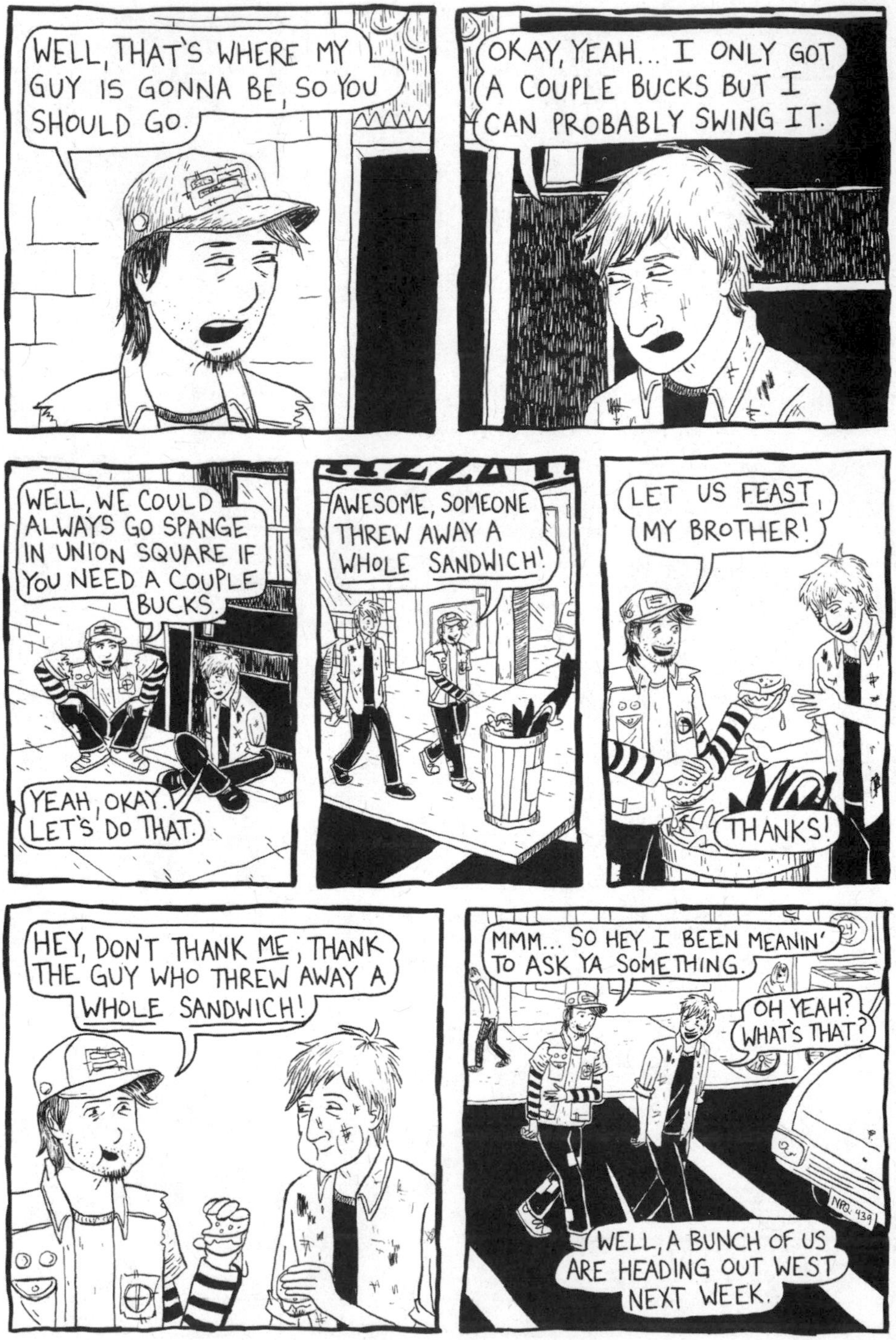
WELL, THAT'S WHERE MY GUY IS GONNA BE, SO YOU SHOULD GO.
OKAY, YEAH... I ONLY GOT A COUPLE BUCKS BUT I CAN PROBABLY SWING IT.
WELL, WE COULD ALWAYS GO SPANGE IN UNION SQUARE IF YOU NEED A COUPLE BUCKS.
YEAH, OKAY. LET'S DO THAT.
AWESOME, SOMEONE THREW AWAY A WHOLE SANDWICH!
LET US FEAST, MY BROTHER!
THANKS!
HEY, DON'T THANK ME; THANK THE GUY WHO THREW AWAY A WHOLE SANDWICH!
MMM... SO HEY, I BEEN MEANIN' TO ASK YA SOMETHING.
OH YEAH? WHAT'S THAT?
WELL, A BUNCH OF US ARE HEADING OUT WEST NEXT WEEK.

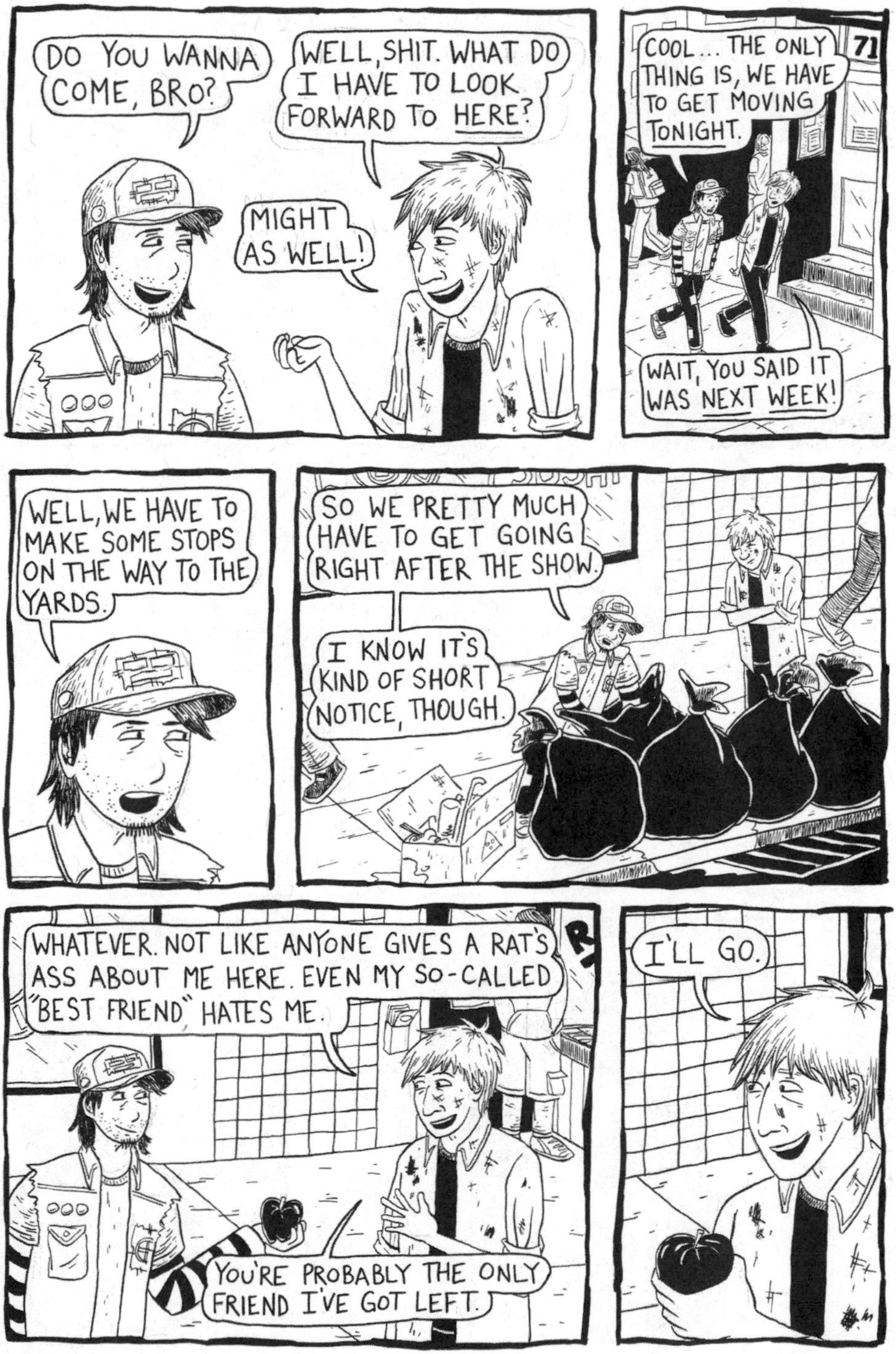
DO YOU WANNA COME, BRO?
WELL, SHIT. WHAT DO I HAVE TO LOOK FORWARD TO HERE?
MIGHT AS WELL!
COOL... THE ONLY THING IS, WE HAVE TO GET MOVING TONIGHT.
71
WAIT, YOU SAID IT WAS NEXT WEEK!
WELL, WE HAVE TO MAKE SOME STOPS ON THE WAY TO THE YARDS.
SO WE PRETTY MUCH HAVE TO GET GOING RIGHT AFTER THE SHOW.
I KNOW IT'S KIND OF SHORT NOTICE, THOUGH.
WHATEVER. NOT LIKE ANYONE GIVES A RAT'S ASS ABOUT ME HERE. EVEN MY SO-CALLED "BEST FRIEND" HATES ME.
YOU'RE PROBABLY THE ONLY FRIEND I'VE GOT LEFT.
I'LL GO.

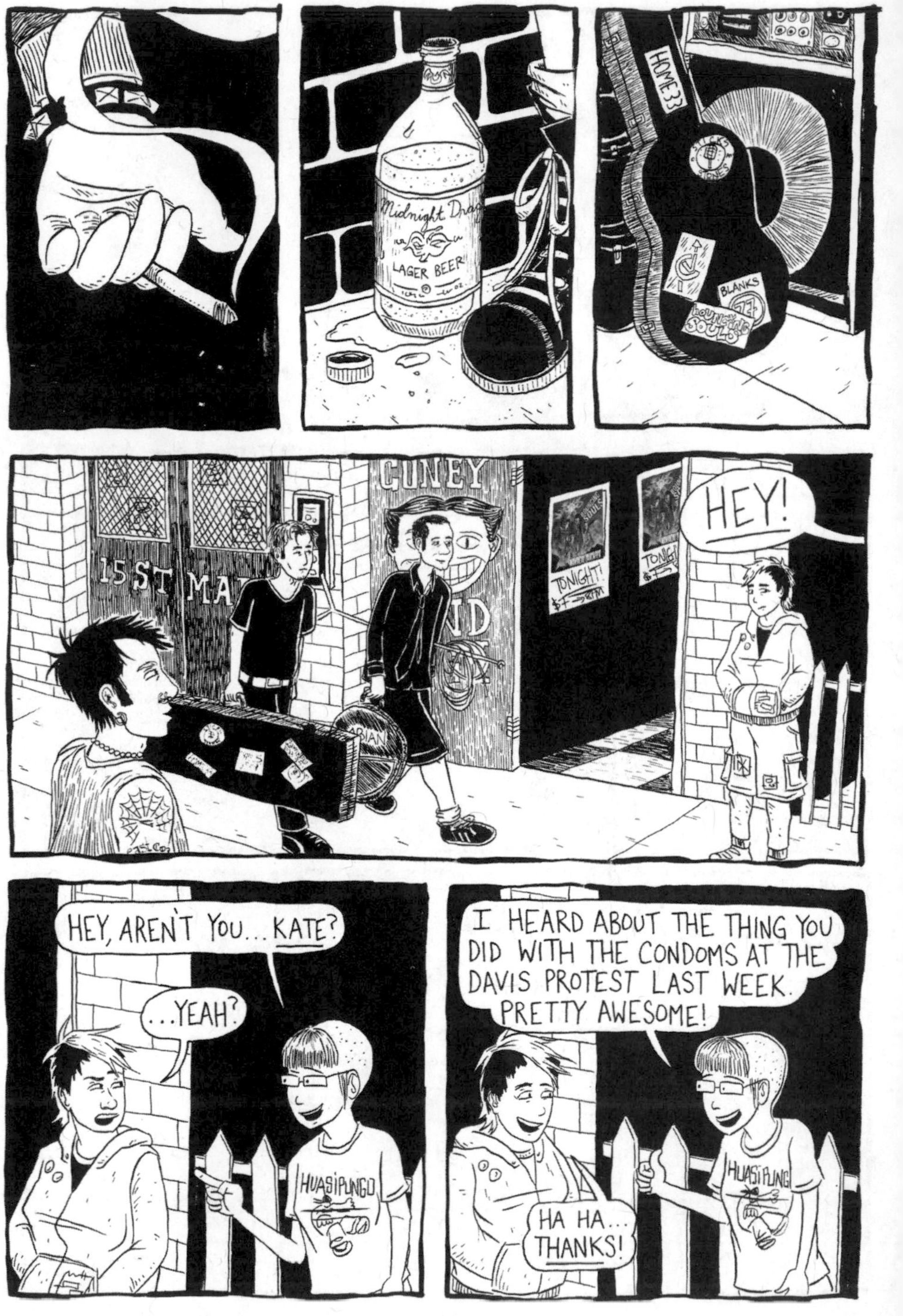
LAGER BEER
HOME33
BLANKS
CONEY
TONIGHT!
HEY!
HEY, AREN'T YOU... KATE?
...YEAH?
HUASIPUNGO
I HEARD ABOUT THE THING YOU DID WITH THE CONDOMS AT THE DAVIS PROTEST LAST WEEK. PRETTY AWESOME!
HA HA... THANKS!

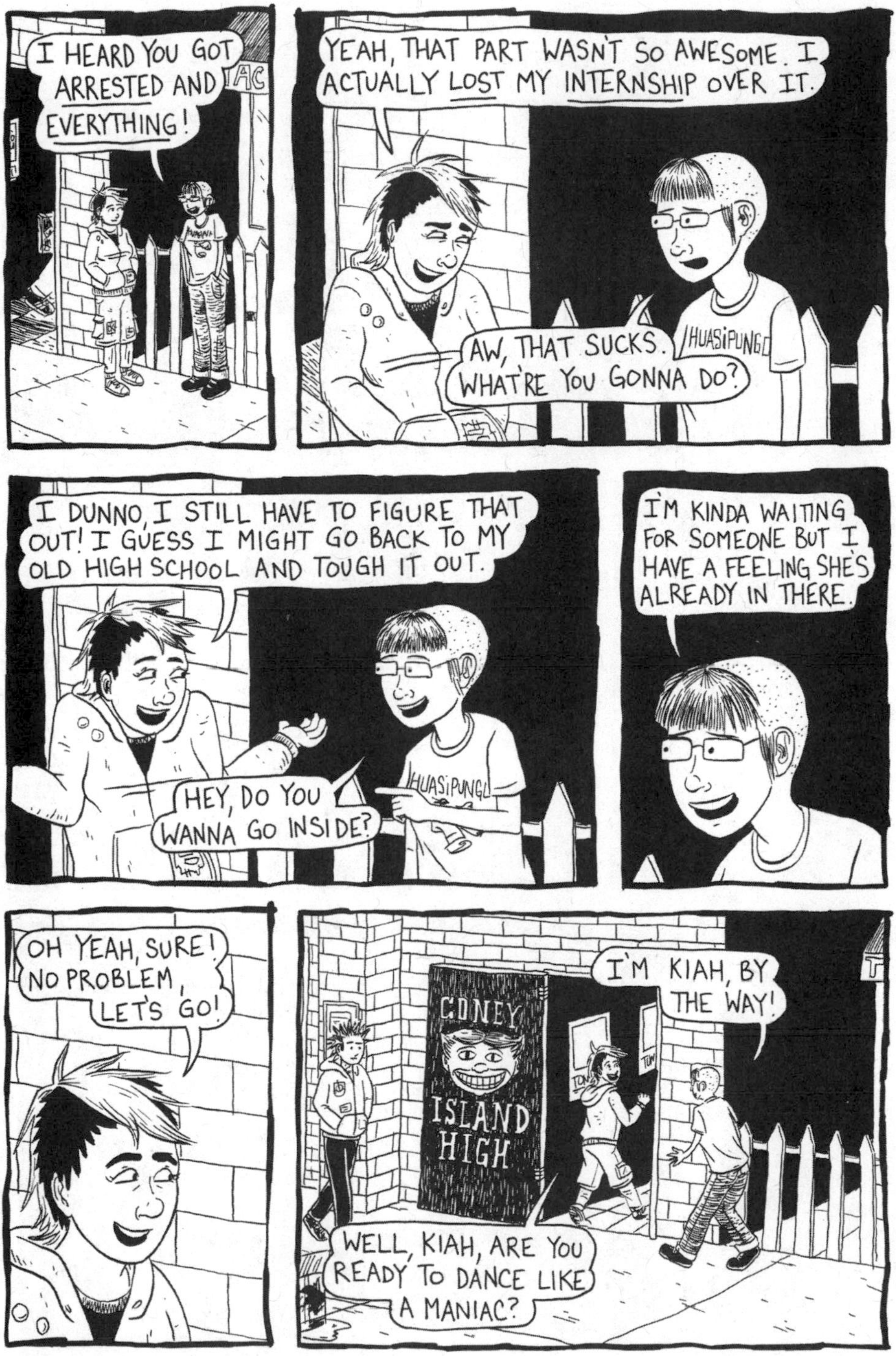

I HEARD YOU GOT ARRESTED AND EVERYTHING!
YEAH, THAT PART WASN'T SO AWESOME. I ACTUALLY LOST MY INTERNSHIP OVER IT.
AW, THAT SUCKS. WHAT'RE YOU GONNA DO?
HUASIPUNGO
I DUNNO, I STILL HAVE TO FIGURE THAT OUT! I GUESS I MIGHT GO BACK TO MY OLD HIGH SCHOOL AND TOUGH IT OUT.
HEY, DO YOU WANNA GO INSIDE?
HUASIPUNGO
I'M KINDA WAITING FOR SOMEONE BUT I HAVE A FEELING SHE'S ALREADY IN THERE.
OH YEAH, SURE! NO PROBLEM, LET'S GO!
CONEY ISLAND HIGH
I'M KIAH, BY THE WAY!
WELL, KIAH, ARE YOU READY TO DANCE LIKE A MANIAC?

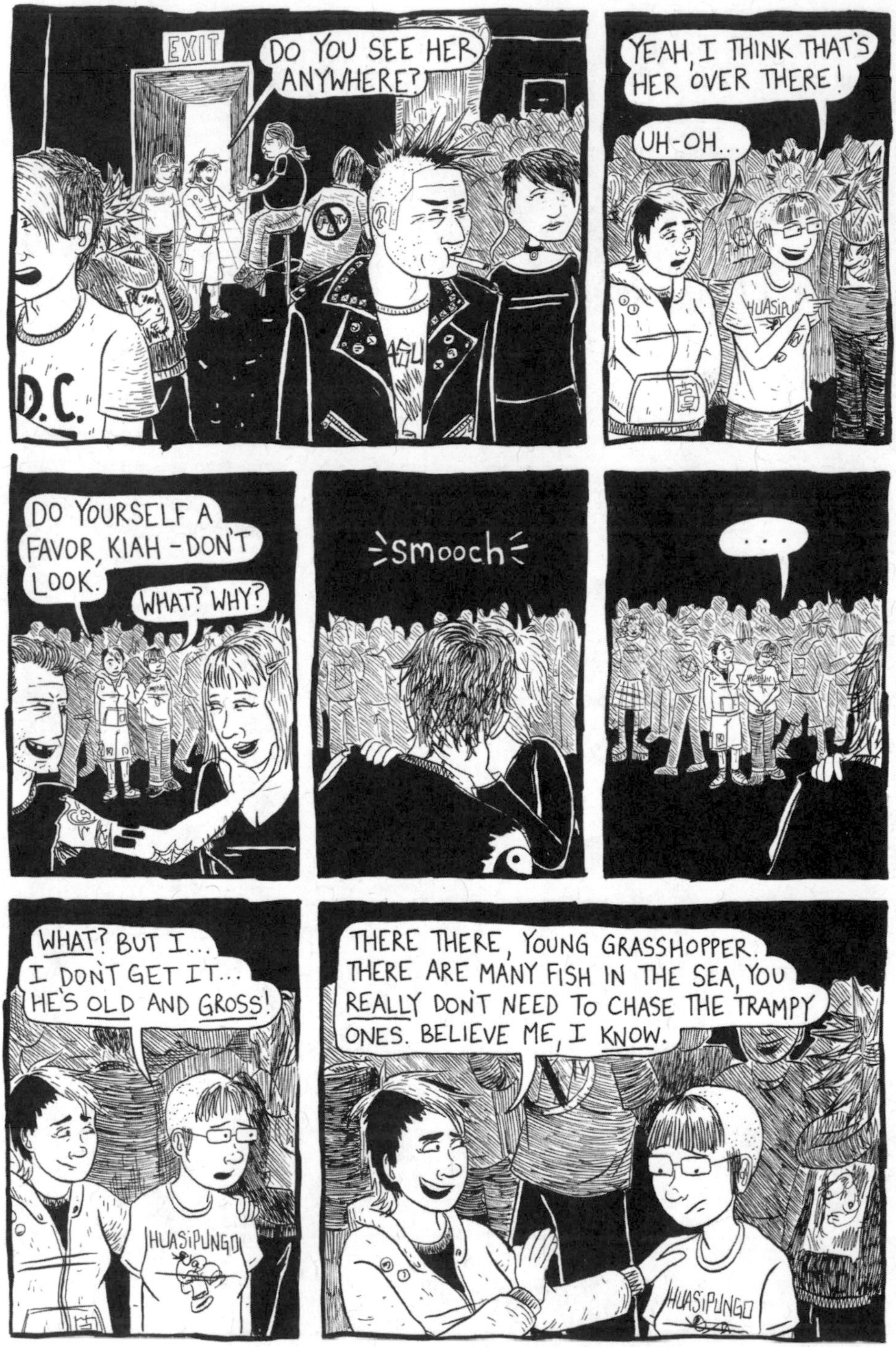
EXIT
DO YOU SEE HER ANYWHERE?
D.C.
YEAH, I THINK THAT'S HER OVER THERE!
UH-OH...
HUASIPUNGO
DO YOURSELF A FAVOR, KIAH - DON'T LOOK.
WHAT? WHY?
smooch
...
WHAT? BUT I... I DON'T GET IT... HE'S OLD AND GROSS!
HUASIPUNGO
THERE THERE, YOUNG GRASSHOPPER. THERE ARE MANY FISH IN THE SEA, YOU REALLY DON'T NEED TO CHASE THE TRAMPY ONES. BELIEVE ME, I KNOW.
HUASIPUNGO

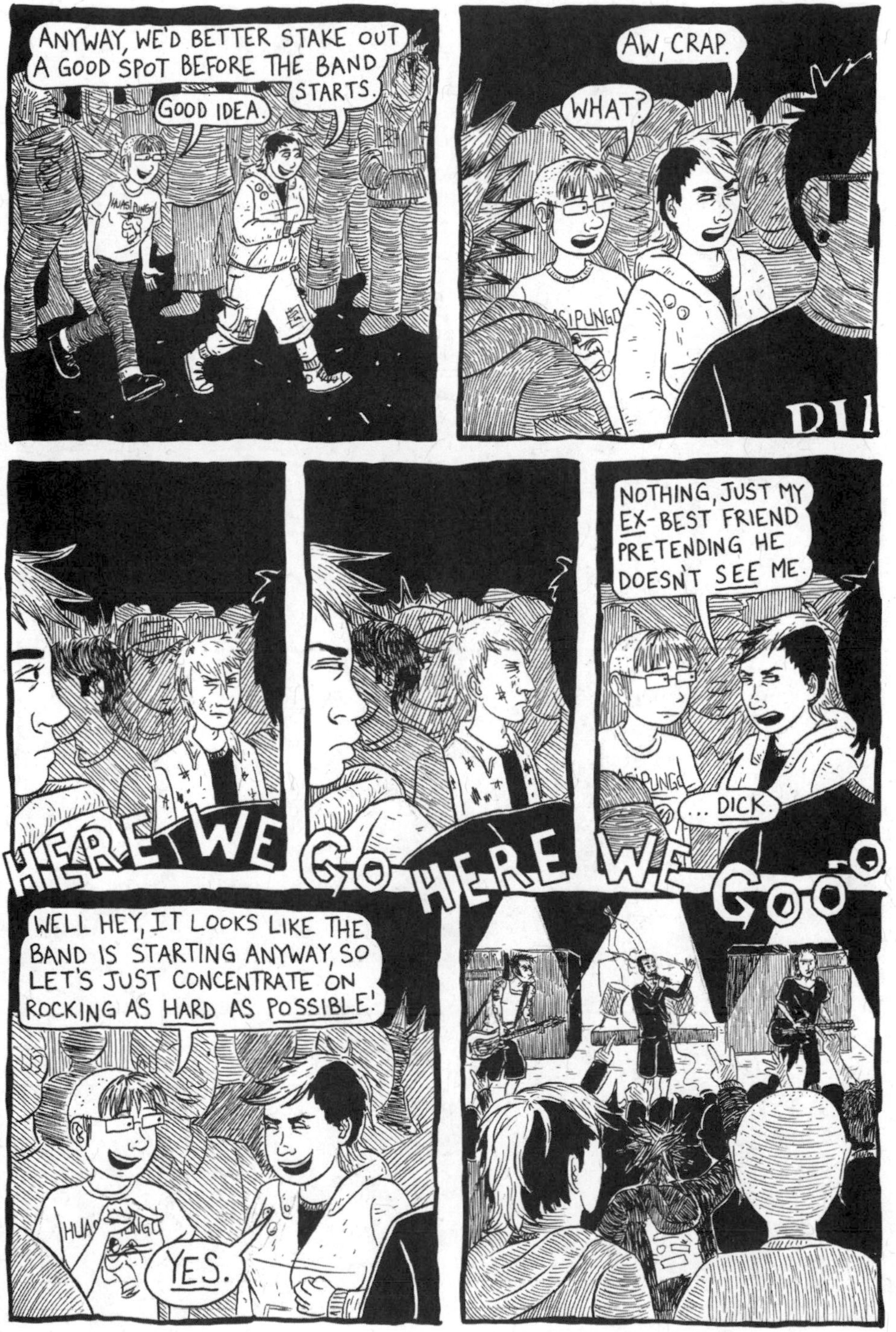
ANYWAY, WE'D BETTER STAKE OUT A GOOD SPOT BEFORE THE BAND STARTS.
GOOD IDEA.
HUASIPUNGO
AW, CRAP.
WHAT?
ASIPUNGO
NOTHING, JUST MY EX-BEST FRIEND PRETENDING HE DOESN'T SEE ME.
... DICK.
HERE WE GO HERE WE GOO-O
WELL HEY, IT LOOKS LIKE THE BAND IS STARTING ANYWAY, SO LET'S JUST CONCENTRATE ON ROCKING AS HARD AS POSSIBLE!
YES.

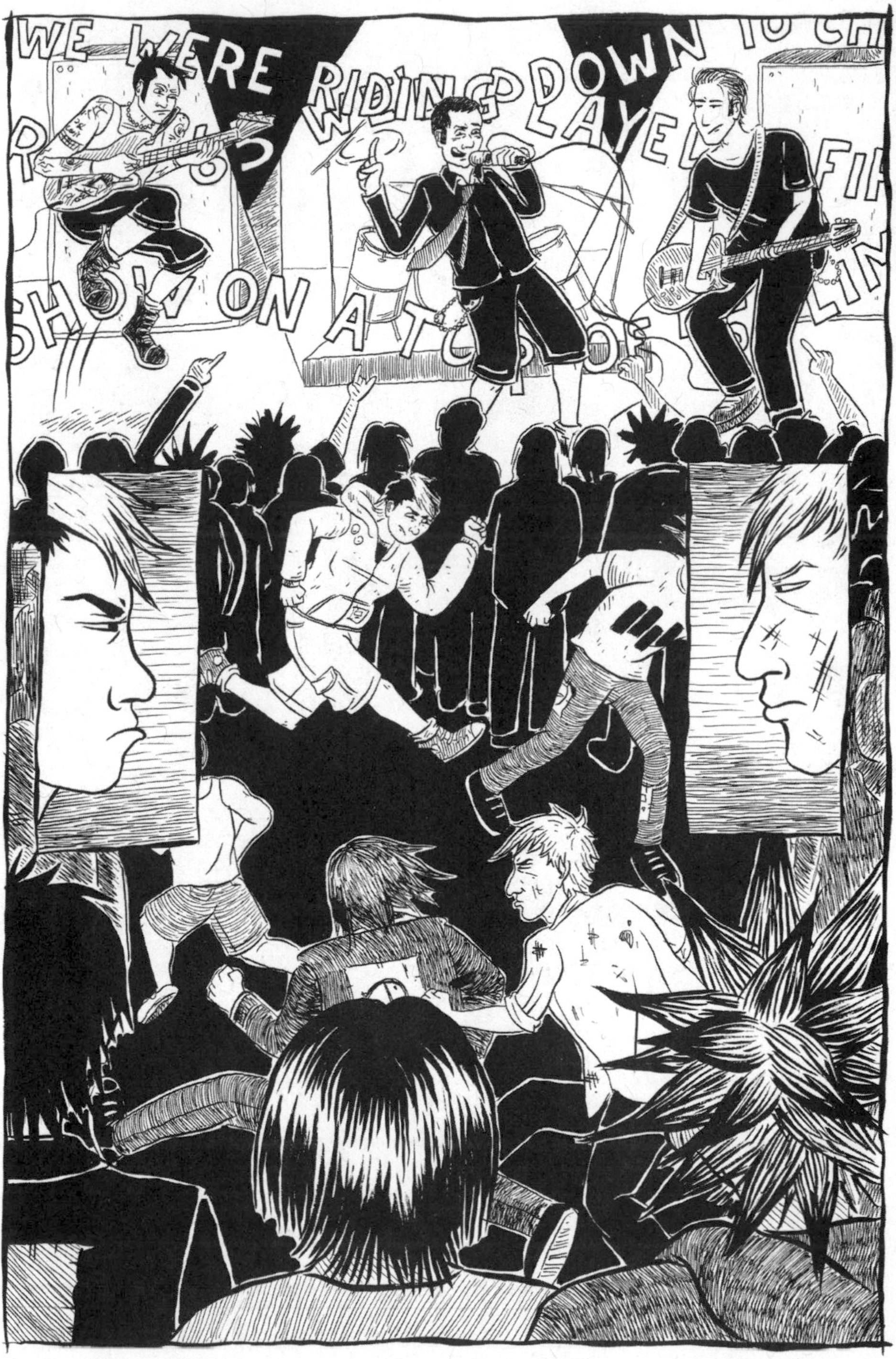
WE WERE RIDING DOWN TO CH
SHOW ON A

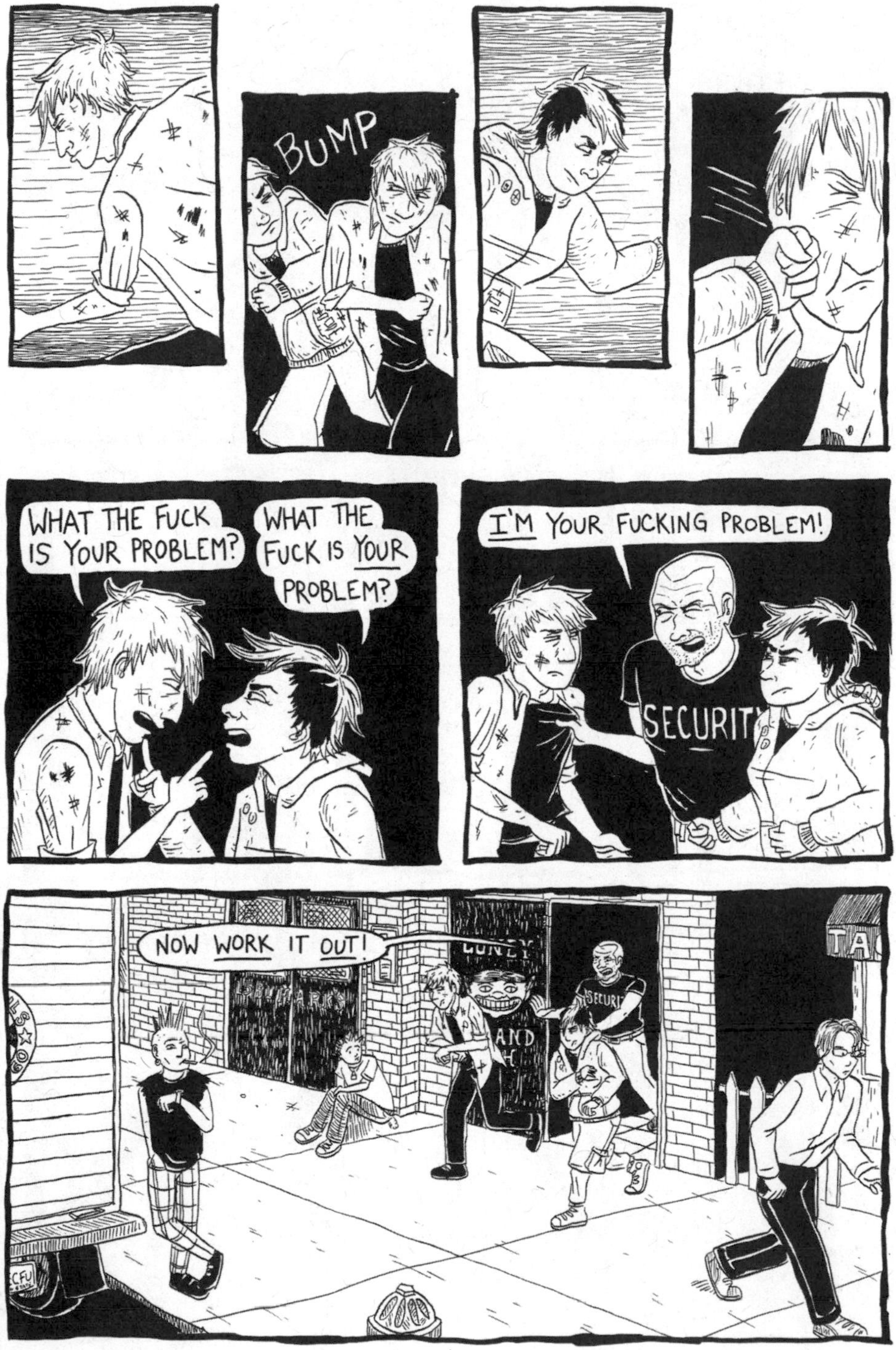
BUMP
WHAT THE FUCK IS YOUR PROBLEM?
WHAT THE FUCK IS YOUR PROBLEM?
I'M YOUR FUCKING PROBLEM!
SECURITY
NOW WORK IT OUT!
SECURITY

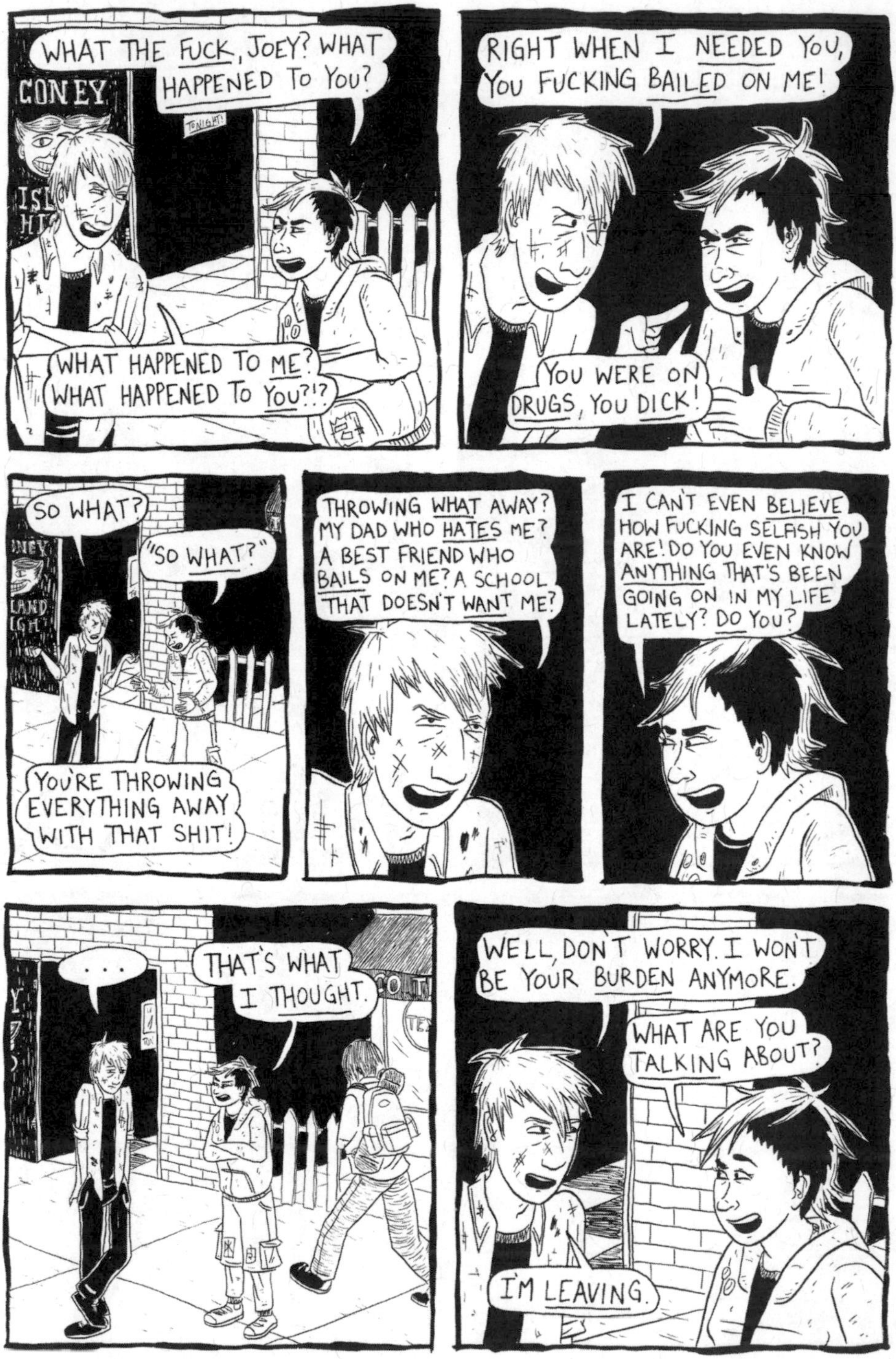
WHAT THE FUCK, JOEY? WHAT HAPPENED TO YOU?
WHAT HAPPENED TO ME? WHAT HAPPENED TO YOU?!?
RIGHT WHEN I NEEDED YOU, YOU FUCKING BAILED ON ME!
YOU WERE ON DRUGS, YOU DICK!
SO WHAT?
"SO WHAT?"
YOU'RE THROWING EVERYTHING AWAY WITH THAT SHIT!
THROWING WHAT AWAY? MY DAD WHO HATES ME? A BEST FRIEND WHO BAILS ON ME? A SCHOOL THAT DOESN'T WANT ME?
I CAN'T EVEN BELIEVE HOW FUCKING SELFISH YOU ARE! DO YOU EVEN KNOW ANYTHING THAT'S BEEN GOING ON IN MY LIFE LATELY? DO YOU?
. . .
THAT'S WHAT I THOUGHT.
WELL, DON'T WORRY. I WON'T BE YOUR BURDEN ANYMORE.
WHAT ARE YOU TALKING ABOUT?
I'M LEAVING.

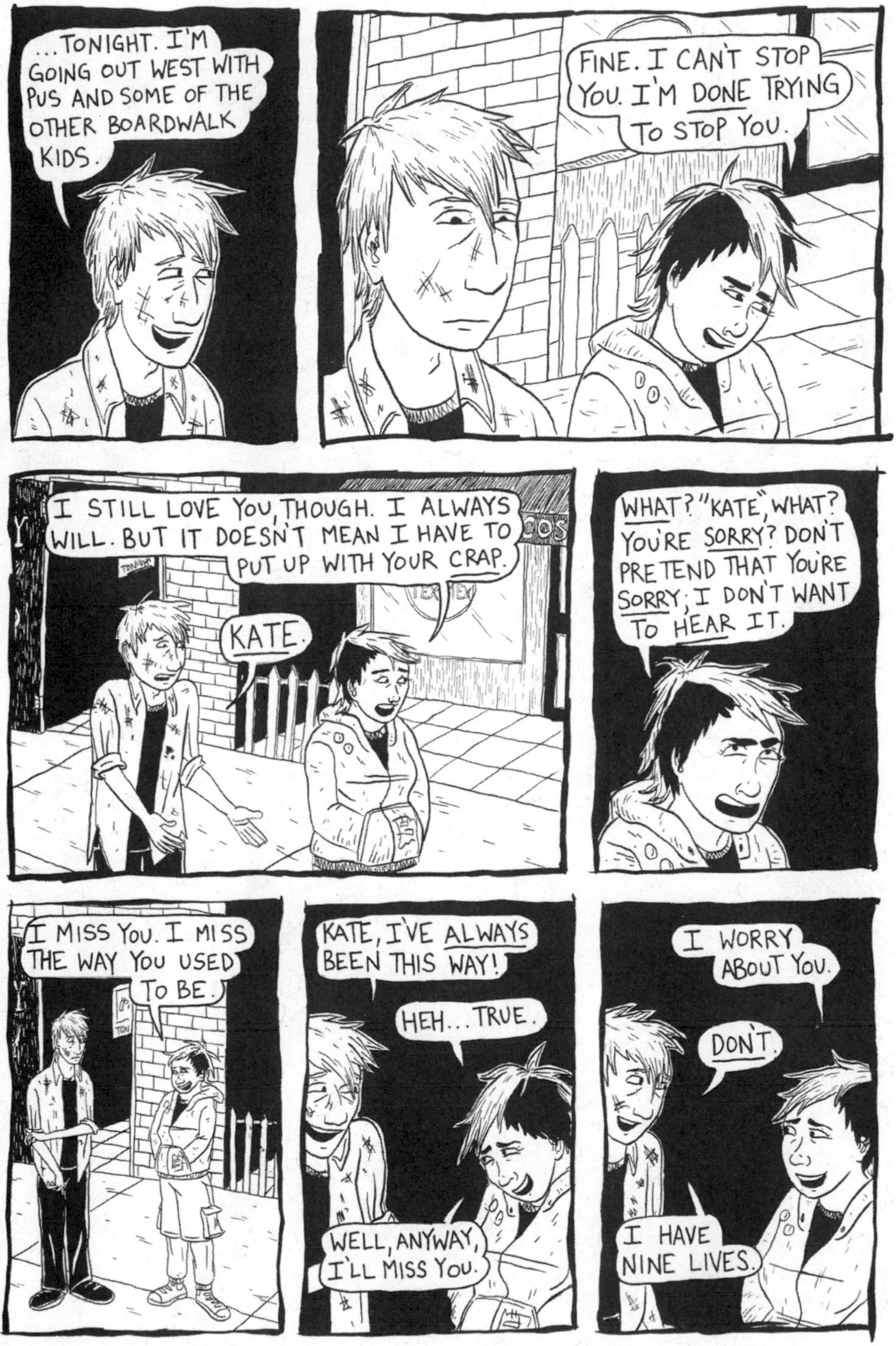
...TONIGHT. I'M GOING OUT WEST WITH PUS AND SOME OF THE OTHER BOARDWALK KIDS.
FINE. I CAN'T STOP YOU. I'M DONE TRYING TO STOP YOU.
I STILL LOVE YOU, THOUGH. I ALWAYS WILL. BUT IT DOESN'T MEAN I HAVE TO PUT UP WITH YOUR CRAP.
KATE.
WHAT? "KATE", WHAT? YOU'RE SORRY? DON'T PRETEND THAT YOU'RE SORRY; I DON'T WANT TO HEAR IT.
I MISS YOU. I MISS THE WAY YOU USED TO BE.
KATE, I'VE ALWAYS BEEN THIS WAY!
HEH... TRUE.
WELL, ANYWAY, I'LL MISS YOU.
I WORRY ABOUT YOU.
DON'T.
I HAVE NINE LIVES.

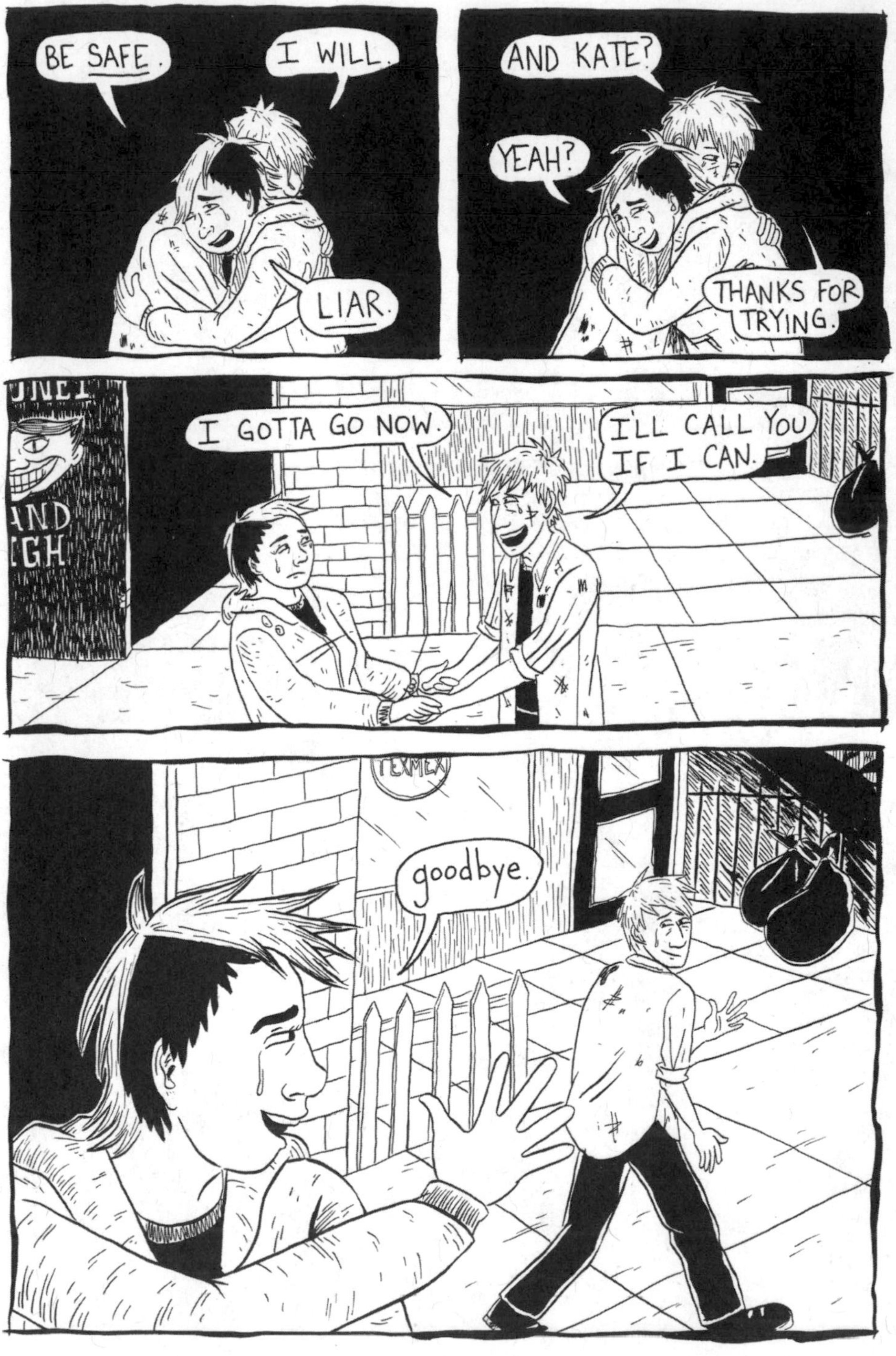
BE SAFE.
I WILL.
LIAR.
AND KATE?
YEAH?
THANKS FOR TRYING.
I GOTTA GO NOW.
I'LL CALL YOU IF I CAN.
TEXMEX
goodbye.

WHERE ARE THEY NOW?

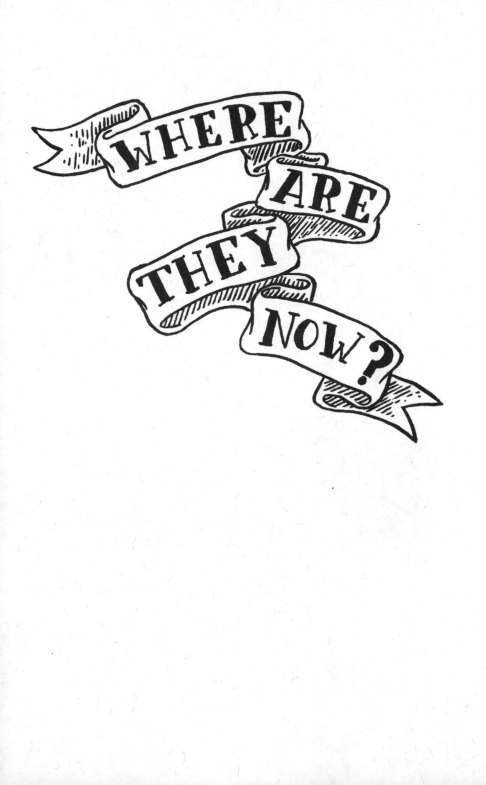

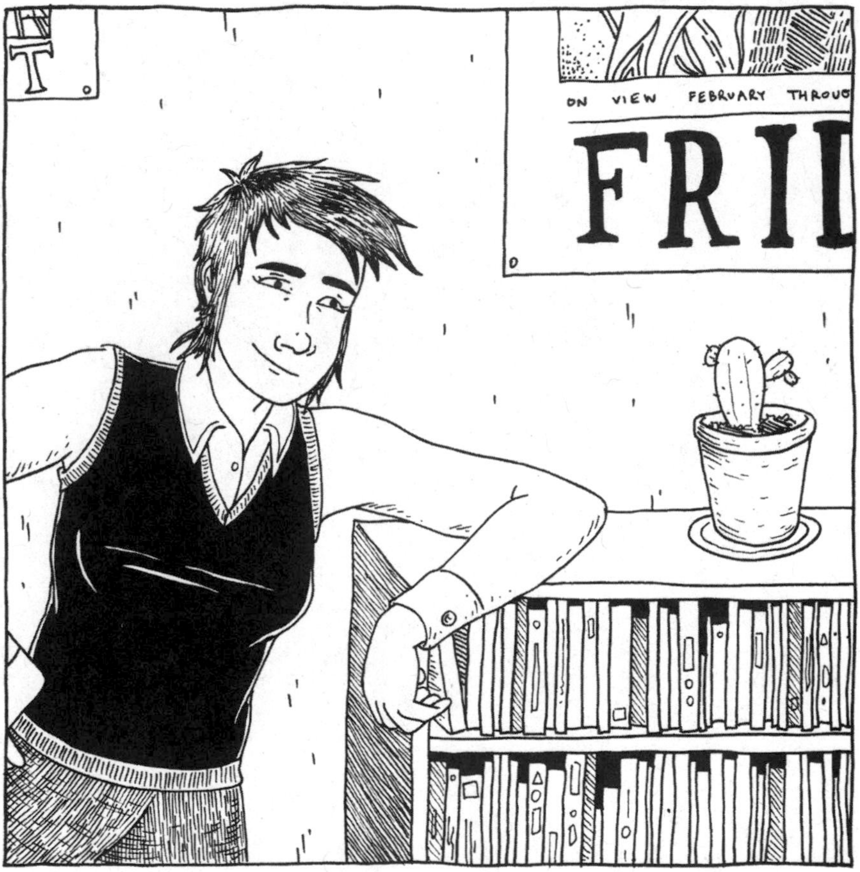

ON VIEW FEBRUARY THROUG
FRID

KATE CALLAHAN

AFTER BEING EXPELLED FROM HER INTERNSHIP-FOR-CREDIT PROGRAM, KATE RETURNED TO HER FORMER HIGH SCHOOL, WHERE SHE EVENTUALLY GRADUATED. SHE WENT ON TO BECOME A GENDER STUDIES MAJOR AT SMITH COLLEGE AND ALTHOUGH SHE DROPPED OUT FOR A YEAR, SHE AGAIN EVENTUALLY GRADUATED. SHE CURRENTLY WORKS AS A PROGRAM COORDINATOR FOR A YOUTH PROGRAM IN BOSTON, WHERE SHE LIVES WITH HER GIRLFRIEND RILEY. SHE HAS NOT SPOKEN TO JOEY SINCE THEY SAID THEIR GOODBYES WAY BACK WHEN, BUT SHE OCCASIONALLY STALKS HIM ON FACE-BOOK.

JOEY KAISER

AFTER A FEW YEARS TRAVELING WITH THE FRIENDS
HE MET UNDER THE CONEY ISLAND BOARDWALK, THE
HEALTH PROBLEMS RELATED TO HIS HEAD INJURY (ES-
PECIALLY THE SEIZURES) BECAME A PROBLEM. RATHER
THAN MOVE BACK HOME WITH HIS DAD (WHO HE HAD NOT
SPOKEN WITH SINCE LEAVING HOME) HE MOVED INTO A
PUNK HOUSE IN MICHIGAN AND STARTED WORKING AS
A BARBACK, SLOWLY MAKING HIS WAY TO BECOMING
A BARTENDER. AFTER A FEW YEARS, HE DECIDED TO
MOVE BACK TO NEW YORK CITY, WHERE HE CURRENTLY
WORKS AS A WELL-LOVED BARTENDER IN BROOKLYN. HE
IS CURRENTLY SINGLE.

VERONA MICHAELS

VERONA ENDED UP STUDYING ART HISTORY AT NEW YORK UNIVERSITY, DURING WHICH TIME SHE LANDED A SUMMER INTERNSHIP WITH A PROMINENT GALLERY IN CHELSEA. UPON GRADUATION, SHE TOOK A JOB AT THAT SAME GALLERY, WHERE SHE MET AND BEGAN DATING THE ITALIAN SCULPTOR, CARLO FURNARI. THEY ARE ENGAGED TO BE MARRIED THIS FALL IN ITALY. THEY LIVE TOGETHER IN A BROWNSTONE IN PARK SLOPE, BROOKLYN.

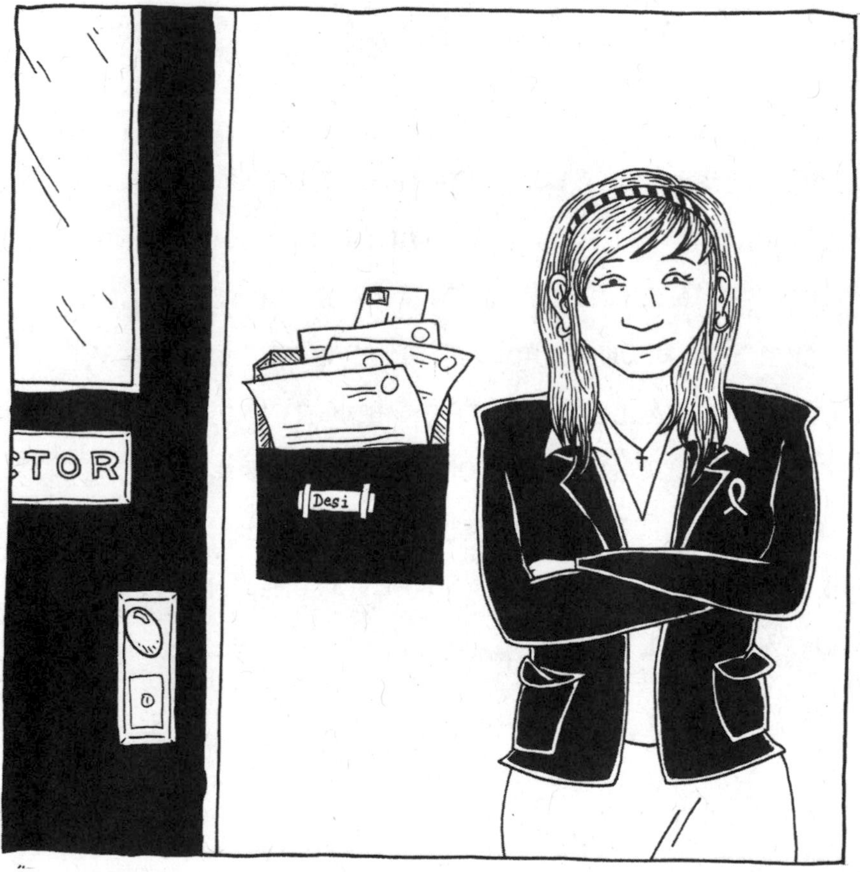

CTOR
Desi

DESDEMONA MACHADO

DESI CONTINUED TO EXCEL AT SCHOOL AND EVENTU-
ALLY ATTENDED THE CUNY SCHOOL OF SOCIAL WORK
ON A FULL SCHOLARSHIP. SHE GRADUATED WITH HON-
ORS AND CURRENTLY WORKS AS AN ADMINISTRATOR
FOR THE NEW YORK DEPARTMENT OF HEALTH. SHE AND
KATE RECONNECTED AND BURIED THE HATCHET ABOUT
FIVE YEARS AFTER THEY BROKE UP AND HAVE REMAINED
VERY GOOD FRIENDS EVER SINCE. DESI IS CURRENTLY
SINGLE AND LIVES IN OZONE PARK. SHE NEVER CAME
OUT TO MAMA, WHO DIED IN 2001.

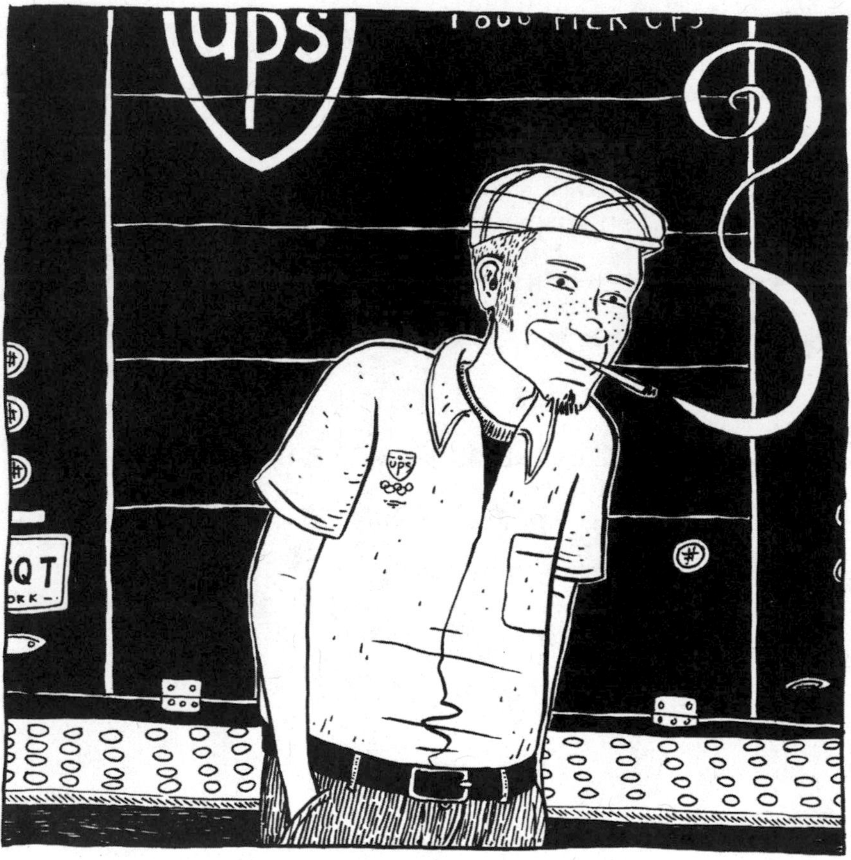
ups

NATHAN SHAUGHNESSY

AFTER BARELY GRADUATING HIGH SCHOOL, NATE CHOSE
NOT TO CONTINUE ON TO COLLEGE AND INSTEAD BEGAN
WORKING IN HIS UNCLE'S HARDWARE STORE IN THE
BRONX. HIS UNCLE DIED A FEW YEARS LATER AND HE
CHOSE NOT TO CONTINUE THE FAMILY BUSINESS. IN-
STEAD, NATE BEGAN WORKING FOR UPS, WHERE HE
STILL WORKS TODAY. HE LIVES WITH HIS GIRLFRIEND
AND THEIR GOLDEN RETRIEVER, HENRY, IN THE BRONX.
AFTER A FEW YEARS IN THERAPY (AT HIS MOTHER'S
REQUEST), HE BECAME A MUCH MORE PEACEFUL PERSON
AND NO LONGER TALKS ABOUT HIS VIOLENT PAST.

MARCUS EMERSON

AFTER GETTING IN TROUBLE WITH JOEY, MARCUS
WAS OUTED TO THE ENTIRE SCHOOL AND MERCILESSLY
BULLIED, WHICH ACTUALLY ENDED UP TOUGHENING HIM
UP QUITE A BIT. AFTER GRADUATING HIGH SCHOOL, HE
ATTENDED RUTGERS UNIVERSITY, WHERE HE WAS AN
ENGLISH MAJOR. HE IS CURRENTLY EMPLOYED AS A
MODERATELY WELL-KNOWN INTERNET SEX ADVICE
COLUMNIST. HE LIVES IN BENSONHURST, BROOKLYN
WITH HIS BOYFRIEND DAVID AND THEIR ADOPTED
DAUGHTER, OPHELIA. MARCUS HAS NOT SEEN OR SPOKEN
TO JOEY SINCE THE DAY THEY GOT IN TROUBLE SMOKING
AND FOOLING AROUND IN THE BATHROOM AT SCHOOL.

Extras

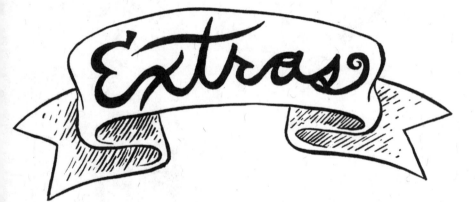

VARIOUS SKETCHES OF JOEY OVER THE YEARS

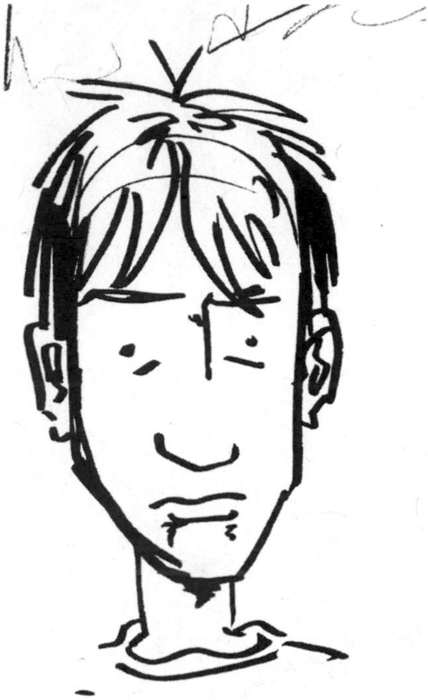

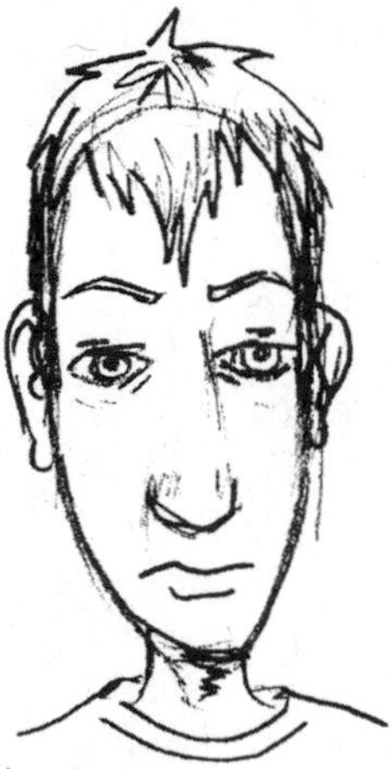

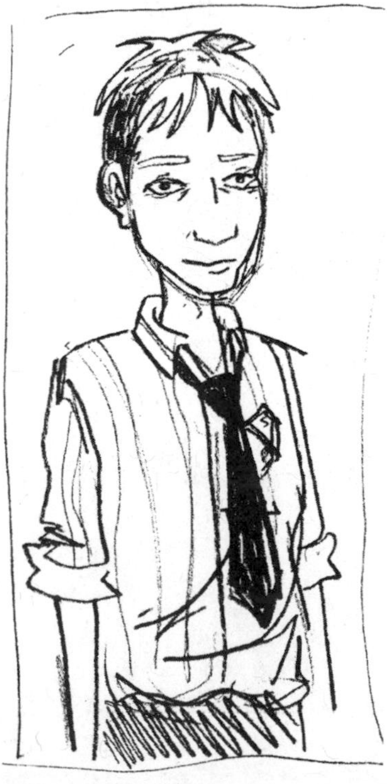

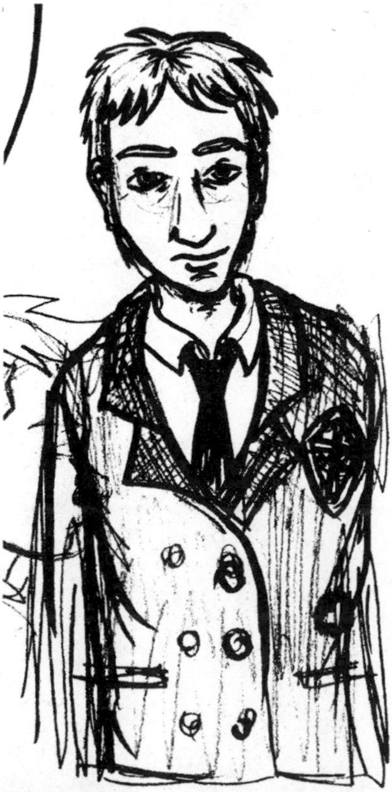

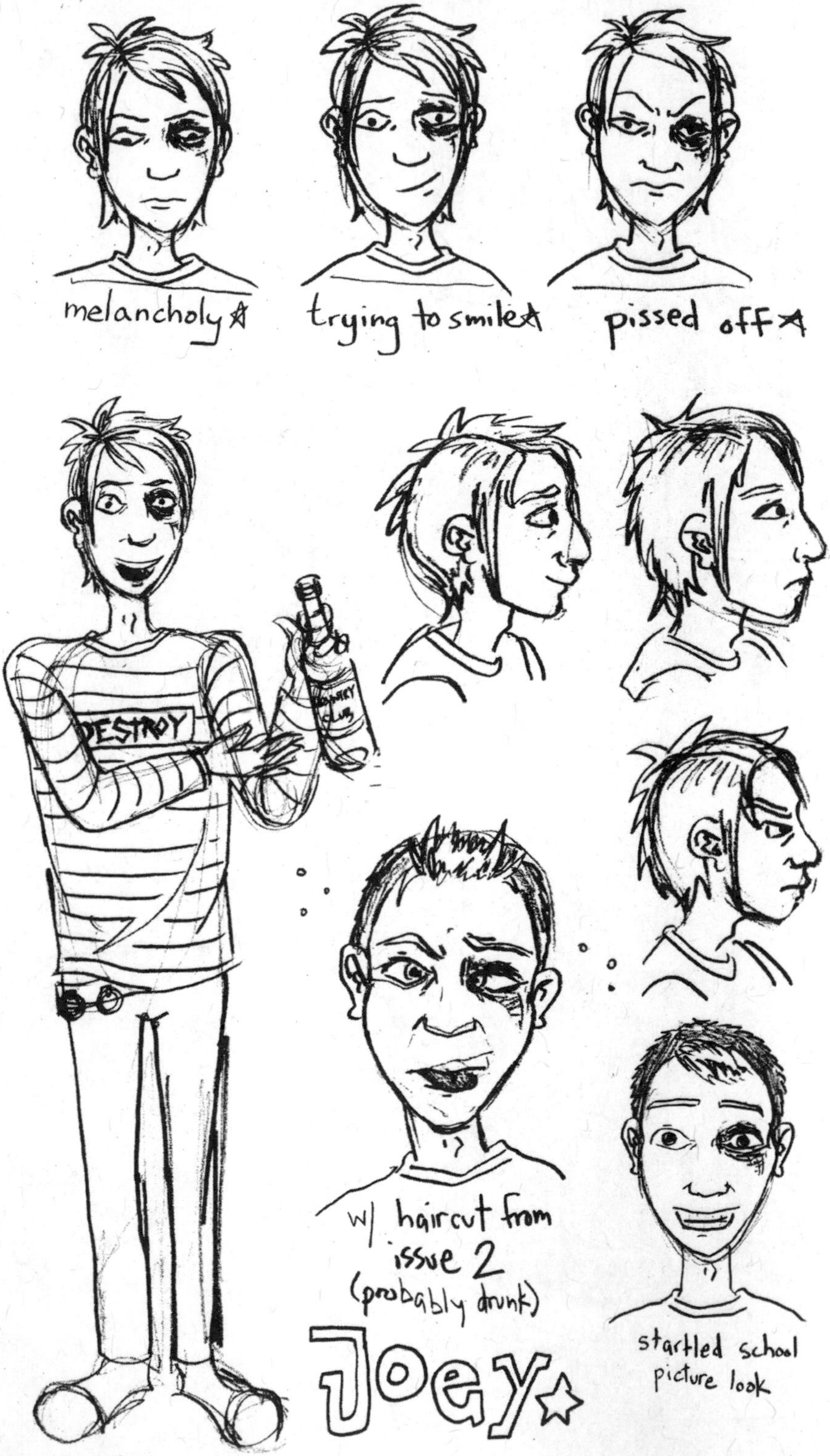
melancholy
trying to smile
pissed off
DESTROY
w/ haircut from issue 2 (probably drunk)
Joey
startled school picture look

ODDUCK COMICS GROUP MAY 2002 1

VARIOUS SKETCHES OF
KATE OVER THE YEARS

hang in thole!

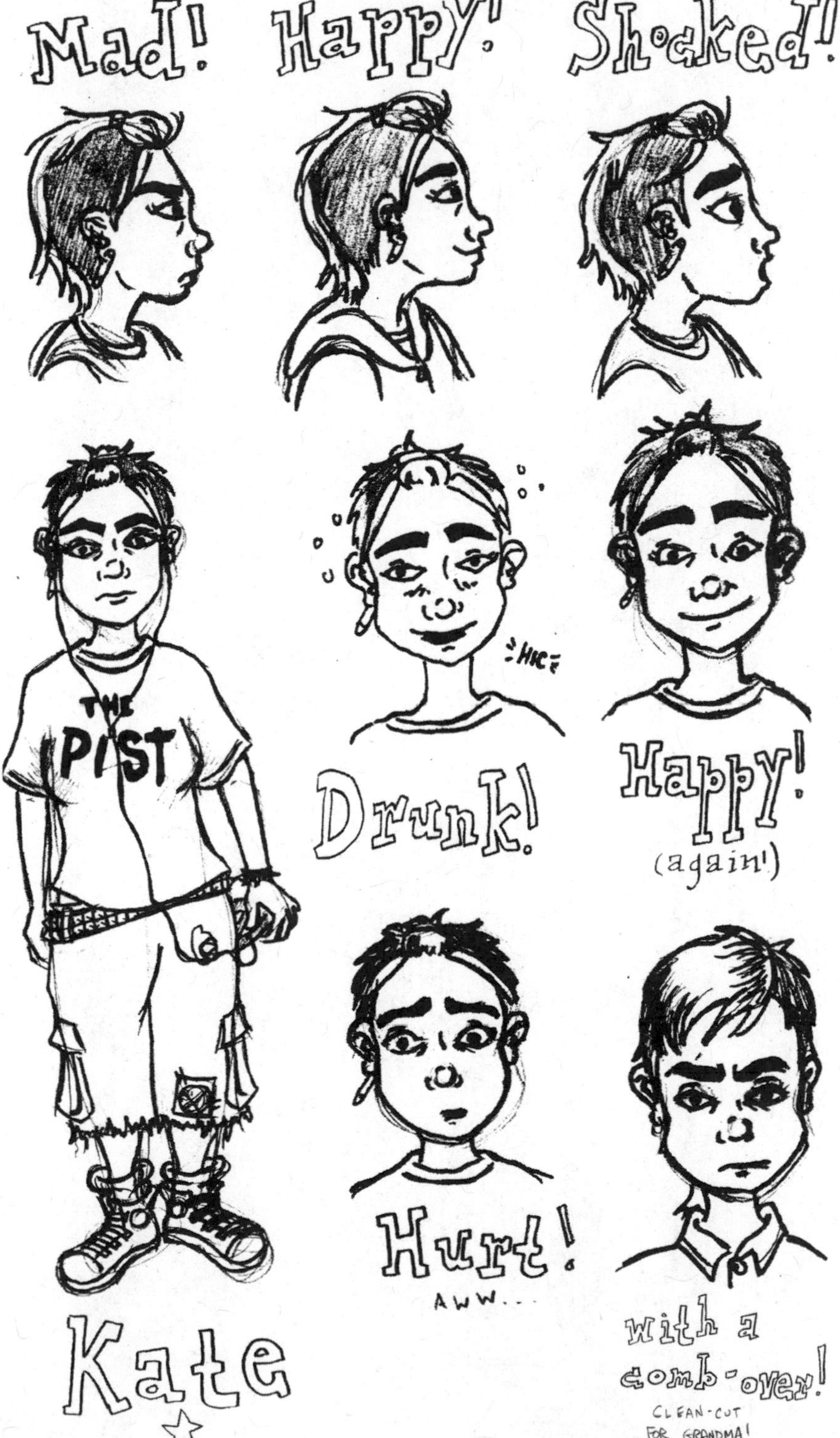
Mad!
Happy!
Shocked!
THE PIST
Drunk!
HIC
Happy!
(again!)
Hurt!
AWW...
Kate
with a comb-over!
CLEAN-CUT FOR GRANDMA!

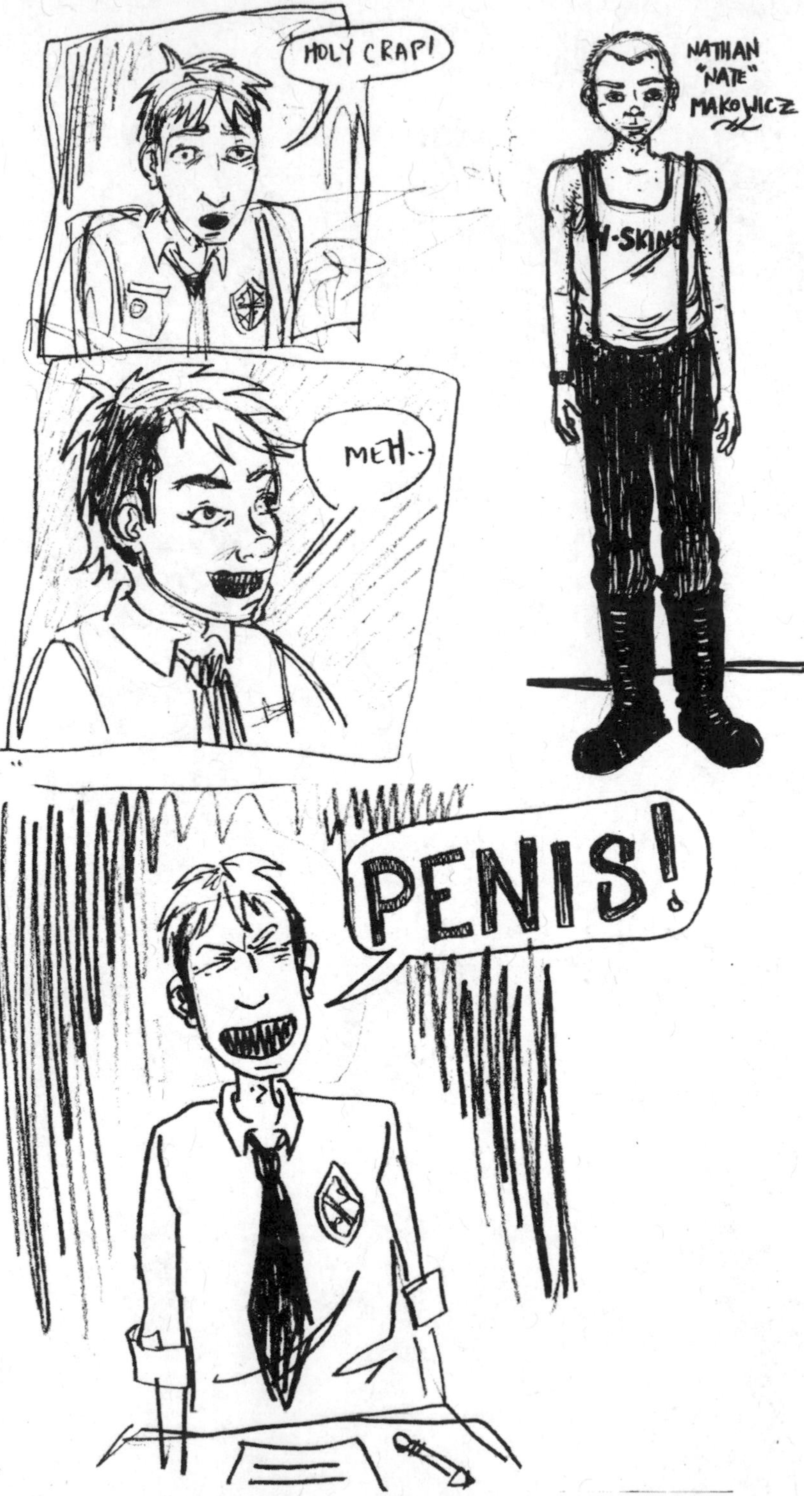
HOLY CRAP!
NATHAN "NATE" MAKOWICZ
MEH...
PENIS!

THE FIRST APPEARANCE OF KATE IN A SHORT COMIC DONE FOR A SCHOOL ASSIGNMENT AT SVA (WHICH, AS YOU CAN SEE, I NEVER FINISHED)

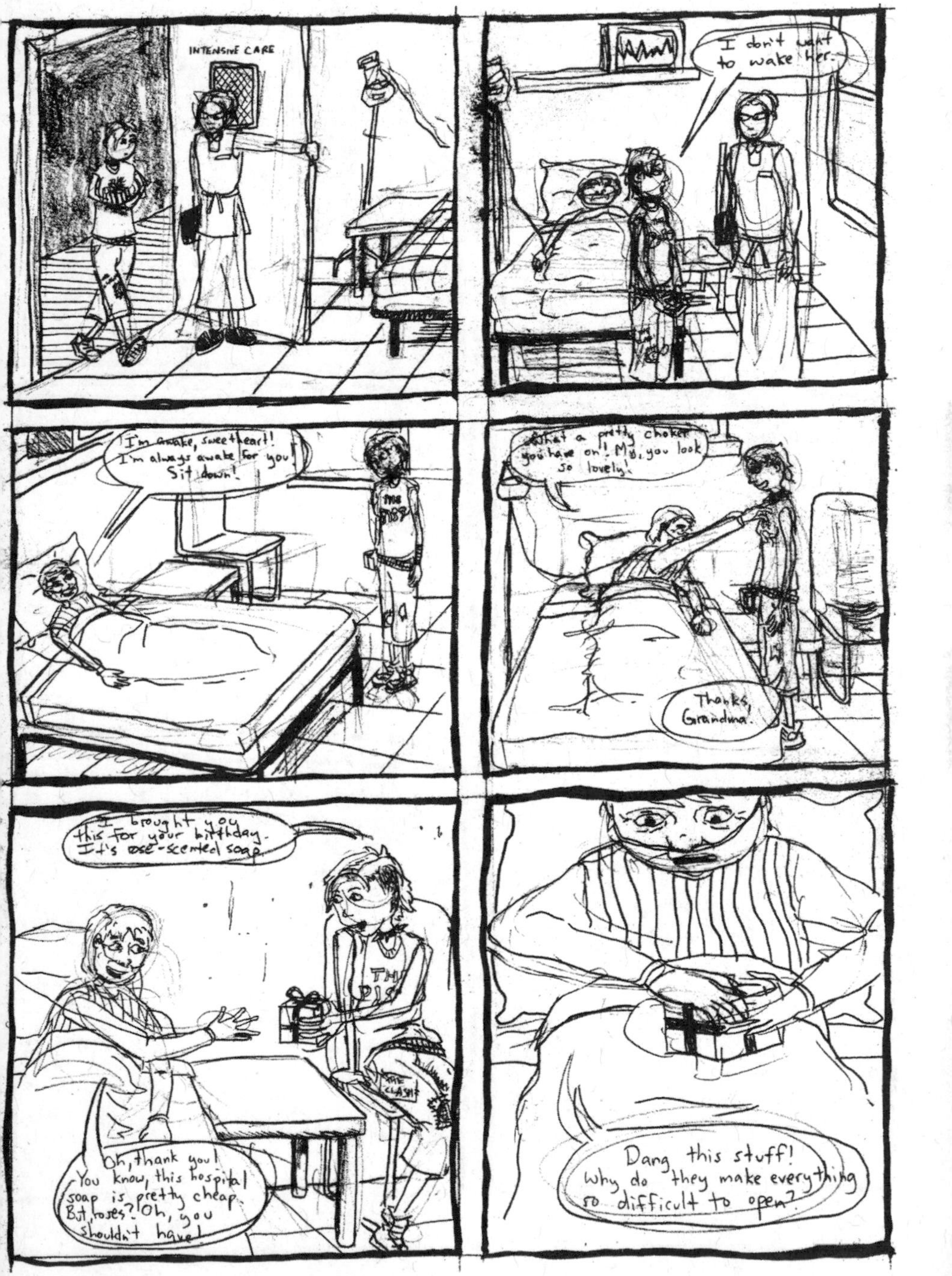
INTENSIVE CARE
I don't want to wake her.
I'm awake, sweetheart! I'm always awake for you! Sit down!
What a pretty choker you have on! My, you look so lovely!
Thanks, Grandma.
I brought you this for your birthday. It's rose-scented soap.
Oh, thank you! You know, this hospital soap is pretty cheap. But, roses? Oh, you shouldn't have!
Dang this stuff! Why do they make everything so difficult to open?

THE ORIGINAL SCRIPT

Liz Baillie

Page One

Panel One

Caption - none

Visual - Kate sitting in a hospital waiting room, holding a small gift wrapped box. She looks out of place among all the older, more well-dressed people in other parts of the room: combat boots and a mohawk worn down kind of make her stick out. She looks up attentively as someone calls her.

Dialog

Nurse: Kathleen Shaughnessy to see Josephine Fitz?

Kate: That's me!

Panel One

Caption - none

Visual - Kate being let into hospital room where her grandmother is lying in a bed by the window. There are a few other beds in the room. Kate looks nervous.

No Dialog

Panel Two

Caption - none

Visual - Kate stands in front of her grandma's bed holding the gift but looking at the nurse.

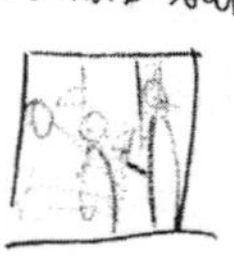

Dialog:

Kate - I don't want to wake her.

Panel Three

Caption - none

Visual - Nurse walks away as Kate stands in front of the bed.

Dialog

Grandma - I'm awake, sweet heart! I'm always awake for you! Sit down!

Panel Five

Visual - Kate sits in a chair next to the bed and hands over the gift. Grandma reaches for it.

Dialog

Kate - I brought you this for your birthday. It's rose-scented soap.

Grandma - Oh, thank you! You know, this hospital soap is pretty cheap. But roses! Oh, you shouldn't have.

Panel Four

Visual - Grandma reaches out to touch Kate's dog collar and smiles

Dialog - Grandma - What a pretty choker you have on! My, you look so lovely!

[illegible]

~~Panel Six~~

~~Visual - Close up of Grandma struggling with the gift wrap.~~

~~Dialog~~

~~Grandma - Dang this stuff! Why do they make everything so difficult to open!~~

Page Two

Panel One Visual - Grandma places gift unopened on table next to bed.

Dialog

Grandma - I'll open it later. So tell me, how have you been, Eileen? How's Florida? You know, I really miss those fresh oranges.

Kate - Grandma? ~~I'm Kate, not Eileen.~~

Panel Two

Visual - 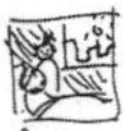 Grandma looks out window in foreground. Kate in background sitting on chair. City skyline is visible out window.

Dialog

Grandma - It's so beautiful here. I'm glad we moved South. Florida is so nice this time of year. Don't you agree, Eileen? I much prefer this to Brooklyn.

Kate - ~~Eileen is my mom!~~ Grandma, this is New York! And I'm Kate, not Eileen!

Panel Three

Caption - I remembered something someone told me once: sometimes, when people are close to death, their mind puts them in the place they love most. I guess for Grandma, that place was Florida.

Visual - 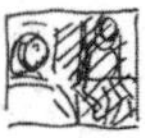 Grandma in light from window looking serene. Kate in shadow sitting next to her looking upset

Dialog

Kate - Grandma?

Panel Four

Visual - Nurse bursts through door suddenly

Dialog

Nurse: Okay, visiting hours is up! Everybody out!

Panel Five

Visual - Kate is the only visitor in the room. The nurse holds the door open for her. Kate looks back at Grandma, who is still looking out the window.

Dialog

Kate - Bye, Grandma!

~~Panel Six~~

~~Visual - Kate walks down hall towards exit. She passes an elderly woman being pushed~~

Panel Six

Visual - Grandma continues to gaze out Window at city skyline. There are no palm trees visible.

[redacted] DIALOG - Nurse (off panel?) - It's ~~time~~ medication time, Mrs. Fito.

[redacted]

AN ALTERNATE (AND EVENTUALLY SCRAPPED) FIRST THREE PAGES OF ISSUE 2

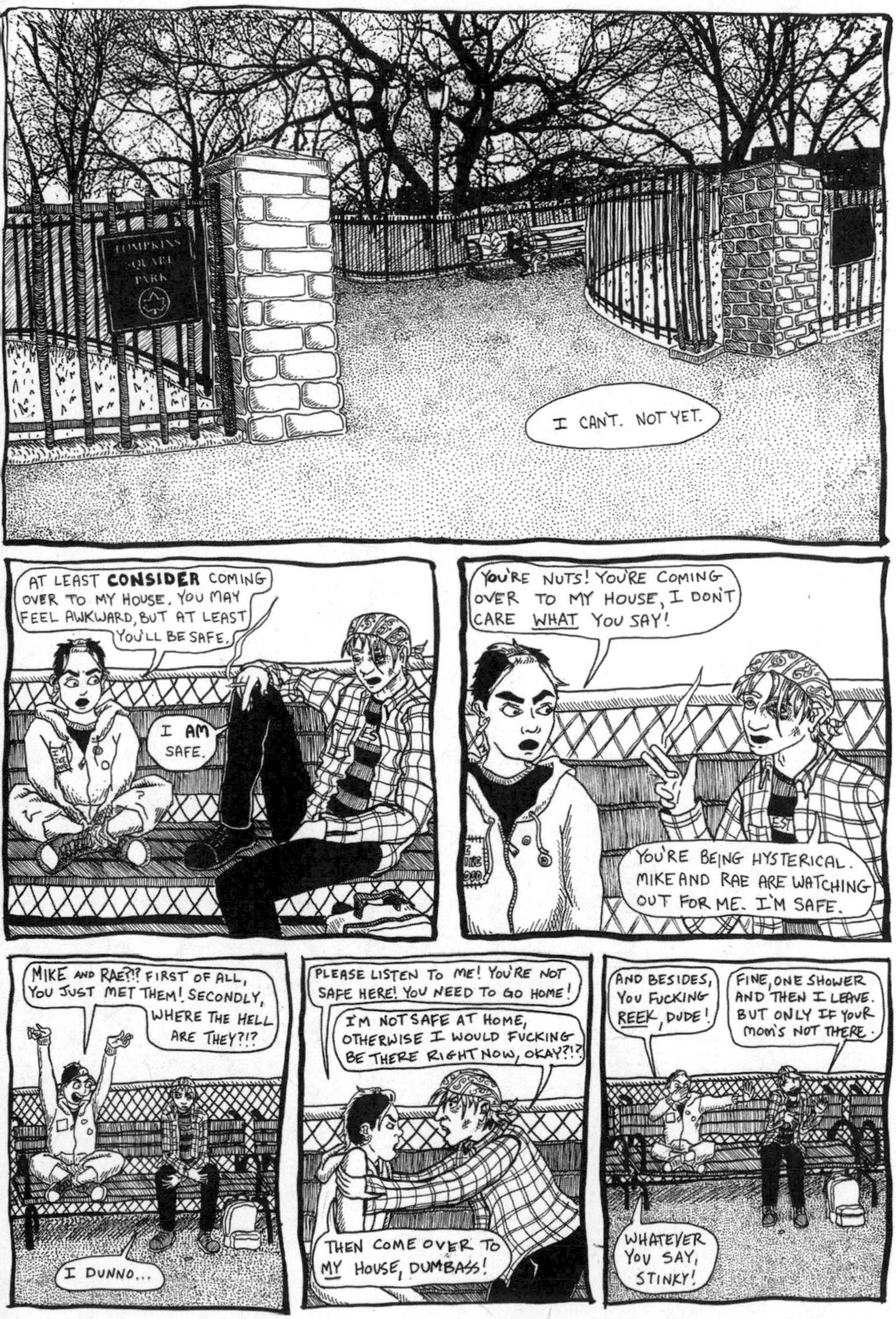
TOMPKINS SQUARE PARK
I CAN'T. NOT YET.
AT LEAST CONSIDER COMING OVER TO MY HOUSE. YOU MAY FEEL AWKWARD, BUT AT LEAST YOU'LL BE SAFE.
I AM SAFE.
YOU'RE NUTS! YOU'RE COMING OVER TO MY HOUSE, I DON'T CARE WHAT YOU SAY!
YOU'RE BEING HYSTERICAL. MIKE AND RAE ARE WATCHING OUT FOR ME. I'M SAFE.
MIKE AND RAE?!? FIRST OF ALL, YOU JUST MET THEM! SECONDLY, WHERE THE HELL ARE THEY?!?
I DUNNO...
PLEASE LISTEN TO ME! YOU'RE NOT SAFE HERE! YOU NEED TO GO HOME!
I'M NOT SAFE AT HOME, OTHERWISE I WOULD FUCKING BE THERE RIGHT NOW, OKAY?!?
THEN COME OVER TO MY HOUSE, DUMBASS!
AND BESIDES, YOU FUCKING REEK, DUDE!
FINE, ONE SHOWER AND THEN I LEAVE. BUT ONLY IF YOUR MOM'S NOT THERE.
WHATEVER YOU SAY, STINKY!

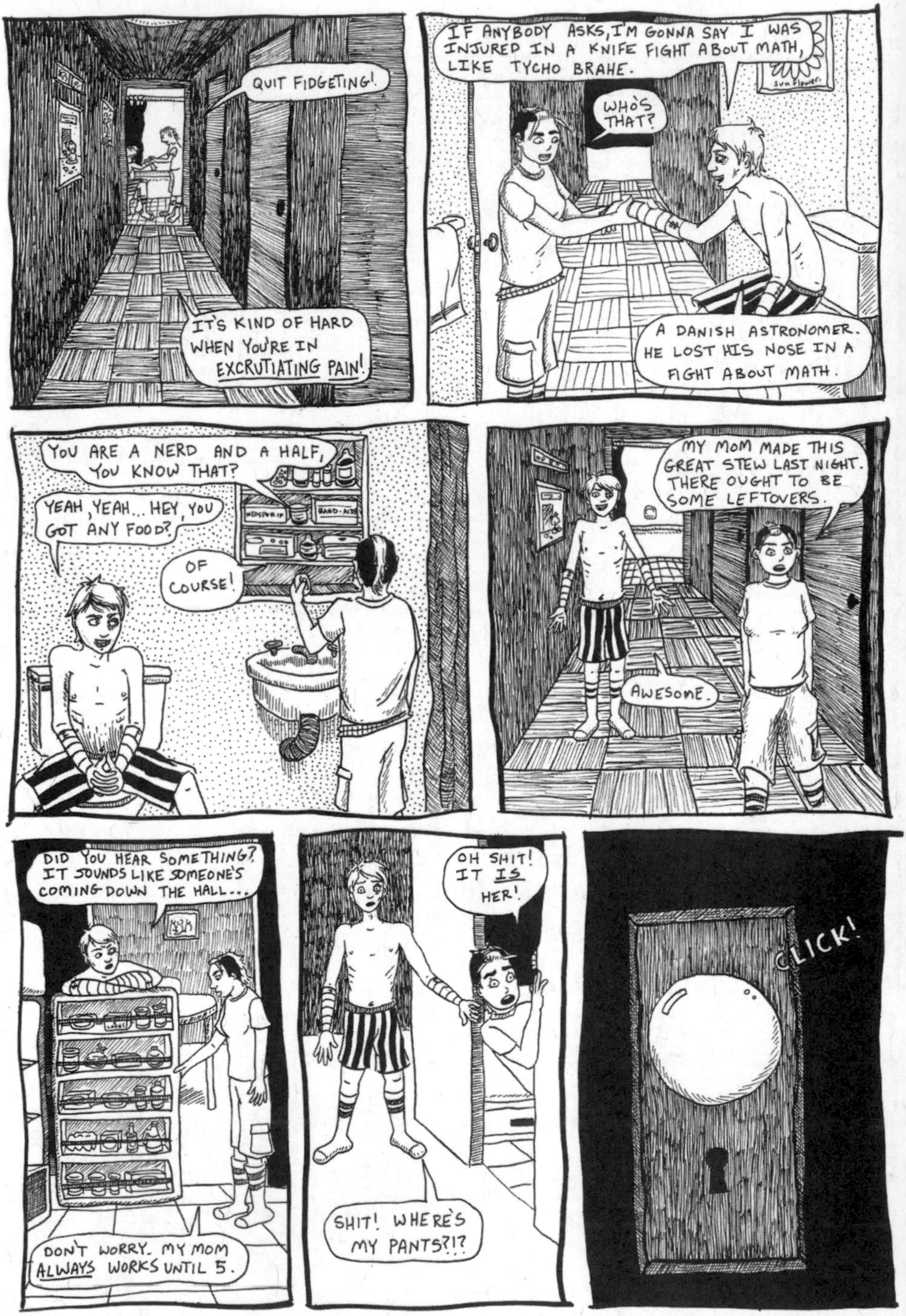
QUIT FIDGETING!
IT'S KIND OF HARD WHEN YOU'RE IN EXCRUTIATING PAIN!
IF ANYBODY ASKS, I'M GONNA SAY I WAS INJURED IN A KNIFE FIGHT ABOUT MATH, LIKE TYCHO BRAHE.
SUN FLOWER
WHO'S THAT?
A DANISH ASTRONOMER. HE LOST HIS NOSE IN A FIGHT ABOUT MATH.
YOU ARE A NERD AND A HALF, YOU KNOW THAT?
YEAH, YEAH... HEY, YOU GOT ANY FOOD?
NEOSPORIN
BAND-AIDS
OF COURSE!
MY MOM MADE THIS GREAT STEW LAST NIGHT. THERE OUGHT TO BE SOME LEFTOVERS.
AWESOME.
DID YOU HEAR SOMETHING? IT SOUNDS LIKE SOMEONE'S COMING DOWN THE HALL...
DON'T WORRY. MY MOM ALWAYS WORKS UNTIL 5.
OH SHIT! IT IS HER!
SHIT! WHERE'S MY PANTS?!?
CLICK!

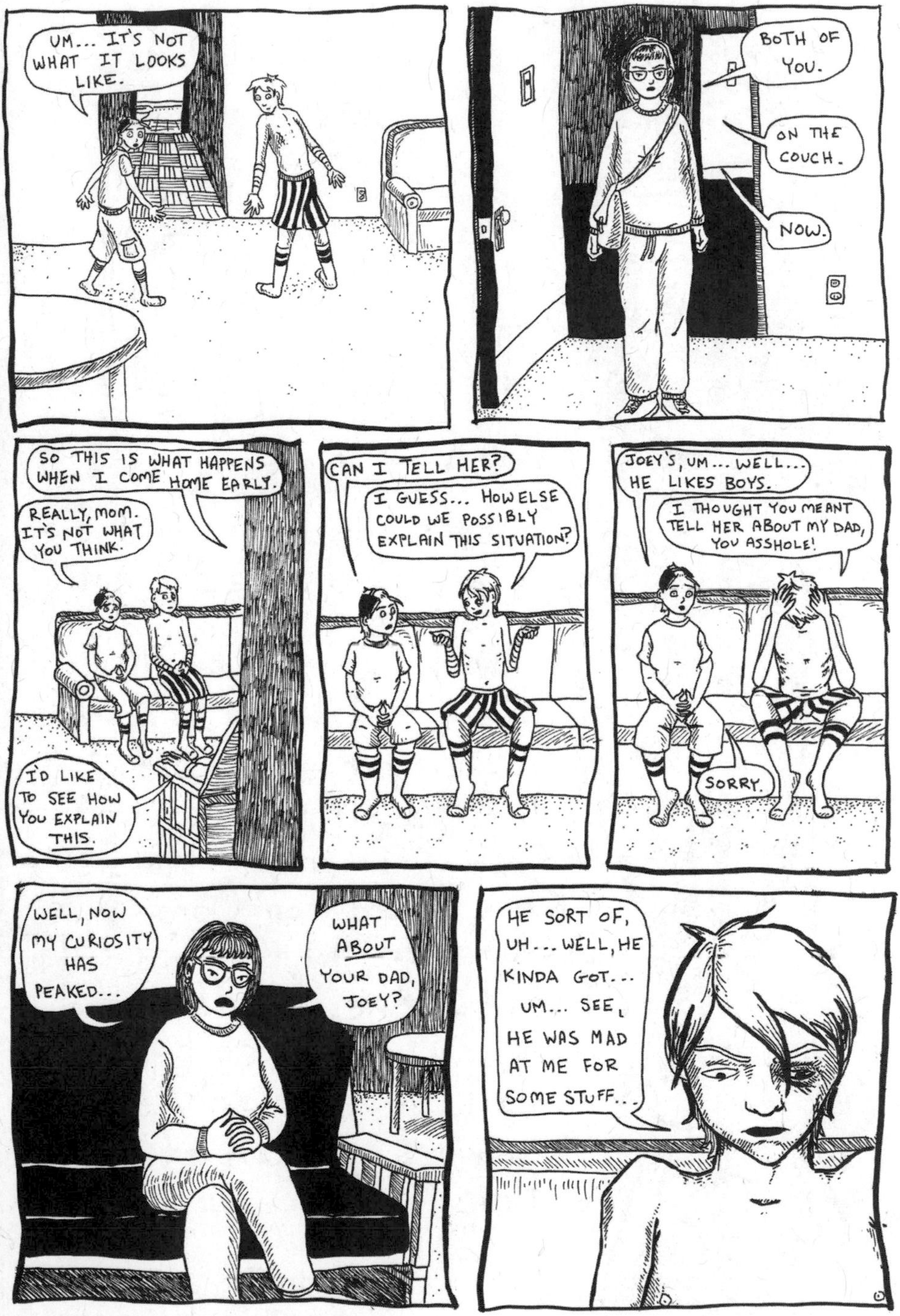
UM... IT'S NOT WHAT IT LOOKS LIKE.
BOTH OF YOU.
ON THE COUCH.
NOW.
SO THIS IS WHAT HAPPENS WHEN I COME HOME EARLY.
REALLY, MOM. IT'S NOT WHAT YOU THINK.
I'D LIKE TO SEE HOW YOU EXPLAIN THIS.
CAN I TELL HER?
I GUESS... HOW ELSE COULD WE POSSIBLY EXPLAIN THIS SITUATION?
JOEY'S, UM... WELL... HE LIKES BOYS.
I THOUGHT YOU MEANT TELL HER ABOUT MY DAD, YOU ASSHOLE!
SORRY.
WELL, NOW MY CURIOSITY HAS PEAKED...
WHAT ABOUT YOUR DAD, JOEY?
HE SORT OF, UH... WELL, HE KINDA GOT... UM... SEE, HE WAS MAD AT ME FOR SOME STUFF...

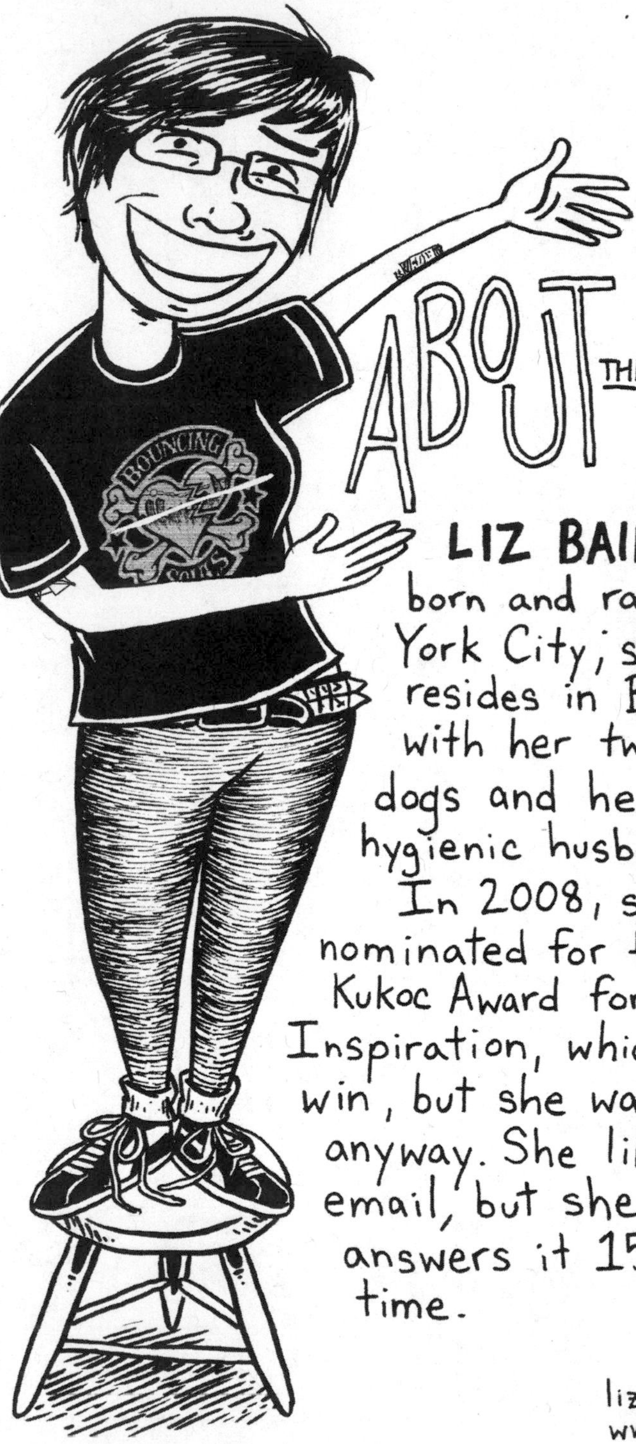
BOUNCING
SOULS

ABOUT THE AUTHOR

LIZ BAILLIE was born and raised in New York City; she currently resides in Brooklyn with her two smelly dogs and her far more hygienic husband, Zane. In 2008, she was nominated for the Maisie Kukoc Award for Comics Inspiration, which she didn't win, but she was flattered anyway. She likes to get email, but she only answers it 15% of the time.

liz@lizbaillie.com
www.lizbaillie.com